WHY SHE LEFT US

A NOVEL

RAHNA REIKO RIZZUTO

Rahna Reiko Rizzuto

HarperCollins*Publishers*

Chapter 12 ("Purple Hearts") was first published, in a slightly different form, in *The Asian Pacific American Journal*.

HarperCollins books may be purchased for educational, business, or sales promotional use. For information please write: Special Markets Department, HarperCollins Publishers, Inc., 10 East 53rd Street, New York, NY 10022.

FIRST EDITION

Designed by Kris Tobiassen

Library of Congress Cataloging-in-Publication Data

Rizzuto, Rahna, R.
Why she left us : a novel / Rahna Reiko Rizzuto.—1st ed.
p. cm.
ISBN 0-06-019370-0
1. Japanese Americans—Evacuation and relocation, 1942–1945—Fiction.
2. World War, 1939–1945—Concentration camps—West (U.S.)—Fiction.
I. Title.
PS3568.I87W49 1999
813'.54—dc21 98-54634

99 00 01 02 03 ❖/HC 10 9 8 7 6 5 4 3 2 1

To Craig, for being there

OKADA FAMILY TREE

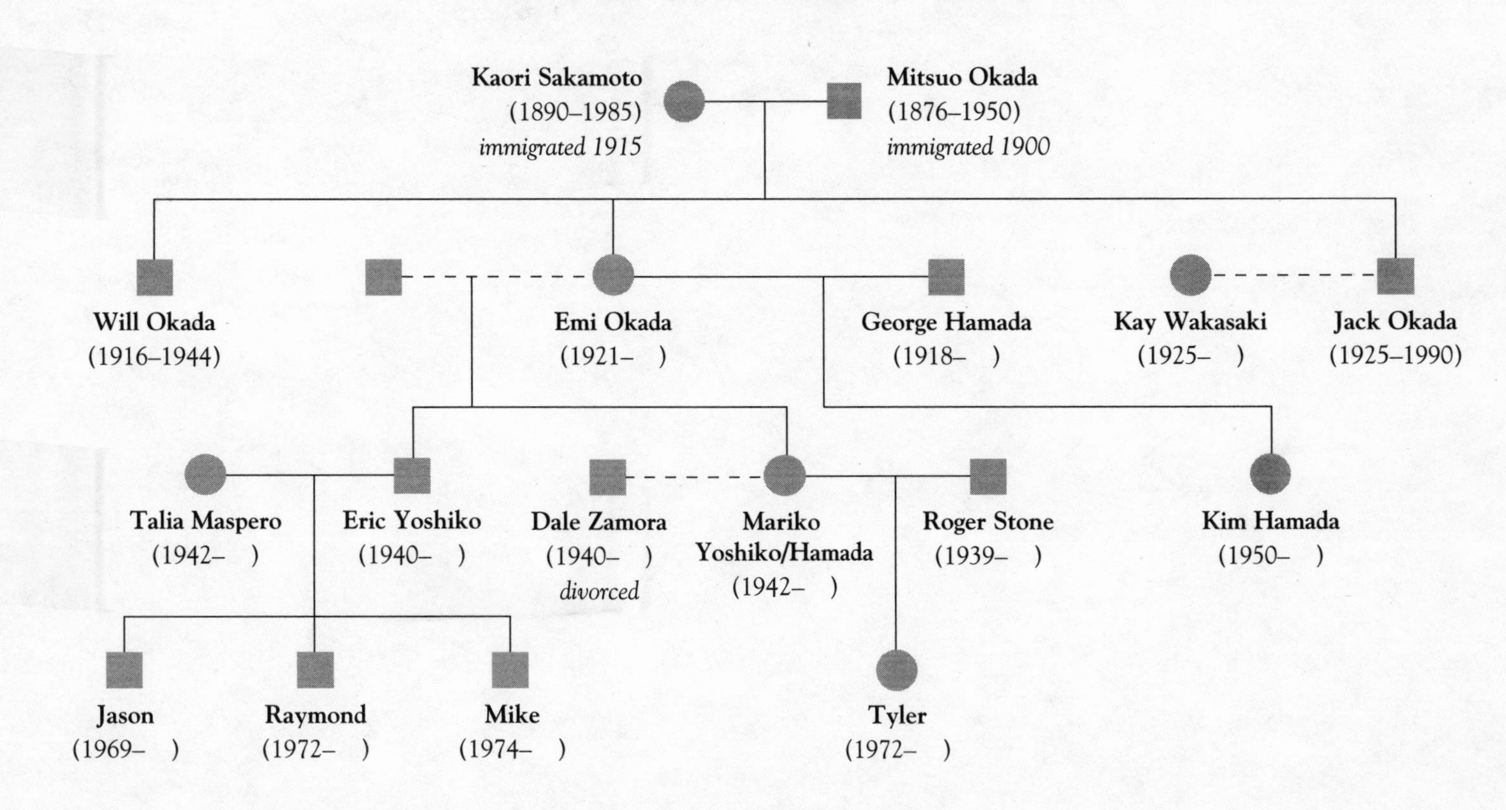

CONTENTS

ACKNOWLEDGMENTS

This book is a work of fiction. It was inspired by a pilgrimage I made to the internment camp where my mother and her family lived during World War II; it was informed by many generous Japanese Americans who shared their stories with me. Although I scoured public and university libraries in Los Angeles, Berkeley, New York, and Hilo in my quest for historical accuracy, in the end the events described in this novel were colored by the many necessary shades of memory. The characters bear no resemblance to people I know, living or dead.

That said, I have many people to thank. For entrusting me with their memories: Dick Arimoto, May Fujii Foo, Jim Hamaji, Reverend and Mrs. Hojo, Ralph Iwamoto, Richard Konda, Fusaye Mayeda, George and Eugenia Mukai, Mariko and Gerry Shibata, Dorothy Takakura, Misaye Yamaguchi, and others, especially those at the Amache camp reunion in Colorado and the Kimochi Senior Center in San Francisco, who shared anecdotes but not their names. For their support and friendship, my cheering section—Eric Anderson, Kris Anderson, Ann Close, Carol Dixon, Eloise Flood, Julie Gibbs, Janice Goldklang, J. Hammons, Tim Thomas, and Stephanie Tooman—and the Asian American Writers' Workshop, for making sure I was not alone. Thank you Bino A. Realuyo, for countless nights of caffeine and inspiration; Elizabeth Schmitz, for going far beyond the call of duty; Tandra Nakamura and Michael Nakade for helping me with my Japanese; and Jenny McFee, for resetting the clock. My deepest gratitude to Susan Bergholz, fierce agent and friend, and to Terry Karten, an instant believer.

Finally, my abiding appreciation to my family: grandparents, Great Aunts and Uncles, great Aunts and Uncles, in-laws, and siblings who were called upon to house me, squire me around while I was doing my research, arrange for interviews, unearth books and articles, and to read. To my parents, two writers who still surround me with their love for words. And to my husband, who makes everything possible. I could not have written this book without you.

1

ERIC

HOLD YOUR BREATH, 1946

Eric's heart is going to burst. His heart is holding all his breath. Except, his cheeks are holding some, and more floats across his eyes. The cars outside keep passing, vague and dizzy through the parlor window. Eric's head is light now.

He has to let it go.

His breath breaks out, pulling his lungs with it until he can gobble another one. He presses his small hands to his mouth to contain it this time. Last night, when he lay in bed, he chose this spot on the otherwise slumped-over couch; it was the best place to watch the moving picture outside the heavy curtains. Now, his nose near the glass, he is close enough to feel the street sounds zoom through him.

Eric is looking for a new car.

Mama's profile flickers through the doorway, tossed clothing hanging over the basket on her hip as she slips down the hall. Eric sees the smooth bun of gray hair she has twisted against her neck, wrapped in a thick, blue ribbon. The ribbon confirms everything he knows about the day. She, too, is expecting something, though she's still in her housedress and isn't quite ready. He freezes, straight and tingling, hoping she will pass, and knowing he's never been that lucky. She doesn't even pause to drop the laundry basket as she steps into the room.

"What are you doing in here?" Her palm swings in a wide wing to slap his mouth. "Get off that couch."

The slap misses his mouth and tears his hand away; it tears his feet off the ledge and his body follows, his shoulders hunching while the rest of him stands still. "Waiting for my mother," he says.

Mama sways toward him again, but doesn't strike. "Who said . . ." Her voice trips, her thought unfinished. In a peek, Eric sees she looks pale. The lines in her face stand out strangely, like little rivers on a map, and his dizziness returns once more. It's not a bright light in his head this time, more like worms, like Mama's wrinkles, and they tickle as they make their way to his stomach.

As time stretches this unexpected moment, Mama kneels in front of him and places the laundry basket at her side with some effort. Their faces are at the same level, peeking over the top of the sill. They are close enough to touch, but he doesn't expect it; they never do. Eric watches, indirectly, as the light turns silver in one of her black eyes.

"Your mother?" she asks finally, taking the hand she slapped to rub it lightly between her own.

"Jack says I have a different mother. Last night. He said she's coming here today." Slowly, so she won't notice, Eric parts his lips and draws a new breath to hold.

Mama withdraws—he can feel it—until she is far from him, far even from her own stroking hands. Sadness pulls at her singsong syllables when she finally speaks. "What were you doing, Eric?"

"Jack . . . my mother—" Eric bursts, another wish released. "I asked Jack if my mother was coming to live here. He said, 'Hold your breath.'"

Mama leaves Eric by the window and calls for his Uncle Jack. He can sense her anger in the quiet that crushes her words. In other houses on the block, Eric knows, arguments scatter with yells and the crash of objects into walls, but Japanese is different. Not a language to be shouted. Maybe the words fly apart and lose their meaning, he doesn't know for sure.

As Mama and Jack begin to fight, Eric finds his little sister, Mariko. He tucks her thumb into his fist and leads her onto the scrawny patch of grass between their house and the street. Cars whoosh by on black pavement. Eric expects to see army trucks and jeeps, even after a year of living outside the internment camp, but these cars are low and shiny. They look like bubbles, with half-mustaches over their spoked, skinny wheels, and they drive too fast to see inside. Eric's world is smaller now that they moved to Los Angeles. There are so many bright and painted houses and no prairie that runs forever through the barbed wire.

His house is a good change though, with everything, even the toilets, right there inside. There's a kitchen with flowers on the walls and two magic boxes: a hot one, called an oven, and one that's icy cold. The floors are made of wood stripes so smooth and clean he can lay on them. They don't hurt the way the brick floors at camp did. More than anything, he loves his new floors.

Under the tree, Mariko grabs the swing Jack made for Eric one day when he was in a good mood and could remember Eric's name. Her first jump up misses. "Help me, Eric."

"Jump higher. You're knocking the seat away."

His sister's impossibly round eyes examine the wood plank, then she smiles. "Please?"

"All right." He wonders why he always gives in to her. "But don't get dirty. Our mother is coming."

Mariko yanks her head toward the house looking for Mama. "Not." She is pleased with the wiggle she's made with the swing and shakes the ropes to broaden it. "Swing me."

Eric sighs. "Mama will push you later," he says. She is not yet four—too young to understand that her mother was missing and has been found. He didn't know either, not at first, until Jack pointed out that Mama was an old lady, as old as a grandmother, which was what she really was. Eric's grandmother. But it was the words *old lady* that stuck and reminded him that Mama had always been too busy for anything he wanted to do. Like last month, when she wouldn't help him make something for sharing time at school. She gave him her Bible—a book filled with tiny drawings of faces and shaking leaves, stickmen and falling boxes. He made up an entire story using just the first page, but Mrs. Morris, his first-grade teacher, stopped him before he was partway through. She told him the drawings were Japanese characters; he was horrified, suddenly Japanese again when he was trying so hard to be American. He wished she'd take back the words, let him sit down gracefully, but as each second passed, he was standing there. In front of the blackboard, in front of the class, with each tick on the smiling clock, still unable to read the book. And with nothing left to say.

Eric's sister hangs from the wooden seat beside him, waiting. "Swing me."

"I can't, Mari, you aren't big enough!"

"I am, I am," she sings, dazzled by her lifting legs. "Swing me."

Since this isn't what he planned, Eric says, "I have a secret. You want to know what it is?"

He waits for her nod. "Then come over here."

Mariko slips off the wooden seat and settles between his legs, facing the driveway. "What is it?" she whispers.

"A surprise. You'll see."

She considers his words, then says, "I'm going to swing."

As she tries to rise, he holds her down. "Someone's coming," he says. "We have to watch for her car."

His sister nods, narrowing her eyes at the road. "Is that her?" she asks as one passes.

"No, she's coming here."

"Oh." And then, three cars later, "Sing me the red bird song."

Eric is stuck in the first verse when Mama and Jack come out of the house. Jack is first. His crisp uniform shifts over his better leg, then the braced one as he hops, skips, and jumps down the sagging porch steps and along the short path to the car. He stumbles a little, kicking at the cracked concrete. He is in the car by the time Mama gets to the front door.

"Jack!"

"I won't speak to her."

"Please."

"I don't want to see her face."

"She's your sister, Jack."

"Not anymore. She killed Will."

"Don't be foolish."

"It's true. He couldn't live with her dishonor anymore."

"No," Mama says, but Jack's words are a fist; Eric can see it land on her, see her begin to slump and crumple. "Don't," she repeats, but Jack's window is closed. Jack never follows Mama's orders, Eric knows. They watch as his car races out of the driveway.

"Don't move," Eric tells Mariko, knocking her backward as he untangles his legs from around her and runs across the grass. Mama leans against one of the carved white posts that keep the house from falling onto the porch, just on the edge of one of the two terribly tall windows. Her eyes are closed; she doesn't open them even though Eric's footsteps announce him clearly. He wants to ask her who Will is, and who the "*she*" is who killed him, but Mama's stillness stops him. She seems to be melting into the parched wood siding and he watches her go. Gray hair, dress, gray peeling paint.

"Mama." Eric plucks her skirt. "I'll stay with you." He pulls more firmly when she doesn't answer. Her stockings, darker at her ankles, steady him. "I'll stay with you, Mama," he says. "I promise. Play with us, we can wait for her together."

Eric keeps his gaze on Mama's heavy shoes until he feels her hand brush his hair. When he looks up, her eyes are soft on his. "Watch your sister for me," she says quietly. Then she kisses the top of his head, something she has never done. The kiss uncurls the dizziness inside him and sends it crawling up his back.

He will watch Mariko, Eric thinks, trying to shake off Mama's sudden weakness. His sister is little; she needs him to protect her and help her understand. There have been so many changes this year already. They have a new home, in a new state, in a house filled with soft furniture and the smell of food. They have tile, a tub, and water whenever they want it. They have a family who speaks their language in a city that does not.

Today, though, they will have more. All last night, Eric watched the gauzy track of the moon through his bedroom window and imagined that he was the child in his baby-sitter's story—looking for his mother. Only his mother was looking for *him*.

Mariko doesn't know any of it, though, and Eric wonders whether he should prepare her, or if it's too much for her to understand. She has a pile of grass in her skirt and seems intent on counting it. "Er-ric," she whines, holding up her hands, spread, to grab his, "help me."

As he gives Mariko one hand, Eric decides to keep his mother a secret for now. He adds her to his new family, then puts the family in his palm where he can look at them. Mama and his new mother, Papa and Jack, and Mariko. His mother has no face yet, so he makes one up. He keeps his palm flat, in case his family changes again, and as he does, Mariko grabs it.

"I need it, Eric."

He glares at her, such a baby, but can't refuse. She puts one blade on each of Eric's fingertips, then gathers them and makes a pile on her knee. Then she begins again, each time bouncing his family farther away. When they have ten piles of ten, Eric's dizziness, and the people in his hand, are gone.

Lunch comes and goes. Mama made *o chazuke*: rice and hot tea in a little bowl, with pickled things drifting in it that Eric hates. He tries to push them to the side by making waves but the things are stubborn. No matter how carefully he holds the spoon, how quickly he dives past them for the pearly grains of rice, they swoop back in with their sour taste.

"Don't play with your food, Eric," Mama says, but it's a weightless order. Her eyes are out the window. She doesn't tell him to sit straight or pick his hands off the table. From the moment she found him in the parlor, Mama hasn't done a single thing Eric expected. Because he cannot guess what will happen next, he can't bring himself to ask to be excused.

Eric glances over to check on Mariko, but she has made no progress with her lunch either. She is sucking her upside-down spoon—it hasn't moved from her mouth minutes later when they hear an engine grind and a car pull into the drive. Eric and Mama stand to see it; it's like the cabs he's seen downtown. For a moment, he wonders if something's wrong. He was sure she'd come in her own car.

Mama leaves the kitchen without excusing herself. She reaches the front door first, but only because she's in the way and Eric won't push past her. Mariko follows in sections: eyes first, then the arms she stretches to be lifted, then the rest of her in an easy tumble off the chair so she won't be left behind. Eric waits for Mama to open the screen door so that the scene in front of them can burst out of its tiny boxes. Then, together, with Mariko following, they step onto the porch.

By now, the car engine has shut off. A man is getting out of the backseat. He's little: smaller than Jack and sturdier. Maybe older, too, it's hard for Eric to tell. He wears a blue jacket, a white shirt, and a hat. The taxi driver helps him lift two large suitcases out of the trunk.

Then a woman steps out. She is taller than the man, and straighter than any woman Eric knows. Her nipped-in waist and flaring skirt come from the movies Mama took him to when they were living in the camp. Eric watches the red swish around her smooth legs and searches for memories to hold up to her. Everything about her is perfect. He can't believe she belongs to him.

Because he has to, Eric forces himself to recognize her. He thinks she knows her eyes, elegantly slanted, but maybe it's Mama's eyes he sees in her face. The fingers smoothing her skirt are long, with curious, knobby knuckles all her own and one plain gold ring. Her mouth, a tight pout as red as her dress, doesn't feel familiar. Neither does the way her black hair rolls into two curling horns at the top of her head.

The woman stops before she reaches the end of the path, but the three of them stay where they are, on the edge of the two steps that lead down. Her face is as quiet as Mama's except for a brief flicker under one eye. Eric smiles at her, but too shyly to attract her gaze.

Then he feels Mama move. Like an echo, she begins touching her own skirt in the same short strokes the woman is using. He counts them as he waits for her to step down so at least she and the woman are on the same level; when he reaches four, though, it is the woman who steps forward—twice before Mama does, too—and it isn't until Mama's feet hit the concrete path that she finds her hands again and lifts them halfway. Eric sees their dance then; it's the woman's turn to follow. But before he can guess what comes next, they have rushed into each other's arms.

The woman hugs Mama in a murmuring cloud. Now that they are both on the same level, he sees she is taller by almost a whole head. Because she still has not seen his welcoming smile, Eric stays where he is and waits. He holds Mariko with him, for balance.

"Emi, Emi, Emi," Mama says as the women pull apart. The man stands almost beside them.

"Mariko?" the woman asks, straightening. "Eric?"

When at last she says his name, the woman's voice splashes into Eric's chest, cooling his insides down in a rush that reaches his toes. It floods his eyes, too, blurring the perfect lines in her face. He knows her, once her image is gone; it was she who taught him the red bird song. He can hear it flooding through his head and it launches him into her arms.

Mariko follows Eric, squealing and twisting, as the woman kneels to wrap them in her arms. Her skin, pressed against his, feels like bedtime, warm and beating. He squeezes his mother hard.

"Children!" She is trying to stand. "Please!" Then she is up and talking above their heads. "Mama, you remember George Hamada. George, this is Mama, and Eric and Mariko." They are introduced according to age and in the order they stand, trembling with obedience, watching her.

George Hamada's face is friendly. Eric likes the way he crouches to be on their level. "It's nice to meet you," he says, taking off his hat. "You don't remember me, Mariko, but I met you when you were small. I was the first person to hold you, did you know that? You could fit into one hand."

Mariko, charmed by his attention, gives him a proper bow. Her dimples surface as she purses her lips, still too shy to meet his eyes.

Mr. Hamada grins and swings her onto his hip. "You're an awfully big girl now," he says, trying hard to break open her smile.

Eric is itching to be up there, too. "Are you my father?" he asks, hoping to add the man to his imaginary family.

His question drains away the bustle, leaving the grown-ups as still as a picture that doesn't include him. Only Mariko sees him; she squirms with surprise at his words. The man is looking at Eric's new mother as if he expects her to speak, but she doesn't reply. Mama doesn't either. She's waiting for his words to disappear.

The man gives Mariko a reassuring squeeze, then sets her down and takes a suitcase in each hand.

"Eric, you're dumb," Mariko declares, unhappy to lose the man's attention. And, as suddenly as the world stopped, it begins to move again.

Mama covers her mouth like she does when she's smiling. "Eric needs to mind his manners," she says. "Let's go inside. Your father's not too well, Emi, he's waiting in the parlor." She tucks Emi's arm in hers and leads her toward the house, Mr. Hamada behind. Eric and Mariko wait in the yard as the adults begin to shrink, until Mama calls for them to follow.

There is something crazy in the room with them, and it's not only Eric's grandfather. Papa won't speak, and although Mama says that he is too sick to recognize people, Eric knows it isn't true. He doesn't think Emi and the man are fooled as easily as they seem to be, either. Their eyes don't meet. Their bodies stay folded. There's too much space between their words.

Eric's grandfather doesn't seem to like Emi. Every time she speaks, he grunts so loudly she can't hear what she's saying and lets her words sink to the floor. Then, when she turns to exchange helpless smiles with Mama, Papa sniffs his nose and bares his caked teeth at her. He swings his open, eager mouth toward Mr. Hamada. The man stares at him with alarm.

"Papa?" Eric's mother asks. Papa's grimace is gone, but Emi's voice is so polished that Eric thinks she must have seen it.

Mr. Hamada begins to rise. "Emi, perhaps your father . . ."

Papa lets out a growling burp and stands up, nodding toward Mr. Hamada, as if he's expecting applause. His bathrobe hangs open in an upside-down *V* under his frayed belt; when Papa sees it, and sees he is naked under it, he moves to enlarge the gap. Eric squints at the old man's genitals until the hair and skin blur into safe colors, hoping the others will do the same. He can't do anything about the movement, though; he can still see the old man's penis bob as Papa swings himself around.

"Mitsuo!" Mama sees at last what Papa has done and hustles him into the hall, hissing. With the two of them gone, Eric waits for his real mother to speak to him, but, although she's been talking steadily since she arrived, suddenly she doesn't seem to want to look up from her lap. Because she might be shy, he searches for something to say. She'll want to know something about him. But Mama returns too quickly and fills the vacant sound.

"So, how was your trip?"

"Our trip?"

"You know. To Seabrook."

Papa is right, it's probably better not to talk, Eric thinks, remembering what happened when he asked the man his question. The adults have recovered. They are discussing a place called New Jersey. It's colder than Los Angeles, Emi says, but not as cold as the camp was in the winter. Mr. Hamada finished medical school there; now he is a doctor. Doctor Hamada, Eric repeats, pressing the new word into his head.

Details march along as Eric holds himself quiet. Emi—his mother—sits with Mama on the new couch. She picks her fingers as she talks, and floats bright bursts of laughter in Dr. Hamada's direction, inviting him to join the conversation. The man gives her the smiles she commands but holds his thoughts and turns often to the window. Once, Eric catches his glance and probes the face for the answer to the question he asked on the lawn. Finding none, he turns his attention back to his mother.

"I couldn't answer your letter," Emi says. The strength in her voice flares in and out. "There was nothing to say, eh? Nothing to be done." She checks around her, as if she's about to tell a secret. Instead, a question comes out. "Where is he? His grave, I mean."

"Colorado," Mama says. "Fairmount Cemetery. We stopped to see him on our way here."

"I wish I'd known in time for the funeral. Did they give Will one of those salutes?"

"I think so. We didn't . . . they wouldn't let us out of camp to go."

Emi's face, puzzled and scared, looks like Mariko's when something surprises her. The feelings touch Mama, too, but she struggles against them as Emi begins to cry. His real mother is the softer one, Eric sees, more easily hurt. She is more like he is.

"Those bastards. How could they?"

Emi's tears squeeze Eric's heart, then blow it up so big he expects to see it burst from his chest. She steps into him at that moment and takes her place in his very core. My mother, he thinks, savoring the words. He's content to watch Mama hold her and whisper in her ear.

"Jack had an appointment at the War Department," Mama says, lying in response to a question Eric didn't hear.

"That's all right."

"He wanted to change it, but they wouldn't let him."

"We can wait, can't we, George?"

"Sure." Then, because she clearly wants more from him, he adds, "We'll see him tonight when he comes home."

"George really wants to meet Jack."

"Actually, I met your brother several times when we were at Amache."

Eric's mother gives Dr. Hamada a little "tsk." "You know what I mean."

Mama's eyes are warning Eric; Jack's anger is clearly meant to stay a secret. Then, as if she's afraid he'll speak anyway, she says, "Eric, take Mariko upstairs. It's time for your nap. Look, she's already asleep."

She *is* asleep, curled in her favorite blue armchair, but Eric knows he's being dismissed. In case it's a test, he stands quickly, holding his shoulders straight, though the adults don't seem to be watching. He shakes Mariko gently until her eyelashes move. They don't open, though, until he bends close to her ear.

"Mari." He puts a lot of breath into her name so it doesn't scare her. "Come with me."

Eric slips his arm around his sister's soft back, helping her up and into the hall. They leave the adults without a word and head up the stairs—which are longer and steeper than Eric ever noticed—to the room they share. Mariko leans on him, rising and falling at the brink of sleep as they take one step at a time. The voices in the parlor have faded long before they reach the top.

Eric settles Mariko in her bed like he is supposed to, but sleep is hard for him to find with his new family below. They brought suitcases, he reminds himself, one for each of them, which means they plan to stay. And Dr. Hamada said they would see Jack tonight.

Eric brushes his hand against the woven straw wallpaper as he shuffles his family from room to room. Jack has his own room now, but the rest are full of people. Of course Eric's mother will stay in his room. They can get a bunk bed, and she can choose the top or bottom. She can have his blankets and his favorite pillow. He'll have to share his drawers, since the room can't hold another dresser. Then it occurs to him—he could empty one now.

Eric eases his largest drawer open, careful not to disturb Mariko. Then, T-shirts removed, he bends down to make sure the space under his bed is clean. The California sun slants along the bottom edge of the window, past the curtains, and plays in the mirror over Mariko's bed. Eric is sure he's never seen it so low in the sky during nap time. He peers out just as the screen door on the porch slams shut below him. Crisp shoes skip on the stairs outside. He stands on his toes so he can see.

Jack must have returned, Eric thinks, remembering suddenly that his uncle is angry with his new mother. If they fight, she might leave, or Jack might leave, as he often threatens Mama. Beneath him, Eric can see the top of a man's head—shiny and plowed with a comb. It has to be Dr. Hamada, he realizes, listening to his heart. Jack's hair is square and so short you can see his scalp down the middle. Eric watches the man. Once the house is behind him, his steps are aimless and confined to the yard.

Mama must have forgotten them, Eric decides at last. He knows nap time *has* to be over. Would she be angry if he got up on his own? Eric considers the question for as long as it takes him to get to the door. Sometimes she doesn't mind at all.

Besides, Eric thinks as he slips quietly down the hall, Mama was the one who sent him to his room, not his real mother. She wouldn't choose to spend so much of their first day apart. He waits at the top of the stairs in case someone is coming, but the front hall is empty except for a warm path of light coming through the open door. He is imagining the smile his mother will give him when she sees him. Then he gets to the bottom of the stairs and hears her voice.

"I begged you not to try to find him, but you wouldn't listen to me," Emi is saying.

The words, like most adult words, have little impact on Eric. But the ache in Mama's reply freezes him outside the door.

"How can you do this?" his grandmother asks her. "How can you turn your back on family?"

"My back? You made the choice, and I warned you I would never take him back—"

"Choice? Emi. There was no choice."

"I guess you're right, Mama. From my perspective, there was my life, and there was his life. But since I was never important to you, you wouldn't have had to choose."

Eric's mother's voice is shaking. He can hear a stir of footsteps in the room.

"What do you want from me, Mama? After everything you said to me, and everything you let Will do, did you really expect me to change my mind? I asked you for your help, but you didn't want to know what happened. You didn't care then, and you still refuse to ask."

Before he realizes that her voice is getting louder, Eric's mother is standing in the hall. Her eyes seem deeper than they were, not a part of her quiet face but alive. He can tell, from the tight points in her cheeks that hold her mouth in a thin line, that she is terribly angry. He and his mother watch each other, motionless, until Mama appears over her left shoulder.

"Eric, go to your room!"

He stumbles up the stairs, his heart racing his pounding feet. Something awful happened while he was resting, and he expects to see it in the parlor behind the women. In a panic, Eric flies into Jack's room, the first one he can find, and slams the door. He throws himself under Jack's bed and waits to see what will happen next.

Mama told him to go to his room. Her voice said run. But no one followed him upstairs. The voices downstairs seem to have faded.

Then the house begins to talk. Doors, drawers, and a thump from the closet he shares with Mariko tell Eric where everyone is. High heels play up and down the hall. Eric hears a car and sees the cab has come back. The driver gets out and helps Dr. Hamada put three suitcases in the trunk.

"Take her, then, and go," Eric hears. Mama's voice in the hall is strained. Mariko is out there, too, fretting beneath her words.

It must be safe now.

He opens the door to take care of his sister. Emi has Mariko balanced on her hip, trying to bounce her quiet.

"I'll take her, Mama."

"Emi has her, Eric." Mama draws him back against her legs. "Emi's going to take care of her."

"But that's my job." He watches Mariko's face peek around Emi's hair as they go down the stairs. She waves at him, then disappears through the door. "Will they be back for dinner?"

Mama's fingers press into his shoulders, locking him to her. "No, Eric. Mariko's going on an airplane with Emi and George. But you're going to stay here with me." She turns him by the shoulders, talking much more than she usually does. "Like you promised this morning. Remember?"

Eric is tense suddenly, hot and cold. His grandmother has trapped him in a place where he doesn't want to be. "But what about me? I want to go." No longer looking at her, he twists easily from Mama's hands and flies out the front door and off the porch. "Wait, Mari! Mari!"

"Eric!" Mariko calls back, but she's in the car, shaded from his sight as Dr. Hamada helps his mother onto the seat.

"I'm coming! I'm going to come, too. Wait for me." He slides by the man and onto the backseat next to Emi. He made it. It's now Mariko, Emi, and Eric in the back of the car.

"No, Eric, you can't." His mother puts her arm out as if to push him away. "You can't come with us."

"But I want to," he says, "I want to."

Mariko wails as Emi says, "I'm sorry, Eric. We don't have a ticket for you." She is pushing him for sure now, her arm straight, holding him away from his sister.

"But aren't you my mother?" he insists. "Jack said you were. Aren't you my mother?"

As he speaks, Dr. Hamada locks his hand onto Eric's right arm. His mother doesn't answer, doesn't look at him. Eric is beginning to understand.

He's being pulled out.

There's nothing but the door handle left. Eric knows it won't help him but he grabs it with both hands anyway. "Please don't take Mari. Please."

The adults don't seem to hear, but Mariko is reaching for him over the woman's lap. He has her hands.

"Mari, don't leave. Get out, okay? Get out."

"George," the woman calls as she tries to separate them. "George!"

Eric is outnumbered, and suddenly he loses the strength to hold on. Crying, he lets himself be guided out of the taxi. He stands where Dr. Hamada puts him and watches the woman in the car struggle with Mariko.

"I'm sorry, Eric," Dr. Hamada says.

The man gets in the car and shuts the door, sealing Emi and Mariko away behind glass. An image of the orange tree wiggles across them. Mama's face rises into the window beside his, her eyes on Mariko. He won't believe this is happening, Eric decides. His mother has to be coming back.

"Mari?" Eric calls again, in a voice he knows is too small to be heard. He stands where he's supposed to as the engine turns over and the taxi begins rolling out of the driveway—until he can't tell from the movement in the car whether Mari is still crying for him, whether any of them have looked back once.

Mama tries to turn his face toward her, but he shakes her off. She is wavering side to side and speaking, but her words, whatever they are, sail like soap bubbles, bursting over his head as he stares at the spot where the taxi was before it vanished. They'll be back, he promises himself, they have to.

To be sure, he takes a deep breath.

2

MARIKO

FAMILY NUMBERS, 1990

Mariko Stone was safe in her living room. She sank into her bottle green chair and watched the waves of rain splash out of the dense fog and into her three picture windows. There was a war on outside, but not even the *kamakani*—the irresistible bonsai wind that hurled the rain and sculpted one-sided trees all over the island—could shred through those spirits. By morning, Mari knew, her muddy driveway would reappear between her orchids and fire ginger, and with it, the waterfalls and necking places, the acres of pasture no one seemed to own. For now, though, only the fog existed. The world Mari lived in was gone.

She had just come up that driveway, of course, with the groceries she'd traveled more than twenty miles to buy, and the mail. After twenty years in the same house, it was easy enough for her to swing in and out of the horseshoe turns that marked the road to Ahualoa, and to find the log and hog wire gate that protected her home. She had shaken the rain from her hair and put the kettle on for tea: green Japanese tea, which she hardly ever drank. Now she was resting in her favorite armchair, considering the envelope she had just received from the War Relocation Authority as she waited for the water to boil.

The truth about her internment during World War II was in the envelope. Yet the first time she had applied for redress, Mari had been told there was no record of her ever entering the camps.

There could be other, more urgent letters, Mari decided, picking up the rest of the stack. She did a fast sort by name—Roger, Tyler, Occupant, herself. Tyler's name, even misspelled and misgendered on the junk mail, pulled up a sharp parade of images. The red dance of sun in her daughter's soft hair before she left for college. Tyler home for Christmas: pale and shorn almost bald—her declaration of independence, artistic identity, and probably sexual experience—her oblong skull set like a jewel atop a black cat suit but still somehow completely recognizable from the moment she stepped onto the airplane's rolling stairway. Mari had grabbed her—hugged her and held that face she loved in her hands as she searched it for the high cheekbones that were hers, and the tawny flash in Tyler's eyes that came from Roger. Her daughter's face had always been such a mix of them, such a strong cement for her marriage. Now that she was away, though, the best of both of them was gone.

If only the government had found Mari's name in its files the first time, she wouldn't be hesitating now. Instead, they had asked for the number that was assigned to her family, the one her mother had been so reluctant to give. Mari could still remember that confrontation. They had been at Emi's house just north of Hilo for their annual Christmas tree trimming party. It was Mari's sister, Kim, who brought up the internment. She specialized in pushing people past the point of comfort. That day, as always, Mari and her mother were her targets of choice.

When Mari arrived at her childhood home for the party, there were no signs of trouble. She waved Roger around to the backyard to set up the grill, then took Tyler and the groceries into the house. They found Kim in the kitchen, making *musubis* at the breakfast table while Mari's mother, Emi, sliced vegetables at the island near the prep sink. Seeing her mother's unguarded back, Mari noticed that her hair was getting grayer. Whiter, actually, as if she'd been caught in the snow. It reminded Mari of the volcano Mauna Kea: bright on top, sliding toward black just as it reached her shoulders and brushed the top of her blouse.

"We're here," Mari said loudly, announcing her daughter's return.

Emi looked up long enough to give Tyler a quick kiss. "Goodness! Did they do that to your hair in Iowa? Somehow, I expected you to come back in a nice prairie skirt. Maybe a braid." Then she turned to Mari. "Did you bring the cookie cutters?"

"Of course." Mari watched her daughter bound over to greet Kim—her mentor and favorite person. Kim was an artist who had found fame through moss figures and death masks made of jerky. The year before, she was on the cover of *Look* magazine, putting the finishing touches on a mud statue. Her caftan had flowed far beyond her pixie figure; she looked like a cloth cover flung away when the sculpture was unveiled.

Kim's tree-trimming caftan was gold and red, its sleeves long enough to flirt with the saltwater in front of her as she pressed palmfuls of rice into perfect, sticky triangles. She gave Tyler's egg-shaped head and shoulder-length earrings a slight nod of approval, then handed her a *musubi* to roll in the shallow dish of *furikake*.

Mari sighed and settled at the breakfast table with a baking sheet, cutters, and four colors of sugar sprinkles. She couldn't bear to watch Kim take her daughter's love for granted.

"They're doing a show of my masks in Mexico City in August," Kim said, nodding at Mari. "I can't decide whether to go."

"Go."

"The pollution is awful."

"Go," Mari repeated as she tried to fit the point of a star into a gingerbread armpit to save space.

"I would if they were paying my way."

Tyler laughed. "Have you two ever agreed on anything in your lives?"

Kim looked genuinely surprised. "You're too logical, Tyler. We aren't arguing. I'm just saying that money is important. Your mother has some—"

"Hardly."

"Well, you're getting that redress payment from the government. Not that I'd want to get rich that way—living in a horse stall, being imprisoned no less. Of course, you were too young to notice, Mari, but some people around here weren't."

Kim was baiting their mother. She did it often, leaving Mari to come to Emi's aid. This time, though, Mari hesitated. She wanted to hear what her mother would say. Mari's parents subscribed to the notion that the "past is past," especially when the subject was as personal or painful as the war and the internment had to be. In fact, she hadn't even known about the government internment camps until she read three paragraphs about it in her high school history book.

When Emi didn't comment, Mari glanced over toward the sink. The tap was on full blast; there was a chance their mother hadn't heard Kim.

The silence swelled around them.

"Not imprisoned," Mari said at last. "*Interned* is the word they use. They were called *relocation centers* too; people don't refer to the horse stalls."

"Lord, Mari, a horse stall is a horse stall." Kim smiled and placed another *musubi* on the plate. "See, Tyler? That's the difference between us and your mother. Artists rub the dirt into things to see the definition. Mari cleans them up, hoping they'll disappear. Anyway, dear sister, back to the subject. Maybe you could help me get to Mexico?"

"How?"

"With your redress money. The twenty grand. I'd pay you back."

That's when Tyler leaned over, as if Mari wasn't in the room let alone sitting right across from them. "They aren't going to give it to her."

"What do you mean?"

"They say she wasn't there. Weird, huh?"

Even if Mari had wanted to protest, she would have been outdone by Kim's dramatic hand slap on the table and the saltwater circles she sent racing in the bowl. "You know, this government pisses me off," she said. "First they round up all the Japanese *Americans* and make them live in stables just because we happen to be at war with Japan—"

"Kim!"

"Then they wait until half the old people are dead before they even apologize, and they come up with some trivial amount of money for redress, which, by the way, is the only good thing the Reagan administration ever did for this country and you can bet he didn't want to—"

"Auntie Kimberly!" Tyler protested, but with a giggle. Mari's husband, Roger, was a Reagan fan.

"And then"—Kim put up her hand, not to be stopped—"and then they tell the children they weren't there. Now I ask you, does that sound fair? Is that democracy?"

"Kim, Jesus. They just need more records. A birth certificate, a family number."

"What's a family number?"

"I don't know. They gave each family a number, I guess. I was only a couple months old when we were sent to the camps."

"Mom should know it."

"I'm sure she does. I'll ask her later."

"You are odd, Mari. Very." Kim turned to their mother and raised her voice. "Hey Mom! Mom, do you have the family number?"

Emi took her time answering. Mari could tell she was avoiding the question by the way she tried to perfect each carrot slice. "The family number?"

"Mari needs it to get her twenty grand."

At Kim's last words, Emi nicked her finger. "Shit," she said, sticking the ragged edge of her fingernail into her mouth. "These knives are so dull, I'm surprised they haven't killed anyone yet. The dull knives are the most dangerous, you know."

They waited while Emi chewed her nail to smooth out the edge. Mari half-expected her to do them all so they would match. Although she had wanted to hear her mother's story, she was almost happy it wasn't forthcoming. It seemed inappropriate to her that Kim, who hadn't been born, was forcing herself into a past Mari and her parents shared.

"Did you get yours, Mom?" Kim repeated.

"My what?"

"Your records. Did they find you?"

"I think so. I mean, yes. Me and Dad."

"Well, why can't they find Mari? Don't you think that's strange?"

"It's a mistake."

"Well, I think it's weird. And not necessarily innocent, either. I think we should check Mom's stuff for the family number right now."

Emi sighed. "I'll look for it later."

"Later! You and Mari both. You'll forget."

"No, I won't. And Mari will remind me, right?"

"Right," Mari said, a little surprised that her mother had offered the number so freely.

"If they don't find you," Kim counseled, trying, as always, to get the last word, "I think you should sue. Make them pay—even for the dead ones. Grandmama, Grandpapa, and Uncle Will."

Emi had been unusually open that day, but Mari was not naive. She never expected her mother to give her the family number. The possibility was so unlikely that she felt free to push; in fact, she called several times to remind Emi, but it wasn't until she offered to drive to Hilo to look for the number herself that her mother announced she'd found it somewhere and, of course, almost lost it again in the papers around the telephone. When

Emi finally read it aloud, it burned from Mari's ears to her fingers, numbing them so thoroughly that she had to flex them to get them to work. She made Emi repeat the number and wrote it down twice. After all, they were both getting old.

Then, after all her pressure, Mari almost didn't send it in. It seemed impossible that they could find her with it, and the payment was suddenly so unreal. Ever since the government announced the Japanese American redress program, Mari had felt a curious lethargy—a feeling that "it" didn't matter, which alternated with her conviction that it mattered quite a bit. It might simply have been her aversion to being a victim; growing up in Hawaii, Mari felt almost raceless, and she wanted to stay that way. But it was more than that. The whole episode—the redress, the camps, even the war—was so far past, at least for her.

There was no way it could change her life.

Feeling the power of decisiveness at last, Mari slipped her index finger under the flap of the envelope and pulled out several papers. The first was a note, stamped with a script version of some bureaucrat's name, asking Mari to please verify the family information enclosed. The next two sheets contained a list of registration records that ran in alphabetical order through Mari's hands: Oiye, Okada, Yoshiko, Okamoto, Okamura. Birth dates, entries, departures, and family numbers were etched in the thick *a*'s and fading *m*'s of an old typewriter, copied until their names, like their faces, had all but disappeared. Mari leaned against the table as she scanned the page; she read so fast that she missed her own family tree the first time through. She had to stop herself from skimming before the words would come together.

They were not the names she knew, and yet, there they were. The truth on paper.

No wonder they couldn't find her the first time, Mari thought as she set the list down gently and watched the folded edges waver. She wasn't there. Not Mariko Hamada Stone, the person she was now, created by her mother, by George, by Mari herself. She had known there was a secret, but even with the names in front of her, she could barely believe how much her mother had hidden and how deft she had been. It was true that Emi never talked about the internment, but if she had, Mari had thought she knew what her mother would say, and the image she created was so strong she'd been sure some part of her remembered. They had lived at the Santa Anita racetrack and then at the Amache camp in Colorado. Mari and her parents, Emi and George Hamada, and the Okada clan: Emi's parents and two brothers. The brothers went to war—the hero Will, of course, and her Uncle Jack. But until then, they were all there, making illegal biscuits on the pot-bellied stove.

Now, she had no idea where that story came from. The registration records did list the Okadas, nicely set out according to age. Mitsuo and Kaori, and their sons, William Iwao and Jack Toshiyuki. But the second family was not the one she was used to seeing, or a name she ever really knew. Emi Yoshiko, twenty-one years old, was listed with *two* children: Eric Yoshiko, age two, and Mariko. No age. Just a date that showed she was a little younger than she thought she was. She had not been a couple of months old when she was interned in the camps.

According to these records, she had been born there.

If only Tyler were home, Mari thought. Although she had never felt the need to confide in her daughter, she was certain that she could. Tyler didn't mind half sentences; in her drawings, she preferred shadows to hard lines. She wouldn't question Mari the way Roger would, wouldn't pin her down and pick at her like it wasn't her life he was tearing apart. Mari used to find it easy enough to deflect her husband, and the truth was, his unending quest for answers had attracted her to him in the first place. He had delved so intently into her experiences, and she had been thrilled by how exposed she could be. In those days, though, Mari had thought that telling secrets meant sharing burdens, and she knew now that it wasn't true. What it did was give them a life they never had to have. It made them real, and impossible to change.

Since Tyler left for college, it was as if Roger had disappeared.

He kissed Mari good-bye at five-thirty every morning and didn't come home until after dark. She wasn't sure what he was running from, her or the silence of the house, and she couldn't bear to ask. He would only tell her that she was imagining things. If she gave him the chance, he would suggest, once again, that she revive the newspaper column she had written before Tyler was born. But eighteen years ago, when there were barely any newspapers on the island, anyone could be a journalist. Today, she'd be exposed as a failure, not the bright, funny storyteller she was once believed to be.

Mari knew what their real problem was: the house was empty. She and Roger had never had more children, though God only knew how hard she had tried. Roger never talked about it for fear of hurting her, and Mari wouldn't remember what to say if he did. There was so much she had never told him, so many miscarriages she suffered through alone. He knew enough, though, not to propose such a simplistic solution.

How could he imagine that a newspaper column could take the place of a child?

Mari turned back to the camp records. In the time she had spent brooding, the dark had made its way home. She could hear the wind whistling down the furrows of the log walls outside, but there was no hint of the stars or the moon yet, or the headlights that would announce Roger was home. Still, Mari knew that she didn't have much time left to decide what to tell him. If only Emi had told the truth, she thought. It would be easier to help her mother hide what had happened if she knew how close she could skirt what was real.

She must have been eight when she found her birth certificate, Mari recalled. More than old enough to remember. She had been poking around in her mother's desk when no one was home. Now she tried to relax and let those hours become a part of her. It bothered her that she couldn't remember why she had been prying. She could still feel the urgency in her younger self and in how she searched every drawer.

As Mari let her thoughts go free, she saw roses. Tiny ones on well-washed cloth, lit by a lattice of light through a louvered door. The memory came in pieces, like raindrops on her *lanai;* her old tears tugged at her with the unforgettable grief of a dream. She knew the roses came later, once she had crept into her closet with the birth certificate. Their pattern on her skirt was the only remnant of normalcy she had had.

How could the mind play tricks like that, Mari wondered. Bury things it knows so deeply that they seem never to have existed? She could still feel Emi's approaching footsteps pound in her head like they had so many years ago. In a matter of minutes, she and her birth certificate would be found. It was surely the worst of Mari's transgressions up to that point. Now she couldn't remember why she hadn't simply put the paper back.

She couldn't remember, either, why she had been sure it belonged to her. It was, in fact, Mariko Yoshiko's, a ridiculous rhyming name that begged to be corrected. The birth date was wrong; the father nonexistent. There had been no reason for her to search each line, one by one, to be sure that this Mariko was a different, unrelated person. No reason at all to stop at the entry after "Mother's previous live births," or to cradle it carefully when she saw that the number 1 had been typed.

But she was Mariko Yoshiko. Mari knew it then and now, even with that number so clearly in her head. The question now was, who was this Eric? Until this afternoon, Mari had thought she knew the answer.

The boy was her cousin. He was her Uncle Jack's adopted son.

3

JACK

PEARL HARBOR, 1941

Two months have passed since the words were spoken, but they are still there, buzzing Jack, waiting to enter his throat. At night, it is his sister's face that lives in him—her blackened eyes that watch him sleep. In the day, though, she breaks into words. Ugly ones, and the voice is Will's, and then his own.

Emi is a whore.

Jack is awake.

And Will is . . . ? Jack keeps his eyes closed, letting the question grow. He doesn't want Will to catch him "lolling." Jack's brother taught him that word when he returned to the family after Pearl Harbor was bombed—until then, Jack hadn't known how much could be accomplished in the first five minutes of a day. Sometimes, Jack wonders where Will got his discipline, and why he feels the need to impose it on Jack. Like perching himself on Jack's bed—which Will took over immediately—staring down at Jack's eyelids for his first conscious move. His brother could be there now, Jack knows, but even the new head of the family has to breathe sometime. He lets his eyes open.

Outside, the day is sunny, almost summery. Will is gone.

Of course, Jack thinks, today is their evacuation sale. Will has gone to the Civil Control Station on South Normandie to register the family and find out where they are being sent. Yesterday, when the army jeeps put up the evacuation posters, Will guessed it was Santa Anita. When Jack queried him—"You mean the racetrack?"—Will said, "Don't you have friends, Jack? Haven't any of them told you what's going on?"

Yes, he had friends, Jack wanted to answer. Not the kind Will meant—loyal *Nisei*, American citizens, with names like Mas and Hiro and Fut. Jack never hung around with other Japanese. His friends are the fellows who sit next to him on the bench, filling in for the first-string football team and looking forward to their turn next year. Jack doesn't see as much of them now that family obligations pull him home as soon as classes are over. But they still talk—these days about joining the army, though everyone knows the war will be over before they graduate from high school.

A swift victory, that's what the papers have been saying. Jack is surprised the war's been going on this long. Of course, as Will would be the first to remind him, Jack doesn't know much. Before Pearl Harbor was bombed five months ago, he didn't know what a "pearl harbor" was. Jack was hanging around outside church with a couple of fellows that day, killing time before Sunday services, when one of the kids gave them the news. Some Nisei fellow about Will's age said, "The damn Japs. I can't believe it." Jack was with him completely, but the first generation—the *Issei*—didn't know how to respond.

After that, the service was forgotten. Jack put Papa in the car. Mama had been too sick to go to church, so Jack's father would have to give her the news. As they drove through the pre-Christmas streamers of Little Tokyo, Jack and Papa let the rumble of the engine wrap around them as usual. Ever since Jack's father lost his dry cleaning business during the Depression, he didn't say much. Which meant Jack almost never heard him speak.

When they got home, the house was silent. It spooked Jack for the five steps it took to get to the living room. Until he saw his mother sitting on the sofa. Mama in one of her cleaning dresses, in her thick stockings and heavy shoes. She was composed as always—she'd even made herself a cup of tea. She wasn't drinking it, though, just holding the cup in her hands.

Jack nodded to her, his usual greeting. He headed for his room.

"*Nippon wa watashitachi ni sensoo o sengen shita*," Papa said.

Japan has declared war on us.

Jack paused in the wake of the unfamiliar sound. He watched his father fall to one knee in front of Mama, then, as an afterthought, to the other. Papa looked curiously tender, like he might reach for her, but his arms were at his sides. Jack knew his parents didn't love each other—had never met until after they married—and now it was clear that their foreign ways had doomed them. Marriage by mail. What could they have expected? And what could they possibly expect from each other now?

As for Mama, she didn't move toward Jack's father or away. He thought she closed her eyes, but since she was looking down, he couldn't be sure. He couldn't be sure if she tried to rise and ended up falling back against the sofa. He saw her hair distinctly, though—fuzzy and falling out of the bun she twisted at the nape of her neck. Of course, she was sick—it had nothing to do with Pearl Harbor.

Still.

Papa turned on the transistor radio. Jack watched him move to his rocking chair. Watched his right hand feel for the armrest to ease his body down.

". . . of at least four ships on fire. I repeat, these are unconfirmed reports. The Nippon invasion has taken Honolulu by surprise. Civilians are heading for the hills."

Jack listened to the voice, crackled and wavering, and wondered why the dial was set to the right station. Whether Mama had been listening before they got home, or if every station had the news. He wondered what Papa was thinking, why neither of them were moving. They were just sitting beneath the radio announcer's voice, like actors in a play waiting for the scenes to change and the narrator to explain away the boring parts so the action could begin.

". . . just joining us, the Japs struck the territory of Hawaii just before eight o'clock this morning. Pearl Harbor, Hickham Field, and the streets of Honolulu sustained heavy bombing. As of now, there has been no declaration of war, by the Japs or by the president. One thing can be said, however: the Japs have signed their death sentence. If there ever was a yellow-bellied sneak attack, this is it."

It was the glee in the voice that made Jack nervous. The words *Japs* and *yellow-bellied* fit his parents too well. They were Japanese and had never been allowed to become American citizens. And the words *death sentence*, he thought, moving out of the hallway and into the living room. Death sentence for whom?

"Jack," Mama said at last. "What's he saying, Jack?"

"The sky over Honolulu is filled with smoke," the announcer continued. "We now have word that our own antiaircraft fire is making the Japs pay. I repeat, there's been no declaration of war. However, all military personnel are ordered to report immediately to their stations."

Sneak attack, Jack thought. How was he supposed to translate that for Mama? A splinter of cane from the chair he'd chosen poked into his back beneath his shoulder blades. He drove it in farther, wanting the pain to help him decide what to keep in.

"No declaration of war yet," Jack tried to say in Japanese.

"What?"

Why they couldn't learn English, he'd never know. He tried again, wondering if he would have learned the Japanese words for *slaughter* and *antiaircraft fire* if he'd studied the language the way his brother and sister had. "No official order of war."

They stared at the radio. Jack waited for the announcer to read the commercials. They marked his time, said it was passing. And in between, navy ships sank the Japanese aircraft carrier. Unconfirmed reports had the slant-eyes attacking the Philippines. The attack on Pearl Harbor was over, but the descriptions of the dogfights grew.

Mama and Papa sat frozen. No longer expecting Jack to translate, no blood pulsing beneath their skin. They were Japs, sitting in a foreign land. They were slant-eyed and yellow-bellied, and though he knew it was hateful, Jack had the strong urge to flee. As far as Jack was concerned, they hadn't been a family since he was nine years old, when his brother left to go to college and his sister went God knew where. His parents fed him, but as long as he brought home decent grades and didn't get into trouble, he didn't have to plow any fields or even go to Japanese school. For the last seven years, Jack had made up his own world. On the inside, he was American.

On the outside, though, it wasn't looking too good.

Will was sitting in the living room when Jack came home from school the next day. He was unexpected. Jack barely knew his brother. During the last seven years, Will was the New Year's visitor who looked Jack up and down and whistled, who talked about how much Jack had grown since the last time they'd seen each other and how he was getting a beard. Every year, Jack laughed, but he also measured himself against his stocky, deep-voiced brother to try to see why people said the two boys were carbon copies of each other. He wondered what it was like to be twenty-five and so sure of things.

Today, though, Will barely acknowledged Jack. He sat so still he could've been a puppet in Papa's chair.

"Hey," Jack said. He wanted to talk, he needed it instantly. Until he saw Will, he hadn't realized he was lonely. "Welcome home."

"I took my old room back," Will said. "You can share it if you want."

"Thanks," Jack said, deciding it was a joke. He tried one of his own. "So what brings you home?"

Will frowned. A lock of hair dropped over his eyes and scraped his gold eyeglass frames like a question. "Yeah, it's bad in San Diego, too," he said at last. "Threats, you know. Kill the traitors. They were driving down my block last night. Different cars, but they'd come back over and over, you know? Yelling. It's just the beginning."

Jack didn't know—they lived in a Caucasian neighborhood among friends. He wanted to hear more, but before he could form a question, Will asked, "Where are Mama and Papa? Why aren't they home?"

Jack checked his watch. "Mama's usually done with her last house around four-thirty. Dad punches out at the orchard at six."

"They went to *work*? Jesus."

Jack nodded, though it hadn't occurred to him to confirm it with his parents before he left that morning. There was nothing dangerous about cleaning houses, even during a war.

That's when they heard the knocking—the yell, "Hey, open up in there!" Jack got up to answer the door, but a key was in the lock before he could reach it. It was Mr. Beattie, their landlord.

The man paused, caught with his hand on the knob. "The rent is due," he said. "It's late. You think I'm running a charity for Japs, you're wrong. I'm getting enough heat just having you here."

Jack stared at Mr. Beattie, confused. It had to be a mistake. Mama'd rather starve than owe money, and she'd never forget something as important as rent. It might've been lost, he thought, except Mama always delivered it in person. They'd have to wait for an explanation until she got home.

"We paid you," Will said when Jack didn't speak. They were his first words since the man appeared, and they were aimed and ready. Mr. Beattie and Jack both stepped back, surprised to find Will in the hall with them. Jack's brother was bluffing, but he was really in command.

"No, you didn't," the landlord said. He whipped a check out of his shirt pocket and held it in Will's face. Triumphant and not letting him touch it. "This isn't payment. It isn't any good."

"How do you know? You haven't tried to cash it."

"I heard it on the radio," he snapped, pulling the check away. "The banks closed you Japs out, so I am, too. Starting tomorrow."

"How much do we owe?"

"Thirty-two dollars."

Will turned his back on Mr. Beattie. He was halfway down the hall toward the bedrooms before he said, "Come in. Please. The door is open."

In awe, Jack watched him go.

The landlord took a step back toward the door and shoved his hands in his pants pockets. His stomach squeezed through his suspenders as he looked around. "What's he doing?"

Jack shrugged then, feeling the power of Will's silence. He let it settle.

Will came back with a wad of money. "That's thirty-five," he said. "You owe me three dollars."

Jack and Will watched Mr. Beattie struggle with the decision. He was so easy to read.

"I'm not gonna let you off this easy next time," he said at last. He turned to leave.

"If you don't have change, you can keep it until next month," Will called after him. "Then we'll only owe you twenty-nine."

Jack looked at his brother's face. Eyes alight but unsmiling until everything was won.

"I'm not gonna be beholden to no Japs," the landlord said, digging in his pocket for two faded bills and some change. "Next time, I'm gonna evict you."

When he was gone, Will leaned his back against the door. Palms flat, holding it shut. The tips of his hair trembled. He'd been so perfect, Jack wanted to hug him. He knew it was ridiculous—that he was just giddy with the fact Will was home.

"You should have answered him," Will said.

"What?"

"When he challenged you, called us a charity case. You should have done something."

Why? Jack wondered. He was a kid—he was supposed to let his elders lead. In fact, he couldn't remember the last time he'd been held responsible for anything, though he wasn't going to mention that. If it *had* been up to him, they'd be moving their furniture into the street by now.

"Well, I thought you did a great job—"

Jack stopped. Was it disgust he saw in Will's eyes, or just a flash in his brother's glasses as he straightened his immaculate hair?

"Do you know why I left San Diego?" Will asked, pushing himself off the door and squarely on his feet again. "They froze the bank accounts of the Japanese nationals yesterday so none of it could get funneled to Japan. I figured we'd be broke, so I took all my money out."

Jack knew enough to let him talk this time.

"When the FBI came for me, I headed home."

He should've paid more attention, Jack knew—should've listened to his brother when he said, "Always take a stand for what's right, Jack, there's a war going on." But he found Will's ways a little . . . traditional, and it wasn't clear, in a world of curfews and bombings, where even Will drew the line. When Jack had to stop visiting a couple of friends because he wasn't allowed to travel more than five miles from home, Will and his Nisei buddies in the Japanese American Citizens League didn't protest. Jack couldn't tell what was so right about that.

But he never expected the FBI to arrest his brother. Nor could he have imagined that Emi would choose those ten days to return home. That was Will's point—that you didn't know when you'd be called on. But even while it was happening, Jack wasn't sure.

Jack could never change the fact that he was the one who'd heard the doorbell and answered it. And when he saw the woman outside in Salvation Army rejects, he figured she was just a beggar—or someone lost—and it would be easy enough to send her away. Her dress was huge, its empty belt loops strained around her stomach. At first, he felt sorry for her, especially when he realized she was wearing rubbers on her feet. Not even shoes. But then, as he waited for her to speak, he decided not to give her any money. What changed his mind was her makeup—she was wearing so much of it and it was so bold.

It was pathetic, Jack decided, that someone that poor would be so vain. "Sorry. Wrong house," he said, letting the door close.

Then the beggar woman spoke. "Tosh?"

It was his Japanese name.

The word hit him hard enough that he caught the door, looked more closely into the night. Something about her seemed familiar. "It's Jack," he said, unable to project his voice suddenly. He knew the feeling, the fear that had come with the bombing and returned with every new restriction.

"Jack," she repeated. "Aren't you going to let me in?"

She seemed so entitled, he froze. Clearly she thought, at least, that she was in the right place. And she seemed to recognize him, though he was still struggling with who she was. He couldn't see her under all that makeup, in the dark. But he could hear her, and she sounded so much like—

Mama.

It was then that Jack remembered Emi. No one talked about her, she'd been away from home so long. She was born between Jack and Will—which made her about twenty. And there was no way, he thought, no way he'd let her in now.

Then, as his sister waited, it occurred to him that he didn't know her situation. He glanced at her stomach again, too embarrassed to stare. But his mother must, and she would've told him if Emi had married. Especially if she had married, Jack was sure.

Emi wasn't waiting for his answer anymore. She bent her knees slightly, grabbed a suitcase, and hoisted it up the one step into the hallway. Jack was afraid to help her, but he did move aside. Emi stepped into the house behind it—she had to move it, then herself, then move it again. She was too pregnant to carry it with her through the door.

"Mama," Emi said then. She was all business.

Jack turned to see his mother beside him. He couldn't tell when she'd come into the room or how long she'd been standing there. Her mouth was tight, not the slightest gap between her lips. Jack watched her polish her hands together—without a dish or a rag between them. Looking at her profile, though, he realized two things immediately.

Emi wasn't married.

And Mama wasn't the least bit surprised.

"You're home," she said.

"I need a place to stay," Emi answered in perfect Japanese.

Mama would never allow it, he thought. Not an unmarried mother. She wouldn't do that to the family.

Each woman waited for the other to speak, watched the other's face. Mama's was lined and tired but much more beautiful than Emi's. It wasn't just the makeup, Jack decided. Emi's eyes were bloated. Her chin fell into her neck.

Both women held their heads high until Mama came to a decision. "We'll get your things."

"These *are* my things." Emi made a movement toward the suitcase. She gave no indication that she'd just won a battle, had no gratitude toward Mama for taking her in. "This is everything."

"Where's the other one?" Mama asked.

Then Jack was lost. He thought it was his meager Japanese, but Emi seemed puzzled, too.

"The other what?"

"The other child," Mama said.

Emi froze. Jack waited for her to answer or leave, but she did neither. He wanted to ask, *what* other child? There's *another* child? Emi's face was carefully blank; it was clear to him that he was the only one thinking, who could see what had just happened, and what was to come. If he'd known how unyielding Will would be when he was released from detainment, Jack would have found the strength to send her away. But it was done. He had let her in.

It seemed better not to say a word.

All his friends are at school today, Jack reminds himself as he gets up from his blanket bed on the floor. With six days before evacuation, it's only the Jap kids who are staying home. Will has left him a list of chores—the first is to post a sign outside announcing the sale. Jack wonders what Will would think of BUY JACK OKADA'S LIFE. How about EVERYTHING BUT BEDDING, CLOTHES, AND PERSONAL EFFECTS ON SALE HERE, he thinks, remembering the instructions on the poster, but what "effects" are sufficiently personal? He taps the neat stack of his own bedding he has finished folding. Even though Will is at the Civil Control Center, Jack knows better than to do anything that will attract his brother's wrath.

FOR SALE it is, then, Jack decides, and it seems to convey the right message. The Okada's first customer, Mrs. Denney, crosses the street before he can finish hammering the stake into the ground.

"Oh, you poor dear," she says to him, and then, when Mama comes to the door, "Oh, Kaori, it's such a shame what's happening. To you, I mean. We know you're a good Jap."

Mama smiles, waves her into the house. Jack can't tell how much of the woman's words she understood.

"Anyway, I came by to see if there was anything I can take off your hands. I'm sure you can use whatever you get."

She has to know what she sounds like, Jack thinks, following them inside. After all, her best friend, Mrs. Conroy, is the one who put a WE DON'T SELL TO JAPS sign in the window of her grocery. Who jabs her finger at it if one of them dares to pass the store.

"Always ready to help out the needy," Mrs. Denney continues. "How much for the piano?"

"One hundred dollars," Jack says, giving her the price they paid.

The woman's eyes and mouth make rounds in her face. "Goodness, young man, I wouldn't pay that if it was new!" She steers Mama away. "Timmy, my youngest, needs a bureau. Nothing fancy, mind you. You might have just the thing."

It's the perfect time to say something, any of the hundreds of comments Will would make if he were here. Instead, Jack stands speechless as the woman's back disappears with his mother. Then the doorbell rings. Two minutes after he put up the sign.

Mr. Norton slaps Jack on the shoulder and pushes past him when he opens the door. "Saw your sign," he says in his booming voice. "Everything must go, eh?"

They are, Jack thinks, relentless. At times, the house is so full, people have to line up outside. "Doing the rounds," Mr. Norton says, and the others seem to know what he means. No one buys anything for the first price—as the hours pass, their offers drop. The rounds must be like a tour, Jack decides. See the little Jap houses. See how the Japs live.

If they aren't there to buy, the hell with them, he thinks. Mama can run around like a shop girl, trying to wheedle a couple of bucks out of some Caucasian who drops food on her linens and then asks for a markdown, but Jack isn't going to. He's quite happy with the sheer number of things they still own.

Then Emi sells the carved desk in the living room. She gets a fair price for it, too. At first, Jack is impressed—though he's sure the buyer feels sorry for Emi, hobbling around like she is. He slips into the kitchen so he won't have to carry the damned thing out, but he isn't bothered. Not until he returns a few minutes later and finds Emi selling their coffee table to a potbellied fellow in work clothes.

"I know it's a lot," she is saying softly, like she's afraid to be overheard. "Twenty dollars, but it's one piece of wood. It's quality. You wouldn't want anything less."

Jack stares at her. Ten is the price Mama's hoping for.

"I'll come back when the price goes down," the man says.

"Well, we have a place to store things, so we may keep it. But, then, you admire it so much, I might be able to sell it for ten, no fifteen. Fifteen."

"That's too much. Even ten's too much."

"It's a shame, since you said it would fit so beautifully in your home."

The fellow caresses the carved edge of the table with his finger, drawn into the bargaining—he's too stupid to look at her eyes. "I'll give you five."

Emi pretends to laugh. "My mother would faint on the spot. Too bad. I'd like to think of the table where someone can enjoy it, instead of sitting in storage. Maybe . . ."

"What?"

"Well, I said ten. It's my mistake. It's not fair for me to change my mind." Her thin eyebrows draw together when she says it, then she *flirts*. "I'll sell it for ten, but only if you take it now. If my mother finds out, she won't let it go."

His sister is a whore, Jack remembers. They are ugly words for an ugly truth. Emi is standing so close to the man that Jack doesn't know who he's sorrier for, the fellow for being suckered or himself for having a sister who could lie so wantonly and publicly for a couple of bucks. Of course, she has no feeling for what she's selling—it's someone else's furniture to her. But as he watches the man's fat fingers splay against the wood, it is Jack—not Mama—who suddenly cannot bear to let it go.

Jack steps forward, to call attention to himself, but not too much. He gives them time to wonder what he's thinking, waits until the fellow holds six bills in midair before he speaks.

"She's lying," he says. "It's not worth three."

The man frowns, glancing from Jack to his sister, then to the table and the money in his hand. Emi, on the other hand, pretends Jack hasn't said anything, doesn't exist. It's a tactic he's familiar with by now. In case she has more lies ready, though, Jack waits until the man puts the money safely back into his pocket.

Then he takes his eyes off his sister and walks out of the room.

4

KAORI

SO STRANGE, THIS REMEMBERING

My life doesn't return to me in any order. Moments flip-flop, overlap—sometimes they come only in splinters. The searchlights at Santa Anita can still pick me up so fast I forget what I'm thinking. They follow me in pieces to the latrine in the middle of the night, then drop me through the bitter doorway to feel my way around the wooden holes.

Bully memories, that's what they are. Strong, but trivial. Only birth and death can rule my time now. And regret. The things I didn't do.

Mariko. So foolish of me to talk to you when you can't hear. For you, I'm long gone, but I can still see you and I know what you want. The truth—your mother's secrets, even your own. You never asked me when I could still reach you, but if you had, I wonder what I would have said? That your mother was born weak? That I had good reasons for holding her away? When I needed Emi, she ran from me. During my worst moment, and I was never the same.

Secrets seem so important when one is alive. So much is invested in keeping them. Once you are dead, though, they are simply heavy.

And I can't leave until I set the big ones down.

I can see myself that day, standing in the dawn in the doorway, watching your grandfather's borrowed truck disappear. It was 1925, the year before our first harvest when we were still picking the owners' crops to pay off our debt. I was thirty-five years old and Mitsuo probably more than fifty. We had just moved into a two-room shack east of San Diego to work twenty acres of celery and carrots and whatever else we could get to grow.

Mariko, I was so tired. If I had only been injured, or only pregnant, I might not have stayed behind, but I had strained my ankle the night before and could barely hobble, so your nine-year-old Uncle Will went to the midweek market in my place. As it was, I had been waiting for the two of them to leave so I could lie down. Your grandfather didn't believe in resting. He didn't believe in pregnancy either; it was too corpulent for him. Once, I stood all night in Mitsuo's hope that the baby would give up and let go.

With the truck gone, the house relaxed; it felt patient. Your mother, Emi, was lying quietly in her own bed, and there was nothing, finally, that I had to do. I was drifting through sleep with the sound of my breath when your Uncle Jack cocked his leg back and kicked me hard and right into the base of my back. The force of his heel, maybe both of them, spread in a wide, aching band, cinching my belly so tight I couldn't breathe. Then he flipped over and grabbed my backbone with his fingers, as if to pull me inside out through my spine.

The pain came in waves, ebbing into my back where it gathered, waiting to strike, but never disappeared. It was complete, so momentous that I could hear it coming—like the echo of a heartbeat, the drone of dying drums. I had had two babies by then, your mother and Will, and I had never felt anything like it. It beat out of my back, shaking even the floor.

Then the tension seized me again. I heard a moan, then a thin, surprised protest that hung in my ears for mere seconds until the pain ran it down. I knew it had to have come from me—a woman who gave birth to your mother in silence—and I didn't understand how. I was hanging on to the edges of my mind, waiting to exist again when I heard my daughter's voice.

"Mama?"

I have no idea how long she had been speaking.

The girl stood behind the screen that separated our bed from the children's. Emi. She was four years old at the time. I couldn't imagine what she wanted. Nor did I care.

When I didn't answer, Emi waited, choosing to crouch on her haunches rather than leave. She trapped me in my bed as effectively as if she had held me down. I didn't want a witness, especially not one who would always be around. I had never, until that moment, shown any weakness to my children. I had been punished, of course, by your grandfather. But I had never been exposed.

"Leave me alone," I said before another pain could take me over. When it did, I bore down—not to give birth, but to keep absolutely still.

I rolled onto my side when it was over. I could still see her figure drawn on the tight screen. Emi's face was tucked into her knees and she was rocking, but I was too greedy to notice her fear. Instead, I found my attention lingering on the squat she had adopted. It looked instinctive, unconscious, and I wanted more than anything to drop into it myself.

I knew I couldn't. And in the moments when the pain ebbed briefly and my mind was clear, I knew I couldn't stay in bed forever, even if my daughter was too paralyzed to leave. The house was too far from our nearest neighbors for her to get help for me anyway. In effect, she was useless. I had to be strong.

When I stood, though, my legs waved under me. They were strangers—no longer connected—and I had to stare at my bones to get them to move. Hot water, I told myself, bolstered by the fact that I could remember that much. I repeated the words to keep myself heading for the stove.

That's why I barely noticed the girl when I tottered past her. She had frozen in the knot she made and didn't follow me to the cooking area until the fire was lit. I remember turning around to let the warmth into my lower back as I jammed my knuckles into the flesh on either side. Leaning forward helped a little, but I was afraid I would fall if I bent too far.

"Mama?" your mother asked.

She was back, lurking around the door. Her high, smudged voice and her questions made me angry; I wanted to think of myself as alone. I was being swept by longings I could barely control—to push, though it was too early, to scream—and I wanted more than anything to give into them. But the girl was there, still there. Keeping me from letting go.

"Mama?"

I turned away from her, still thinking *hot water*, but the empty bucket was so far. I tried to plot my path through the window and feel each step to the well. "The baby is coming."

She knew the baby was inside me and was looking forward to its birth.

"Stay out of the bedroom," I said, my voice breaking high in the last word as my stubborn son twisted again and my belly seized. "This is for grown-ups, not little girls."

She might have left, then; she might have stayed, I don't know.

I was bent over, trying to die.

I find myself at the well again, staring deeply into it at the bucket of water. I have lowered it to the bottom, and now there's no way to get it up. I could jump down, I think, as if floating might help me, but instead I begin hauling the rope, the wall of my belly splitting open with each tug. By the time the jagged rim has risen high enough that I can see it, tears are dripping off my chin. It takes every bit of will I have to get the bucket off the pulley and onto the ground.

By then, my pains are almost on top of one another. It's as if they have grabbed me by the ears and forced everything from my mind. My legs are bent and wide to keep the rest of me upright. My body takes over then, forcing me to my knees, and still farther, until my hands hit the ground and my belly swings away from my creaking backbone. The weight pulls the roaring in my ears and—miraculously—the pain is gone. I wait, not daring to move or breathe, feeling the dirt press under my nails as I dig my fingers through the grass, but I have been released. I find myself praying. Light streams into my eyes.

When I lift my head, I can see the house. I know I should rise to my feet and walk toward it, but I feel too good where I am. My thighs bump my belly gently as I crawl instead; my bare knees skim over the grass with a delicacy that belies my weight. I bunch the hem of my dress in one hand, freeing my legs as I sway back and forth—so loose, so easy for the first time since the birth pains began. I am in that position, happy as a beast, when the girl reappears and touches my shoulder. I have completely forgotten she is there.

"Ah, Emi, get the bucket." I am happy to see her until I look into her eyes.

Emi doesn't recognize me. She has come outside searching for her mother and is faced instead with an animal on its knees. And she is afraid. Of me. Not with the respect a child should have for her parent, but with revulsion. I can see her fear in the way her eyes flicker toward the fields.

She is too close: breathing, watching, judging me. My skin is hot beneath her fingers, so I slap her hand away. In her eyes, I can see my skirt, tugged up over my bowing belly, exposing the undergarments I have had to tie on. I pull it down, but not before the dirt flares in Emi's pupils, and clings to the sweat on my pale, fleshy thighs.

I am holding the hand I slapped in my own, when Emi pries it away. She runs behind me, and by the time I can turn around, she is gone. "Get back here," I say, knowing she is either in the field or behind the well wall. She doesn't answer, but I can see the top of her head behind the stones.

I can't get the water without her. And from my slow and lumbering turn, I can't judge how long it will take me to get back inside. Dirt stares at me in lidded circles from my knuckles. Emi's eyes are everywhere.

But although I can't bear to see myself through them, I need my daughter. Me, who has never asked for help. If I can erase what she sees, I think, perhaps I can lure her back. That's when I call out, "If you can hear me, Emi, you must help me. I promise, when you need me, I will always help you."

There is a plea in my tone, though I don't intend it. I have no authority she has to obey. That's when I decide to stand to prove I am still her mother. I am barely upright when the pain splinters my spine.

I think I faint then because the next thing I remember, I am lying on my side. Emi has reappeared, finally. Her face is pressed close to my own.

"Mama?" The word itself was the question. "Are you going to die?"

I grab at her wrist to help myself up, but she is faster and pulls away. "Please," I say. The ragged edges in my voice frighten us both, and I no longer remember what I am asking for. My head is filled with tears that pool in my eyes until I am like someone blinded, begging "please, oh, please" until she puts her hand out and helps me flip over. The pain eases, but not as much as it did the first time. Without asking, Emi takes the bucket and attempts to drag it into the house. Water slops out each time she steps and stops. I hitch my dress up and follow my daughter like a dog, but I am clearer than I was and no longer brave enough to stand. By the time I reach the house, I am covered in mud to my knees.

There was no question of boiling the water; less than half of it was left by the time your mother got it inside. There was no question, either, about going any farther than through the door.

Every time I leaned back or upright the stabbing pain returned, so I settled myself on my haunches, not much different from the way your mother had done behind the screen. The walls gave me nothing to hold, and it was difficult to keep my balance. Still, I propped myself in a corner of our entry hall and did the best I could.

"Cloth," I told Emi, reduced to gasping single words. I twisted, motioning her to the chest where I kept sheets and blankets.

She stared at me, mesmerized once again by my weakness.

"Listen," I said, using one precious hand to grab her face. "Get cloth. Do as I say."

She tore away from me then; by acting in a way she understood, I had released her. I could hear her fall on her knees before the trunk and fumble with the leather latches. She returned and dropped two folded stacks of clothing in a pile at my feet. She brought shirts and dresses mostly, light-colored things that would be ruined. I didn't care enough to complain.

"Under me," I directed her. "The baby comes . . . under me." I pushed against my thighs to raise myself high enough for her to lay the clothes in a patchwork under my naked buttocks. She circled my feet with the blouses, since I could no longer lift them off the floor. The last sane part of me resisted the urge to be naked, but, with my dress bunched under my breasts, I may as well have been. We could both see the angry red and white lines on my belly and the way it roiled with a life of its own.

"Get a knife. Go on," I ordered before her face could freeze and she could ask me once more if was I going to die. Just as it had before, my voice picked her up and spun her on her heels. I could hear her scrambling into the kitchen, dragging a chair over to the counter, then jumping down and scrambling back.

By then, I was too weak to stay on my feet. My buttocks dropped to the ground and I bent my knees, forcing my back into the corner. The pain was at the edge of me, in the splitting skin between my legs. My mouth was so dry, I could have stuck my head into the bucket and not quenched my thirst.

"Go," I said when she returned. I could feel Jack's head pushing to get out. There was nothing left for her to do.

She turned, uncertain, the knife still in her grasp. "I want to help."

Perhaps she thought I was going to slit myself open. Whatever her fear, I had no time to explain. Each moment curled me into a ball that wound tighter and tighter until all that was left was the pain and the seizing—I was blind to everything but getting the baby out. It was as if I had eyes in every nerve; I could see the hair on Jack's head, shoving against me, then slipping back inside.

The girl settled opposite me. "I'll be a good girl."

I wanted to grab the baby's hair and rip him out of me. I wanted to rip your mother's hair out, too. She had forced me to stand, reduced me to begging. She was responsible for my humiliation, and now it was a part of me.

I felt my skin rip then and I knew it would be only moments until Jack's head came into the world. I pushed hard, through a white wall of needles that rang through every inch of my skin, and they didn't hurt; I felt almost peaceful. I could see the girl's mouth move. Her arms uncurled in front of her as her body jumped forward. There was a pause, once she reached me, then I felt the baby go. He skidded out in a gush of fluid, too slippery and fast to be caught. I could see it all, as if I was watching from the sky. The baby slid over the girl's forearms and landed on the floor.

Jack started screaming before he hit the ground. At least, that's how I remember it. It was a high-pitched cry of hunger and anger, and the longer I ignored it, the stronger it got. I knew I couldn't hold him; I was shaking so badly my arms could no longer hold me. My hair snagged on the splintered walls as my head slid to the floor.

My free hands moved, almost as if I willed them, out of the blood around me and into the bucket by my side. The red swirled off them, tinting the water that I slurped from my palms. I bent my head still farther, thinking I could plunge my entire face in it, when I felt a tug between my legs. The umbilical cord pulled tight. My son and I were still attached.

That's when I began to cry in earnest. I had come this far—alone, with no one to help me or hold me—and there was further to go. Was it too much to ask? I wondered, to be able to rest? But I couldn't yet; I wasn't free.

Emi, of course, didn't know what to do. She had grabbed a cloth and began wiping Jack's face, but she didn't seem to notice the cord. I remember watching her hand reach toward the pile of clothing—she didn't dig around in it, her fingers merely grabbed the piece on top. I saw the fabric crumple in her filthy fingers, then there was blood on it, too. It was a dress with an indigo ghost-crane pattern that my mother had given me. My last surviving gift from home.

I had no energy to mourn when Emi destroyed my dress. I had nothing left, nothing inside me to feed my son. Perhaps if I slept, I thought. If I did just one thing for myself. But first I had to cut the cord.

"Give me the knife," I said. It was strange to hear a full sentence. I motioned for Emi to push him toward me, and when he was close enough, I saw he was a boy. His scrotum was a bloody red ball. His tiny fingers were blue.

I was so cold, there, staring at his blue fingers. It was as if he took all my heat with him when he was born. And then, I felt the afterbirth leaving almost incidentally. It slithered out between my thighs and onto the floor.

Together, Emi and I stared at the mound of veins. It was a large, dark bag—red and black and blue. She gave me the knife, and I grasped the gnarled cord and cut it. There was very little blood.

"Now take him away."

"Away?"

"Leave me alone."

He was too big for her to lift, so Emi packed some more clothing under him and dragged him a few feet. I waved her farther and she went, reluctantly, but only to the opposite wall. Jack's cries had subsided; now he was only whining. I lay on my side, burying one ear in some cleaner clothing and covering the other one so I could sleep.

"I helped you." Emi said it matter-of-factly. I was so far from saved, I didn't know at first who she was talking to. Your mother was so proud as she tried to lift Jack onto her chest that she seemed to be claiming what little credit there was for my labor. I was outraged that she would try.

"No, you didn't," I said.

"I . . ." Emi paused, her satisfaction lingering on her face, misplaced and fading. I waited for her to continue so I could tell her all the things she hadn't done. If I had, we might have put it all behind us. Instead, I closed my eyes against her and went to sleep.

Funny, when I see her now, Emi looks so young. Her eyes swing repeatedly toward mine; it's how I know she wants me to speak. But I can barely hold mine open, and I know I have a right to be tired. And as I lie there, ignoring her, she decides to be cheerful. She lowers her ear to Jack's breath. She counts his fingers and toes.

Even without my eyes, I can hear her sing to him. She is trying to keep him still. But I can tell he is hungry and I know I must give in and feed him.

Ah, Mariko, it's so strange, this remembering.

It's so hard to tell the truth.

5

MARIKO

PERFECT DAUGHTER, 1990

Mari had parked in the far corner of the lot so that, even if Emi came out of the restaurant to look for her, she wouldn't see the car through the confusion of plants that hung from the rafters of the *lanai*. She was now fifteen minutes late for their lunch date, no longer the perfect daughter who arrived everywhere on time. If Emi knew why Mari had called her, though, she would be less eager than Mari was for this meeting. Roger was the one who had thought it was important. He had some very strange ideas about what Mari needed to know.

When Roger walked in on the night Mari got her camp papers, he didn't mention the fact that she was sitting in the dark. He listened patiently as she explained that she'd always thought Eric was her cousin, while she remembered that she and Roger had seen him at her Grandmama Okada's funeral five years before. She hadn't thought anything of it, then; there were so many people, "calabash" aunties and uncles—friends of her grandmother's from as far back as the war. That was her message: that she had had no warning signals, no clues.

"What did your mother say?" Roger had asked then, after the dinner dishes were finished and they were getting ready for bed. Mari was studying herself in the bathroom mirror, noticing the extra softness beneath her eyes and wondering whether it was finally time to dye the white streak in her hair that she had had and loved since she was thirty, so she was able to watch Roger's question catch her. She could see it dig at her most vulnerable and most exhausted places and understood immediately that she had been trying to distract him all evening with details and noise. Mari knew Roger disapproved of the elliptical relationship she and Emi had—the way she worked so hard to protect her mother when he thought it should have been the other way around. It was one of the few complaints she always felt free to ignore.

"You know she would never tell me anything," Mari said. "You know it as well as I do."

"So show her the proof."

"What proof?"

"The papers, Mar."

She met his eyes, flinching at how intently his reflection met her own. How could her husband understand so little after all these years? "Why would that matter?" she asked him. "I handed her my birth certificate forty years ago and she didn't admit a thing."

Mari had told Roger that story when they met, and he made her laugh about it for the first time in her life. She had laughed again on the day they married, when she realized that Emi was hovering beside the minister and the church register, ordering the newlyweds to go on ahead with the photographers, because she didn't want Roger to see Mari's birth name. Mari could still feel him pulling at her, eager to move, and she wondered suddenly if she had been laughing alone. Had he even realized what her mother was trying to do? Recalling his face now, Mari didn't think so.

Even then, they were living further apart than she knew.

Mari left the bathroom and moved to their bed. She fluffed a pillow and curled against it, dusting her feet so they wouldn't dirty the bedspread, then she grabbed a second one to hug just in case. Roger followed, but not quickly enough. He sat beside her with one shoe on the floor and the other pressed into the bed.

"You're probably right," he mused, "she'll try to avoid it. It'll help if you confront her in public so she can't get away."

"I can't believe you said that." Mari heard tears; ridiculous, useless tears. "How could—" She didn't know how to finish. When had he turned assigning blame into such an art?

Roger hugged her then, pillow and all. "I'm sorry. That didn't sound right."

Mari closed her eyes so she could feel Roger's hands, at last, and his unpracticed voice. He was waiting. "Don't you see? I can't ask her," she said. "It's just not something you talk about."

She knew he would ask, why not? She could hear the question build in his chest, one slow word placed on the next like pickup sticks. He'd never felt the loneliness, the inexplicable threat that came with being ignored. Besides, Mari had never told George Hamada that she knew he wasn't her father; if they never acknowledged it, it didn't have to be true. As old as she was, Mari still couldn't bear to lose her family. She couldn't turn on them, then or now.

"What do you think happened, Mar?"

"I don't know. There was a war. Who knows the pieces?"

"Not you, obviously. It must be awful."

Roger was stroking her scalp, pulling individual hairs by accident; she could hear them crackle under his fingers as he rubbed. Mari hated to pull away. She had to fight herself, literally, and put a hand on his chest, to rise. But she had to; she knew it wasn't going to end there.

"What must be awful?"

"Not knowing."

Mari counted to ten, slowly, getting air with each number. "All right," she said. "Just tell me."

"Tell you what?"

"Whatever it is you're getting at. What you think I want to know."

Roger had taken her hand, then, tightened his fingers around hers, as if he could keep her from falling. "You want to know why. What happened." And then, because Mari had no idea what he was talking about, Roger said, "I mean you and Eric were together in the camps, right? She had two kids. It was right there on paper. So then, clearly, she left him. And for some reason, you were chosen."

Mari wasn't going into the restaurant to see her mother. She had known from the moment she pulled into the parking lot, but she couldn't admit it until now. She simply didn't believe, as Roger did, that by giving Mari the family number, Emi had signaled that she was ready to tell the truth. On the contrary, it meant that her mother trusted her not to ask. Mari had challenged Emi's truth only once, when she was a child, and had barely escaped with Emi's love. She pledged then that she would protect her mother in whatever way she had to. There was too much at stake to revoke that pledge now.

Mari knew her decision was the right one. During the last four days since she had gotten the camp records, she had become keenly aware of how much her mother loved her. She had had a vision, which she viewed as both a reminder and a warning. It began with an image of herself in a red dress.

The vision had been widening slowly. She was walking down a city sidewalk she had never seen before. There was someone with her, too, who wouldn't move into Mari's view. On the drive here, Mari had felt that person slip a hand in hers. The love that came with the gesture had almost driven her off the road.

Mari had no idea if it was an actual memory. She was afraid to tell Roger, mostly because he would think she was crazy, but also because she didn't want to scare the vision away. She wanted to understand what she was seeing first, and she believed that she was beginning to. She looked to be about the same age she was when she found her birth certificate—a precarious time for her and Emi. It was also about that same time that her grandfather Okada had died, and Mari had gone to his funeral with her mother. That was in Los Angeles, so it was possible that the vision was real.

As far as Mari knew, that was the last time her mother had seen any of the Okadas. Whatever had happened to make Emi leave Eric, it had clearly robbed her of more than her firstborn child. It didn't seem fair to Mari, especially if her mother had simply been trying to make a life for herself in the midst of a war. That was only one explanation, of course, but Mari had read recently that adults were released from the camps to work or go to school after a certain amount of time, and she thought it was quite possible that Emi had done so, returning as soon as she was able to care for at least one child. In fact, it seemed so likely that Mari wondered if she had already been given that explanation and had lost it along with the other memories she was struggling to find.

Of course, Emi never did reclaim Eric. But then, there must have been a point when she realized her child's welfare was more important than her own. After years of living with his grandmother and uncle, Eric had surely formed bonds that should not be broken. It must have taken a lot of courage for her to sacrifice her happiness for her son's.

Mari could go into the restaurant and never raise the topic, she knew, but Emi would be anxious and quiz her closely about her delay. Instead, she used the pay phone at the gas station to leave a message for her mother. Her brakes had failed, she told the hostess who answered. No one was hurt, and she would call Emi later from home.

Mari drove directly out of Hilo, over the airplane bridge and toward Ahualoa. She had disconnected herself from her past and her future; no one could ask anything of her for the rest of the afternoon. The last time she felt this innocent was in high school, when she and her girlfriends used to sneak away during open periods to watch the guys surfing. Somewhere nearby, if only she could find it, was their favorite lookout. It was the place where Mari fell in love with her first husband, Dale.

Mari had wanted to believe she was in love, anyway. She had wanted to know what her girlfriends felt when, one by one, they declared that the nondescript boys they had just been dancing with were real men, and then lost their capacities for thought. Mari spent too much time judging the boys she dated to bring herself even to kiss them. This one's pimples were repulsive; she didn't like how that one smelled.

Any one of them would have been kinder than Dale, she knew now. But she never recognized his moodiness, principally because he was rarely around. He was two years older than Mari, so he came to the lookout when he felt like it, leaning into her car window only when his surfing was done. Dale had wanted to be a cop; he wasn't content to work in a gas station. But Mari fell in love with the way he arched his torso when he aimed his board at the rocks.

Why hadn't her parents opposed the marriage? she wondered. She couldn't imagine letting Tyler make such a mistake. But Dale behaved himself, more or less, before they were married. Even then, he never hit her. He found the part of her that gave up.

Mari hadn't realized how unhappy she was until she got pregnant, eight years into their marriage. By then, Dale's cruelties had worn a path in her heart. He'd found her vomiting into the toilet one morning before she had the chance to tell him about the baby. He'd called her a flurry of names and walked out.

Mari had hung over the porcelain ring, letting the grief she had swallowed eddy beneath her as she listened to Dale pack a bag. In the silence that followed, she realized that she'd spent years wishing he would leave. Her nausea lifted; she felt good for a moment. Then she remembered that she wasn't alone any longer, and not even Dale would walk out on his child.

Mari dialed her mother's number, not pausing long enough to

rinse her mouth. Emi made arrangements for her to see Ed Spencer, divorce lawyer and family friend, the following afternoon. Unable to wait, Mari put on the pair of low-slung jeans that her crazy sister, Kim, had sworn were the *thing* among single women. Then she left the house, with a plan to purge every trace of the baby. Mari didn't care whether it was illegal.

She had to make it impossible for Dale to return.

The only good thing about her first marriage, Mari decided, slowing her car to search for the lookout, was that it introduced her to Roger. She had been sitting in the waiting area of Kawai, Spencer and Stone the day after Dale walked out, still wearing her ridiculous hip huggers and crying the tears that had risen the minute she'd heard her mother's familiar voice on the telephone. Ed Spencer was late; his secretary didn't know when he would return. She had suggested more than once that Mari reschedule her appointment, but Mari was too afraid to leave.

She had gone through four tissues by the time she saw a man emerge from the hallway behind the receptionist. He held a glass of water in one hand. Mari looked up with gratitude, but it wasn't Uncle Ed. She curled her feet more tightly under her, trying to hold on.

"Roger Stone," the man said, stretching his other hand to shake hers. "Ice water sometimes takes the heat out."

He meant her face. He sat down in the chair next to her and didn't seem the least bit embarrassed, though she knew she must look terrible. Mari pulled her hand and eyes away and tugged her blouse down to cover the top of her pants. If Roger saw her gesture, he didn't register it. His gaze remained polite.

"Mariko," Mari said, looping her loose mane of hair over her eyes. Her predicament was so enormous, she couldn't think of a last name to use. "I'm a bastard."

Roger smiled. It was a sweet smile in a strong face, and she was amazed to find herself lingering on it. "Most of the women who come in here claim their husbands are the bastards."

"Oh, God—" She had been trying to confess, was at a loss to explain until she realized what he had said.

Mari laughed.

It was a raw laugh, on the edge of tears, until Roger began laughing with her. He tipped his head back, shaking his sandy, softly cut hair so that she could see the few strands of gray at his temples. He enjoyed it so much that she could feel herself responding, evening out her voice until the sound was clear and high. Every time she looked at him, it began again.

"You should pick a different label," he advised her when they had caught their breath. "You're going to be stopping enough conversations as it is. I mean that as a compliment. You know, like when you walk into a party and everyone stops talking."

"A party?" She couldn't conceive of it.

"Well, when you're single again, meeting new people. You can be anything you choose."

"I'm pregnant," she said.

"Ah. Well. There's child support, if you want it."

"No, I meant it's biological. The laughter. I meant I wasn't laughing at you."

"Hmm. Too bad." He tried for a serious tone.

Who was this man who assigned such value to her words? Mari wondered. She could only imagine his reaction if she told him her pregnancy wasn't going to be an obstacle; she was planning to have an abortion later that afternoon. In a way, though, the abortion was consistent with his other comment, that she could be anything.

It was simple. So liberating. "Mr. Stone, right?"

"Roger."

"Stone? As in Kawai, Spencer and?"

"That's me."

"You're a partner?"

"I know. No one believes it. Too young. Hair's too long."

"That's not what I meant," she said, although it was. "I was just wondering . . . Uncle Ed isn't here. Maybe you could be my lawyer?"

"How about grabbing a cup of coffee with me instead? Unless, some milk for the baby?"

"I'd rather you didn't mention that," Mari said, sorry that she had brought it up. It didn't matter, though, since she would never see him again.

"We could go for a walk, then. Pass the time. There's a pretty park around the corner. Lots of banyan trees."

Even seated, Roger was tall. His hands were large, with flat fingers and nails that reminded her of guitar picks. He was the kind of man, she decided, who didn't ask permission for what he wanted. A good trait for a lawyer to have.

"I need to get this over with," she said. "Couldn't I just sign something?"

"Yes, but you should wait for Ed. You should have one lawyer, start to finish. For continuity."

"I can pay."

"That's not my concern. It's just that you look like you need more than a lawyer. And if you need one, I'd rather be your friend."

"My friend?" Mari had the urge to laugh again. Too bad she wasn't the carefree person he saw. She had spent her entire adult life waiting on a man who despised her.

She wasn't brave.

"My friend?"

"Is that so strange?"

"Yes," Mari said. "I guess it is. You can't just become someone's friend." She drew back, as much to protect herself as to look at him. Blondish hair, greenish eyes, more than six feet tall—the partner of a family friend. "You know what my mother would say? She'd say, 'Watch out, he's probably one of those psychos. Otherwise, why would he be so interested in you?'"

"Why would I be interested?" Roger widened his smile when he realized she was sincere. "Just my luck," he said. "You're funny, too."

* * *

Funny, that's what Roger said she was. There was a brief time when she had let him project it into her, but it had been impossible to sustain. She owed him more than that, even then, but how was she supposed to know what was to come? That was the problem with memory, Mari thought. In the glare of the future, the past seemed so wrong.

Mari had had to backtrack to find the overlook she had been searching for. Sometime during the thirty years, the road had been paved. She understood now that she had left her mother to come here, hoping to see something in today's young people that would help her make sense of her actions. But although it was prime afterschool surf time, Mari was alone.

There were no heads bobbing beneath her. No winter storm waves to bring the past back. In the flat silver sunlight through Mari's windshield, she could almost believe that none of it had happened.

Maybe that was the message she had come here for. That neither Mari nor her mother had actually hurt anyone.

It didn't seem fair that either one of them had lost so much.

6

KAORI

HOW SHE LEFT US

Your mother had so many excuses. She could tell ten stories with the same breath. I told her, I don't know how many times, that some things cannot be helped, but she never listened. There was something else I used to tell her, too, that everything's connected: if you turn your back on someone, you turn against yourself.

I don't think I realized how weak she was, though, until the Depression. We had moved the family to Los Angeles by then, and when the stock market crashed in 1929, everything we had was gone. By Christmas, the dry cleaning business where your grandfather worked had been boarded up, and we were eating butter sandwiches and Spam.

We needed our children to survive. At first, no one was hiring. More than a year passed before Will and your grandfather got work picking cabbage outside of the city. By then, I was cleaning houses for food. Your mother could have worked, but instead, she took care of Jack, since he was too young for school. They were close in age, maybe four years apart, so she could keep him out of trouble and keep herself out of the fields at the same time. I let her live off our labor until Jack enrolled in first grade. Then, we needed money. It was time to find Emi a job.

She decided she wanted to clean. It was her choice; she said she wanted to be like me, though I knew she cared more about staying out of the sun. I knew she thought it would be easy, so I gave her the most tedious jobs. Emi hot waxed floors. I taught her to make things sparkle using onion skins. There is an old Japanese saying, "Rain firms the ground," and I thought it was coming true then. My daughter didn't complain once. It was just a hint of hardship, but it seemed to be turning her around.

By the time she was twelve, Emi was so meticulous at finding dirt that the easiest thing I ever did was find her a live-in position. She cried a little, not wanting to leave us, but it was a better job than the rest of us could have gotten: her weekly wages were twenty-five cents over the standard rate, before food, and they offered to let her continue with school. I didn't realize she still needed my guidance until she was almost fired in the first few weeks because she was stubborn—then I made it plain that I wouldn't allow her to return home. If your mother hadn't kept trying, wasting her precious wages on trolley fare to appear unannounced, I wouldn't have had to be so harsh. But I was more comfortable without her around watching me, I can see that now. For a while, she wrote us letters until her Japanese characters became too awkward. I still don't know what happened to her during those years, and I'm not sure I want to.

That's how she left us. That's all I know.

It is late summer, 1940, and I am waiting on Alameda for the trolley to take me home. My hair itches. Even though I know it's sweat, I imagine there are spiders chasing one another on my head—it's the same soft scramble I felt when I was scrubbing Mrs. Hannaford's toilet. I had twisted around to find a fat-bodied creature on the inside of my knee, waiting for my move, or perhaps choosing a direction. It was swollen; there was hair, so I knocked it, expecting a shock in my fingers. Instead, my hand caught its web and it sailed easily, away and then back toward me, climbing higher on the thread with those purposeful legs as it swung. It would have only touched my dress, but I could feel it land on my bare thigh, so I shook my hand and it dropped. My feet were already stamping. I should have realized Dickie was hiding outside the door to see if I would kill his "pet" and that I'd be forced to forgo my pay. So while I'm standing in the heat, which rises from the concrete and beats down, I know a whole jar of spiders are free, or waiting to be freed one by one, in Mrs. Hannaford's house. And I wonder, if there is a spider in my hair, whether I can let it go unharmed.

That's when Emi steps out of the salon.

I am slow to recognize her. Her face is pale, her eyes are much larger and rounder than I remember. Her sharp makeup has etched her eyebrows into wings over bent lashes. She has rouged her cheeks so they seem pointed. She looks much older than eighteen.

Each piece of Emi comes at me—distinct but gone too quickly to prompt a thought in my mind. She is wearing those high-heeled shoes that rattle women's ankles, and precious stockings on her calves. Her dress is a childish pink with an elaborate lace yoke meant to draw the eye. The line of the dress is simple, and the waist, of course, has been let out. Her shoes curve her back and throw her stomach forward; it rolls obviously beneath the surface of her dress.

She is my daughter, so I raise my hand to stop her, but when she pauses, intent on her pocketbook, my throat is seized. By then, she is in and out of focus—she is Emi and she is not. I feel absolutely no connection to the creature standing before me. She is much older and more modern than the gawky child I thought I had, and at the same time so vulgar and crude. As I watch her fingers dive into her purse, I search for a ring on her swollen knuckles and find, instead, pink painted nails. My impulse is to go over to her and yank on her ear until she's dropped to her knees. I imagine that, once I do, she will shed her bloated body and return to me. But I am nauseated at the thought of taking her home in the state she's in.

As I wait for her eyes to sweep over me, and for my heart to beat again, I curse her stupidity and her complete lack of regard for us. She doesn't notice the people around her. Her eyes gaze ahead as if there's something interesting to see. The moment goes on forever, and, strange as it seems, I find I am staring at her neck. It rises off her shoulders like wheat, impossibly long and light. It might be her scooped collar, or the high twist in her hair, but I am stunned by the vastness of her skin. How new it seems, and how free.

The moment is brief. Without trying, I have taken a few steps back, putting space and a heavy Negro woman between us, so Emi doesn't catch me standing there. Once she comes back from her daydreaming, she heads north, striking the ground so firmly I expect to see her heels snap off with any step. The bus doesn't pull up right then, nor does Emi turn a quick corner and vanish from my view. When she is ready, I think, she will know where and how to find us. Still, it takes a long time for her to walk away.

There are secrets that are hard to keep and secrets that are hard to tell. And, in our family, there are so many because we never told the truth. It was something we never wanted to do, to understand what had happened to our lives. It got us through the bad times, and I know it's gotten you through yours, too, but it can't last forever. Without the whole truth, we're like those people who can't see color. There was a woman like that in the camps. She could never find her mess hall because she couldn't read her tag. One day, when I was sitting with her, she asked me to describe it. Green. There were no words. Just a sense of something missing.

So here's what's missing in our lives. If you ever hear this story, Mariko, remember that people can change. Your mother's a better woman now: a mother and a wife. But things went wrong for Emi early and they had to get worse. It was part of God's plan.

Pearl Harbor was also part of that plan. The war brought everyone home. Emi came home one night in February, more than a year after I saw her on the street. She was the last one, and she was pregnant. Again, but for a moment when I first saw her, I thought, still.

There's a single knock on the door, an accidental sound. When the next knock comes, softer and after a pause, I dry my hands on my apron. No one else is rushing to answer the door, and the thought that I am alone makes me nervous. Even then, there is something dangerous about the sound. It occurs to me that I should ignore it, then I chide myself: how bad could it be?

Emi's third knock almost strikes my face when I open the door, but she pulls it back in time. Since there is light behind me, and dark around her, I don't see her hand. I see a shadow, like a fear, that makes me think the war has landed. I expect to see soldiers, bayonets, the enemy on our shores.

She has opened the screen door. It's resting on her back, making it harder for me to see, and it takes me a moment to stop searching the motionless streets and look at her. The makeup I remember is gone. Her hair is straight as a young girl's. She looks hunted, beaten black around her eyes, and the realization that this is Emi, that she's done this to herself, strikes me as she watches. I can tell by the way she lingers on the edge of the dusk that she can see more than the outline of my face. And that coming home is a test she expects me to fail.

Until this day, I don't know why I let her in. Whether it was Eric who guided me, although I didn't know the truth about him at the time, or whether it was the knowledge that only I could save her. I did ask about him, before she even walked through the door, but she pretended not to know what I was saying. It was such an unsettled time, I let it drop.

I was going to be truthful, wasn't I? Well, then, I must have let it drop because of Jack. He came into the room at some point, maybe to help Emi with her suitcases, and I couldn't let him find out about Eric through me. I couldn't bear for him to realize I knew Emi had had a child all along, and did nothing.

I held that secret in for days while Emi sat in the room we cleared for her. She was pretending to be ailing, avoiding even supper, the only meal where we sat together like a family. She never gave me a moment, and I was finding it difficult to wait—for her health or her courage—when there was so much other waiting to do. I slept the same fitful sleep I had in the years we were farming, knowing the crops weren't in and the cold was dropping down. Do you know what I mean? Something out there needs to be gathered. Every morning, it might be gone.

I was exhausted in those days, too, why else would I have waited? I made myself sick wondering how she could sit in that room knowing her child expected her to return. That's what I imagined, that she'd left him in a rented room, promising to be back soon. Maybe she had told him to bar the door, that she was leaving to get food. I spun it all out—they were starving; the boy was so thin. Baby, not boy. I had a hard time seeing him because I didn't know what he looked like. I hadn't given him a face at that point, and I had to keep thinning him down in my mind. I do remember he was almost dead before I forced my way into Emi's room.

She hesitates before she says, "Come in," and when I open the door, I find her writing. She's curled on the bed, a light quilt buckling over her feet, using her knees as a desk. Her lap ripples with her tiny script, and as I come near, she turns the top page over. She smiles, as if to start fresh.

I don't sit in the plain chair that stands between us. Time is running out. I ask my questions, and when she tries to evade them, I tell her, very plainly, that she's a liar.

"I saw you," I say. "I was on the corner of Alameda, not last summer, the one before. You walked right past."

Emi flushes and sets her pen down, as if every movement will give her time. I can imagine the tight guilt in her breast as she remembers how she looked that day. "You saw me?"

"You'd gotten your hair styled."

"I walked past? Why didn't—why didn't you say anything? Why didn't you stop me?"

Her pregnancy has pinned her in the corner, leaving only her face and thin arms for defense. She stares at her page, looking for instructions or an answer. I look, too, at the loops and curls, the precision of it, and know, though I can't read it, that she will explain.

Then she says, "It was a boy."

I make her repeat it. Her plunging voice, and the word *boy*, which is tired and mostly breath, make me think the baby must have died. Her sadness is so convincing. Then she says, "I gave him up for adoption."

My knees still roll when I hear that word. I see the little boy from my imagination left in the rented room to die. I see Eric himself, as he was when you were born. Touching your week-old hair, clapping to make you jump. He liked to show me your fingernails when we three were together in the internment camp. They were the smallest things in the world to him, and I often found him straightening your fingers so he could wave them around. It didn't hurt you. He was learning sizes. I can still remember how Eric screamed whenever Emi pulled him away.

That was the future my daughter was trying to destroy, though neither of us knew it then. Still, Emi must have suspected something as she stared out the window, trying hard to send herself somewhere I was not. What I saw in that stare, in her eyes as dull as stones and as far, was that, while she was gone from us, she had gotten what she couldn't have. Shouldn't have had. She had stirred right and wrong together until all the edges were gone. I couldn't imagine how she could create life and leave it in someone else's arms.

"Where is he?"

She turned toward me then, annoyed at being pushed, but she knew what would happen next. She was just gathering the strength to get through it. "I said I gave him away. Do I have to say everything twice?"

"I asked you where he is. You answer me."

"Mother, he's fine, all right? I know he's fine. I gave him to a nice couple."

"A nice couple."

"I met them myself, at the hospital."

Her insolence, her attempts to persuade me even for a moment, were making my head pound. "Who are they?" I asked. "Give me the name."

"No."

I stood there, searching her bloated features, waiting for something I recognized, some piece of my daughter to emerge.

She tried whining. "Why? What right do you have to demand things of me?"

"I'll go to the hospitals. I'll go to the law."

"No."

"No. What does 'no' mean coming from you?"

"No, you can't call them. You can't."

"Emi, you don't give away your child! Do you understand me?" My hands trembled at her stubbornness, wanting to slap her with every word so they would sink in somehow. I saw pieces of her only. Lank hair. A tarnished smile, and Salvation Army work shirt. "He's not a doll to set aside and forget. He's family."

"Family." She spat the word, gathered herself into anger. "What's family to you? What about me? Aren't I family? You see me in the street, and you don't stop me. You send me away for years, then you don't even say hello! That's what family means to you." But she couldn't have believed those words because she backed away from them as soon as they were out. "He's better off where he is, Mother. You wouldn't understand."

"I?"

"Yes, I can't explain it—"

"I wouldn't understand? You're the one—" I saw Emi's face again on Alameda, her pink fingernails, her satisfied smile. I thought of how I could have shamed her, and how, instead, I'd let her go free. "You are going to tell me where that little boy is or get out of my house."

I wasn't gambling. There was no chance she would leave. It was February—the FBI still raided houses, and people spat on us in the street. We were living in military zones. "Tell me or get out."

"Mother, please, I'm sorry. I'm sorry for what I said." She'd felt the shift, knew she was weaponless but didn't understand. "If I tell you, you have to promise you won't do anything, okay?"

I turned my back on her.

"Wait, all right?" she said. "Okay. The last name is Kurakawa. They live in Glendale. It's a nice place. They're nice people."

She paused, then in a child's voice, she said, "You have to leave him there."

"You don't give away a baby," I repeated.

Emi rolled around her stomach and got up from the bed. Hesitating. She came to where I was standing, so close that it seemed she wanted to touch me. "Mother, please listen to me. Don't try to get him. He'll be happy where he is."

I stared past her, through the sharp light of winter and into other people's houses.

"Mother, please! Don't do this. Please leave him alone. Please."

"Don't beg, Emi," I said. "How many times have I told you not to beg?"

"Oh, God," she said. "Don't beg? What else can I do? I need you to listen." Her image was coalescing: her distended stomach hung off her shoulders, pulling her skin tight against the bones.

"Why won't you listen?" she pressed. "Why are you doing this? You don't know. Do you realize you haven't even asked me about it? What happened? It's not important to you, is it? Not important to ask about your own daughter? Talk to me, Mama, please. Can't we talk about this?"

She'd put her hands on me in her begging. She was desperate to stop something that had to go forward, and she wanted me to take the blame.

I pushed her away. "We're past talk, Emi. We're long past talk."

"You have no right to do this. No right. You can't make me take him. I swear, I'll have nothing to do with him. If you do this, he belongs to you."

"He'll always belong to you," I told her. I was at the door.

Again she changed, persecuted and surprised now, as if I had closed the door in her face. "Mother, wait. Please, listen to me. You can't— Why are you doing this? You don't understand. You don't know what you're doing."

Then, finally, she gave in. She dropped back onto the bed, her head wobbling, talking to herself, trying to curl. Her words were bubbles on the water, but her tears fed them and they grew. "Oh God, I knew I should never have come home," she was saying. "I should never have told you. I should have stayed far away."

I felt no pleasure standing over her like that. There was no reason for me to stay.

As I closed the door gently behind me, Emi screamed one last time. "Mother, please! You can't do this! Mother, please! Mother, talk to me!"

Talk to me, she said. It was her most common, most insistent demand. But that's all we said about what happened, then or ever. That's how Eric came into our lives.

7

ERIC

RUNAWAY, 1950

The best thing about boats, Eric thinks as he lies facedown on his bed going over his escape plans, is that barnacles live on them and they have to be scraped off. That's a job for boys, stowing away across the ocean, who can hold their breath forever and swim. He can swim. He can coil the rope on deck, too, lugging it heavy into loops between his legs—one leg in the circle, one dragging around it—to make a ready lasso for the sailors. He can even hang from the rope when the barnacles grow back to scrape their heads off when they peek above the waves. There will be plenty to keep him busy, then, until he reaches Hawaii and his mother.

"Eric!"

Why can't she learn to say his name? Eric wonders as the sound Mama makes, *Eh-lick-oo*, pulls on him until he can see his room again, but not far enough to feel his bed against his back or the sticky California morning sneaking down his collared shirt. She will call again, he knows. Maybe twice.

Now, when he's so close to leaving, Eric can't be interrupted. He tests the latch on his bedroom door before he opens his second drawer. The two worn white shirts he stole off the clothesline are undisturbed. They belonged to Mrs. Grolsh, one of the ladies who pay Mama to do their wash in the early morning, but Mama once said Mrs. Grolsh was so rich she couldn't remember half of what she owned. Eric's mother is like that, too—rich—at least she was the last time he saw her, and so is Jack's new wife, Kay. Always wearing store-bought clothes. Not like his, which Mama makes too big so he can grow into them. Which she sews hard buttons of thread into each time she mends a hole.

Under the shirts, he has a few things for survival: the rabbit's foot Jack gave him and a wooden whistle to raise a ruckus, get a cop. It has carved eyes—he stole it from Papa's room since the old man can't leave the house anymore. Eric knew he'd never notice it was gone.

He has eight bucks and twenty-two cents, too—collected over time from the cracks in the sofa at Kay and Jack's house, and the ground on his walk home from school. It's all in coins, in a sock so it won't jiggle much, tied with Mama's wide blue church ribbon. She knows *that* is gone—she turned the house upside down looking for it until Eric almost gave it back. After all, why would he want to be reminded of someone who betrayed him? But he kept it, at the last minute. Nothing else could hold the sock so tight.

"Eric," Mama yells again from downstairs, "what are you doing?" It's a full sentence. That means trouble. He can hear her footsteps coming as he shoves the drawer shut and cracks open the door. He's plumping his pillow proudly when Mama steps into his room and looks around.

Her wet hands leave marks on her hips. She already looks weary, and not in a mood to overlook anything. Eric holds himself still. His bed is made. His schoolbooks are neat on his desk. Everything seems safe, but he's not sure. Mama's good at seeing things he thought he covered up.

"Are you always late like this?" she asks.

"No, Mama."

Usually she's gone by now, but Tuesday is laundry day, when Mama sets a tub on the stove to boil, then pours it over a pile of other people's clothes. Eric likes to watch, and not just for what he can steal. He likes to see the sun come up on the line of scarecrow shirts, their arms reaching down to their bottoms. But when she's in a bad mood, which she has been since his mother sent the pale pink letter, laundry day gives Mama time to order him around.

"Did you feed Papa?" Mama begins ticking off Eric's jobs as he nods. "Did he eat?"

Eric nods again. It's a lie, but he doesn't care. Grown-ups lie, too. He isn't going to shove the food into the old man's mouth, and he isn't going to get blamed for it either. Papa can't tell on him.

"Good," Mama says. "Is the garbage ready?"

Eric nods.

"What about the milk bottles? Did you wash them out?"

He's moving his head, but he's losing her words. Mama speaks in a tangle of Japanese and English, the first filling in for her adopted language whenever she can't find a word. Which is often. And since he's forgetting more and more of his own Japanese now that they're not in camp, he isn't always sure what she's saying. Sometimes he blocks her out completely and nods only when he hears a break in her questions. He picks a piece of her—her right hand, her calico hip—and makes it grow until it fills the room. Today it is her forehead: the lines on it wave like the sea and he can pretend her gray hair is foam on a shore. Of course there are times when he understands fine—he just doesn't want to. That's when he pretends he isn't there and sends himself off to his mother's home.

"You have your homework?" Eric nods again, his attention snapping back. "Then what are you waiting for? You'll have to run all the way to school."

He almost says, I wouldn't be late if it weren't for you, but this is Mama. She wouldn't hear the words. Besides, it doesn't matter. He's tired of waiting for his mother to return for him. Today is the day he is going to her.

Mama watches him straighten his shoulders and shift his books. He waits for her to let him go. "You'll be on time," she says. "You're a fast runner."

She stands aside to let him pass. "I made your favorite tonight. Chicken and noodle." Eric feels her hand touch his hair, then flicker down to his shoulder, then fall away as he walks by, but he won't look at her. "Real American," she says. "Make sure you put it in the oven when you're finished with your chores. Jack and Kay are coming for supper."

Eric skirts the softball field on his way home from school. It's a reminder of all the reasons he hates his Uncle Jack. Eric used to play there with the best team in the league, and if Jack had come to a single game, he might have realized how good he was. But these days everything is about what Jack and his new wife want—they don't care about Eric at all. Kay was the one who told Eric she and Jack were moving, and he was happy to see them go until he realized who would be left behind. Taking care of Papa became Eric's job, along with all of his others, and although he reminded them that he was already ten and could do the chores *and* play softball, Jack insisted it was too much.

Then of course, there was his mother's letter. It had come to the house just before Jack and Kay moved. When Eric brought the mail bundle in that day, he had seen her return address. It was from her, Emi Hamada in Hilo, Hawaii. He knew her name.

Eric was surprised she would write, since Jack hated her so much. But she sent the letter in a pale pink envelope with a flowery smell. It was a sign to Eric that she had something important to say. She *had* to be coming for him at last.

He started to rip it open, then stopped. It was addressed to Mama, and if she found out he had seen it, she'd be too angry to ever let him leave. Smoothing the tear between his fingers, Eric set the envelope in the kitchen where surely Mama would see it before Jack or Kay did.

Mama didn't know he was watching her when she came home that day. He pretended to be busy peeling apples, so she didn't know he saw her slip the envelope into the bosom of her dress. She knew how important it was. When she left the room a few minutes later, it was all he could do to keep from trailing her up the stairs.

Mama didn't want to be interrupted, that's what Eric figured. He even had this idea that she'd gone upstairs to pack for him. He thought she was sad, because she'd miss him when he was gone, and she didn't want him to see that. But she'd call him when she was ready. He was so sure.

He must have waited at least a week after the letter came. And each day, he wondered a million times when his mother would arrive. If she would just appear, like she had when he was five. He wouldn't have time to pack his things while Jack tried to kick her out the door, but maybe she'd thought of that. Eric imagined her laughing, and telling him she had a room full of clothes, all exactly his size.

Then one night, Eric was sipping his broth at dinner, juggling people around in his head. Mama sat across from him, with Jack and Kay in opposing chairs, so it was the four of them making corners on the round kitchen table. There was no room for his mother. He couldn't find a place to put her. But he didn't mean to say anything, and didn't realize he had spoken until everyone looked at him.

Jack put down his spoon. His face was red. In the silence, Eric could hear his own question, just as he'd asked it.

"When is my mother coming?" He couldn't take it back now.

Jack had sighed, extravagantly, as if he was having a hard time getting Eric's attention. "She isn't coming, Eric. Get that through your head."

Kay jumped like she'd been struck. "Jack!" she said, turning on him. "How could you? What a cruel thing to say to a child!"

"Well, it's true," he said, glaring at Kay, not bothering to look at Eric.

Eric hated him. So what if he'd asked before? He was waiting for the right answer.

Kay seemed to be waiting, too.

"Christ, Kay, don't do this now," Jack warned. "We used to talk about this every night!" He took a swig from his water glass and set it down too hard. Water slopped up the side and onto the table, but Jack didn't see it. "Didn't we, Eric?"

"Leave him out of this," Kay said.

"Leave him?" Jack gave a harsh laugh. "I thought this was about him. Isn't it about him? Didn't he start it?"

"No."

"No?" Jack leaned back in his chair. "You know, Kay, sometimes you are so—"

"So what?"

"What I want to know is, why is this suddenly *my* fault? Emi made this mess. You want me to change it, but I can't change it. So what do you want me to do? You want me to lie?"

Kay put both her hands flat on the table and pushed. She rose to her feet, knocking her chair onto the floor in the process. She bent to pick it up with shaking hands. She looked as if she might cry, but she didn't apologize.

Eric had never seen her like this. He was riveted.

"Don't you dare take it out on the boy," she'd said in a low voice.

"What?"

"You've been screaming at people for weeks, and you don't have any idea what's wrong."

"What's wrong then?"

"I'm not going to let you do it, Jack."

"What?"

"I'm not going to let you ruin my life like you ruined yours."

Kay left them without words. Eric, Jack, and Mama stared at one another, feeling a void swirling between them. Separating them. Eric was filled with amazement at Kay and how *brave* she was. It was the first time he'd ever seen anyone stand up to Jack, but she did it the same way he imagined his mother would. He was sure Kay was right, though he had no idea what was going on.

Jack stared into the hall like he couldn't believe she was gone.

"Eric, she's not coming," he said at last. He didn't pull his eyes to meet Eric's until he'd gotten the whole sentence out, but his voice was gentler. "We thought she would once, but we have to let that go now. Mama's your mother. She's brought you up, you should appreciate it . . ." Jack stopped and ran his hand through his hair, then leaned toward Eric across the table. They both knew that argument by heart. Then he said something new, as if answering his own silent question. "I don't know why she won't come, Eric," he said, "but she won't. She doesn't want you. They're happy where they are."

Eric just stared at his uncle. If he let the words touch him, the tears standing in his eyes would release and fall. But he didn't have to listen, because Jack didn't know about the letter. His mother wanted him. And she was coming all right.

He turned to Mama so she could explain. She sat there, eyes a little wider than usual, but that was all. "Mama," Eric began. There was a question in his voice.

Mama shook her head. Her face was closed like a door.

She was afraid Jack would try to stop him from leaving, Eric knew. She didn't know that Eric's mother was stronger than any of them. Emi was coming for him, and she was bringing Mariko, too. And when they were finally together, they would ban Jack from their house, just as he had banned Eric's mother from his.

It would serve his uncle right for telling such awful, aching lies.

Eric's house is in sight now, four driveways up on the left-hand side. He feels heavy merely walking up the path. Inside, he places his books on the kitchen table and listens for Papa. It's the part of the day, the chore, Eric hates the most. Some days he postpones it until just before Mama comes home. But the feeling that Papa's *around*, hovering in the air, is too much for him today.

Eric takes the key to Papa's room from the kitchen drawer and goes to the door.

"Papa!" he calls, knocking at the same time to warn the old man he's coming. "Papa, it's Eric! May I come in?"

That's Mama's idea: "May I come in?" She thinks politeness counts, even with crazy people.

Eric turns the key and the door pushes open. The curtains are drawn. Eric's fault—he didn't open them this morning. Blurry boxes drift on the wall in the gloom as the curtains sway from the inch of open window. The wall switch flicks uselessly. Papa must have turned the light off at the lamp.

Eric hears rustling in the corner, but Papa doesn't speak. As the familiar smell of musk and rot reaches him, he finds he can't let go of the doorknob. He has to walk in, open the curtains. And he has to lock the door behind him, in case Papa tries to escape.

He does consider leaving, but he slams the door instead and plunges into Papa's darkness. He's in the room, wondering why, holding his breath like he did when they went to the ocean. Like he's dipping into the dark for a second, then coming right up. He runs for the window. Eric's chest is clenched, wanting air, as he feels for the curtain pull near the top. Then he has it. Light falls into the room.

Gasping, he turns and looks around.

Papa is sitting in the opposite corner. His legs are bent, folded tightly against his chicken chest. He hugs them with his arms, his knobby elbows, and stares out the window just over Eric's shoulder as if he's amazed at the light. The sunken eyes seem to be smiling. The mouth, which usually hangs open like he's forgot it's attached, smacks gently to show his pleasure.

Eric tries to go to his grandfather. He's quiet today, even docile, but his face is that of every monster Eric's read about or seen. It's like a skeleton, shifting and lunatic. It follows him to sleep. One of the things Eric dreads most is the day Mama's face sags low and becomes as empty as Papa's, and he has two of them to care for.

The bed stands between Eric and Papa. He's ripped off the

sheets and blankets again, and thrown them to the floor. Papa crouches against the wall he painted one day with the watercolors Mama thought would keep him busy. There are still traces of the blue boat and the other thing, which Eric always thought was a weenie, but Mama insisted was just something unfinished. She *had* scrubbed extra hard to get it off, though. After that, they gave Papa crayons, then picture books that he tore to shreds. Now they can't even keep an extra set of clothes in the dresser because he rips them and throws them around.

"Papa." Eric takes a few steps forward. "It's a nice day outside."

He isn't sure if his grandfather understands, or if he cares, but the talk is more for him than Papa anyway. Walking in as if Papa is a baby or an animal is something Eric can't do. He can barely stand to touch Papa's papery soft skin to begin with, so he pretends that he's visiting. That his grandfather isn't so old. And still not dying fast enough.

If it's a pretty day, and Papa seems a little reasonable, Eric is supposed to tie a rope around Papa's waist and take him out into the yard. The rope is to protect him, but it doesn't stop him from stumbling. Eric can still remember the first time Papa fell. He wasn't hurt, only scared, but it froze Eric to the spot, watching the old man weep like that. Eric patted his head and said, "It's all right," and the other things Mama used to whisper to him when he was sad or hurt. It was embarrassing to hear them come so easily out of his mouth.

Anyway. They haven't gone out in the yard in a while and they aren't going today.

As Eric approaches Papa, he smells shit. It's the absolute worst thing about old people. When Mama first talked to him about this chore, she said, "I did it for you when you were a baby." Like it's his turn now. He wonders if he can ignore it today and pretend it happened just before Mama got home. He got away with that before. Mama never accused him directly, she just mentioned the rash Papa developed, and how painful it must be. The last time, she made Eric look at it—all the bumps and smeared flesh. She made him put on the cream.

Cupping his left hand over his nose, Eric pulls the old man to his feet. Papa follows easily down the hall and to the bathroom. He seems to know what's happening and stands in front of the toilet, waiting for Eric to undo his belt and pull his pants down.

He can't do this today, Eric thinks. He wants to run away *now*. His grandmother is sick to make him do this. He just knows that, if he told someone, they'd find a way to make her stop.

Eric's heart is pounding, telling him it's ready to run if he is. Papa waits, plucking at the buckle on his belt. He looks at Eric and smiles.

"Okay, all right," Eric says, yanking Papa's belt open hard. Just once more—it'll be his going-away present. He unzips the pants, letting them fall to Papa's feet. The smell, of earth and acid, bounces up around him in a cloud. Then he unpins the diapers around Papa's small buttocks and dumps the contents into the toilet.

Papa stands there, shriveled and half-naked. There's a streak of shit on his hip. "Of course," Mama told Eric when they changed Papa together for the first time, "that's what a diaper is for."

"Sit down," Eric orders his grandfather. "On the toilet." He's trying not to breathe very often. He pushes Papa's shoulder gently, then opens the can and tosses the diaper in. At least Mama takes care of *that*. He washes his hands and soaks one of the rags in the water. At least Papa can still follow instructions, though he can't always remember to do things on his own. Eric wrings out the rag and passes it behind him.

Papa looks at the rag. Nothing's going to be easy today, Eric thinks. Not a single thing.

"Go ahead," he says. "Clean up." Eric makes the motions to show him what to do. The old man smiles, understanding.

Eric moves out into the hall. Behind him, Papa begins to chatter. It's nonsense-words in Japanese that aren't words anymore. He's talking to someone who isn't there.

It's almost over. Eric goes back into the bathroom to open the lid to the diaper can. He tells Papa to dump the rag in. He flushes the toilet; he always waits until the end in case Papa remembers what it's for and decides to use it.

Eric picks up a fresh diaper and helps Papa rise. He thrusts it through the old man's sagging white legs and pulls the corners together on one side. Slipping his fingers under the cloth like Mama showed him, he pins it. First one side, then the other. Papa's still chattering, pleased to be clean. He's behaving well, Eric realizes. Probably well enough to go outside.

Well, that's just too bad, Eric thinks, yanking up Papa's pants and closing them. He promised himself he'd get out of there and he isn't changing his mind. Still gently, because he doesn't want to frighten him, he takes the old man's arm and leads him back down the hall to his room.

The eight dollars and twenty-two cents are now in Eric's pocket. He's slipped the rest of his treasures into the Sunday jacket he has on. His mother doesn't know he's coming, but he wants to look his best when his ship arrives. Then her neighbors will see right away it wasn't his fault he was left behind.

Eric slips down the stairs quietly, though he's sure Mama won't be home for quite some time. When he reaches the hall, he remembers he didn't put the casserole in the oven. He hesitates, unsure whether he should do it. He doesn't want to ruin his clothes.

It'll give him more time to escape, Eric decides, going into the kitchen. He can hear Papa from there, singing like he does when he is happy. Like piano keys in no order, banging in his head.

Eric strikes a match to light the stove fire and blows it out carefully when the flames take hold. He doesn't want to burn the house down with poor Papa locked inside. The old man is going to have a bad enough time once Eric is gone. With only the window for company on the days he remembers how to draw the blinds.

The idea of leaving Papa alone makes Eric pause. He couldn't care less about the others, but the old guy's at their mercy like Eric is; he never hurt anyone. Checking the strength of the sun through the window to make sure Mama isn't about to walk in, Eric considers his options. He can't take Papa with him, but he could free the old man.

The sun is pretty low now, Eric realizes—no time and no need for a good-bye note. He can still hear Papa singing that horrible song. He goes to the bedroom door and unlocks it.

The bolt pulls back with a click in Eric's ears. He thinks he may have heard a pause in Papa's song, but there's no signal that the old man heard it. To really let him go, Eric thinks, he would have to go in there and drag him out.

As he's deciding whether to brave the dark and the smell to get Papa, Eric hears the crunch of shoes outside in the drive. He freezes, cursing his daydreaming—he'll be in big trouble if Mama finds him all dressed up. When the sound doesn't repeat itself, Eric moves cautiously in the window. There's no one out there. He still has a chance to leave.

He makes one last check through his pockets, then he's ready. He definitely doesn't have time to go back down the hall and coax Papa out of his room. He wonders again if the old man will make it. He decides to give him one last chance.

"Papa!"

Eric doesn't expect his grandfather to answer, so he is all the way to the front door when the old man appears. He stares as Papa comes toward him, the hems on his pants puddling at his feet each time he sets one down. But his eyes seem clear. Eric's yell must have jolted him back, however temporarily.

He'll take him as far as the yard.

"Papa, come here."

Outside, defenseless, Eric tries to explain why he is leaving. His mother sent for him, but somehow, he's still here. It's Mama's fault, he tells his grandfather, talking through the hands the old man holds up to shield his eyes from the sun; his grandmother is plotting against all of them. "You have no leash on, Papa," he points out. "You need to get away now."

Papa isn't listening, of course. He's just a crazy old guy. Eric knows he should take his grandfather back inside, but he's too worried about the time. "I'm going now, Papa," he says. "We'll never see each other again. Escape to the Johnsons' house or Mama will surely lock you up again."

Eric backs away, then hesitates. If the old man can't keep his head, he'll never make it alone. But Papa's eyes do seem clear, and sad—they hold on to Eric's until he can't bear it.

Good luck, Papa, Eric thinks, turning to run from the house and his grandfather.

There is nothing to hold either one of them anymore.

8

JACK

SOLDIER IN WAITING, 1943

"I am not the enemy," Will says, leaping onto one of the mess hall benches stranded in the crowd. He surveys the sea of frayed, overgrown pea coats and wool pants around him—the heads of the other families who came to hear him speak. He is one of them—just another Japanese American internee holding off the cold in borrowed military castoffs—and yet, as humble as Jack's brother is, he is the undisputed leader of the Nisei in the camp.

Will will win this fight, Jack knows. Not even Donald Tateishi, Will's nemesis and the voice of the "no-no" boys, has such a natural flair for drama. Besides, the camp boycott Donald is trying to organize is wrong. The loyalty questionnaire the president wants them to sign may be insulting and poorly written, but it isn't a trap.

It's a way to clear their names and set them free.

Of course, people do have reason to be skeptical. The evacuation was supposed to be temporary, just a precaution to weed out the enemy spies. So why build the internment camps, when people had already settled into the racetracks and fairgrounds?

It must have been a case of government infighting, Jack thinks—after all, he's come across plenty of Caucasians who don't like the Japanese. But after three months, they were moved to this factory-stamped settlement in Colorado. The Amache camp. In the desert. On a clear day, they can see the Kansas border through the chain-link fence.

Now, only six months later, the army recruiters are here. And the questions: Will you forswear allegiance to the Japanese emperor? Are you willing to fight for America in the war? For Jack, the answers are sure, sure! So many of the young fellows are itching to join the army—sure they're worried about leaving their parents, but no one's actually going to ship them back to Japan while the war's going on. It's a chance any one of them will take—Jack included—to regain their honor, fight bona fide enemies. In battle, there is no second-guessing. No family to worry over or avoid.

There are even some soldiers reenlisting—fellows who were discharged a couple of weeks after Pearl Harbor was bombed. Jack is pretty sure Donald was one of them, which is why it makes no sense that he's taken the other side. There's no use fanning the fears of the old folks who are afraid of being left without a country when they all know any resistance will reflect on everyone. If the boycott happens, the whole camp could be exiled or jailed.

"I am not the enemy," Will repeats. "You are not the enemy. Why shouldn't we prove it? Answering 'no-no' gives them an excuse to deport us. 'Yes-yes' means we can fight, and we will win."

Jack basks in the icy breath around him. They are listening—the fishermen, migrant workers, railroad laborers, peasants. Will's hat is off, and his coat is open. His tiny sentences punch through the air.

"Fight?" asks Donald Tateishi. His sliding Japanesy voice is unmistakable. It creates a ripple on one side of the mess hall. As

Donald moves toward Will, the few supporters he has press in, carrying Jack with him and into Will's view. Jack knows he should leave. He isn't supposed to be at the meeting—because he isn't the head of the family, and more importantly because Will forbade him to come—but with Donald there, Will will need him. The no-no boy is the only fellow who can make Will lose his cool.

Besides, Jack decides, he doesn't want to hear about Will's triumph from the gossips tomorrow. He ducks behind a mushroom hat and keeps his eyes down.

"Fight and be cannon fodder," Donald says, taking a cheap jump onto one end of Will's bench. He is taller than Will—the crowd laps at his waist. "They'll ship your parents to Japan while you line up for someone else's guns. We let the JACL lead us once, and where did that get us? They couldn't have forced us to come here if the League wasn't so eager to show their loyalty and urge everyone to go along."

"That's bullshit and you know it!"

"Ooh, the golden boy's getting angry! The truth hurts, doesn't it?"

"We would've been arrested," Will insists, pushing his words into the gaps where there should have been air. "You know that as well as I do!"

"*Would* have been?" Donald mocks. "Okada, are you denying that the FBI came for you, too?"

"What he's saying is, they were shooting us in the streets," a new voice calls no more than a few feet from Jack.

It is Jim Tanaka, Will's friend. A rare fellow, half Caucasian and hard to miss with his angular face and long nose. He's a good guy, and Jack is glad to see him. The odds are more even now—there are three of them against the rest.

"I was there, Donald," Jim continues. "I saw it happen. Houses burning, one on my block at Berkeley. Just for kicks."

That stops the grumbling around them. People remember what they went through. Simple truths offer simple victories, Jack thinks, satisfied. This is what he came for. To cheer.

"So you're talking about protection!" Donald says then. "We're locked away for our own good? And I suppose the armed guards are only here to shoot our enemies?"

He gets laughter on that one.

"We're talking loyalty!" Will corrects. "Service to our country. How many of you here long to stand up straight again? We can do that if we fight."

"Do you, Will? Do you *long* to stand up straight?" Donald asks. "And why are you so ashamed?"

The questions are steps—each one closer to danger. Will's face looks like Papa's, closed and lidded, so motionless and smooth. He seems to know what's coming. "We are talking about the loyalty questionnaire, Donald," Will says, letting each word stand by itself. "I don't think anything else—"

"But I do think it's relevant. You're trying to send every man in this room to war because you were dishonored."

"I am *not* dishonored."

"Aren't you?"

The question hops from ear to ear, wanting an answer. No one seems sure how things got so personal, or exactly what Donald means. No one, that is, except Jack—when the words find him, they strip him raw.

Donald is talking about Emi, Jack is sure. She's their dishonor. And by the way gossip spreads through the barracks—in handfuls—they have only a few seconds until the others begin to understand Donald's words.

Jack looks to Will for a signal, but he's frozen where he stands. His face is a puzzle—just a zero where his mouth should be. Donald has hit home, Jack realizes. Will will be run out in seconds once the crowd turns.

It's up to Jack to figure out what to do.

"Shut up!" Jack's voice is higher than he wants—a little squeaky—so he yells as loud as he can. He does it for Will, because his brother seems unable. Will is too caught up in the truth.

Donald makes a big pretense of laughing as he turns to find Jack in the crowd. "Why should I, little man? You think they would let you fly an airplane? Serve in a submarine or on a boat? You aren't even old enough for them to kill."

At that, Jack throws himself at Donald. A second-string football tackle, true, but serviceable. As he dives, he yells something like, "You don't speak for us!" He can't wait to taste the guy's knees.

Everything flies then. Donald knocks over two benches and hits the ground in his effort to put them between himself and Jack. The sleeve of a green overcoat that could be Will's catches Jack's eye, but too many fellows are shoving one another for Jack to be sure. He can't find Will's face, but he doesn't need to see him. He knows that, wherever his brother is, he and Will are finally side by side.

Then Jack turns on Donald, who's still picking himself off the floor. "Come on, come on, Mr. JACL," Donald taunts. He has to know Jack will reach him before he can move. "Take a swing at me. Show me what a good soldier you are."

Jack obliges, pushing off the men around him. Fighting is something he knows how to do.

At the last second, though, Donald spins away. Jack's elbow hits the concrete floor first. Then his shoulder, then his head.

Every piece of Jack is heavy. Most of it, too heavy to move. When he opens his eyes, red and gray swirls around the edges of the room. He can hear Jim asking if he's all right, but the sound is clogged and quiet. Jack sees his father, and wonders if the old man is proud of him, standing up for the family the way he did. Papa's face has no expression. It's replaced almost immediately by Will's.

"Jack! Hey, Tosh. Toshi. Can you hear me? Are you there?" Will's voice is soft as he slips his hands under Jack's hat and around his head, feeling for the wound. When he finds the tender spot, Jack jumps, knocking unexpected tears from his eyes. Quickly Jack puts his own hands there, wrapping them tightly to steady the pounding so his brother won't think he is weak. His skin is hot beneath his fingers, but there isn't any blood.

He closes his eyes for a moment, and when he sits up, the crowd is gone. Will is kneeling in front of him, his firm hand on Jack's shoulder to keep him upright. As his head dips close enough that their cheeks brush, Jack readies himself for his brother's praise.

"What the hell did you do that for?" Will asks.

Jack hears the words but isn't sure what Will's talking about. Instead, he tries to focus on the heat of his brother's skin. "You heard what he said," Jack begins. "About Emi—"

"Christ! Jack!" Will glances around, but Jim Tanaka is the only other person near. "What an idiot! What the hell are you doing here?"

Since he has no acceptable answer, Jack ignores the question. "I thought we were supposed to stick up for—"

"Well, you're wrong."

"But I was trying to protect you."

Will pulls Jack closer, moving his lips into Jack's ear. He can feel the words going in. "Jesus, Jack. You better snap out of this high school stuff. When I'm gone, it'll be up to you to take charge of the family. You can't make such stupid mistakes."

"But I want to go, too—"

"Listen to me. *You* are not enlisting. You have no idea why a man goes to war."

Will's words hiss in Jack's head even after he rocks back and releases the hand on Jack's shoulder. Jack closes his eyes again, humiliated. He doesn't want his brother to see his tears.

"Jack," Will says, farther away now but still softly and on his level, "when I come back, this whole thing will be over. All of this—the slate will be clean."

Jack doesn't move until he hears Will rise and leave him. Someone else, Jim Tanaka, takes a step, too. In the glance they exchange, Jack sees how close they are. Jim's knowledge of Will is like a band around Jack's temples, tightening as Jim stays to help him to his feet. Jack looks again for Papa, but he sees nothing, as usual, to tell him how the evening disappeared.

Will has left Jack. Abandoned him. And all that's left is to throw an arm around Jim's waiting shoulder and, with his help, to take his father home.

His father could be his salvation, Jack assures himself the following afternoon as he heads for the room his parents share with Emi. So what if talking to the old guy these days is like trying to read haiku? Jack might get five syllables here, or seven there, but the only ones he needs are "yes, you can enlist." He isn't betraying Will, exactly, but he isn't going to stay with the family either so his brother can be a hero alone.

How could Will say that Jack has no idea why a man goes to war? Haven't they lived together in the bachelor barracks for months? If Will ever bothered to notice him, he would see Jack's world has folded down and disappeared just as Will's has. He needs something normal, people he can count on. Family is not a possibility. He doesn't know where else to look.

Jack's only other option is work release, and from what Will says, it isn't something to look forward to. His brother left camp once to harvest sugar beets in Idaho during the first fall of their incarceration. Every day, Will worked every lighted hour with the other laborers to rush the sugar production for the war effort. Every night, they cowered in the shed they slept in, listening to the town teenagers threaten to burn the "Japs" out. He said, and Jack will never forget the words, that they boasted it would earn them "a purple heart." Before he arrived, one of the fellows had been beaten into a two-week hospital stay.

Will told Jack about it late one night when they lay in their cots. He usually didn't talk to him at all unless he'd been out playing cards. Will had made friends with an administrator who worked on the fire squad, and the fellow used to sneak them liquor. Since the internees weren't supposed to drink, their game was the most popular one in camp.

Thinking about that game as he watches his boots punch in and out of the snow to his knees, Jack has to admit that Amache's not exactly a prison. There's a hospital at the northeast corner toward Holly, and a variety of stores, along with the coop, in the center of the grid. There are a couple of churches, two schools, and a post office. A police station and a fire station. Almost as if no one expects them to leave.

And yet, especially in the winter, the place feels barren. The barracks stick out of the snowdrifts like machine parts on end. Six families in each building, twelve buildings in each block. More than thirty blocks, Jack knows, each with its own mess hall, showers, laundry, and little pad of what's supposed to be grass. The snow has wiped those out, buried the hollowed half-tunnels between the buildings and the fenced-in gardens that mark each front door.

Everywhere Jack turns, he sees the same white-trimmed windows. He has always used Papa's garden to identify their room. It's the rock patterns more than anything that distinguish it. Tiny circles within circles all over the ground.

Finally spotting a familiar curtain, Jack knocks on the door. He blows into his hands—he likes the way the frost rises. As he begins to wipe a clear spot into the window, Emi opens the door.

She is carrying her son, Eric, holding him against her shoulder. She raises a finger to keep Jack quiet, but he isn't planning to speak. His first reaction is surprise, even dread. Mama is always with the children when he comes.

Jack looks both ways, in case Will has engineered this situation so he can accuse Jack of consorting with the enemy, despite the fact that Jack hasn't said two words to his sister since they arrived in camp. If Emi notices the movement, she doesn't say anything. She leaves the door hanging and backs into the room.

Jack follows, ducking his head, though he can easily clear the door frame, stamping the excess snow on the floor Mama has shellacked, brick by loose brick, to keep out the dirt. They are in a middle room, a midsize room, but Emi makes it look small. There are four beds in the space, all pushed to the edges to clear half the floor. Two bookshelves and a pencil drawing decorate one wall.

The last thing Jack wants is to stay. He doesn't take his cap off, just steps up to the potbellied stove.

Emi is wearing wool pants and a cotton sweater, not unlike some of the other Nisei girls. They are bold, too. There's something irrepressible in their laughs, though Jack is sure Emi doesn't laugh much anymore. But there are traces—definite traces—of Emi in the girls he's begun spending time with. Even the ones he likes, so he gives his sister a conditional smile.

When it seems he might stay, Emi smiles back and motions to the only chair in the room. "Try to keep your voice down," she says, "if you can. I just got them to sleep."

Jack doesn't want to sit with her. If he could do anything, he would turn on his heels and leave. "I didn't expect to see you," he says, stalling for time.

His voice is cold, even to his ears. Emi stiffens.

"What I mean is," he begins. What does he mean? "Is there something wrong? Is he sick?"

"No, it's just a cold. But he's been coughing and miserable for days." Emi's words have no inflection. She isn't fooled.

She sits on one of the beds next to a lumpy cotton blanket—Jack guesses the baby is underneath—and waits for him to speak. He gives in, dragging his cap off from the back so it won't tug his hair too far out of place and holds it in his lap to have something to squeeze. Emi looks tired, her eyes soft. When her head tilts toward him, Jack can trace the faint bump on the bridge of her broken nose.

Jack was there when she broke it. He can still hear the crunch in his mind. Like everything about that evening—not long after Pearl Harbor when Emi returned home—his memory of the noise is completely wrong. He never heard it, didn't realize her nose had broken until there was no longer anything he could do.

"Are things okay, then? With you?" His words are no longer charged.

"Yeah." She begins to shrug the shoulder Eric is resting on, then lifts one eyebrow instead. "I can't wait to get out, but that's nothing new. How are you?"

"Okay," he says. It's such a normal conversation. How are you? I am fine. They are talking like there's nothing bad between them. "What do you mean, 'get out'?"

"Get out. You know, work release—it was the whole point of the questionnaire. I was thinking of school, if I can get in. I never had time for college, you know?"

Will will never let her go, Jack knows, but he isn't going to say it. He can soften the blow. "It's not so great out there."

Emi laughs. "How can you say that? How can it be worse than being here?"

"Well, you're safe, for one." He decides not to tell her about the purple hearts and Idaho. She won't handle it well. "You know, with Mama and Papa."

"Yeah, safe. Just what I wanted to be. Safe and protected."

He sees a flash of her nose breaking again, and everything else that happened that night. He can feel the tucked end of the banister in his right hand even though he didn't actually hurry Mama up the stairs. He can see Emi facing Will down in the kitchen. There are carrots everywhere: cut into flowers; falling in thin slices off the knife's steady footsteps; splashing into her lap. "No, of course not," he says, her know-it-all tone making him argue. "You wouldn't want to be safe and protected. Not you."

The comment hits. Emi flushes. He can see it clearly, the Okada look, the still-crawl of anger through the eyes. He must look just like her.

They are on the edge of it, too close. If one of them speaks, who knows what will come out? So he pulls back, tries to pull her back, too.

"Well," he says, "I, ah, I hope he gets better." They are back to Eric.

Emi won't look at him. She isn't very graceful in these situations, or helpful in getting back on course.

"Do you know where Papa is?"

She shrugs. "Does Papa know where Papa is?"

"Does that mean no?"

"What do you need him for?"

"I need to talk to him. It's important."

She looks up, then, and reaches for Jack's arm. "You *did* answer the questionnaire, right? You know they're going to throw those no-no boys in prison?"

Her concern is nice, familylike, even though she has no idea what she's talking about. "Of course. Hell, I'm no traitor. I'm going to fight if I can. That's why I need Papa."

"Why?"

"Permission. I can't wait around until I'm eighteen. The war could be over."

Emi pulls her eyes away to bounce Eric. "Why not ask Will? Isn't he the head of the family these days?"

He tries to act casual. "I'll find Papa myself."

"No, you won't." Emi says it like it's obvious, but then relents. "He's by the wind break."

"Wind break? As in trees?"

"Do you know where the cemetery is?"

It must be clear he does not. "Emi, there aren't any trees."

"I know. They all died. That's why Papa goes there. I think he's trying to plant them in the snow. Let me take you."

Jack is surprised by her offer and less than eager to walk with her through camp. "I'll find it."

"No, you won't. Here, hold him." Emi thrusts Eric at Jack, then slips around him out the door. The boy is heavier than he expects. He has a sweet, soapy smell.

"Carol?" Emi's voice asks in the room on Jack's right. "I have to go out for a little while. Will you listen for the babies while I'm gone?"

"Are you going past the store?" The voice is young, speaking English.

"On Ninth. I could go down to Seventh Street if you need something."

It's just like Emi to try to get her own way, Jack thinks. He can't call out with the sleeping boy's head on his chest, and he doesn't want Carol, whoever she is, to see him either. When Emi returns, he's holding Eric at arm's length. "Here, take him back," he says in a low voice. "I said I was going alone."

She lays the boy on the bed with a finishing pat. "You don't want to be seen with me?"

He wishes her voice wasn't so loud. "It's not that."

Dragging a pair of snow boots from under her bed, she says, "Jack, if you want to enlist, you should enlist. You have to get to Papa before Will does."

Jack watches Emi shove her feet into the boots one at a time, surprised at how well she understands. He can go with her, he decides. It doesn't have to mean he's switching loyalties. He can use Emi without owing her anything. Will never has to know.

Emi has on her coat, hat, and mittens. She gives him a smile. "Well then. Let's go."

As he steps outside, Jack sucks his breath and holds it to help his lungs absorb the shock of cold. They are surrounded by snowmen. Jack looks around. One is missing a head. Another, used for target practice, is largely buttons in the snow. He doesn't point them out to Emi, merely follows her in the newly tamped tracks of a supply truck until they turn down Seventh Street. There, she waits for him, since the snow is worn enough to walk on side by side.

Jack hesitates, then falls into step with her. There's no obvious reason not to—even on this, the main drag, there aren't people crowding around. Outside the dry goods store, a small group trades gossip, saying hello and good-bye. Jack doesn't recognize anyone—they're mostly old ladies. So he doesn't think about them much.

As he and Emi approach the building, the group stops talking. Trying to see who the newcomers are, Jack thinks at first, getting ready to greet them. But as they draw closer, the faces stay carefully blank. It's like walking toward Papa, only weirder, since the women are looking past them, though they can be seen clearly now. It isn't just the women's eyes—the narrow voids—that make Jack cringe, but also their stillness. Even once Jack and Emi pass, they don't turn.

Jack can feel the judgments—they crawl up his neck and into his hair, then turn and make their way into his stomach. He knows the women are the biggest gossips—mostly the ones from the boonies, too. People from Los Angeles, the people that matter, would never stare like that.

Still, he wonders what they're thinking—if they've guessed he is Emi's brother or think he chose to walk by her side. More than anything, he wants to ignore their reaction, but he needs to check his theory that Emi's dishonor was the subject of Donald's taunt.

"People sure were staring at us," he says once they are safely alone and near the edge of the buildings.

Emi gives him a bitter smile. "At me. You're a cute fellow, Jack, but—" She lets her words hang, forcing him to pursue them, and he does—not to satisfy her but because they are rubbing against his heart.

"Why would they stare at you?"

Emi watches her boots stab at the snow a while, trying to pick a path no one else has used. "Did you know that there are over a hundred of us?"

"Who?"

"Unmarried mothers. Women of ill repute."

She delivers the words so casually, Jack is unprepared for their sting. "You're crazy," he says, twisting his neck to get away from her, hearing the grains in his voice.

"It's true. I'm working in the clinic now. I get to check the records." She keeps her own voice light, raises her eyebrows like she can't believe it herself.

Jack realizes then that she doesn't care if people know. Maybe she wants to pull the whole family down with her—maybe that's why she tricked him into walking with her here. "People could think you had a husband, you know. A lot of families got separated."

"You want me to be a liar, too, Jack? I know that would help you. But Mama hasn't exactly made it easy for me, has she?"

Jack has no idea what she means, unless it's the fact that Mama was the one who found Eric and brought him home. But Eric isn't the problem, at least in the camps—it was Emi's pregnancy people reacted to. They knew that, if she had a husband, he would have been here at such a crucial time. Still, she didn't have to do everything the hard way. It would have been easy enough for her to hide if she never came home.

They have reached the cemetery. Jack can tell by the drifts of snow, cut on one side and deliberately placed, and by the three markers that have been recently brushed off. Before they arrived here, it never occurred to him that people would die in camp. Not once a year, or once in a lifetime, but sometimes every day. He remembers being shocked to hear the wailing when the first old man died. That time, the family petitioned to have the body cremated so they could take it home.

Home, Jack thinks. He can't seem to escape the word. Or the memory of Emi returning, or the blame for letting her in that night. With Will gone, Jack was the man of the house; she was his responsibility. He decides to ask the question that has been haunting him. "Why did you come home?"

He waits for her answer, trembling, afraid to know how important her reasons might be. As he does, he looks at the graveyard, scanning for Papa, smelling a tang of incense skim past him across the snow. Answer, he wills her, sure that the navy blur on the horizon is his father, knowing he's getting ready to leave. It's his one opportunity to find out what she knew, what she expected, when she returned.

"I'm not very lovable, am I?"

By now, Jack is familiar with Emi's habit of answering a question with a question, but he can't imagine where her mind goes to make the kind of flips it does. Except that she doesn't want to answer, doesn't want to bare herself that way. Instead, she looks at the markers on the graves around them—wood crosses, no stones. Emi's face is pensive, but it holds no clues about why she is thinking about love. Or what it could possibly have to do with coming home.

"He's over there," she says, pointing to the blur Jack has already spotted. "Good luck."

The tone in Emi's voice is Jack's first sign that he has moved away from her. Released, and thankful she isn't following, he heads into the white field.

9

MARIKO

THE DAY THAT NEVER WAS, 1950

Miss Kana has a mole on her left cheek, a really gross one with hair sticking out of it. From her desk in the third row back, Mari can see the hair sweep through the air as Miss Kana talks. She can't believe she's never noticed it before.

"Mariko, I asked you to please come up to the blackboard and do this problem," the teacher says, pounding the thick finger of chalk against the wall behind her.

Mari stays inside her 9-shaped desk, safe from long division. She has never been able to figure out how a larger number can "go into" a smaller one, and it isn't fair of Miss Kana to ask. It is even more unfair of her to call Linda Banks, who Mari hates, to the blackboard in her place. Mari watches Linda's dirt-colored ponytail bounce with each chalk stroke as she makes the ten into a one hundred and fits the sixteen inside it. The teacher nods at Linda and walks over to her desk, her knees make little ripples underneath the long *muumuu* she's wearing.

She doesn't look at Mari again.

* * *

Every day, Mari sits next to the window so the sun can touch her. She likes to put her forearms flat on the desk and let them bake there until her hairs lie down. Until today, though, she's never noticed how thin the glass is, or how the noise from outside can turn off Miss Kana's voice. The high school kids are having their break now, and Mari can see everything. If she leans back and to her left, she can hear words from outside.

Outside, Mari sees her neighbor, Cindi Amos, the girl with vanilla ice cream hair. In her sleeveless dress with green and blue fish, Cindi could be the ocean, Mari thinks. Her hair could be the surf on the beach.

As Mari watches, a boy comes up to Cindi and they begin to walk together. Cindi's skirt swishes more than usual around her tanned knees with each step. Mari remembers her mother's insistence that she stay far away from boys and never let them touch even her fingers. She looks for a dark stain to appear, the kind her mother always says you can never get off, but Cindi and the boy are too far away.

Miss Kana has moved on to composition when Mari's attention returns to the room. She wants the class to write a paragraph about a member of their families.

"Think about description," Miss Kana says. "What color eyes does the person have? What does he like to wear? Description can also mean what the person does during the day. Anything that makes that person different from you." Miss Kana smiles at Mari as she talks, forgiving her for not knowing math. She always puts a big star on Mari's English assignments.

Mari won't get a big star today, though. Not with her family. One week ago, Mari found her birth certificate, and ever since she hasn't been able to think about her father without feeling as if she's being pulled into the night sky. She has nothing to say about her mother, who refuses to answer any of her questions, or her sister, Kim, who was born last month. She could write about her grandfather's funeral, which was just held in Los Angeles, but he died mysteriously and they never met.

Then Mari has an idea.

My brother is a fireman she writes. *He is big and strong and a hero too. When there is a fire in our town, my brother goes into the house and saves all the people. He won a medal from the fire department. When there are no fires, he stays home and plays with me. He has black eyes and black hair. He looks just like me.*

The words come out so fast, it's like they're hidden in Mari's pen. It serves her mother right for telling her to set the table even when she asked her, "But isn't Dad my father?" and not in a whiny tone of voice. Mari kept asking, "Mom? Please? Say something, anything, yes or no?" though she knew she wasn't going to get an answer. Emi bent down, clutching both of Mari's hands in hers, and stared into Mari's eyes. By then, Mari didn't care about the question. All she wanted was for Emi to release her and leave the room.

While the rest of the class finishes their compositions, Mari studies her paragraph. It is short, but it has all the important details. Everyone knows what a fireman looks like.

Miss Kana notices she's done and comes over smiling. She leans so far forward to read the paper that her curly hair brushes Mari's skin.

"What an interesting description," the teacher says. One hand brushes back and forth on Mari's shoulder; the other lifts the paper off the desk. "May I?"

Mari lets the paragraph go, though she knows Miss Kana will read it in front of the class and that most of the kids know she has no brother. Someone will tattle, but it doesn't seem important. Mari watches Miss Kana collect a few more papers and waits for the recess bell to ring.

Outside, the day has been drawn sharply, pulling Mari's attention to color. Yellow paint coats the buildings and the walkways, and green grass lies splintered on the ground. On the playing field, a group of boys are running with those wide-open screams that seem to start the moment they hit the school yard. Mari looks for her best friend, Jeannie Tono, among the girls who are gathering under the trees. She is winning the game of jacks they started in the halls this morning with Jeannie's new ball.

When she finds Jeannie, Linda Banks is with her, admiring the ball's twirling colors.

"You're on tensies," Mari says as she takes Jeannie's hand. She is too polite to say that she herself is on double "round the worlds."

"We goin' start one new game," Linda says, her stubby, bitten fingers on the ball. "Jeannie goin' let me play."

Mari looks at Linda, feeling Jeannie and the game slip away. Suddenly, she is furious. Linda and her long division, she thinks. Linda and her fake pidgin English, which she speaks on purpose because she's a *haole* and she has to wear hot *haole* dresses and patent leather shoes. Mari's mother would slap her mouth if she came home talking pidgin. "If you want to play, get your own jacks," she tells her, holding her hand out for the ball.

"Mari, it's okay if she plays, yeah?" Jeannie says, but hesitantly. She can't quite get her eyes off the ground. "You can win. You're winning anyway."

"Nobody's gonna let me win," Mari says. "Give me the ball."

"No!"

No one is going to take her best friend from her either, Mari vows as she grabs for the ball. Linda Banks starts to run, but her legs aren't strong and she doesn't get a good head start. Mari's on her within seconds, rubbing Linda's dress and frilly white socks in the dirt as she digs her fingers into the hand holding the ball.

Linda is screaming and whining, most of it jumbled noise, but Mari hears "*tita*" and "get off." Linda's the *tita*, Mari thinks as she focuses on the ball. It rolls out of Linda's stubborn grasp and into Mari's as the two girls are yanked apart. The gym teacher has got Mari by the arm, but Miss Kana is there, too, demanding they stop.

"She wen' start um!" Linda cries. "She wen' pick on me!"

"It's my ball," Mari says, refusing to surrender it to Miss Kana.

Her statement is going to get her into worse trouble, but by the time Mari reaches the principal's office, she believes that it's the truth.

Mrs. Oates, the principal of the Hilo Elementary School, looks just like somebody's grandmother. Her gray hair sticks to her head in waves, and her hands are little twigs that steer Mari softly into the deep leather chair alongside her desk.

"Mariko Hamada," she says, leaning back and rocking as if Mari should fill the silence. Mari waits back, surveying the office around her. It's not such a scary place. There are some books on the shelves and a blown-up photograph of the playground.

"Mariko, how are things at home?"

Mari's mother usually gets right to the point when Mari's in trouble, but the principal is clearly trickier. "Fine," she replies.

"You have a new baby in the family, right?" Mrs. Oates asks. "Is it a boy or a girl?"

Mari has no idea what her family has to do with fighting during recess. The principal is confused, she decides, but she doesn't correct her in hopes that she'll receive a lesser punishment.

"A girl," Mari says. "I even change her diapers."

"Mariko, Miss Kana brought me an assignment you did in class today," the principal says. She has the paragraph about the fireman on her desk. "Can you tell me about what you wrote?"

Mari waits, very still, for the next words or movement to tell her what to do. She feels like she's hiding in the last corner of a safe room, and Mrs. Oates is coming to drag her out of it. She wants to be invisible.

Mari's toes are tingling. She's felt that before. Sometimes when she stands at the top of the stairs, or hangs over the third-floor railing at her father's office and looks down, Mari yearns to throw herself over. It's never a serious urge, and she isn't sure if she expects to fly or to go splattering onto the ground, but she savors it anyway. It starts with exactly the same feeling in her toes.

"Do you have a brother, Mari?"

There it is, the clue Mari was waiting for. A sweep of clear air passes into her head, filling her with stories. "Well. He's not really my brother. He's just, uh—" No words come to end the sentence. "He's someone else. Like a calabash brother. A cousin or something."

"And he's a fireman?"

"Well, not yet."

Mrs. Oates is staring hard at Mari. Her face doesn't like what she's hearing.

"He will be when he grows up. He doesn't live with us yet, but he will. I know it." Mari's voice catches on the lie. "I didn't make that part up."

If Mrs. Oates is talking, Mari can't hear her. She is watching a little scene in her mind. In it, her brother is playing with her. She knows him, she just can't see his face.

"That's not true, either," she says, the truth pushing its way out of her mouth. "I don't think he's coming at all."

Now everything is worse. Mari is crying, and every time she tries to stop, it just gets louder and more furious. The truth is supposed to make things better, but black waves are crashing on her head, and she's stuck just above the sand. She keeps thinking, don't leave me, don't leave me here. But she won't say it, she never would; she doesn't even know what it means. No one is leaving her. The principal's not leaving. It's the coming that scares her, the fact that her parents will be called and then the truth will come out.

Mrs. Oates puts her arm around Mari and hugs her. She lifts her and leads her to the couch against the window. Mari is terribly ashamed, but there's nothing she can do. At least, curled on the pillow, she can breathe.

Mari must have fallen asleep because her mother is here. She can smell her shampoo, so close that if she opens her eyes, Emi's face will be looming over her own. Emi's tone is disapproving; it goes with straight lips and wrinkles in her forehead. She isn't talking to Mari, though. She's talking *about* her.

"You should have called me sooner," Emi is saying.

"Barb Kana thought it was just a phase. Mariko is such a good student and usually so cooperative. But this essay disturbed us. I can't repeat myself enough; I think it's very important."

"I can't imagine what you're suggesting. Certainly not that Mari has a long-lost brother." Mari can feel her mother's anger twist toward the principal, ready to choke her.

"Of course not," Mrs. Oates says. "But whatever has been bothering Mari might have to do with the family. Maybe it's the new baby. You know children take time to adjust to a new addition. I'm not telling you what to do, but I think Mari is acting out something she can't talk about."

Mrs. Oates is making Mari's punishment worse. No one tells her mother what to do.

"Mari is fine with Kim."

"Perhaps. Keep her out of school for a day or so, though," Mrs. Oates says. "I'd like to know what's going on before she comes back." Their voices are loud enough to rouse Mari if she wasn't already awake, but it's the principal's demand for an explanation that opens her eyes.

Emi is standing in front of Mrs. Oates's desk, her back to Mari. The fingertips on her right hand are drumming against the top. It means "hurry up"; she does it instead of speaking. Mari dreads the moment her mother turns around.

Mari's body has a great weight when she moves it: swings her feet over, sits up, clears her throat to attract their attention. Even before Emi holds out her hand, Mari can see her red nail polish. It doesn't match her navy blue dress, which means she left the house in a hurry when Mrs. Oates called. Emi's fingers are tight, but not digging; her narrowed eyes seem to be seeing Mari for the first time. She points to Mari's book bag, asking her without words to pick it up. The principal watches them carefully; she is so interested in what they're doing that Mari and her mother turn automatically to her, side by side, so she can easily see. Emi squeezes Mari's hand in little pumps, sending a message Mari can't understand. She feels like she's been shoved under a cold shower; she's trying to keep her skin warm and dry, but the cold is reaching every inch of her, running through her hair, sheeting down the tender skin on her *opu* and into her belly button, turning her to ice.

"Mari," her mother says finally, giving her arm a shake, "aren't you going to say something?"

She shakes her head no. She's never going to say anything to anyone again.

"Apologize to Mrs. Oates."

"I'm sorry, Mrs. Oates. I didn't mean to cause any trouble."

"And it won't happen again, will it?"

"It won't happen again. I promise."

The principal smiles. "Well, Mariko, I hope to see you under happier circumstances next time."

Mari's mother doesn't comment. She walks to the car with anger in her legs, first yanking Mari along as they go, then dropping her hand. She doesn't care if I come with her, Mari thinks, imagining her mother driving off alone. She has to get in that car.

Emi is already there, getting in behind the wheel. She doesn't stop Mari from opening the passenger door, though; she seems to be waiting for her to get settled. Mari puts her book bag at her feet. Now that they're alone, they can dispense with the sign language. She can hear the list of crimes she has committed: forcing her mother to rush to school in the middle of the day; causing Mrs. Oates to give Emi a lecture; and, of course, exposing the family secret.

But with each mile, Emi doesn't speak. Mari decides that her mother must be wishing she'd gotten to the bottom of things last week when she found Mari in the closet. Mari can still feel her lifting the birth certificate off her lap; all Emi had to do was flip open the folds to see what it was. It seems impossible that she didn't, but Mari's eyes were closed, so she can't be sure. She does know that her mother didn't say a word about the paper. Instead, Emi held out her hand to lift Mari and said, "There you are. I need you to help me set the table. Didn't you hear me when I called?"

As they near the house, Mari watches the center ribbon of grass on the gravel road get sucked under their front fender, then listens to the whine of the motor die. Although she has turned off the car, Emi doesn't move except to shift her hands on the steering wheel and slump a little. Mari looks at the fine cobweb lines that mark the bone under her mother's eyes, then tries to see why her mother is staring at the powder green vertical plank wall of their house and the wood lattice skirt that hides the crawl space under the floor where the mongooses live. Slowly, Mari lifts her thighs one at a time, peeling them off the blue vinyl seat of the car, but quietly so her mother won't notice.

"Mari," Emi says. Her eyes and mouth are tired.

She is about to begin with the list. Mari wishes her mother would pinch her arm instead and banish her to her room. Anything to get away from the hot ticking of the car as it settles into stillness, and the thick threatening air.

"I can't believe you did that. If you ever—"

Don't say it, Mari begs in her head. Take away my supper. Make me hang the laundry, fold it, iron it. Make the beds for a year.

Just keep me.

When her mother finally speaks, her voice is hollow. Memorized. "I've worked hard to be a good mother. I don't suppose you know that."

Mari doesn't know how to respond. You're a great mother. The best, most perfect. "I'm sorry, Mom."

"Then I get a call and find out that you're sitting in the principal's office—"

"I'm sorry. Truly."

"And that woman—you have no idea what she said to me."

"I can explain—"

"I don't want to hear your explanation."

"But I didn't mean it. I wasn't thinking."

"No you weren't thinking, were you? Look what happens when you don't think."

Emi stops talking until Mari is sure the silence is going to smother her. Then she asks, "How did we bring you up, Mari? To get in trouble? You know how good Japanese girls behave."

"I didn't mean it."

"I should call that poor girl's mother and make you apologize."

Poor girl, Mari thinks, catching her next apology before it escapes. It takes her a few seconds to remember Linda Banks. There was a fight over Jeannie's ball, she remembers, but why would her mother care about that? "I'm sorry," Mari offers, wondering if her mother's words are a trap.

Emi nods and looks out the window. "If I ever find out that you attacked someone again, you are going to be very sorry."

They aren't talking about the same thing, Mari realizes. It's strange that her mother doesn't notice. "I won't, Mom. I promise."

"A promise is important, Mari. You better not break it." Her hand moves to the door handle and pulls, not hard enough at first to release the door. Then she shoves it, and the door swings wide, snapping on its hinge with a low-pitched groan. "God, this has been a shitty day."

Mari's mother walks into the house and holds the front door open, waiting. Mari follows obediently, marveling at the swear word, and then, when she finds the power to move backward in time, at the fact that her mother didn't mention the paragraph she wrote. She heard Mrs. Oates talking about it. She heard her mother say the words "long-lost brother." Mari reviews their private sign language, wondering if she missed a signal. She can tell Emi is hurt by reading her mother's gestures. But Emi is pretending it never happened. That must be the message. She wants Mari to pretend, too.

Mari scoots under her mother's arm, hearing the swollen door squeak behind her. Emi throws her purse on the sofa and Mari lowers herself next to it, staying in sight but not in focus.

"I left your sister with Mrs. Ohana," her mother says, her hand pressed against her forehead. "You can watch her for me when I get back."

Emi must have run through the trees to Mrs. Ohana's house when the principal called, Mari realizes. Her flat white shoes are dusty. One is streaked with green.

"I can get her."

Emi sighs. "I'll be right back. Sit there and *don't* get into any trouble. I have enough of a headache as it is."

The house is still and big around Mari. She's been reprieved, but it feels heavier than punishment; as if she's supposed to figure out how to heal her mother on her own. Left alone, Mari pulls a broom out of the kitchen dust closet. She tests the hard bend of the bristles on the floor, then flips it over so she can clean the clouds and strands of dust that someone left behind. As she drags the stiff straw against the kitchen floor to catch the crumbs that have fallen from the round breakfast table and are hiding between the legs of the chairs, Mari wonders who could have used it. She thinks of the broom as her own.

Mari sweeps ten times on one side, then ten times on the other, promising with each stroke that she will never hurt her mother again. She has found a rhythm: her hands are far enough apart that she's not jerking the broom from the center of the handle; her sweeps are so smooth she can almost see the tracks of clean floor. She squats to see if any stray dirt is standing off the surface, then she's ready to move into the hallway. Before today, she might have been bored and on to something else before she finished, but the good Mari knows better.

The good Mari will finish sweeping the floor.

10

ERIC

WHAT HE IS, 1956

If Kevin doesn't shut up, they are never going to get there, Eric thinks, refusing to turn around and face the white boy. The kid never officially joined the gang in the first place, just hung around behind Moose until they got used to his pinched-up face. When Moose was with them, Eric acted like Kevin didn't exist, like he wasn't worth the trouble. Besides, he liked the perversion, the way Kevin obeyed the colored kid with legs like tree trunks. Tree trunks. Eric read that somewhere, or saw it in one of those Mickey Spillane movies, and it sure fit Moose. Moose has arms like tree trunks, hell, even fingers. This should be Moose's gang, but Eric's the smart one. He doesn't get caught.

Now Moose is upstate—or downstate or wherever the juvenile center is—and Kevin's a real pain in the ass.

Eric flicks his fingers at the collar of his leather bomber, lightly so the guys won't notice but hard enough to make sure the thick zippers haven't turned it back down. He loves the jacket, as much for its looks as for the way Mama burst into tears when she saw it. He hadn't planned it that way, but still it was a gas. She's taken to calling him a hood now—she means it as a warning, as punishment for the money he spent, but he likes the way she spits out the word. Everything he is is such a disaster for her, and she has no idea what he's really done. Like what happened to Papa. He killed the old guy with his running-away stunt. And Mama was so flustered, she never even noticed Eric had gone.

Eric likes having something he can admit to. The term "hood" is a label he's worked to earn.

"This is stupid." The white kid keeps repeating it, as if they don't have ears. "Why are we bothering with a music store? What are we gonna do with a bunch of instruments?"

"Gee, Kevin, maybe you're right," Eric says, twisting his mouth in a way he knows looks threatening. "Maybe we should rob a candy store, huh? Then we can sit around and pop your pimples afterward." He stares, without turning, out the windshield of the old 1940 Chevy he borrowed from Jack. The guys are in suspense, he can hear it—Lonnie and Pete crowding Kevin on both sides, shoving their shoulders out at him now as they wait on Eric's words.

Tapping a cigarette on the dashboard, Eric lights it and sucks, the smoke hits the back of his throat like a branding iron. He holds his breath, then blows the smoke in a disappearing draft. He wants to pop his chin, blow a smoke ring, but he's never learned how. He isn't sure, either, if it's cool.

"Throw him out, Lonnie," Eric says, imagining how Kevin sees him, a back-lit head in a cloud of smoke. Mama would call this *gara ga warui tokoro*, a bad neighborhood, but Eric couldn't care less. If Kevin's smart, he should survive.

"Goddamn Jap!" he hears amid the scuffling that says the kid's outside. "Yellow inside and out, you damn Jap traitor!" The voice is a whine, a high insect sound he could swat easily. He rolls down the window, notes the neck of Kevin's undershirt is damp.

"Hey, Kevin," Eric says, making his voice almost agreeable. "*Sayonara*, shit head."

Then the gas pedal is pressed and they're gone, peeling out toward Larry's Music Store, just the four of them now. About to graduate—from public school punks to guys with real power. Eric's been dreaming about this for months. Not answering to anyone, just making his world up as he goes along.

As he drives, Eric hauls up his anger and polishes it in his chest. He's glad Kevin called him a Jap—it'll send him into overdrive. Kevin's too stupid to realize insults only make him dangerous. They grab his throat, and march him to where he needs to be.

Eric can see his anger in the way Dobbs bounces on the front passenger's seat, tapping his fingers on his knee. Dobbs is wiry and quick like Eric, Mexican maybe, but in this group no one talks about race. He was arrested once for shoplifting, but they grabbed him before he left the store, so he got off. "Gee, Officer," he said, replaying that innocent voice for them in the school halls, "I *was* going to pay for it." And he did pay, right there, so they couldn't do a thing. Whatever he took, it was something Dobbs didn't even need.

"So the plan is the same, only Kevin's not around to watch from the car," Eric says as they near the store. "We don't need to keep the motor running anyway. We go to the back door. Dobbs picks the lock and he's the lookout man. Lonnie and Pete grab some records, anything small enough to take. I'll get the cash register. Easy, right?"

Lonnie's nodding in the backseat. "Then we go to Benny's, right? Order some burgers, right?"

"Right." Eric smiles. This is big. It's almost the biggest thing he's ever done.

The biggest thing was revenge against the guys in junior high. A different school than now, very proper and rah-rah. Three Irish guys picked him out the first day, calling "ching, chong, Chinaman." Hitting him, just roughhousing, they said. There was no way he could match them. He didn't get a lot of support, either, not even when he came home with a black eye. Jack told him violence was wrong—his eyes glanced off Eric's when he said it, like they did when he was lying, but Eric knew he was a pacifist. Ever since Kay dumped Jack after Papa died and he'd returned home, he was always mooning around like he lost something and didn't think it could be found. He was always trying to talk to Eric, telling him to talk things out, as if any problem he might have would lift into the air piece by piece as he spoke.

Meanwhile, Mama wanted Eric to stay at the good school. Where he could use his brain. So next time he saw the guys, he called them over. He made a lot of noise, cursing and dancing away until he liked the size of the crowd, then he took a swing at the biggest, dumbest one. The guy broke Eric's nose, and gave him a cut on his face that bled forever. Then even Mama and the principal had to agree to a transfer.

Mama got quiet after that. Without enough money for private school, Eric's been skipping classes at a mixed-race high school downtown, which is as good as any for him, but somehow, it's all become his fault. Especially the no-money part. Things got even worse when he grew his hair long and slicked it back—for Mama, that is. At his new school it only built his reputation further and got him some friends.

It was more than a year after his transfer when Eric took his gang on a little visit—Moose and Lonnie were with him then—and cornered the guys. Eric watched, no dirty hands for him, as they got exactly what they'd given him, no more, no less. All he did was taunt them, "Chinaman, who's a Chinaman now?" to make sure they understood.

That was his biggest thing, what made him "Japan." Like James Dean but tougher, not a guy to cry in the end. He has kamikaze blood—he's a mystery to friends and enemies alike. He can ace a test without studying if he wants to, or hang out in the bathroom smoking and doing pull-ups on the pipes while he tells the guys what the answers would have been so they'll know he chose to fail. Girls love him for it, even more when he ignores them. He's always finding love notes in the books he leaves strewn around the dingy school halls—hearts and flowers and curlicue handwriting—

he lets them get that close. Not any nearer, especially not the white girls. He knows plenty of guys who have tried to date them. They have too many crazy rules.

Eric pulls off the road and into the parking lot behind Larry's Music. It's Columbus Day, and Larry should be having a sale. But he's closed, and his little block building's on the far side of the lot, like a die that chance rolled off the table. Eric parks close, less than twenty steps away, so they can get in and out without being seen.

They've been around and in the store often enough to know what's there. No alarm. Larry shares a guard with one of the stores in the strip, and the man's too lazy to check on the place more than a couple times a day. None of the other cars are close enough for anyone to get a good look. Eric parks sideways. That way, no one'll see Jack's license plate.

The guys are ready. Dobbs slips on a pair of gloves, palms his slender lock pick, and swings out of the car with a grin. He walks to the door in no hurry.

"So far, so good," Pete mutters in the backseat. He and Lonnie have laundry bags in their laps, white muslin puddles waiting to be filled. "No one's paying any attention. This is a great plan."

Eric accepts the praise, careful not to let his pleasure at Pete's words touch his face. His eyes are on Dobbs, standing by the door, unlocking it like he's a salesclerk who maybe forgot something and came to pick it up.

The door swings open.

Then the three car doors open, like they're on the same hinge.

"Easy, now. No running."

Dobbs is watching from inside the store so they can stroll the twenty steps without glancing behind them. He slips the pick to Eric. "I want that Bill Haley record," he says to Lonnie as they pass. "Don't forget."

The gang fans out, collecting. When he reaches the cash register, Eric tries to maneuver the pick the way Dobbs showed him, but his heavy gardening gloves get in his way.

Dobbs comes over. "I'll do it."

"No!" Eric smashes his hand into the round button keys. "We need you at the door. It's these stupid gloves, that's all." Quickly he strips them off so he won't look so clumsy and tries again, after telling Dobbs to look the hell out the door and not over his way. The kid is getting cocky, thinking he should do everything. Trying to take away Eric's piece of the heist.

In a minute, the register releases and the iron drawer slides open. He pulls all the money out and ruffles through it. One hundred and thirty-seven dollars. The tray is loose, so he lifts it to make sure he doesn't leave anything behind. Smart move, he tells himself when he sees what's underneath. A fifty-dollar bill.

Eric's pretty sure he's never seen a fifty before, so he takes a careful look before shoving it in his pocket with the rest of the money. President Grant. He'll remember that.

Slamming the cash register shut, he swabs the keys with his gloves, obscuring any fingerprints with dirt. "Everybody ready?" The bags, full, hang on Lonnie's back. Dobbs's eyes are sparks in his face. Eric knows what he's feeling. It's delicious standing there, postponing the moment, as if they could get caught but never will. It makes him want to laugh with them, to play some music loud so anyone in the parking lot could hear. There is no one there, and he knows there will never be. They are free to dance on this edge of danger, where they cannot be touched.

"Let's go then. Slowly, close the door and walk to the car." They follow him exactly, and they're in. Then they're driving down the road. And then they are gone.

The gang stays at Benny's long enough to show their faces, to sop their adrenaline in burgers and fries, to divide the loot. Dobbs makes junk yard noises, trying to play the harmonica like Sonny Boy Williamson, as Eric looks through the stuff for something Mama would enjoy. It's not as easy as picking out a record; they don't have a hi-fi set, just an old piece-of-junk radio. Besides, if she guesses that his gift is stolen, she'll call the police herself.

After they stuff themselves with food, Eric takes the fifty—his part of the money since they can't break it right away. It's more than Mama makes in a week. Then he kicks the guys out of the car and roars away from the drive-in, still carrying the warmth of a dying fire inside him. He wants to get home on time. For his alibi, but also to please Mama and keep his peace.

When he swings the car into their driveway, its dim headlights show Eric the house he grew up in not as tall, lopsided, and peeling, but as home. Gentle lamplight skims over the parlor furniture inside, knitting the threadbare coverings closed for the evening. The house smells of ginger.

Putting his book bag down, Eric walks into the kitchen and stoops to kiss Mama on the cheek. She feels like ruined silk under his lips for a split second before she whirls to face him.

Alarmed, her eyes race over his face.

"Eric! What wrong?" She turns his face from side to side. "What did you do?"

He should know better than to show his feelings, Eric thinks. In his family, they keep things hidden to the grave. "What did I do?" he asks, pushing her hand away to sit at the kitchen table. "Christ, all I did was say hello."

Normally, he wouldn't get away with swearing, but since she was expecting the worst again, she lets it go. "Did something happen?"

"No. Nothing." Eric frowns, retreating to his usual terse style as he tries to come up with an answer. "I did well on a test, that's all."

Suspicious, Mama's eyes search his as she rubs her cheek with two fingers. "What test?"

"History." He shrugs, as if it's no big deal, leaving the silence between them.

Mama pauses for a second before she decides to believe him—since she's finished with her questions, she nods and turns to the stove. She's very deceptive, Eric thinks, watching her straight back. First, she's tiny. Chests of drawers are taller than she is. And the pillow of hair floating around her face throws people off, too, especially now that Papa's dead and every strand has turned milk white. His friends think it's sweet the way she trips over her English. They think she is cute—like a pet—and just as harmless. And she does look harmless, like any little old lady. They never guess that she's a monster.

Can be a monster, Eric corrects. Since Kay left Jack, Eric's uncle has taken to understanding everyone; Eric doesn't know how many times Jack has urged him to see Mama "through the filter of her life." Once, when he was younger and being punished, Eric asked Mama why she bothered to go to the orphanage to bring him home. She slapped him, of course, and didn't speak to him for days. It didn't answer the question, though. Eric knows his mother doesn't want him. Jack turned out to be right about that.

The last time Eric saw his mother was at Papa's funeral. He didn't know she was coming, didn't know who she was until his uncle said her name. She had greeted them politely, gave both him and Jack light hugs before she drifted to the other side of the grave. She stayed a day, and talked with him, but there was no mention of their relationship, no invitation home.

From the way she studied him, though, Eric could tell Emi knew he had killed his grandfather. She was the reason he'd left Papa alone, he was too obsessed with returning to her—his mother—to imagine what the old man might do if he was free. Eric had run away believing she would want him to make it to the shipyard, then he wasted two hours in an empty lot, crying because he couldn't hitch a ride. He wasn't thinking about his grandfather, couldn't feel what was happening at home. By the time he gave up and made his way back to Mama's, his grandfather was dead. The ambulance was leaving. And his grandmother was so bewildered that she didn't notice that he had been missing. She simply took his hand and rushed him upstairs so he wouldn't see the blood.

Six years ago, Eric was young enough to believe that his mother's abandonment of him had had to do with Papa. Now, of course, he knows that whatever wickedness his mother recognized in him was there long before his grandfather died. Like Jack says, she is happy with her life without him. Eric no longer expects her to walk through his front door.

As Eric watches Mama cook, Jack walks into the kitchen wearing the suit jacket he went to work in. His uncle closes himself in his room every evening until supper is almost ready. Eric doesn't know what he's hiding from, or even if his uncle knows he is hiding, but he figures none of them truly want to be home.

"Did you get the stuff moved?" Jack asks, reminding Eric that he told him he needed to help the drama teacher move some props for the school play. "You didn't mess up the car, did you?"

"Eric got an A on his history test," Mama says.

"I didn't say an A." He forgets for a moment that the test doesn't exist. "I said I did well."

"It's the same thing, isn't it?" Mama asks.

"Well, no, it's not the same. A B-plus is a good grade, too, isn't it, Eric?" Jack's in a good mood. He wants Eric to confirm his grade. "Even a B's okay. It depends how hard the test was."

The grades, Eric thinks, are not the problem. It's this attitude that he has to be so good. They want to pretend that he's a bright, responsible boy, when they all know he isn't. That he is, or should be, a dutiful son.

Jack chats about his office to distract Mama from Eric's stillness. He never says a thing about what he does there—if Eric asks, he just says he's an accountant. Eric's point, not that Jack gets it, is that his stories are full of what other people said and did. It's like he's living the other people's lives.

He's getting that just-over-thirty paunch, too, Eric notices. Not a lot, but enough to suggest that he should cut down on the beer and pool halls. He never talks about that either, but maybe because he knows Mama wouldn't approve.

While Mama finishes cooking, they leave Eric alone. She won't let him help and he doesn't have to talk—yet. Dinner's when she wants to hear about his day. All the little details that mean nothing unless you add them, which is something she'll never do. Still, it helps her think that she's keeping tabs on him, and that keeps her off his back.

Tonight, though, Eric's still bubbling inside from the heist. He wants to shake her up a little. Entertain her. He remembers his excuse for taking the car, they're going to ask him about acting class sooner or later. Maybe, he thinks, he could do a little performance for her. The problem is, he doesn't know any plays.

"I was a hit in drama class today," he says, once the food is served.

"Before or after your history test?" Mama's intense about details, and she remembers every word. It's like she's trying to be there with him.

"Uh, after. It started when Mr. Edwards was assigning roles. He wanted me to play the—ah—good brother, you know, Aaron, the one his father loves. And I wanted to play Cal."

"Cal?"

Eric sighs. He tries to sketch out the story without getting too deeply into it—he doesn't want Mama to get sidetracked by the mother who leaves the family to be a madam and run a bar. He's seen the picture at least four times, but the last time was over a week ago. Mostly what he remembers are the fight scenes, and the time when Cal climbs off the moving Ferris wheel, but you can't get one of those onto a high school stage.

"Eric! Why couldn't you be the good brother? You'd make such a good hero if only you would try."

Jack looks as if he wants to speak, but Eric shakes him off. He's pretty sure Jack won't pick up on what he's doing, but he wants to get through this first in case he does. "It's a wimpy part, Mama. He goes crazy in the end."

"But the villain!"

"Cal's not a villain. He just has this, thing, inside him that makes him restless. Anyway, Mr. Edwards said I wasn't handsome enough, so he wasn't going to let me be Cal."

"So did you play the hero after all?"

"No, Mama." She just can't let go. He'd shut up, but the vision in his mind's so strong, he needs to get it across. "Listen to me. It's not about heroes and villains anyway. The important thing is, the way I argued. I told him, I can play this part because my Mama showed me how."

"*I* showed you?"

Eric pauses to give her the chance to reprimand him for talking back to the teacher, but he has hooked her by mentioning her name. She's listening to him.

Eric takes a chance and gets to his feet.

"Yeah. You know why? Because Cal wants to do something to help his father, so he plants beans, see, right before the war. He goes to check on the field just about every day, and when the crop comes in, he's so happy he lies in the dirt!"

"On the beans?"

"No. In the furrows. He lies down between them, in his suit, and he peers down the rows like they're the barrel of a gun or something. Watch." Eric messes up his hair the way Cal's always is, so Mama can see the picture clearly, then demonstrates on the floor. "And then," he says, looking up at her, "he gets up and starts dancing in the fields!"

Mama's stunned, but Eric rises, holding his spirit safe from her disapproval. He dances the way Cal did, goofier and goofier until, like a miracle, her laugh shatters out. "Eric! You can't dance on the beans. Be careful, you might crush them."

Eric dances harder, twisting side to side, showing her how he avoids the tiny plants around him. "Remember what you said about when you were farming?" he asks her. "How the dirt was so rich and clean you wanted to wash your face in it? Well, that's what I did." He drops to the floor, on his knees and panting, and looks into his Mama's smiling eyes. That's all he can see now, her eyes, and the tiny hand she holds over her mouth so her teeth don't show when she laughs. He can hear her laugh rise over his beating heart. Then he bends over, knocking his cupped hands on the ground, and splashes the imaginary dirt in his face until he can taste it.

"And guess what? I got the part!"

Gasping for breath and giggling, Eric misses the sound of the car pulling up. Mama and Jack miss it, too, until there are red and white lights chasing each other over their walls.

"Maybe there's been an accident," Mama says, still excited, still so happy with him. She doesn't look at Eric's face.

She doesn't know.

But Eric can feel Jack's eyes on him as his laughter drops at their feet like a stone. He glares at Eric, blaming him for everything that's about to come through their door. Jack waits, through the knock, but he can't scare Eric into a confession. He remains on the floor, still on his knees, the dirt in front of him long gone. Neither one of them moves.

"Jack, get the door," Mama fusses. "Maybe someone's in trouble."

As Jack rises, Eric's mind is strangely quiet. He sees the house the way the cops will, shabby, hopelessly out of style, not even a television. He feels exposed, and angry, too, with Mama and all her little questions, never any of the big ones she should ask. She's never recognized the truth, never once has cared anything about him. If she did, she would know the cops were there for him. She would have seen on his report card that he wasn't enrolled in drama class.

"Is this the home of Eric Yoshiko?" an officer is asking. Jack nods, and two men in uniform step into the house looking around, looking for him.

"There's been a robbery, and we need to ask him some questions," one of them says. He sounds sorry. "We'll have to take Eric to the station."

No one could have seen them, he thinks as he watches Mama fight off the words, the plan was too good. Kevin must have turned them in.

"Robbery?"

"Yes, ma'am. Uh," the cop turns to Jack, expecting him to translate, and—although they both know that's not what Mama's problem is—he does.

"G*ootoo*."

Mama looks from Jack to Eric, making it clear who he is, in case the cops didn't notice. They must be wondering who these crazy people are, why this kid is kneeling on the floor. Mama puts out her hand, as if she is blessing him, but he can see how scared her eyes are, and at the last minute she pulls away. Everyone waits as she shifts her thoughts in her head, Eric watches their progress in her eyes, as they dart faster and faster, and in her arms, which creep almost imperceptibly into her lap until she is so tight, she's about to explode.

"Nooo!" The way it twists out of Mama, it's barely a word. "He's innocent. He was at school, at acting class." She looks wild, but hollow, about to splinter. "He's innocent."

Can he still get out of this? Eric wonders as the men approach to escort him to the car. If it's Kevin's word alone, he might. He took off his stupid gloves, but the surface of the cash register was like fine gravel. They'd never get his prints. If they didn't catch the gang with their loot, they should have a chance. Which brings up an important question, one that startles Eric as it rises.

Does he want to get out of it?

Mama's at his side before they can touch him, almost crouching in her need to keep them away. "You can't take him away. Why can't you ask him here? I'll bring him to you, then. He's innocent." She skips through her principal thoughts, unable to string them together. One of the cops appeals to Jack, but he seems unable to move.

"No, I'll go," Eric says. They're his first words since the police walked in, and he delivers them as he rises, towering over his grandmother until he's in easy reach of the cops. He isn't thinking, really, but he can see his mother's face the way it was at the funeral, and then his sad, crazy grandfather's, and it feels like the right thing to do. "Don't come, Mama, I'll go alone."

She stares at him, no longer seeing him as Jack goes into the hallway to get his coat. "I'm coming with you, Eric," he says. "I'll take our car and follow you, and I'll be with you right away. Don't talk until we see what this is all about."

"It's a mistake, that's what it is," Mama says softly as they leave the house. "He's innocent." Standing on the dark lawn, shining in silhouette against the police lights, Mama looks like a child. Confused and alone.

Innocent. Eric slips into the car before the cop can touch him, struggling with the unfamiliar word. If it wasn't for the guys, and the fact that they might be safe, Eric thinks, he would answer her. He would tell her everything he's done, force her to see him as he is. Jack, too—his war hero uncle who bears no sense of guilt or evil.

To just say it, once and for all.

11

KAORI

BRINGING HIM HOME

I failed to reach your mother, Mariko. I think you can tell that by now. She spent her youth trying to bend the world to her instead of bending to the world, and her mistakes were so profound. But I warned her when she returned after Pearl Harbor was bombed, and when she refused to hear, Will tried to reach her, too. She scorned both of us, and she suffered for it.

We all did. We were a family after all.

That was a long time ago. And because those days were better put away, whole sections of them, whole events are gone. Emi stayed locked in her room because I didn't tell her I had kept her secret. It was easier for me if she held herself apart. I thought about it for days—it was a harder decision for me than your mother ever knew. I had sworn once, after our first harvest, that I would never interfere with fate again, and this seemed to me to be a test. But then I realized that the blame was already mine. My daughter had come home because she needed me. She couldn't reverse things on her own.

I made my plans once I decided, but, of course, my plans went wrong. I called the telephone operator to find the Kurakawa family in Glendale, and she put me through without warning. If I'd been prepared, I'm sure something about the conversation would have seemed suspicious. Her husband wasn't there, Mrs. Kurakawa said, and she never answered when I asked when he'd return. I said I needed to see her about an urgent matter, and she invited me to come, as though she had expected me to call. She was so polite, her Japanese was so perfect, that I thought it would be simple. I thought we were lucky, that at least the boy was safe with a good young girl like her.

I was dressed by the time the minister called to say he couldn't drive me—in my blue linen, which I smoothed before answering the door, and my church hat. All I needed was to see his face and the faraway pain that wasn't for me and I could tell without listening that there were too many crises, too many old people trying to die before something worse happened. He handed me a pass for traveling, but there was no more he could do to help. It was the morning I was to pick up Eric. I was suddenly on my own.

I let him go without a word. My smile lasted; I aimed it at the empty door because I understood that he couldn't wait. I was the only one in California who was waiting anymore. The boy in my mind who wasn't Eric yet was fading, taking all my help and all my hope for Emi with him as he did. I wasn't thinking about what would happen next. I asked Will to drive me.

I know I should have told him where we were going—and why—but I never quite found the words. Will had returned from his FBI questioning only days earlier, and I didn't know how dangerous he could be. Even if I had, if I knew how Eric and Will would spiral together, that we'd trace the rest of their lives to what happened on that day, I still can't tell you I would have changed what I had done. Without Will, I never could have rescued Eric. From the moment he walked into that house, he understood what I never would have guessed.

* * *

We have driven for a half hour in silence by the time we reach the address the girl gave me; I check the mailboxes for names and tell my son to stop in front of a large house with wood lace trim on the front porch. The Kurakawas even have their own parking place. They have a small garden, too, with rose and azalea bushes, but the human shape in it is gone.

The girl—that's how I have come to think of her—greets us. She is as small as I. She has stockings on her legs and no makeup, signs of wealth and good breeding, and her face is one of those beautiful ones with a high, wide forehead that dips shyly to her chin. Her eyes are not too wide, but deep as charcoal. I am surprised to feel myself relaxing when she bows.

"Thank you for coming." She leads us into her drawing room. "May I offer you some tea?"

"Oh no, no thank you."

"I insist. You must have refreshment."

"We are far too much trouble."

"The water's about to boil. Please sit down."

She leaves us time to inspect her home. It was finer than ours once, but I can count the furniture that remains on my hand. A rug the width of two men standing lies in front of the mantel, a rocking chair and wood-framed sofa face each other off its edges. The rug is worn, but in its center, a low, lacquered table is topped with a perfect rose. The rest of the space, easily half the room, is empty. At the far end, a brown carpeted stair reels up toward the second floor.

That's what I see. Will settles into the rocking chair as I sit on the sofa and begins his own survey of the room. I do notice that the wall behind him needs paint, that a pattern of white shadows marks a set of missing pictures. And I see the two empty hooks above the carved mantel, but I know what it's like to be poor and to sell things, and I approve of what she kept and the cozy way she has arranged what is left.

The girl returns with a tray and places it on the table, then she kneels neatly in front of it and begins wiping the tiny bowls. I also drop to my knees to be close. From her quickness, I realize the water *was* about to boil, and wonder how long she's been waiting for us. When she holds out my tea, I take it, knowing I can't mention Eric now without disturbing the peace. She sways back on her heels to serve Will, but just for a moment. His tea wisps where it sits, rejected, on her table. His rudeness stuns me.

She pours for herself and waits only until my first sip has reached my belly before she speaks. "Please talk freely. In these past few months, I've realized how short time can be."

She's right, of course. I introduce myself, and Will when he doesn't speak, and thank her for seeing us, before I pause. "We've come to discuss a delicate matter," I say at last.

"You've come about Ken."

"Yes. Your son, Ken."

"My son? My son is Eric."

I'd presumed. "Eric, then. He's my grandson. My daughter's child."

The six words tell Will why we're here. I know they hit when his chair begins to rock in tiny brush-stroke motions. I can hear it crackle against the floorboards, drawing up tight after only inches in either direction. That's when I realize I should have warned him, but I can't bring myself to turn now or explain.

The girl nods lightly, deflating. "I'd hoped it was about Ken." She has missed Will's tension and seems not to guess our purpose. I don't know how to begin again.

"So how can I be of help?" she asks, at last.

"He's my grandson."

"Yes."

I use different words. "It's unfortunate."

"Oh, no," she says. "I take good care of him." Her face is unlined, and I realize she doesn't understand. She thinks we are there to thank her, perhaps. "Would you like to see?"

Yes, I think. I would like to see. I have been dreaming for days about Eric, wondering what he looks like. I have seen his skin as sheer as fresh pearls, his mouth puckered and a little blue.

I have imagined the things I will bring him, the sights I'll let him see. And though I know there are hard words between those moments and now, I hear myself say, "Thank you. That would be very pleasing."

I dare not look at Will when the girl is gone. Instead I listen to her shoes click, and when the stairs swallow that sound, I count, keeping her pace in my head so I'll know how far she's going by how long she has been gone. The bowl of tea has cooled quickly in my palms. The carpet has all my attention.

"Here we are." It's the girl's voice, but I have heard Eric's already in the idle, nonsense song that gathered as he came down the stairs and the room opened up to him. His shoulders are turned forward, trusting that the girl will keep him on her hip as he looks ahead. A red block waves in an outstretched hand.

The errant, tufted eyebrows are familiar, but even without them, he's a beautiful boy. There is something of Will in his confidence. It is clear, though he's only a year old, that he feels this is his house, and his mother. Will and I are only strangers here.

"Say hello, Eric," the girl is saying. She nudges one arm so that it moves up and down. He watches it, and us, as if nothing is connected.

When she sets him on the rug, I notice how his flannel nightshirt matches the blue squiggles in the rug. Eric has spun over and is pulling himself up, holding on to the table. I want to cradle him. I want to cheer his strength, but instead I say, "I'm so sorry."

The boy is intent on rising, but the girl has gone still. Her hands pause where they are on the floor, ready to scoop him back from either side. Her eyes hold him. Then, she gathers strength and lifts her head to me.

"Don't be sorry, he wasn't asleep." Her words are rounded, willful. She has finally heard me.

I have a vision of her then, Eric in her arms, flying out the window and away from us like a woman in a village tale. In it, her hair is swept into a low neck bun; she's dressed in soft white from her kimono to her *tabis*. The clarity of the scene and the funeral robe are frightening and make me wonder what I would have done in her place. Eric, on his feet but swaying, reaches up idly to touch me, as if the world hasn't settled for him yet. When he realizes who I am not, though, he turns again for her.

"I have a legal contract," she says. "It came just before Christmas. A present, you could call it. It's all in order." Eric has stooped to touch her thigh. As I watch, she raises her hand and lets it hover above his head, barely grazing the hair that sprouts up from his nap. He straightens, then falls back on his diaper and rolls, content that she's in the room. Their contact is complete.

It is the way he is with her, the way he hasn't looked at me, that forces me to be direct. "We've come to take the boy back."

"Back?"

"Back to his mother. She can care for him now."

The rocking chair begins to scrape the floor in longer strokes. Mrs. Kurakawa turns to it, and then away when it's only Will. She seems confused, and I can tell, from her lack of fear, that she can't read him. Neither of us know what he's capable of, but I can feel how violently he disagrees with me.

"I can take care of him, too," she says. "I am. I have been."

"Yes. But she's his mother. She wants him back."

The girl is waiting for something further, some explanation she expects me to give, but I have made my point. There's no reason to be hurtful. When nothing else is forthcoming, though, she seems to relax. "That's it?" she asks. "That's what you came for? To say she's changed her mind?" Each question comes with greater ease, and when I nod, she asks another. "Why didn't she come herself?"

"She's been sick. With the war getting closer, she didn't want to wait."

"Yes," the girl agrees, "the war is getting closer." She finds safety in my words and uses it to meet my apologetic eyes. "I'm sorry, Mrs. Okada. It must be very sad for your daughter. But you can't have my son."

"He isn't your son."

"You shouldn't even be here. This is illegal."

"This isn't about law." I am struggling to figure out what changed the balance, to find a word she understands. I think of appealing to Will for help, but instead I look to Eric. I can see his uncles, even his mother, in the pillow beneath his skin. "It's about blood," I say, trying to capture that feeling.

"His *blood* gave him away. I love him, and your daughter doesn't. Or didn't. This family is best."

"We are best," I correct.

"Why didn't you take him before?"

"What do you mean?"

"When he was born. When your daughter needed you? Why didn't you take him then?"

"Why?" She has so many questions. Her face becomes a child's top—her domed forehead, her pointed chin, the way she skitters from my words and spins hers around me with an indecent amount of force. "Why do you ask?"

She picks up the teapot. "Is this about property? The family name perhaps?"

"No. Just family."

"Well, you didn't want him then and you don't deserve him now. Not that it matters. I am Eric's legal mother and I would never give him up."

She drinks so calmly. I search for the pride I need to leave rather than suffer her insults, but time is short and I need a plan. Watching Eric push his block in lines on the rug, my thoughts grow crazy. I can steal him, I think. Sometime, she'll have to sleep.

Then Will asks, "Where's Ken?"

He hasn't spoken since we left our house, and I can hear the rust in his voice and the fury, though his casual words try to mask it. I look over, finally, to see him sitting forward, the chair frozen on the tips of its bows. His head is cocked to disarm her, his elbows crouched ready on his knees, but I know he isn't listening. I recognize it all then—the coil and the trap—from my life with Mitsuo. In that instant, Will has become as unstable and as righteous as his father; my son has become the way my husband was in his early years, as Mitsuo must have been before I met him. I know them both, and their demons, and have no courage to stop what's to come.

The girl, cautious, tries to match Will's tone. "Who?"

"Ken. Your husband. The one you thought we'd come about, remember?"

"Oh. Ken. He's not here right now."

"Of course he's not," Will says. "Why don't I tell you where he is?"

His words crowd her, though he himself doesn't move. All of us feel them, and when they reach her, she does exactly the wrong thing. She rises. "I think you should leave."

Still on the tips of the rocker, Will threatens to break it with his stillness. "Ken was arrested, wasn't he?"

"Don't be ridiculous."

"Everything's gone. Pictures, books, papers. There was a samurai sword above your mantel. On those hooks. Does the FBI have it or did you get it down in time?"

The girl keeps her voice low. "My husband is no business of—"

"Mine?" Finally Will stands, releasing enough tension that I can breathe. "Why not? You said our family isn't good enough for the boy. *Our* family."

"Well, you left him—"

"So did your husband."

"You know nothing about it—"

Eric stops pushing his block when he hears her raised voice, looking from the girl to Will to see if he should cry. We all hold our places—Will for the power of it, the girl and I to reassure Eric. I could try to hold him, but I know I can't help. He ducks under the table, staring at Will's feet.

My son keeps the pressure in his flat voice steady. "No? Where is your husband?"

The girl moans. "He isn't—"

"No. He isn't here. Did he run, or did they take him? What would we find out if we asked?"

My own arms are numb. The shadow of her fear has me frozen. "Please," she says. "This has nothing to do with Eric."

"No? Does the adoption agency know about the arrest?"

"I told you. Everything's in order."

Finally, Will moves. "Did they take him, or did he run?"

"You can't reverse it," she says, "I signed the papers already—"

"Did they take him, or did he run?"

She backs away, losing space. "Please, you don't know—"

I believe, then, that he will scream at her, keep repeating "Did he run?" until we both become mad, but he moves forward instead, like a hammer, worse than words could be.

"Stop it!" she screams, and as she does, a thin wail rises from under the coffee table. She covers her ears with her hands, but it slices through their fragile shelter. "Stop it! They took him. All right?"

She doesn't glance at Eric, but I do. His face is porcelain smooth, the sound of her voice a beacon. He's too afraid to cry.

"We're taking him home," Will says.

"No, you can't. That's kidnapping."

"I *will* report you to the adoption agency if I have to. Maybe they'll deport you, too."

Will walks out of the house then. In the current of the slamming door, I have risen. I am alone with the two of them, still trapped in the ebbing wail. The girl stands as if she might never move, and I recognize the moment: when the action you hate most is the one you have to take.

She scooped Eric in the easy motion I'd imagined and moved toward the stairs. Her feet sank in the carpet; they were so small they teetered and fell between the tufts. When she got there, she paused, then stopped again on each step for so long I thought she had forgotten her purpose. She might have returned in minutes with Eric and his suitcase, and handed him to me without a word. But she might have run.

The girl must have felt my heat behind her, but she didn't

turn. Perhaps by then, she knew I was her fate. Whatever the reason, she took me to the nursery without a backward glance. Eric was quiet because she was, but he held her with both hands as we waited to see what she would do.

It was a small room, and so full. There was a huge rug in the middle and a bin of toys that flowed over and across the floor to my feet. The bright yellow walls glowed and birds flew through the air on strings above a large, carved crib. On the largest wall, illustrated pages from books, carefully framed, hung in rows that read down to the floor. There was a rabbit at my knee, and a frog. And a prince at my ankle. I could see how she must have crawled on her stomach to nail in the bottom ones.

The girl set Eric in his crib and moved to the window where she could watch Will smoke and stand guard. She folded her arms, protection against the sight of him glaring at the front door. "He's so cruel," she said flatly.

"No," I said, though I knew she was right. "He's strong."

Her eyes were full of tears. When they spilled over, she touched them, puzzled. "Kenichi was a journalist for the *Rafu Shrimpo*," she said. "The last time I saw him, three agents were shoving him out the door. He was trying to explain that he hadn't written anything unpatriotic, but they had his arms twisted behind him, so I guess they didn't hear."

I watched her balled-up fingers pick the skin around her nails. Two were blood smeared.

"I know some people who were taken, too," I said. I didn't tell her one of them was Will.

"But they've come back, haven't they? Or at least sent word. If only the agents hadn't come so quickly. If they'd given us Christmas, we would be fine."

The girl's focus on her husband, rather than on her little boy, was confusing. She was hung up in the past, replaying a nightmare she needed to change. I didn't know then what it was, just that it had to do with Eric. I didn't register the word *Christmas*, or know enough about the adoption "contract" she had mentioned or the law. All I knew was, she wasn't holding him like I would have. I realized then that, if I were her, I would not have let him go.

I would have stalled. The truth of it came to me coldly; maybe it was me with Eric in my arms who was trying to fly away. Standing in the window, Will's paces ticking in my head, I had to admit I would have done anything to keep the child. There was something in the frenzy of the glances Will was throwing at the window that upset my idea of who was right. Suddenly, I realized I was searching for ways to help the girl. I had it all figured out, how to lock her in safely with the boy when she said, "We'd have been safe."

Her words must have marked the end of a dream for her because, when she heard them, the tears really came. She yanked two suitcases out of the small closet behind her and threw them open on the floor. Outside, Will was pacing the length of the car. Over and over, a timepiece gone mad.

I moved to the window to catch my breath as she tugged the top drawer of a dresser that came away too easily in her hands. She fell back, spilling it into the suitcase, then dropped it to the floor. I thought she'd pull out the next one and start throwing clothes, but instead she reached into the bin. She snatched toys in each hand, tossing them into the second suitcase, then going to the crib for more. As the space around him emptied, Eric watched her, waiting to be next. He didn't move when she took the mobile down. She stood over him, unwilling to collapse it. His eyes bobbed with the birds.

"He's my son, you know," she said. She looked exhausted. "I think of him that way. He's so clever. He can say a few things now, and he laughs. I just, I've always thought of him as my son."

I had decided for her, and she had decided for me. I would live with it, never knowing what might have been; even later, when I found out her husband never had the chance to sign the contract, that moment never allowed me to feel good about what I had done. It was over. Since she didn't have the strength to, I walked to Eric's crib, afraid, in the back of my mind, that he would cry out when I touched him and make a choice himself. But he came without protest. I settled him on my hip like I'd seen the girl do and took him down the stairs, leaving her to follow with his bags.

And that was it, the quick end we both wanted. Except that, when we got to the car, she pressed the flying birds into my hand. I thought it was a trade, that she wanted to hold Eric one last time, and I wasn't going to let her. When I looked up, her eyes were on Will.

"You are a thief, you know."

"And you're a liar."

Then she said, conversationally, easily, "Perhaps I am. But your sister is a whore."

I looked up to catch the words in the moment before they disappeared. Before they were sucked into Will's fury, erased by the absence of movement, of sound. They were not words he could forgive, or even respond to, so I expected him to strike her as I had feared he would for so long. But in the immediate silence, the girl seemed incapable of saying something so ugly. She seemed weightless, herself just a child.

The girl turned to me then, as if she had just stepped onto the driveway. As if the world was one minute younger than it would ever be again.

"Protect my boy," she said as she released the mobile into my care. "Don't let your son break him the way he's broken me."

That was the last word; Will gave it to her. He seemed marginally more human as we got into the car. And though I didn't dare speak to him once on our long trip home, I wasn't frightened. I thought it was over. Will had won, after all, and I imagined that both of us could let the girl's words go.

12

JACK

PURPLE HEARTS, 1944

Jack dives. Screaming shards of tree tear off behind him as he hits the logs over the slit trench and drops inside. His legs snag, he hears a snap, but he's okay. Just a thud. No pain. Facedown, inhaling mud, Jack knows he's fine. He's sure he can walk, but right now his helmet is pressing on his neck and he's drowning. Shifting, thinking he should have left the strap loose after all, Jack gets his nose up. Don't wipe it, he thinks. It's one of the few tricks they taught him, finally handy. Jack is passing out, he's vulnerable. He needs to look dead.

The first thing Jack knows is, the mud in his nose is dry.

He opens his eyes, but the fog is in. Fucking fog, he thinks, always in. The Jerries' best weapon. Night, day, you can walk right by them. They wait and get you in the back. It's all one-arm wrestling in these mountains, all blind man's bluff. Without ears, you're dead for sure.

Jack waits for details. No breathing near. Just the demon wind in the pines and the rustling, never-ending rain. A Japanese American soldier dying, crying for his mama. "*Itai, itai.*" It hurts. There are a couple of others, too, desperate, their moans syncopated, heart-beating. Grenades holler in the distance. There are no medics, no patrols out walking in the nightmare.

No, it's just Jack and the night noises. And the hint of soundwaves gathering to break? a breath holding?—that picked him up and launched him here on the front edge of the tree burst. They have a knack for torture, those Germans. With their mines and traps. And their tree bursts: showers of wood splinters and metal flinging blood like rice. Hitting the enemy isn't enough for Jerries. They aim at stretchers and Red Cross helmets going down the hills.

Jack's legs ignore his mind's attempts to move them, but he can feel his fingers. The nubby, running wall of the slit trench has come into focus. Crusts of ice shatter against his fists as he tries to turn over. Old rain laps at his ears. Just shock, he thinks, looking up toward a sky that isn't there yet. His legs, he has them. He has to. They taught him that, in basic. Didn't they teach him something?

Basic training, Jack thinks. What a lie. For days, he's known: all the single-digit days of his war. At Shelby, what did he learn? Creeping and crawling. He learned to slog through swamps, wear mosquitoes without flinching. To hang on to his rifle through the fire and kick, launch mortars, read maps. None of it as easy as it sounds. He learned tricks: "fire for effect," like playing tic-tac-toe with mortar, and he was so damn happy to get it right he never thought about what happened to the Xs and the Os. They didn't mention that.

They didn't tell you what to do then, when the shells are on you and you're screaming before you hear the damn things fire. Sure death was out there. Men would be "lost." But he didn't understand, somehow, that people were going to die. Friends were going to die. He didn't know what that meant.

Now, Jack's in mud again, he's been sitting in it for days. Mud and shit and piss and blood. And the last time his clothes were clean, the last time they were dry? It's the shock, Jack thinks—can't keep his mind straight. The toes on his left foot are beginning to burn. He hasn't tried to see them yet.

His rifle, frozen, is still good for something. Barrel down, Jack uses it to pull his torso out of the water and lean against the dirt. It's too dark and wet to see blood. He can count the feet, three, that rise out of the water in front of him. Squinting doesn't erase one; he concentrates, thinking, "two."

Two days ago, Jack had two legs and two days of rest before they were called back into the forest. Eighty measly fellows left in K Company, and they were supposed to be heroes. Rescue the lost Texan battalion. Jack fell in line and marched: up and down, through the dark, in the rain. He held Shimmy's pack so they wouldn't lose each other. Trees, identical and tall, burst out of the fog and hovered before sinking back. Through the thinning curtain of dawn, cliffs fell off his path.

First, it was just snipers popping at them. They lost their scout, but when the medics tried to reach him, K Company was taking everything—artillery, flak gunfire, grenades, the "meemies" that screamed. Fellows were going down in a dozen different sounds. The column scattered, Jack fired by ear, keeping Shimmy in sight. Getting lost in that damned forest felt much worse than being dead.

He'll be both soon, Jack thinks, he gets to be both. But what an honor for his folks. A Purple Heart, to recognize his many days of war. Not like Will's months, Will's real valor. Jack's brother was first, he joined the Hawaiians even before the 442nd sailed. Will was at Anzio, Belvedere, Livorno. He crossed the Arno River and liberated Rome. Combat was something Will painted on his face. Exhaustion, too. Grit. Jack was in the last pack. Clean, shipped off, and delivered with training still to do. Taking his last chances for the fellow who didn't get another chance. And all around him, fellows who'd seen people die. Who'd killed.

Back home, it had been impossible to understand. Impossible, too, to halt the choking horse-infused cars on the train ride to the staging area near Bruyères. But Jack had joined them now. He got to France in time to see what dying's like. Men die pissing. They break like dolls. They tear along seams and into fragments. Puzzle pieces and bile. In camp in Colorado, when Jack was being held behind barbed wire, he'd been so sure there was honor in dying. Maybe he'll believe that again. But now, death just feels vulgar.

In basic training, they learned to follow orders. But Dahlquist, their division commander, was insane. Never letting the flanks catch up, attacking uphill, screaming "Advance, advance!" on the front line to get them out of their foxholes. Take the objective. They were lost, too, once, without backup or communication. They didn't teach you that at Shelby.

At Shelby, you didn't ask either. You trusted. You never guessed that your commanding officer would kill your best friend. Like on Hill C, where Henry died. The Hawaiians had the hill, but Dahlquist pulled them off, and the Jerries grew back like the trees. They had to take it again, they formed a special task force just for that. Jack wasn't there when Henry went down, so he didn't know. Which men were wasted? Which ones?

So bitter, Jack thinks. Better to die right out. To be killed while killing someone. Or saving someone. Will had been right; Jack was a fool to think he could ever be a soldier. He was a fool, too, to make friends. They should have warned you about that in basic training. At least that. They should have told you not to make friends.

Henry died on Hill C. Shimmy died rescuing the Texas battalion, the first day when K Company crossed paths with the tank.

Shimmy knew it was coming. He'd been having trouble sleeping, waking Jack and all the fellows with his nightmares. Empty barns without straw, a bus rolled in a trench. Nothing Jack recognized. Jack told Shimmy he was asking for trouble. There was too much death around him, aiming at him, Shimmy replied. "Today's my turn. I know it." "Go down and you'll take me with you," Jack warned. But he didn't get through.

They had expected a rest, but the orders came anyway. So that night, they smoked. Even the fellows who'd never smoked before; the room was lit like the skyline of downtown L.A. They debated—helmets? fastened?—and one stuffed his helmet full to keep it out of his eyes. They told secrets. Some gave treasures away. One of the fellows whose girlfriend had just dumped him was begging to be forward observer until the sergeant said, "Do it on your own time." Meaning suicide. A young fellow too, a *Skeebo* Jack didn't know. He knew Henry Otaga, who was dead, and "Shimmy" Shimizu. Replacements. The others had been scattered.

He must have left something undone that night, Jack thinks. It was morning too soon. The team jumped off in the utter darkness: trench foot or no, half-strength or no, everyone was on the move. Ice rain dripped off Jack's helmet. His soaking boots announced him when he walked. He waited, blind, surrounded by ambulances in reserve, as the story filtered down. A battalion from the Texas 36th was cut off by Jerries and dying. A rumor followed; who knew if it was true? The top brass was sending the Nisei on this one so they wouldn't have to deal with their offspring.

That helped. Something to prove wrong. The whole team fanned out for a banzai charge. Right into Jerries. They were caught on a ridge in a splatter of bullets with no plan but forward. The way was supposed to be clear.

Jack and Shimmy charged together, over trees, behind trees, not breathing. Shells wailed like race cars around them, the sounds reflecting and deflecting until no one could tell where they were coming from or when. The ground was plowed by shells, kicking up mud, gravel, branches; they were furrowing a field in the underbrush. Jack saw them hit in a puff of fog, a rain of blood, guns and boots, a flurry of flesh to blanket the trees and cling to the tiny leaves and branches at their feet. It was magic. The fellow with the stuffed helmet blew so far up that nothing landed and Jack didn't even slow down.

He wanted to. He wanted to get help, call for time-out. He wanted just to stop and think, but the Vosges Mountains didn't give chances like that. There was no safe base. No safe tree even. There was a quiet moment though, a heartbeat moment every time a shell hit. There was a moment when he could see fellows fly, sprout blood, land in several places. When the sizzle hung alone in the air.

It was strange how that happened over and over, Jack thinks. Strange because war is a din too loud to hear through. In war, you rely on your eyes for orders. When the fellow in front of you goes, you go.

It's quiet now in the trench, but Jack is not alone. He can see and hear every death. Every kill since he started. Henry is with him, like he was on the boat. So anxious to join his brothers in the war. So drunk on the whiskey they were passing he thought it was stars that were flashing in their wake. Henry had been talking about his father again, and how he got to see him at Crystal City before they were shipped out. Jack could have told the story himself, but he listened while Henry remembered how they made him take off his uniform to be searched. While he marveled again that the Japanese at that camp were speaking Spanish—most of the prisoners weren't even American. Henry's father had sat down across the table without a movement to greet him. They hadn't met eyes, they didn't speak until a guard came by. His father mouthed the unfamiliar English words, "I am fine. I am fed and taking care," before he broke the rules and switched to Japanese. He got out, "Fight for your country. Fight with honor, or don't come back at all," before the guards dragged him away.

Jack pokes the legs in front of him. His are burning now. Shrapnel. The tree burst did get him, then; he didn't outrun it. His left leg seems broken. Probably the snap on the camouflage logs. The price of living through the night, if he does.

When Jack gets to the third leg, it comes out of the water in his hands. It's much heavier than his own, there past the knee. A piece of silky flesh, shorter than his fingers, swings on the joint.

Jack scoops some water to rinse the mud away; he has to scrub around the bone to get it clean. Is it a casualty? he wonders. It could be all that's left. On the other hand, the rest of the fellow could still be out there. He might even want it back.

The first time Jack saw a man die, it happened right in front of him. Maybe two, three men up the line. They were being shelled, the fellow panicked and ran off the cleared path. He should have known about the white tags, that there were mines out there, but he didn't. It was a bouncing betty, a chest-high shrapnel spitter, and he was falling, so he took it in the head. Sliced him into meat right there. Scooped out his face: nose, jaw, everything was gone. His body jerked so much hitting the ground that Jack thought he must be alive, but it was only spasms. Jack stood there. He couldn't take it in.

There were shells everywhere, he remembers, about to hit his spot because they hadn't yet, and shells were always hitting the spot where you had just been standing. Someone tackled him and dragged him down as he screamed for the medics. He didn't need to, they saw it on their own. They were in the field, armed. Even the cook was armed.

In basic training, they told you to wait for the medics. You had a first aid kit, true. But they didn't give you any tips on how to put a nose back on or spend a night bleeding to death in a trench. They didn't tell you what to do about the pain either. Pain was good, a sign you were a soldier. You lived with it, hell, you stole back to the front despite it. Instead, they taught you not to leave fingerprints on the salt and pepper shakers. No shit. One of the lieutenants used to inspect them with a magnifying glass.

Jack would give anything to be back in basic now.

It was the tank that got Shimmy, the first morning of the rescue. They were moving on the ridge and suddenly a Panther rolled into the valley not a hundred yards away. Aimed right at them, infantry behind. The fire it sprayed was everywhere.

K Company took it all. Fire slashed through the fellows Jack had smoked with. He watched them explode, one by one, saw daylight bloom inside them. Jack's fear took him to the ground, smothering in the taste of burned and blasted flesh. Shimmy just stood there shooting, and the tank stitched him right through the middle and kept going.

Dirt had caked Shimmy's eyes when Jack reached him. He was pumping blood from his gut, but he was trying to hang on, literally—he had his hands stuffed through his belly button. The rest of his arms seemed okay to Jack. His legs were okay, too, nothing twisted when he fell. A medic spotted them and scrambled over without a litter. It was a good thing Shimmy skipped breakfast, Jack remembers thinking. He didn't want to see food spilling through his fingers. It was too loud for Jack to get that thought across to the medic, though. Nor could he hear the fellow's words, understand why he moved on. Jack grabbed for him, screamed at him, "He's alive, you asshole, come back," but his hands came away empty and no one heard. The ground groaned as someone hit the tank and it ignited. Jack took cover, pulling Shimmy to a tangle of roots.

Then he heard Shimmy laugh.

The sound rose through Jack, tickling his ears, making him laugh, too. He felt as if water was flooding his face, running off it. He was surfacing—a fool again, but safe. Afraid for no reason. Jack was so pleased, until he turned to greet his friend and found it wasn't a laugh; the sound was rising from Shimmy's gut. Or maybe his lungs. It seemed important to know, but then, one was no less deadly than the other.

Jack needed help and he knew there was no one left to give it. He was shrouded in blood, they both were. Hot and soft. Cloying. Iron scented. He held on anyway, searched the blur of fellows still dying until the gurgle faded. Or the battle picked up. The rain picked up, too, that was his thought until he realized, "Stupid. It's only tears." And since he had nothing better to do, Jack talked to Shimmy.

Jack said the human things that Shimmy would have, each word pulling on a wire around his heart. "Tell my mother I love her." "Tell her I died for my country." It didn't matter that it was *his* Mama who Jack was thinking of, not Shimmy's. He said it like that so Shimmy could rest hearing it, thinking it came from him. Jack pressed Shimmy tightly to him, too, head in his lap, touching him so that if he could feel, Shimmy would know Jack stayed. That Jack understood, and they could just forget that drowning laugh. So that Shimmy could find God in the abyss with the knowledge that it was so much better to die himself than to see a friend die.

He would finally find the place where he belonged.

Now, it's morning. Between the bars of camouflage logs, Jack can see white sun shimmering through the fog. Lighting the rain like Christmas. And he's still alive, Jack thinks, a miracle or maybe just a curse. He has one thing left to do.

Jack drags his body high enough to see out of the trench but not be seen. Picking up the extra leg, clean now for someone to use, he strokes it and settles the heel in his crotch, the knee on his shoulder. With love, he pulls the shoelaces loose and uses them to tie the leg to his wrist so it can't be left behind. Just you and me, buddy, he says in his head. Count on me. Tired, thinking he's probably lost some blood, Jack sees a trio of white butterflies hopscotching in the beams of light. Dancing above the carnage, unaware of the men and the blood. The leg can go home in a box, he thinks. Shimmy's box, Henry's. It died young, it deserves that much. It can fill a grave, a heart, a hope—it can stand in for anyone's missing pieces. It can even heal, Jack thinks, make up for certain things. Like the man Jack found and killed right after Shimmy died.

The only one of Jack's whole war.

13

MARIKO

THE WOMAN HE SEES, 1968

When Mari reaches the top of the wide slatted stair of the Shriver family's home and her Uncle Carroll's medical clinic, she glances down the wraparound *lanai* in case her Aunt Dee and her calabash cousins are there. The large plantation house is quiet except for the ceiling fan shooing out the last of the day's heat. She peers through the half-pulled curtains but can't tell from the lights whether Uncle Carroll has sent them away to protect her. His office hours are over; the orchid sun casts the world in its best light of the day.

They are gone, Mari decides, letting the cricket song rise and fall in her heart as she follows the CARROLL SHRIVER, M.D. sign to the back of the building. Uncle Carroll isn't going to fight her anymore. In a few short hours, she will be free of Dale; free, as that young lawyer in Ed Spencer's office encouraged her, to take an interesting class or two. Roger Stone was right when he said she could do things she hadn't dreamed of when she got married. She could go a little wild.

The waiting room is empty. Mari moves through it quietly to find Uncle Carroll in his office alone.

His eyes are closed, his white hair softer and brighter than his coat. "Am I too early?" she asks softly. She hugs him, holding him as if she hasn't seen him for years. He hugs her back, and as she breathes in the warmth of his skin, Mari realizes how much she needs this.

"You can still change your mind, you know," he tells her gently when she pulls away. "There's no shame. The important thing is to make the right choice."

"I know," Mari says, remembering how hard she had to work to convince him. It wasn't until she told him her husband left *because* she was pregnant that the doctor agreed to let her return.

Mari follows Uncle Carroll farther down the hall, feeling messy and small against the white walls. His examining room seems bigger than it did the day before, when he gave her a pregnancy test; the bench is covered in plastic for the blood. She stands in the doorway, breathing in the spare doctor smell and cool surfaces while he lays out a gown for her and silver instruments for himself.

"Do you have to cut me open?"

"No, no. Nothing so drastic."

Mari hugs herself, not moving, and tries to place the objects in the room. "I've never even had a tooth filled."

"Maybe we should talk this over some more."

"No." The hostile glow of his instruments is making her nervous, Mari knows. And Uncle Carroll, watching from so far away, giving her so much room. "I want to do it," she says with more conviction. "Maybe some music will help."

"You won't hear it."

Mari switches the transistor on and tunes it, ignoring the doctor's sigh. "I want to be awake for this. I want to know what's happening."

"Put the robe on with the opening in the front. I'll be back."

When Uncle Carroll returns, he is carrying a long leather strap with a loop on each end. "This is to keep your legs up, since you won't be able to hold them," he explains, scooting his stool toward her. "Put your feet through these loops, see? Bend your knees and I'll slide them up your thighs." He raises her head, sliding the middle of the strap behind her neck to keep her legs from dropping. "Does it feel okay?"

"Sure." Mari shifts her shoulders to get the strap to lie flatter. Her legs wave a little, pulling on her hair. She's surprised at how precarious her position feels, how limp and uncertain her legs are. Still, there is something secure about the grasp of the leather. "I feel like a horse."

"I'm sorry. They don't make equipment for this procedure. I'm going to numb you up, so if you could put your legs together and roll over to the side? It's going to hurt."

For just a moment, Mari wonders what she's doing: whether she's being so stubborn to ward off Uncle Carroll's sadness or whether she wants the chance, now that he has given up, to change her mind. The hesitations, if that's what they are, come from too far away for her to feel them.

The needle burns, then Uncle Carroll helps her turn back over.

"It's okay, it's okay," he murmurs. "It's just not very dignified, is it? Take some deep breaths and think about something pleasant."

Mari wonders why he is trying to soothe her, especially since the concern in his voice is summoning tears. It's not until he says it that Mari remembers there isn't anything pleasant about her life. She's lying on a table with her knees yanked back, stabbing into the air, and her butt growing numb in front of her father's friend. Uncle Carroll is right, Mari realizes. There's no dignity in this. There's no control.

"Breathe, Mari. Take some deep breaths." He's washing his hands, bringing his instruments closer. He tents a sheet over her legs so she can't see, then rubs something cold on her inner thighs. "This will keep things as sterile as possible. Tell me if you feel any discomfort, but try not to move."

"Right."

And then his head dips and it is happening. Mari braces against the pain. Her nerves are looking for it, wanting to savor it as the price she must pay, but she feels only pressure: a few pokes and jabs. Any minute, she thinks, but time crawls and she can't feel anything. She tries to hold still so she won't bleed to death, but it's hard for her to concentrate. She keeps forgetting to breathe.

"Your cervix is dilated. You're doing fine."

"Is it over?"

"No. I'm going to scrape the inside of your uterus now. Think about a song you like, or a book you just read. Don't think about this or it'll take even longer."

Mari can feel the scalpel in her elbows. It's everywhere but where it's supposed to be: ringing in her ears, brushing against her teeth. The pain is a shadow. It isn't there, yet she can feel each stroke precisely, carving out the inside of her heart.

Real pain would be better than this, Mari thinks. She grinds her lip between her teeth, tasting salt as her skin breaks in a small throb. It dissipates but makes things bearable. Less lonely.

If only she had a part in this, an assignment, Mari wouldn't feel so uncertain. The sheet, brushing her belly, has slipped so far she can see Uncle Carroll's white hair bobbing between her legs. He has so many instruments—they click as he moves them. He has something to concentrate on, but she is cheating. She has nothing at all to do.

"Relax. Put your head down." His hand is warm now, pushing on the tightening lock of her legs. Her knees fall to the sides, her thighs finger-painted with blood.

"Listen to the music, okay?" He begins to hum, pulling a song out of the radio and wrapping it around her. It is the same hum, the same head, that visits her home with his family in tow. The same hands, too, that shake her own and make perfect imprints on her legs. Reassuring shapes, she tells herself. Made of blood and nothing more.

She sees herself again, lying in sin on the table with her legs strapped to her neck, with Uncle Carroll there to witness it. She should be mortified, but instead, he is company. He is family in the doctor's office, someone to take her hand when she's finished falling, when the clandestine operation is over. If it is ever, finally, over.

"How are you feeling now?"

Mari opens her eyes and realizes he's washing his hands at the sink. She moves her lips, but cannot speak. Time has passed, and she has lost it.

"No pain?"

She tries again. "No."

He comes back with a warm cloth and wipes her legs. "It's going to be uncomfortable for a couple of days. I'll give you some painkillers. And you'll be bleeding like you have your menses. You'll need to rest."

Mari lifts her head, aware of how slow everything has become. "Can I move? Is it over?"

He nods. "All *pau*. Let me get you out of this harness."

She flinches at his touch. "No."

"Mariko." His face looms over hers. "Are you okay? How do you feel?"

How does she feel? she wonders. Does he truly want to know? She feels like the straps have become a part of her. Without them, she will fall apart. She will be Mari again, without a purpose and completely alone.

"You can move a little, Mari. It won't disrupt anything. It won't hurt."

Mari lifts her head to let Uncle Carroll remove the straps and pull the plastic lining out from under her. Her legs fall heavily against the bench. She looks at the sallow skin on them and her crude wiry hair as he clips a sanitary pad onto the back of an elastic belt then slips it down her thighs and beneath her buttocks. She watches him thread the sheer tag of fabric through the front clip and pull until it's tight. That's it, Mari thinks, a little piece of gauze to cover her and she's not a mother anymore. Not a wife, not anyone really. From here, she has nowhere to go.

"I'm not going to move you yet. You can rest here for a couple of hours, then I'll let you go. Who's coming for you? I'll call and tell them when you'll be ready."

He had asked her to have a friend come to get her, someone she could trust who would stay with her. "I . . . ," she begins. She can't see his face. "There's no one. I couldn't think of anyone."

"Well, then. You'll have to spend the night. I'll tell Dee."

"I'll just lie here—"

"We'll set you up in the house. The best thing for you now is some rest. I'll come back in a little while with some soup."

"I don't want to be a burden." She knows she should be embarrassed, but she can't help thinking about the soup.

"No burden. I was worried about letting you go anyway. I don't want anything happening to my favorite girl." Uncle Carroll picks a cotton blanket off the stool it sat on throughout the operation and tucks it around her. He pats her shoulder, puts a pillow under her head.

"Are you leaving?"

"Do you want me to stay?"

"What if something—"

"Nothing will. The worst part is over." He strokes her arms, trying to relax her. "It gets better from now on."

This isn't what she hoped for. She wants to go into his house and curl up on his sofa; she wants people around. She knows that means they'll guess what happened, but not even shame could keep her away. Instead, she lies stiffly on the bench because, having planned to stay here, she can't think of a reason to keep him. Uncle Carroll smiles. She feels his touch fade.

He leaves her in the dark, with the hall light aching in an *L*-shape around the cracked door. She is too drained to fight the rising room.

Mari is alone. Every time she opens her eyes, tears flee down her face and into her ears. Her breath boils out of her, pitching her chest as it pushes past the fist clenched against her mouth, past the fingers that rub her teeth because she can't keep her lips closed. She can feel a fire building, a fuse lit around her heart, too deep and moving too fast to be put out. Mari wraps her soggy arms around her body; when that doesn't work, she curls and grabs her legs to tamp it down. She has killed her own child, she realizes. She killed the only thing she might have lived for, and she's giving up for good.

The first knock is perfectly civilized. It drifts into Mari's head like the taps and rings of the others who have been trying to reach her, then passes through without anything to catch on. It doesn't matter who it is: her parents, Dale, even Uncle Carroll checking to see if she's healed. She isn't healed, Mari knows, jarred to the edge of her greedy sleep; she can't be.

It is the second knock that rouses her—a more hollow sound Mari can hear at her back door. The man is circling her house, trying to get in. She knows it's a man by his heavy heels. She presses her pillow around her ears, waiting for the noise to go away.

For four days, Mari has been floating in a blissful darkness, with nothing to measure herself against and nothing she has to reveal. All the pieces of her body, each knuckle and hinge, have come undone. When she first returned home, pronounced "fine" by Uncle Carroll, she could smell herself rotting. She has tried to erase herself so thoroughly she can't be found.

"Mariko! Mar-i-*ko*!"

The voice is far away and strange; whoever the man is, he can't pronounce her name. She imagines, for a moment, that she's in danger, which would be only slightly better than being saved. Fear is an indulgence in her slowly fading state, though; if she was threatened, her neighbors would call the police. In fact, most of them would call the precinct and ask for Dale.

"Hello! Mariko! Hello!"

It's the threat of Dale himself arriving in his flashing, braying car that rouses Mari from her bed. Her head sails off her body as she does; she grabs it with both hands to remind it where it should be. "Go away," she says, in words that stay inside her mouth. Her voice tastes dusty. "Leave me alone."

Mari drags herself through the quilted hall shadows toward her front door. The small window in it has been pierced by a long red jewel. She squints at the dust dancing in the column of sunset that stretches toward her, wondering whether she can postpone this until it is dark. She feels light, so disjointed; she checks around idly, sure she's dropped pieces of herself on the floor.

"Mariko, hey! Open the door."

There is a head eclipsing the light from the window; whoever it is can see inside. Mari opens the door obediently, letting in the world. She swings away as it floods by her, hunches with her eyes closed behind the wood.

"You *are* home. I knew you would be."

Mari waves the voice in with one hand and doesn't open her eyes until the man is standing in her hallway. It's the cute lawyer from Ed's office. Roger something. Roger Stone.

"Taking a nap?"

"Oh. Yeah." When Mari straightens, her fingers brush the bottom of her T-shirt. She looks down at her bare legs, suddenly, deeply aware of the wadded pad just out of sight. She remembers that this man knows her, so it will be easy for him to see what she has done. "This isn't a good time."

He nods and steps past her. "It's pretty dark in here. Can I open a shade?"

She says no, but he doesn't hear her. She wants to pull her T-shirt down, only she's afraid it will slide up and expose her from behind. Instead, she stands in the doorway of her living room on two even feet, framed like a schoolgirl as Roger pulls her curtains one by one. The fabric swings no louder than a kiss against her old floor. Her toes revive as the sun flashes on them.

Her sofa is suddenly blue.

"You missed your appointment with Ed," Roger says when Mari doesn't speak. "We've been trying to reach you for days. Well, two days. I've been trying to reach you. You said we could be friends."

He looks so pure, standing there. So unaware.

"I'm not presentable."

"Do you need help? Can I . . ."

He must sense something is wrong, Mari thinks. Maybe she *is* dying, but he doesn't seem sure. She imagines herself melting; red clots spinning down her thighs on their blood-thin webs; Roger lifting her out of her telltale footprints; her legs staining his shirt. She can see him holding her, a broken bride to carry across a threshold. Since there is nowhere he can take her, she shakes her head, then ducks it quickly to make sure her feet are clean.

"I'm sleeping," she mutters, disappointed by her vision. She realizes he won't call Dale; he's a man, and they never ask for help. "Go away." Each step she takes down her hall feels safer until at last she's in her thick, dark bedroom where everything she owns ran together days ago. She curls around the ridge of pillows in the center of her bed with her back to the open doorway. She lets herself dwindle down. First her body, then her mind.

He'll be gone soon, Mari thinks, closing her eyes. He's nice. He'll go away.

When Roger enters Mari's bedroom, her curtains have fused. The world has lost its pricks of sun. "Hey. Wake up, sleepyhead," he says from behind her. "I hope you don't mind. You had nothing in that kitchen so I went to the store."

"Umm." She must have drifted off, she thinks, unable to turn and face him. She can't imagine why he hasn't left. "I'm sleeping. Do you mind? I have to."

"Have to what?" He has flipped her bedside lamp on, shifting the shade so the light's not in her eyes, but she can feel it spreading across her; and all his energy, his weight on the bed, forces her around. She slits her eyes so they don't burn and tries to see him. He's brought two glasses of lemonade.

Have to leave, have to go—Mari doesn't remember what she was thinking. Taking the glass he holds out, she runs it along her inner arms. Her skin tingles, like a wind picked up somewhere. It raises ridges on her body until it connects her head and ears. She didn't expect this, all this feeling. She sighs, knowing she has lost to him, and lets the ice bump against her lips.

"Drink it, don't smell it. I'm making some food. It comes in a box."

The whole encounter is so peculiar. In real life, she would never have let him in. She barely knows him, has spoken to him only once, and yet she answered the door in her nightshirt and let him settle onto her bed. He didn't even offer his help so she could reject it. He has simply taken over.

Mari shivers as the cold liquid spreads across the floor of her stomach. "Umm." Roger hands her the second glass, and she finishes it, too, automatically. Her organs are awake, despite that fact that she's tried for four days to put them to sleep, but she feels good and as if she could watch them working through her skin.

"You look like you need it. And I'm always happy to help."

"I should take a shower," she says, knowing it's an intimate thing to say, but she wants the cool fingers of water to comb through her hair. A new sensation, she thinks. Sinking into her back and shoulders to steal her soul.

"No." He brushes her arm. "You might fall over."

"But I'm dirty."

"It's okay. I'll bring the food here when it's ready. Which should be soon. In fact, I'll check on it now. Do you want anything? More lemonade?"

She shakes her head. She is tired; she needs to lie down. But it's harder to sleep with the lemonade inside her. When she holds her hands up, they don't disappear as quickly, as if the ice in the glasses has made them solid again. It's Roger's doing; it's amazing how he doesn't really see her. He has a remarkable ability to summon what he wants.

Mari can smell the food slipping smoothly down the hall and into the room; it enters a step before Roger. She tries to smile at the bright orange clouds peeling off the bowls. Macaroni and cheese, she thinks. How vile.

"How's my patient?" he asks, resettling.

Mari's arms, stretched out to take the food, begin to tremble at the word. She snatches them to her chest to rock them, keep them on. He must know about the abortion after all, though she can't imagine how. And just when she was beginning to believe she was strong.

"What makes you think I'm a patient?"

"I just meant—well, I'm nursing you today—"

"Who talked to you?" she insists. "Why are you here?"

"No one talked to me. Hell, I stole your address out of Ed's file."

"Well, why—"

"I wanted to see you, that's all. I didn't expect this."

"What? Expect what?" she asks, but she's unable to hear what she is pushing him to say. In the short time he has been here, Roger has pulled her so far out of her wretchedness that she can no longer bear to return to who she was. "There's a flu going around," she says, watching his face carefully to see if he knows she is lying. "It's the damn flu."

He is eating, his face impassive. His eyes don't meet hers, so she can't tell what he thinks. She waits, aware that he is taking forever to chew. She wants him to gobble it, to face her with the truth.

"You should eat." He gestures to her untouched fork. "If it's too rich, I can make toast."

He is so gentle it takes Mari a moment to realize that he has accepted her story of the flu. It makes her uncomfortable, the way she lies so easily, but she can't tell him the truth now. All she can do is to try the macaroni. She turns her fork to twirl the cheese strings, but the orange merely dribbles off.

Roger watches her until she swallows. "Good isn't it? My mother's favorite recipe."

Mari tries not to gag as she searches for something to say. "Big family?"

"No, just me. Mother was a career woman—way ahead of her time. We had a girl to do our cooking, but I used to make supper on her birthdays. My gift to her. Macaroni and cheese."

Mari tries to imagine a little boy in a kitchen but fails. "What about your dad?"

"He was there. Always checked my schoolwork, but he wasn't one to play with kids."

"It must have been lonely."

"Maybe. A little. When I was young, my mother used to let me sit with her while she got ready for school. She was a teacher. I don't know if I said that. Anyway, when she had time, she let me brush her hair. And then she put a dab of perfume on my nose and said, 'Now you won't miss me.' When they got home, she and Father would have a cocktail in the parlor every night before dinner and I'd get to sit with them. Mother told such vivid stories about the boys in her classes. I was so jealous. I think Father was, too."

In the several seconds of silence that follow Roger's story, Mari listens for his message. She likes the bond he described between mother and son. Examining this new man, the full lips, the forehead that didn't wrinkle when she yelled, Mari checks around inside herself and finds she likes the way he talks to her. She was no one before he showed up at her door, full of opinions and confidence. Now she can choose to be the woman he seems to see.

"Why didn't she have children?"

"She had me."

It is the surprise in his voice that makes Mari realize that three is not her idea of a family. "Yeah, but no others."

"Well, maybe I was enough."

"Mmm, I don't know about that," Mari says. And then quickly, because he seems hurt, "Maybe you were. Don't you want children?"

"Sure. One. Maybe even two. Depends on how good they are."

"Me, too." She smiles and he returns it, holding her eyes until she is sure he is talking through them; he has established a link, connected their minds. He has dumped his mind into hers, really; she can feel his desires reviving her brain. Because it feels right, she asks, "Isn't it amazing how we both want exactly the same thing?"

Roger tosses his head, his smile deepening if that's possible, inviting her to bury herself inside. "You mean one or two kids and a wife with a career?"

"Well, what else do you want?"

"Not much, I guess. Maybe play a little softball now and then with the guys."

"And bring your kids to watch?" She is gone, released from who she was. It doesn't feel like a risk to add details of her own.

"Watch? He'd be out there playing. We'd win a couple games, then come home for a celebration dinner."

"Oh. Well, what if it's not a boy?"

"A boy, a girl, it doesn't matter." It seems to Mari that he hesitates, but then he adds, "A girl could play, too."

"I think a girl would be nice," she says, trying to steer him just the tiniest bit. She can see herself as the child she was in pictures, an older version of herself by the child's side. It's a strange sight, but oddly comforting. In her mind, it's just the two of them—Mari and Mari—young and restored.

"Maybe. I could see that. A tall, bullheaded boy just like me, and a feisty little girl. Maybe with jet black hair." Mari notices that he won't give up on the boy, but she forgives him when he turns and says to her, "You know. Just like you."

14

KAORI

THE BEST THING THAT EVER HAPPENED

We reported to the Japanese Union Church to be evacuated on the last day of April 1942. None of us knew where we were going when we boarded the Greyhound bus. Your mother, Emi, took half of one seat with her son perched on what was left of her lap. My family was whole: Emi and the boys, Eric, myself, and your grandfather Mitsuo, who was convinced that we were going to our deaths and didn't care. There was ruin all around him, in the way he didn't notice his shirt bunched at the waist, or his shoes untied. His weary eyes, his slump, said this time it was too much. First Pearl Harbor, then Emi's disgrace, and now this.

And when I think of Mitsuo then, I remember how your Uncle Jack once said that the war was the best thing that could have ever happened to our family. He gave the words a mystery, daring me to question him. I never did. Maybe I had too many worries of my own, maybe I simply wasn't strong enough to accept his as well. At that moment on the bus, however, the war became a new target for Jack and Will, and I was grateful to be placed just slightly out of range of the haphazard family anger that blazed from man to boy, to boy, to man. I had often imagined it that way, that Mitsuo had burned himself out. It would have been a just end for him, would have put things in balance. But too late to spare those of us in his path.

The buses took us out of town in caravan, toward the jagged San Gabriel mountains. Past palm trees—I remember them because they looked so clean. They were outside, where real life was going on. Where people moved and breathed; they stared at us from their houses and the sidelines along the roads. Outside, clothing had more color. Voices could carry, and when our bus slowed, we could hear them along the road talking about the "Japanese monkey farm" at the end of our journey.

The Santa Anita racetrack.

In my mind, I still see it. Low matchbox barracks fill the parking lot, their rooftops overlapping in a blanket of tar paper that seems to stretch for acres. As our bus inches forward through the barbed and twisted gate, rows of clear space open between the buildings and they fall into diagonal lines like a puzzle solved. Rising behind them is the grandstand, freshly yellow and green. It stands, framed in turn by the hazy mountain range, displaying its turrets and arches and frosting-edged rooftops. There is a fountain, too, pumping merrily beyond the ticket booths and turnstiles, and I remember looking at the splash of flowers around it and thinking, how could they do this? How could they give this up for us?

We wait on the bus until they've unloaded our baggage, then fall out the door, past the soldiers and into a line that winds around the edge of the asphalt. Tags still around our necks. Men hold their hats; I see gray, with wide brims and black bands. Their jackets are unbuttoned and their ties swing against white starched shirts—it's not until later that the fearful searchers will yank those same ties to the side. I have a hat on, too, with a bunch of silk flowers. I'm wearing sturdy shoes and socks in the heat, standing just under the two guard towers at the main gate seven times higher than a man. Inside, the sun beats us, and I think of the monsters children make from wood scraps, of fragile, awkward spiders pushing their bodies toward the sky.

In my mind, there is no noise, nothing but tiny, proper movement, but I know we were frantic. We were ordered around, we had to open our bags, stand in line for that, too. I know we were yelled at when we spoke Japanese, that it was forbidden by the soldiers. We didn't look old and young to them, I guess. We couldn't make them feel how willing we were to follow. But I don't remember speaking, just the times I almost spoke. I was afraid of the words, of the sentences I could form. Of the things they could teach me that I didn't want to know.

So there we are, standing in the parking lot in lines, women and small children in one, men in the other, for vaccinations and a health exam. The buses are behind us, our bags are piled high. While we wait, we lift our arms from our sides, sagging in the heat, and soldiers pat our bodies down, seizing cameras and searching for weapons. In front of us, curtains are hung in the shape of a box. The nurses wait inside them. Each time we move forward, someone is disappearing and the curtains shudder, holding in the elbows and knees that jostle and press as the people inside falter at the sight of whatever is to come.

I went in before Emi and her little boy because I was the mother. I was rushed in just as the foot of the woman before me slipped through the curtain and out the other side. There was a nurse waiting, seated in the only chair, wearing one of those folded hats that look like paper. She asked me to undress.

It was not like I had never been naked, Mariko. I was fifty-three years old. I had given birth to three children. But I had never stood outdoors, without walls, before a line of people who could see my every shadow and movement. My coat shook as I slipped it off. I had to drop my belt on the ground. Then I made a pillow of the coat and set it down, too, flat to protect my other clothes from the dust. I unbuttoned my dress down the front, it was all buttons in those days and so slow, and placed it on the coat. I balanced on one shoed foot at a time, then, with my hat still on, removed my undergarments.

The nurse waited while I did this like I wasn't there. When I was ready, she stuck a tongue depressor in my mouth, flashed a light around my throat and eyes and ears, and gave me a slip of paper. No healing words for me. No touch, skin to skin. Not even a glance of sympathy or disdain for my softening body, shaped and misshapen by years of gravity. I had nowhere to put the paper then, so I just held in it my hand while I got dressed.

I don't remember what happened then, but I see us in the late afternoon walking through the camp toward our new home. Mud rims my shoes. We have left the parking lot and are heading for the horse stables, wading through the water and sewage that runs freely between the buildings in this older part of the racetrack. Here, the wood is weathered—and the internees are, too. They have been there for weeks, and are so used to new arrivals that they don't look up as we pass by. I watch their heavy feet as they do, feeling my own begin to drag until I am startled by a small pack of boys throwing mud balls at a line of fresh laundry. One screams, "Lights out, lights out, the Japs are coming." The others laugh, then they disappear. They are gone before any of us can stop them.

I am disquieted by their game and their bad manners but am too preoccupied to say anything. Our family has been assigned to the horse stables. Since Jack is allergic to animals, he and Will will be housed in a bachelors' barracks somewhere, leaving Emi, Eric, Mitsuo, and me alone. It is the prospect of losing my sons that makes me slightly dizzy, not the long stables that slope in front of us, thick and blunt, each stall with its own door. The walls seem windowless until I am close enough to make out a few streaks and fingerprints in the opaque panels placed near the roof, but I've lived in worse. That first year in America, when your grandfather and I lived in a shack, ten by ten, with two men sleeping on the other side of a hung blanket.

My boys are with us as we step through one of the short swinging doors into our stall. Jack has insisted on coming, hoping his allergies have faded in the years since he was a child. I can see the guilt on his face; he wants so badly to be a provider. Like his brother. In those days and the days after, Jack measured everything against Will.

It doesn't work, of course. Not even sunlight can fight its way over the hay and dust hanging in the air; it dies less than five steps into the building. Jack's eyes water, then he sneezes, and he's back outside before mine can adjust to the light. When they do, I realize the scurrying that greeted us isn't the sound of rats but of people. I can see shoes under the two-foot gaps between the side panels of our stall and the floor. The horse stalls don't reach the ceiling either. Our only privacy is in the panels, about four feet high, suspended from post to post.

The stall was divided in half by swinging doors. I don't know how we would all have fit into it anyway. As it was, I guessed Eric was going to have to sleep with Emi and I wasn't looking forward to fighting with her about that. Will stood against one wall with me, inches from a huge lacing spiderweb. Dirt wavered around him, marking his shirt each time he moved.

"Mama," he said.

"Hush," I replied, knowing he wanted to renew the fight he'd begun with the man who assigned us our quarters, and knowing he would lose. "We'll be all right." I could still see the bristling machine guns in the hands of the soldiers and the boredom in their eyes.

"We'll just see where they're putting us. Take our things there. We'll be back."

"And we'll do just fine without you," Emi broke in. She wasn't assuring him. Her voice was cold.

My son froze. His face floated in the half-light, his eyebrows up and curling. And I thought, It's coming again. I looked down instinctively, knowing I couldn't—and wouldn't—help her, not when she goaded him the way she did, but when I raised my head, Will hadn't moved. He was glaring at Emi with eyes polished black as stone. He turned then, grinding his foot as he did, and left without a word. He left the form of a butterfly in the dirt on the floor.

Emi followed Will, but only as far as the stack of luggage the boys had left outside. She dropped to her knees and extracted a bucket and a whisk broom she'd thought to bring. I could see her legs in the gap above the ground, could see strands of horsehair and bugs where they had been whitewashed into the swinging doors between us and the half-walls all around. Rusty nails for holding tack still stuck out of the wood. I was grateful for Emi's energy toward the filthy stall. Mitsuo, Eric, and I watched her assemble her supplies, then stood out of her way as she began with the floor.

The floor planks were set apart at least an inch and separated by wisps of grass and weeds from the ground below. As Emi worked, they began to peek through the layer of dirt in arcs, made partly by the broom and partly by the bottom of Emi's shirt hanging low over her belly. Standing there over my daughter, what I noticed most was her hair; it was falling from the glossy black twist she'd fashioned in the same way it used to fall from her ponytail when she was a child on the farm, jumping row after row of beans on her way up the hill. The smudged film on her face and arms reminded me of how she looked as a young girl learning to clean toilets, and how determined she had been then to discover herself in the work.

Maybe her isolation was wearing on me—with the boys' departure stretching before me I was beginning to feel a little isolated myself—but I wanted to help her. I had come to count on her company in the short time since she'd come home.

"Why don't you go out?" I suggested to Mitsuo, putting Eric's hand in his. "Take the boy. It's no good for you in here."

My husband took Eric's hand, although I'm not sure if he

understood who the child was. They shuffled together, testing their feet, then paused at the door, blinking. I knew Mitsuo was afraid suddenly to leave the darkness for the light, but I waited, knowing it was best not to urge him to go.

Then I turned to Emi. "You'll need water," I said.

"I have to get the dirt up first."

She was misunderstanding my offer. "I could get it."

"It'll just make mud."

Emi didn't look up. She was hard in those days, and clearly unable to sense the mood around her and act accordingly. At first I thought my gesture had simply taken her by surprise—after all, she could not have expected either my charity or goodwill. Besides, it was so unlike her to reject me. All her life, your mother had been demanding, constantly asking me for favors, answers, sympathy I couldn't give. Even as a child she needed me so much I would have described her as weak, and her attempt to give up her son had done nothing to change my mind.

Then my daughter straightened from a crawling to a kneeling position and leaned against her feet. She braced her lower back with her hands and nodded to the door. Mitsuo and Eric stood just outside it. Apparently, they hadn't yet settled on someplace to go. "If you want to help, take them away."

Her voice was matter-of-fact. She didn't want me there.

We had all lost so much—our home, our lives, our dignity—that I had thought we might help each other. What I hadn't realized until she rebuffed me, though, was that Emi had never had as much as the rest of us to lose.

"He's your son," I reminded her before I left her there. But in the sunlight, Eric followed me, so she got what she wanted after all.

It is after lunch, about two weeks after we arrived at Santa Anita. I am standing in line for the latrine. We have learned a lot of tricks by then, but it's one of those times of day when there is no place to go to avoid the lines. We are a chain, stretched the length of the building and then some, and I am back in the loose links, where the line still twitches. I am guessing how long each woman will take. Not for any reason, just for something to do.

The girl ahead of me wears a white smock with a red cross on her back. I am looking at her, but also through her, as I watch the latrine door, so when she turns, I don't see her. It's more that she rolls into my vision. I see her chin first, a strong chin, and then her nose, and I notice she's pretty in a young way, but she's blocking what I expect to see. She has turned by then; she can see me staring and counting. She must think I am crazy.

"Mama?" she asks.

I look at my daughter, ashamed. "I was counting. To guess how long this will take."

"Take my place. I'm not in a rush."

"No, I'm not either. I was just counting."

We smile, with growing honesty, about running into each other like this.

"Are you working?"

Emi has the courtesy to look embarrassed. "I've been volunteering at the clinic they just set up, looking after children, mostly, when the mothers have to be seen. This was the only thing that fit my . . ."

"I see," I say, to stop her before she can gesture to her bulging stomach. It's hard to imagine Emi would offer to care for a child. "And Eric?"

"One of the girls has a sister. She watches him."

"You know I'll take him. You shouldn't leave him with strangers."

"He's fine. You should get a few days off." She changes the subject then, wanting instead to justify her job. "There are so many sick people. I saw Mrs. Tateishi there. The older woman who collapsed in the mess hall the other day? I know she's a friend of yours."

"You do?" The woman and I often played the one hundred verses—the tanka from old Japan. I'd say the first line and she'd try to match it, then it would be my turn to finish her verse. We did one each day, whenever we passed each other. It was fun.

"She has diabetes. I can take you to see her, if you'd like."

I was surprised that Emi knew so much about the old lady, and that she'd invited me to come to the clinic with her. As we moved up the line, your mother was animated—airy and humorous when she was talking about the clinic and gossip, and indignant about camp politics and the recent riot. I followed her words closely, searching each anecdote for clues about who her friends were, and how she spent her time. It was like meeting someone new.

When we got to the front, there was a lady hovering outside the door, first in line, but always, at the last minute, letting the women behind her take her place. She was first generation, and much older than I, hunched over so far she wouldn't have reached higher than my shoulder. Her white hair was gathered into a bun at the back of her neck, thrusting her pale face forward more quickly than her body. She kept twisting to look down the line, picking up the bag she was carrying, then putting it down at her feet. I guessed she was waiting for the line to get shorter, but it was clear she couldn't wait much longer.

The latrine was a large open space with a cement floor. In it, two long lines of toilets had been set up, rough holes in a broad wooden box over one communal cesspool. The seats were unbearable to sit on, splintered and soaked with smells. Worse, each hole was open to the others, piled nearly on top of one another, forcing us to sit side by side and back to back. We'd asked for some walls to be put up around the seats. We'd asked and asked.

When our turn came, a group of four women came out together. The old lady who'd been waiting in front of us went in with Emi and me and one other woman. I remember each moment of what happened next.

Inside, the lady lingers at the door. Emi stops, waiting for her to select a seat. It's terribly rude of Emi to notice her hesitation, but she doesn't do it on purpose. It's my guess she's distracted. I think it's possible that she's seeing the woman for the first time.

There are three open seats in a row. Emi and I walk over to them, pull our underclothes down to our shins and sit, arranging our dresses as modestly as we can. The empty seat is next to Emi.

Finally, the old lady moves. She makes a queer mourning sound and walks to one corner of the room. From under my downcast eyes, I watch as she puts the bag on the floor. She bends from the waist, as if she's pulling rice, but she's removing camp store supplies from her bag. She places each one neatly onto the floor; large items like dried soap go down directly; the smaller sundries, like toothpaste, are set on top so they'll stay clean. I am wondering at each item, a man's razor, some thread, a comb, and what I'm waiting to see is toilet paper, since we have to bring our own.

No toilet paper comes out. Instead, she's built a rickety arrangement in the corner and what engages her is making sure it stands. When she's satisfied, she straightens, bringing the empty bag up with her in one hand. She walks toward us, then stands near the open seat next to Emi. She faces away from it, inching backward until she's almost touching the wood. Then, sighing, she lifts the bag and plumps it up.

She places it over her head.

Blinded by the bag, the old lady fumbles with her undergarments, then stretches her arms awkwardly behind her to feel her way down. She puts her fingers right where other people sit.

We wouldn't have looked at her. None of us would. I wouldn't even have looked at your mother if she hadn't sounded like she was choking. Down the line, I could see Emi, then the lady wearing the bag, then, just as background, three other ladies staring into their laps. Emi was crying.

Before I could react, your mother yanked up her underclothes and burst out of the latrine, not waiting for me. She moved surprisingly quickly for someone who was eight months pregnant. I followed when I could, calling after her as I ran along the dusty path.

At last she stopped and stood immobile, her shoulders squared and arms cinched tight around her belly as she stared off into the distance. She was biting her lips softly, her mouth was a narrow, toothless line.

"What are we supposed to do, Mama?" she asked. She looked damaged.

What could I say, Mariko? I barely understood what she was asking. "She's old, that's all. She's not used to it here."

"Used to it? That's the solution? I guess if we stay here long enough, we can get used to pissing in public into a open hole."

Emi's chin was quivering—her whole face was alive and shaking, though with anger or sorrow, I didn't know. It was her eyes I remember most, huge with tears, glittering, on the verge of spilling into the world. It might have been the courtesy she had shown me while we waited in line, but it was the first time since she was a child that I wanted to hold her. I knew, even at the time, that she was talking about herself.

"It was bad enough before," she continued, spitting out her words like they were dirt on her tongue. "All the rules—the things we could and couldn't be. Then, finally, everything changes, but it doesn't get better, does it? It just gets worse and more humiliating."

"It can't be helped, Emi," I said, touching her arm. "You know that. There's nothing we can do right now. We just have to make the best of it."

But she wouldn't stop demanding, not my Emi. She jerked away from me, rejecting my comfort as if it were a joke. "I'm serious, Mama, I'm tired of hearing that. You of all people should understand. You've just accepted everything that's happened in your life, and where has it gotten you? Has it helped you? I lived with you, Mama. I know. And what about me? Has it helped me?"

All those questions and no answers. She was staring at me, searching my face, and I could feel the pull of her eyes and something in my own belly turn. Has it helped you? she'd asked, and I was breathless with the storm of what she released. That I could be innocent, when I'd spent so much time understanding my guilt. The thought that our lives were not destined, but a series of accidents, was too foreign to me. I needed to believe there was a purpose, that someone, somewhere, was in control. The freedom that Emi suggested held too many possibilities. I couldn't stand in the face of them; they weren't something I could consider outside the latrine.

I pushed them away. Instead, I held on to your mother's eyes, because I could find guilt there. I could find a reason for Emi's anguish that I could explain.

As for Emi, I don't know what I said to her in that timeless space as she searched my face and found me. Surely nothing in words. I steeled myself, knowing I was about to disappoint her, but knowing, too, I couldn't open myself that wide. I couldn't bare myself that way; I needed to be tight and strong. I remember how lonely it felt, to push that self back without tasting it. But when it was gone, it was gone.

Emi's face drained in our silence as we stood there. After a moment, her eyes were dull. I had seen the piece of her that wanted to fight, but it was beaten. She didn't see me anymore.

"There isn't any right and wrong, is there?" she asked. "Is there? That's the secret to all of this. There's only wrong."

With that, my daughter walked away from me, dragging the toes of her shoes in the dust. Her offer to take me to the clinic was forgotten, and I needed to let her go. In her borrowed Red Cross smock, she could have been anyone. No one I had to soothe or answer to.

I don't think either one of us had any idea where she was going.

15

JACK

WELCOME HOME, 1945

The crowd at Union Station clears out in eddies. Some hisses, but nothing Jack can't ignore. Someone whispers, "Go back where you came from, Jap," but he can't read the words in the turned faces around him. It doesn't matter. He heard it, and worse, on the long train ride home.

Jack's winter in the trenches is over. And his summer in London, in a makeshift hospital with men whose names he doesn't know. Staring day after day at a city torn by strafing. At walls leaking onto the pavement between others still untouched.

He is home. Surrounded by red tile, white stucco, and not a sign of war. The looks he gets—the way his uniform startles people—makes him realize that here in Los Angeles, the war has never been real. Americans might believe in it because they are told to, but anyone who suffered or died is a long way off.

Not even the bigots have changed. When Jack reaches the bus stop on Macy Street, the driver won't let him on. "No room for handicapped, see?" he says, shutting the door on Jack's arm. "No room for your kind."

He should raise hell, but he is tired. Instead, Jack wiggles his arm to release it and lets the bus go. The driver takes off so fast he leaves a few Caucasian passengers. They look at Jack, then away.

As he wonders what to do then, a young fellow offers Jack a ride. Sandy hair. A civilian. He might've seen what happened and decided to work out his own guilt. The fellow helps Jack and his duffel into the car—Jack won't let him take his crutches, though, and once he says where he's going, he doesn't say another word. Doesn't look out the window at Little Tokyo, either, not once he sees the burned-out storefronts and the Negroes in the streets. None of the internees can return, Jack realizes. He closes his eyes.

An old bent-over Japanese man replies to the horn as they pull up to the church that Mama told him to go to in her letters. Almost at a run. Jack wishes his driver hadn't announced them, but there's nothing he can do. The old fellow is pulling on the handle, opening the door.

"*Okaeri!*" he says. "Ah, welcome, welcome home!"

Jack can feel how eager the fellow is to claim him. He treats Jack like a hero, like he's done something good. It's the thing he dreaded most coming home—the happy face, the moving-on face they expect. He's the same fellow, from the same family, just a little older and crippled now. If he could have any wish come true, he would choose never to be Jack Okada again.

If he had a wish, Jack thinks, he would travel. Into Europe, into the filth and leftovers of it all. He would live without a name even, until he found one gleaming in a shattered window, stamped on a grave marker. In the rusted, twisting metal of a car tossed off the road. He would recognize it, he was sure of that, if he walked long enough. Through towns that didn't know him, wouldn't care, would let him pass. He would look to the ruts of a mountain road to find his face, into the open mouth of a farmhouse surprised by a grenade. Jack would pick a new self in the remnants of an exhausted Europe. Something tainted, common. Something that fit.

The old man reaches out, not to help Jack but to pull him into his world. Jack swings his crutches, a little hard, and hits him on the foot.

"Sorry."

"Oh, please. Oh, so sorry," the old man murmurs. "*Gokuroosan datta na.*"

"I don't speak Japanese," Jack says, glancing at his driver.

"You must be very tired. Thank you for your efforts . . ." The translation trails off when it's clear Jack isn't listening.

The sandy-haired man has taken Jack's bag out of the trunk and put it on the grass. "Well." He doesn't seem to know what to do.

"Thanks for the ride."

The duffel is in the old man's hands now—he is banging and jerking it on his leg with each step. Jack shrugs at the driver and follows, relieved to hear the car start up and pull away. At the steps of the church, the old man waits, averting his eyes from the crutches and the limp. "Yuchi Murikawa," he says when Jack is near enough. "Karl Honma, Mas Kodama."

Names. They have to be. The names of missing soldiers. "I don't speak Japanese," Jack repeats. "I need to rest."

He takes his bag and lowers himself onto it inside the front door of the church. He forgot Los Angeles was so hot. Even inside, where he's protected from the sun, the air is too dense to move. If there was anywhere else he could be, Jack thinks, but he no longer has the energy to continue, not with the old man hovering over him. He keeps his eyes closed. His left leg throbs.

Eventually, the man's steps move away.

Jack doesn't know how much time has passed, except that he can hear a few people tiptoe by him, or start toward the door until they see him and turn. Finally a set of deliberate feet come toward him. He rouses himself to watch a young woman walk down the hall.

"Your mother will be so happy you're finally home," she says when she's near enough. "She calls me every week."

Jack doesn't bother to rise, since he's sure she has no idea who he is. She's barely more than a girl—probably a nice girl, after all, she works at the church. Her hair is smooth and plain, and her dress is neat. She holds a folder behind her crossed arms.

"She does," he says as a challenge.

The girl lets her arms drop far enough to read the front of the folder. "Mitsuo and Kaori Okada. Your mother is a wonderful woman. She, well, she needs you at home."

Jack keeps his eyes on the low, sensible shoes in front of him. He doesn't want to think of Mama calling every week to find him, and what that could imply. "How did you know it was me?"

"Your name tag. And she gave me a picture of you, from when you were young."

The girl smiles, but Jack might as well have been walloped. He knows the picture she is talking about—it was taken just before he left for the front. Mama pleaded with him for it, she kept insisting she needed it to keep him safe. He hasn't bothered to look at himself in so long, it never occurred to him that he is older. One year ago, he was so dangerously young.

"I'll take you to them," the girl says. "Don't worry, it's not a bother. I'm happy to."

She is more sensitive than he gave her credit for—she has the ability to break him before he gets home. But he owes her something for her kindness.

Finally, he stands. "Thank you," he says. "I guess it's kind of tough these days to get a ride."

She drives Jack south, out of the city, until he's sure they'll run straight into the ocean. They travel farther than Jack has ever been, pass signs for towns he's never heard of. The last sign he sees before she turns off the main road reads LOMITA.

As they pass the sparse wood buildings that line the pocked road in the center of town, Jack wonders how much worse it can get. Then the girl sets out on a dirt trail and the barracks slide into view. They are basic military issue like the ones at Shelby, only the tar paper is ripping and the floors sag on either end. He notices a few trailers among them—dumped in uneven rows on a field of tarmac, connected rooftop to rooftop by lines of clothing, since there isn't anywhere to sink a pole.

The girl drives until they're halfway down the rows of buildings. "Welcome home."

"You're sure?" he asks. Meaning the welcome.

The girl sighs. "It's just temporary housing until people can get settled. When they closed the camps, well, we couldn't place so many people at once. And there are problems with the old neighborhoods, too. Some of them have been taken over, and now there are laws . . . Anyway, yours is the first one. Twenty-one."

The door the girl points to has a boy dangling from it, his arms tying him to the doorknob, keeping him safe from the world outside. Emi's boy. The stopped car has attracted his attention. He watches Jack fumble with his crutches, then get out.

"Thanks," Jack says to the girl, dismissing a driver for the second time that afternoon. She figures it out faster than the fellow. Whatever is coming, he doesn't want her to see.

Jack picks his duffel off the pavement and then drops it. Emi can get it for him—it's better than hobbling home on one crutch. As he approaches, the kid grows wary, waiting for Jack to walk by or turn. Jack watches him consider his options, try to be tough, then get scared. At the last minute, when it's obvious where Jack is headed, the boy slams the door.

Jack gets the end of his crutch in. "Wait. What's your name?" He can't find it in his memory.

The kid presses against the door like he can keep Jack out.

"Mama!" Jack yells, pissed off, shoving the door open.

"Mama! Mama!" the kid echoes and turns tail, leaving the house defenseless. Jack's mother appears. She walks toward the door, pulling at the strings of her apron, tucking a wet rag in its front pocket. She is taking her time, as if she is readying herself to greet a guest.

"Mama," he says again from the doorway, softly this time, to test her hearing.

Her hair is completely gray, and her face—when she turns it toward his voice—is almost the same color. Only her eyes stand out dark as ever, but they seem smaller, overrun by the pouches in her eyelids and the sagging below. Her chin droops to one side as she cocks her head and crosses her arms lightly in front of her.

Jack steps through the door so there is light on his face, but not far enough to have to struggle with his crutch. When her expression doesn't change, he takes off his dress hat and runs his fingers through his damp hair. He releases the matted strands and prepares them to be seen.

Mama doesn't move then, but her nose trembles. Jack watches the relief spread across her face, beginning with her eyes. He didn't expect tears, but there they are, before she can speak, running so fast they reach her chin through her long laugh lines.

"Ah, Toshi-chan! Jack!" She fumbles toward him, talking in Japanese. Praying maybe. Over and over, thanking God. She trembles around him, pressing his arms, squeezing them to make sure he is there. Her fingers are so light. They leave wet marks on his uniform, and when she sees them, she giggles, one hand over her mouth. "*Mizu de nureta te de nurashite shimatte, sumanaine!*" she says, trying to wipe the marks away. "So sorry."

"Mama. It's fine." He grabs her hands.

Jack's mother pulls him into the room until he can see the Salvation Army furniture. They are poor again, but this time it feels right. He wants to sit on the green striped sofa, let his arms patch the holes where the stuffing sticks out. He wants to hold his tattered mother there, maybe have her hold him. That close, he can see the lines in her face again and how deep they are—she has aged perhaps more than he in the time he's been gone.

"Where is everybody?" he asks.

"Where are your things? Your clothes?"

"Outside. I'll get them. I just didn't want—"

"No, no. You rest." She is pushing past him.

"Mama!" He follows because she is too frail. "Here, let me have it. At least let me help." She gives him a handle and they both take the bag. When they have hauled it to the door, the boy is there again, his tears dry, hanging on the knob.

This time, Jack remembers. "Eric," he says, tucking the crutch firmly in his armpit as he brushes his hand across the kid's head.

With the duffel in and the door closed, Jack is home. And it's awkward, not knowing where to begin, where even to put his hands. Mama is urging him to drink tea. To eat. She's trying to sweep him over to the sofa, telling him how hungry he must be. She will make something, she assures him. She can make it better if he waits.

In the old days, it didn't matter what Jack wanted. Now, she fixes him the cold drink he asks for and lets him stand at the kitchen door while she cooks. It's been years since he's seen a real kitchen. It seems so small. The stainless steel basin is dented and leaking—it wobbles when she leans on it, but she doesn't seem to care. She is chattering about their neighbors, about who went where and how nice the minister has been. Jack watches her hands chop cabbage and scallions on a wood board. Then a small piece of fish. When the water boils and she stirs in the miso, he can smell it loose in the air.

Jack isn't eager to talk about family either. Certainly not about Emi, but not even about Will. The last time Jack saw his brother, when their companies served briefly together in the Vosges, Will didn't recognize him. Too many Japanese boys in the forest to pick one out right away. When Jack called out, though, they got to say a few things before Will had to go. His brother was clearly still angry Jack had enlisted. He let the rain and the dull throb of artillery pull him away.

Will wasn't the only one who forgot what Jack looked like. When Papa shuffles, drooping, toward the kitchen, he blinks like his son is an unexpected light. The fear in the old man's eyes reminds Jack that Papa was already having bad spells before he left for Shelby. Of course he's confused to see his son in uniform, home so soon.

Mama coaxes the old man into the living room and serves dinner on a rectangular coffee table in the middle of the floor. The room is cramped with furniture, but still, things double for other things. Jack sits across from his father, among the stains of earlier meals on the cutoff piece of carpet that covers most of the floor. The old man smiles and waves, as if he knows Jack now, but he could be waving at someone else, someone Jack is standing in for.

He hasn't left the living room yet, and the house already depresses him. They are doing well and poorly at the same time. The place is furnished with a sofa, a table, and three straight chairs backed against different walls, like they expect company. A watercolor hangs on one wall, a snow-capped mountain that could be Fuji or one of those Colorado mountains. It strikes him because it's placed low, at the height of his chest, and it's still the highest thing in the room. The room is like an hourglass—the top half empty, the bottom chock-full.

As they eat, Emi's other kid plays at what should be their feet. She won't eat from her own plate, but when something appealing is about to disappear into someone else's mouth, she tries to waylay it into her own. She's too smart to do it with Jack, and she has the most success with Eric anyway. She insists on noodles—no broth—and makes the kid pick out the green things before she will eat from his spoon.

Jack finds himself wanting to protest without knowing why. The words "You would've slapped me silly if I'd done that at her age" occur to him, but he lets them go. It's not his place to tell his parents how to act. But they've never seemed so feeble. So in need of direction.

While Mama clears dinner, Papa gathers himself and the children together and herds them into a different room. Jack watches him wave and close the door. When Mama is finished, she begins to apologize. "I didn't know you were better. We don't have a bed."

"I'll sleep here on the couch," he says, trying to soothe her, still reaching out. "I'm a grown-up now. I can live without a bed for a couple of nights."

Mama nods and looks at the door Papa closed. "You can have ours. Our room. There's no place for a bed. No money."

"So where'd you get all this furniture?"

"Ah! Emi gave me money."

It's the last thing Jack expected. Emi doing something right. "Where is she?"

"Working. In a fish place. Fish sticks."

"Well, fine. I'll get a job and we can move out of here. Get more room."

His mother shakes her head. "No jobs now. Not even cleaning. Nowhere to live."

"I'll get something. I'm a soldier. I mean, if Emi can, I can."

Then Mama understands. "Emi lives in New Jersey. Since she left camp."

"In New Jersey?" Jack knew she'd planned to go there. "But, what about you? Shouldn't she be home taking care of you?"

"She's in New Jersey," Mama repeats.

"But her kids? Why did she send them here? Couldn't she at least take care of them?"

"She didn't send them," Mama says, puzzled. "We've always had them."

"Oh, God." It is then he realizes Will isn't home yet. That taking care of the family is, once again, up to him. "They were with you the whole time? In camp? You took care of them?"

"She sends money when she can."

Oh, please, let me leave, he thinks. Let me walk out the door. Jack searches the room for a way back out, taking in every detail of the hand-me-downs and cursing Will in his mind for being right about Emi after all. "That's helpful," he says finally, in a voice more bitter than his own. "That's really very helpful."

"She has a job," Mama says, patting the air in front of her like she wants to calm him, but is afraid to touch. "And there's a man, a doctor—"

Jack's anger surges to fill the holes Mama's odd submission has left. He's afraid he'll smash something. "A man. Of course. There would be a man. That's all Emi was ever good at, eh?"

It's Will's voice, he knows. Will's words. They made him cringe when he heard them the first time, but he was just a child then, he can see that now.

"That's probably where she's getting the money," he continues, glaring at his mother, willing her to speak. "From the man. Don't you think? Still just a little whore."

When she doesn't look up, he takes two clumsy steps forward to stand in front of her. "So it's just me then? I'm the one. I broke both my legs. I damn near died, but it doesn't matter, does it? I'm the one who has to stick around."

Her head is bent, almost at his knees. He wants to yank her hair, force her to see him, but he's shaking so badly he could pull her head right off.

And then she does look up, and Jack can see she is terrified.

"Will—was killed," she says. "He was killed in battle."

Jack doesn't see her mouth open. She remains hunched over, her arms wrapped around her stomach. Watching him. She might not even have spoken.

Did she? he wonders. Did she say his brother, Will, was dead? Jack has returned to the clouds, to the fog in France. Huge sweeps of white in front of him, hiding what he doesn't want to see. He wishes he could stay there, in the white, but like the Jerries, he knows, Mama's words will find him. He can hear them coming for him now.

Will's face emerges from the fog. His cutout face, face cut sharp by war. And Shimmy's, Jack's best friend, who has haunted his dreams since they pulled Jack out of the trench and saved his life. He can see the blood that oozes from Shimmy's eyes every night—even though Jack knows where he was hit, how he died. No one plucked out Shimmy's eyes. No one plucked Will's out either—Jack is sure of that—but his face is next to Shimmy's and he's screaming, "You let them kill me. You let me die," and all Jack can do is bow.

Accepting it, knowing that it's true. Just as it happens every night in Jack's dreams, part of him wants to run, but he can't. He could try—pull up his feet to wake himself, deny it was real. And he's sure they would disappear if he said *no* real loud in his head, but as he says it, lets it burst into full volume, Jack is forced to his knees. He's forced to wait and do nothing as his brother marches toward him. Howling. "It should have been you," is what he is saying.

Jack is the weak one.

Mama hasn't moved. She's still there, and he can ask her the millions of questions he has—how Will died, where, when, who, what—but somehow it doesn't matter. Jack can feel the emptiness of the house around him—how its heart is no longer there—and it knocks him down, each piece of him, one limb at a time. Every shield he ever erected, every excuse, disappears.

Will was the best of them, the most noble. And Jack is never going to see him again.

Jack goes to sleep that night thinking about Santa Anita, and the day Will saved him from the crowd. It was a riot, actually, their first and only true one. It was about irons and household appliances. Whatever the reason, the soldiers came.

They couldn't have been in camp long at that point, but people were all riled up. They didn't have any warning. The soldiers stormed into the barracks and started grabbing people's possessions—big bags full of it, at least that's what they were saying at the time. Later the camp administrator said they had merely confiscated the illegal appliances because the electricity was always going out.

People went nuts.

Whispers about the protest reached Jack and Will at about the same time they heard the calling. "Come and gather, come and gather." First one man, and then a chorus. Packs of men responded, converged on the administration building. And on Jack and Will, who were standing nearby and together for a change. The mob came straight toward them.

The leaders had almost reached the two of them when it happened. Someone turned on someone else, and the scene exploded into dust. People were surging everywhere. A window behind Jack smashed, jolting him enough to notice the rocks flying through the air. He ran for the safety of a nearby doorway and looked for Will.

Young men, old men, even some young women were screaming and coming faster. They crashed into one another as they poured through the narrow lanes between the stables. Some in anger, some just struggling for breath and to stay on their feet. The mob was sweeping in old ladies emerging from the latrine. One of them—she looked like Jack's mother but he knew she couldn't have been—was struggling with her kimono. A young woman grabbed her arm, and the two of them bumped back and forth, trying to protect each other. The crowd covered them, and as Jack tried to wave them toward him, a typewriter lifted into the air.

It was thrown into the sky, the dull iron back tumbling over the spidery underside. All framed in blue. Jack watched it roll over and over, saw the round keys flash in the sun. It couldn't have happened that way, of course, but that's what Jack remembers. Because it was heading straight for the old woman and the girl.

Jack yelled out a warning, but no one heard. He launched himself into the crowd, knocking the protesters' shoulders and knees. He was still trying to reach the two of them when the typewriter hit the old lady square in the face. He watched her fall, the girl falling with her. Watched her sprout blood from her nose and mouth, and from a cut above her eye.

Then Jack was on the ground. Someone landed a blow to his stomach strong enough to send him rolling at the dusty feet of the crowd. Other people were down, too. He could see their faces and hear their frightened cries and moans of warning. Someone was dragging the old woman to her feet and coming toward Jack. Then he was lifted.

"Jack! Hey, Tosh. Toshi. Can you hear me? Are you there?"

There it was—Will's voice and the same questions he would

ask Jack on the night of the "no-no boys" debate at Amache when Jack stepped in to help Will. But he doesn't want to think of that—he wants to stay with Will. His brother, who just saved the two women. Will had the old lady braced against one shoulder, the girl still clinging to her kimono.

"Jack!" he called. "Are you hurt?"

Jack held his stomach. "Uh, no. I think I'm okay."

"Take them then," Will ordered, shoving the women at him. "Get them to the side."

"Them? Umm, I don't think— Can't you?"

"Jack, look around you. I have to go. Don't you see?"

Jack looked from the bleeding woman to Will. He wanted Will to save them, for his brother to be the hero, but this was something he was going to have to do. To make it up to Will—there was something he owed, some way he had wronged Will, but he couldn't remember how. "Okay, I—" But when he tried to ask Will what exactly he was supposed to do for them, his brother disappeared into the crowd.

"Will!" he yelled at nothing. "What do I do?"

He heard his brother say, "To the door," though he could no longer see him. "Take them to the door."

Or had Will said, "Take them, they're yours"? In a way, they *were* Jack's—his responsibility at least. So he nodded and yanked the old lady toward the side. He could hear Will yelling to the people around him, and he wanted to go to him—to help—but he had a role now, and he couldn't leave the women until they were safe.

"Get back inside!" Will screamed. Just like the last call, this one began to echo. "Back inside," the crowd replied in two languages. The faces between Jack and the door looked confused by the new order, but something made people follow it. They let Jack pass. He got the old lady and the girl to the doorway. When he turned around, he saw the surging had stopped. Bodies trapped on the ground were beginning to rise.

It seems like a dream, like a fairy tale. Like Jack couldn't have witnessed his brother calming the crowd. Couldn't have seen him part it, touch it like a wild thing, bring the people back to themselves. From the doorway, as the sobbing woman dripped blood on him, he watched Will in the street. Calling for a miracle. Calling, "Get back inside!"

And as Jack readied himself to leave the women and find Will, the crowd shook itself. It stood quiet. Then, Jack heard it roar.

"Get back inside!" It was one voice, the voice of the crowd. The riot was over.

Will had vanished.

Jack was alone.

16

ERIC

TALIA, 1967

She was supposed to take him home, but her chair is empty. She knows it's the only one he can see from the hall. It's for Eric that she picks it, so he can see her, no surprises, half of her in the wide bullet-proof window that separates the visitors from the cons. Usually, she is reading—her book in her lap, letting her brown hair cross her face like a curtain. The guards have to tap Talia's shoulder to get her attention. If they simply speak, she doesn't hear a word.

"No money, it says right here," the desk cop says as he shoves Eric's wallet across the counter.

It skids on the wood-grain Formica and falls at Eric's feet. "Lying piece of crap," he says, but the days when he could feel that kind of emotion are long gone. "Fifty bucks I had." His words are single notes, over and over. He looks around for Talia.

Every week, when she came, he told her not to. It's how he's always lived, letting his mouth take him places in case they're better than where he is. This time, though, she must have caught a flat or something. Tough luck for Talia—and more common lately. Eric doesn't know the particulars. He's not the kind to ask.

"Fuck off, Yoshiko," Slick tells him.

This whole time, Eric knows, he's been staring into Slick's eyes. The cop can't get him to rise. It's Eric's greatest strength, that he is untouchable, but he gets no satisfaction from it today. He is hassling Slick over a lie just to buy time for Talia. Stupid to do it, when he's only going home to get his stuff.

"Fuck you, too," Eric says, leaving the empty wallet on the floor in protest, choosing a direction in his head. Once he turns, Talia's name matches his heel-toe rhythm. The sky is so gray, the exhaust looks clean.

It's a perfect day to leave jail.

If he hadn't been arrested a year and a half ago, Eric would have left Talia then. They'd been together on and off since high school, but he'd only moved in with her to save on rent. Of course, it didn't hurt that it had almost killed Talia's father, so old-world he was always telling Eric what Talia expected and what she deserved. A husband to provide for her, children, pretty gifts—the list never stopped. A home, a two-car garage, but apparently not the kind of home Eric chose.

The day they moved in together, Talia cried. But when he pulled the car up to the building, it was Eric who freaked out—he didn't want to have a home at all. To shake it out, that strange fear, Eric left the boxes where they were, grabbed Talia and carried her through the door like a bride. He laid her down on the living room carpet—she was giggling by then, so he put his finger on her lips and lifted her shirt halfway until it wrapped her face. Polyester puffed gently off, then on, her nose. Beneath it, her eyes had closed.

They christened the place with the windows open. Clothes everywhere, and Eric reared up and thrusting, so anyone could have seen his head bouncing up and down if they looked.

He felt so good that day.

Eric can't have walked five minutes when a dark green '66 Chevy pulls over in front of him. Shined up by someone with nothing to do. Out-of-towners, probably grandparents, lost enough to pick up a hitchhiker in front of the jail. He walks to the driver's side, even though it's in the street. An old guy rolls the window down.

"Where ya goin' son?" Midwestern accent, Eric decides, crew cut hair. The wife bends forward to see through the window. The doors are locked.

"Just a couple of miles up the road, sir. Huntington. I'd sure appreciate a ride if you folks are going that way." He can see a black purse lying on the seat between them. Its gold chain strap loops half in and half out of the open zipper.

"We're going to West Hollywood to visit our daughter," the old lady says.

"Yes, ma'am. That's the same direction." Eric takes his hat off, holds it over his heart. He crouches so she can see his head clearly, to beam his smile in good, and she turns to pull the lock latch up. So easy, it always happens like this. The door is open.

How do they stand it, Eric wonders, being so defenseless? They have a convict in their car who can tell what they think and what they're going to say before they say it. They think he's a soldier, what with his hair so short it pokes his fingers when he touches it. His hair used to be flashy, commanding—Talia said it was her favorite thing about him. But if the cops hadn't shaved it off, the couple never would've picked him up.

He makes up a rank and serial number. The old lady says they only have girls.

"It must have been so, well, I just can't imagine," she says. She's turned right around so he can see her age scribbled on her face. A grandma like Mama, maybe younger, he decides. "Still, we're proud of you, and grateful, you know, for fighting."

Eric shrugs and sits back against the seat. "Well, it's a duty, right?" he asks, feeding them his Uncle Jack's old words. "Simple as that. Still, you can't imagine. Unless you've been there."

"Phyllis," her husband warns.

"I'm sorry. I didn't mean to pry."

"It's okay," he says. "It's hard to talk about sometimes. The memories at night, other things."

"I'm terribly sorry." She seems reluctant to turn away.

Eric waits a few minutes, letting the whine of the tires direct their thoughts, then throws in the punch line. "My best friend," he says. He rubs his face like he's waking up. "I had to tell his family how it happened."

"Oh," she says, back again. And then, "Are you going home?"

He told them Rosa Street, but when they pass the pink stucco house where Mama and Jack live, Eric feels like a ghost, like if he gets out of the car, they won't see him standing there. He hasn't smelled plumeria since before prison. He didn't mean to come here, but when the old lady said "home," he was still thinking about his best friend in Vietnam, a human firecracker blown ten feet in the air. He was selecting a name for the guy, and trying to imagine the sadness, so Mama's was the only place that came to mind.

Eric rolls down the window to feel the wind on his face, not the air in the car cycling over and over from their noses into his. Her interest in him is making him tired. "Could you drive me around the corner?" he asks. "I want to get my Mama some flowers."

The old lady thinks that's so nice, and the old man shakes Eric's hand with purpose when he gets out. He gives them real directions to West Hollywood this time.

"It'll feel like you're turning around," he says, throwing in a salute just for kicks, "but that's just the way the streets around here run."

He is back in the neighborhood. Two minutes walking will take him to Mama's. He can go there. If Jack had his way, she still doesn't know Eric's ever been in prison, but then, he was small-time before, so it was easy to hide. She will feed him and ask how he's doing, and she won't say a word about where he's been or why he disappeared for more than a year. He can't show up in blue jeans with his shaved head and not a dime to his name, though. Too risky. Home, in Eric's family, is not a place where they have to let you in.

Fuck, damn, Eric thinks in no order. He should have rattled the grandma, let her go a little worse for wear. He could have stolen their money or conned them, he could have taken a different role. It's a question always, whether to give people what they want or the last thing they expect. Roles, rules, expectations. He can't think anymore without them.

Growing up, he had his role. Redeeming his mother, and it stuck. Any mistake, any sign of selfishness or weakness, and he knew what they were thinking. Mama got to be the good one, the one who took him in. Jack was the good one, too, taking care of his mother and Eric, sacrificing his life. After a while, Eric refused to play their game, but Mama never let it go. Jack knows he's a fuckup but he keeps it from Mama. All Eric wanted was to be allowed to be honest—several years ago, he'd planned a whole evening so he could drop the phrase "this guy I met in prison." But he never did. He felt like a terrorist, unable to blow up the building. Like some asshole standing on the Golden Gate, afraid to jump off.

Prison's better, Eric thinks. There are rules, right out there, printed on paper even. You want to stir things up, you break a rule, and maybe you're high on it for weeks, and maybe they beat the crap out of you. You don't have to sense and gauge to get away with something, like at home.

Families, Eric thinks, are deadly. He heads toward Alameda, walking, looking at the quiet, listening to the air. It's not empty, like in prison—it's full of sound and no people. He can't place half of it, just crickets, cars rolling out of carports far enough away. As he walks, he counts the yellow useless lights in the windows of the houses. The heat's rising. The asphalt under his shoes is still cool.

He should have made the old guys take him to the track. He

could walk to Orange Street instead, but would Talia be there? She could be waiting for him at prison. The cops probably wouldn't even tell her he was gone. He could slip into the apartment, pick up some essentials—hell, he could pick it all up, all her stuff. It would serve her right. She wouldn't report him, but she'd know he was there. Touching her things. Taking the ones she loved best.

Eric imagines himself unlocking their front door. Then walking into their bedroom, opening her top drawer. Under the puffs of black lace that smell of her perfume, he would find Talia's diary. In the nine months they lived together, he hadn't touched it once.

He could have—it didn't even have a token lock on it—but the burden of sharing her feelings kept him away. Now that he is leaving, though, it's the perfect way to keep a piece of her. When Eric shuts the door in his imagination, Talia's diary is all he has.

He can hear his footsteps again, and see he's walking nowhere. He could check out the Black Rose, he thinks, hook up with some of the guys. Eric has been looking forward to a double scotch for 547 days, but he doesn't want to be spotted yet. He's about three blocks east of Mike Tardish's. As good a place as any to take a piss.

Mike must have been dead asleep. "Hey, man, Yo!" he says, stepping aside when he realizes who Eric is. "Yo, wow, you're out. Hey, congrats." He flicks the light on.

Eric winces, aware that he's made a mistake. Mike's a friend, but now that Eric sees him, he remembers that Mike's a loser, too. Not someone you want to talk to, because he's always changing his answers. He's a fringe guy, a janitor with plenty of time to hang around Eric and the guys at the bar in case something rubs off. "Who's doing your cleaning these days, Mike?"

"Look whose talking."

Eric sits in a wounded yellow chair. "Old news," he says. "Got anything to drink?"

Mike kind of limps into the kitchen and returns with some Johnnie Walker Red. "Looky here, two matching glasses to welcome you out."

Mike pours, then pours some more. The scotch slinks down

Eric's throat and into his empty stomach, where it curls up, warm and beating.

"So," he asks, "what do you hear?"

Eric does it all the time—asks a question, then doesn't hear the answer. He uses the time for other things. Like comparing shapes and colors in the stains on Mike's ceiling. The place is still a dump, even if he has a woman. Eric looks around, expecting her to pounce on him for being there.

As Mike runs down the news, Eric remembers he was one of the guys who thought Eric should dump Talia. The night he got arrested, things started rolling with Mike's silver fob. Mike wanted Eric to fence it, but there was a party going on and Eric couldn't be bothered. He told Mike it was a mickey mouse job and to get himself a drink.

"He doesn't fence anymore," Dave had said so Eric could hear him. "He's gone clean."

Eric stopped, jarred out of context. "What the hell?"

"When was the last time you took anything?"

"It's a piece of crap trinket."

"Still."

"He's in love," someone else had said. "He doesn't have time for us."

"He's pussy-whipped," Mike corrected.

It was true, Eric realized. He'd been a good little doggy, happy pissing in his cinder block home. It wasn't shame, so much as fear, that voiced his challenge.

"What's on for tonight?" And then, when the guys just shrugged, "Come on then. Let's get something on."

Eric sits on Mike's couch drinking steadily, even when Mike falls asleep again, and later when he leaves to pick up a pizza and another bottle of Red. An hour past happy hour, he's still in Mike's living room when he remembers the drinks at the Black Rose are about to go up. Eric rises, and finds his toes are drunk. They refuse to help his feet walk, so he shuffles to the bathroom to splash some water on his face. It's so late that *Gilligan's Island* is on television. What morons, that they can't get off the stupid island, Eric thinks. He always thought they'd brought an awful lot of clothes for a three-hour tour.

The building falters as they try to leave it, but once on their way, the breeze shrinks the alcohol in Eric's skin and he feels better. Mike's a better guy now, even though he's talking about plumbing. It hasn't been such a bad day.

The Black Rose looks good, too, more so because it's started raining. The dark and the sweet smell of drunks rushes them as the door opens. Eric sends rain skittering off the stubs of his hair as he looks around. The place is too full, and with a bunch of people he doesn't know. He hesitates, trying to think up somewhere else to go, until Dick waves him over from behind the bar.

"Yo, it *is* you," he says, slapping Eric on the back. "I figured, with Mike, who else could it be? You drinking scotch? How the hell are you?"

Eric drinks the scotch and relaxes slowly. His eyes catch on the new things—the extra glasses behind the bar, the coatrack right up front. He finds he is staring at the suds in the sink, and Dick's arms thrusting in and out of them, making them quiver as he talks. Nobody's there.

"Frank's been working night security," Dick says, appreciating the irony. "Brady, you might've seen in the can."

"Yeah," Eric says as Mike leans forward to hear. "He's got a slide. A month, I think. He looked good. Seen Pete lately?"

"He comes in."

There's a girl at one of the tables with hair like Talia's when she was in high school—heavy down her back, not a lot of fuzz. They were seeing each other in those days, what passed for dating then, but he didn't let opportunities go by. Not even at the prom. Some other girl, Laurie something, asked him to be her date, and he was so surprised he said yes. That's what he told Talia; the truth was that, when he'd been asked, his hand was all the way down Laurie-something's pants—beneath her lace undies and in where the heat was. He was just trying to see if he could do it, with her backed against the wall between the lockers the way she was, and it was easy, so easy. Like silk. She'd let him go further if he promised to take her. It was quite an opportunity.

He can't remember how Talia found out, but she screamed, threw things, beat on his chest with her gentle hands. They were at a drive-in, walking back with popcorn, and she sprayed it like fireworks on a nearby car. It was cool to see, but the guy in the car got out, so Eric dragged her into his car and took off with her still crying. When they got to the street, she snapped the chain his ring was on and flung it in a gutter. That's what attracted him, the way she wanted him so bad. The next day she started a catfight in the halls with Laurie-something—little Talia, Italian princess with her hot roller curls. She won, too. It was a shock to her poor dad when she was suspended from school. They went to the prom together, Eric as her prize.

Talia was beautiful that night. She wore a tight-on-top dress with a swirling skirt—it was green to match her eyes. He brought her a corsage, Jack had insisted, but since she had no collar, he had to stick it through the dress. He stabbed his fingers with the pin twice—he'd slipped them under the fabric like a gentleman to shield her skin. Her skin burned the backs of his fingers all the way to the gymnasium. He left a tiny spot of blood on her dress.

If the prom had ended there, things would've been different, but Talia wanted to dance, and he wasn't going to look like a jerk. She got those hurt eyes, like she couldn't understand him, then she started dancing with some other guys. Eric ignored her, talked to his friends. She couldn't affect him. That's what he thought until she got to Laurie-something's date.

Talia danced with the guy on purpose. There were names for the ways they danced, and they looked good, too—their hands didn't tangle and the guy always knew which way she was going to move. Eric watched their feet step, one-two-three, without hesitation. Then Laurie grabbed Eric's hand and pulled him onto the floor.

When he and Laurie started, Eric was watching Talia, and the way the rose he gave her brushed against the guy during move after practiced move. It wasn't until the next dance that he noticed Laurie at all, until her hips pressed into his. He stepped back at first, thinking he'd gone wrong again, but she followed him with a purpose, wiggling in the fast dances and stroking in the slow ones. He heard her breath puff out of her fat lips and remembered how she'd slid his hand under her blouse in the school halls and let him touch her under her bra. Eric looked at Talia's bright eyes, heard her laugh with yet another partner. When the music stopped, she pulled a thick rope of hair off her neck so he could see the little curls pasted against her skin before she whirled away. They held him until Laurie pouted, then he remembered that he'd never had a blonde before.

He had one that night, in his car, under the parking lot lights. He had white flesh mashed in his hands, an ass so soft that he could really get it going and sink it in deep. She was biting him, and she cried out when he did, announcing their fuck to the world.

He didn't see Talia again for two years.

When the pool table in the back opens up, Mike wants to play eight ball, so they do. Sort of. They play who can get eight balls in first, any color. Eric is drunk again; more than his stick wobbles, but Mike is drunker. He is bending at the waist, lying on the felt. Eric helps Mike up, sends him to the bathroom; then he takes Mike's turn for him and wins the game. Stealing the game reminds Eric of stealing from Talia. He can see himself standing alone in their apartment as the outlines of her life pop out of the dark. Fitting like puzzle pieces into a whole. He's not looking just for her diary this time, and it's a while before he thinks of Mike again. Who probably has his head in the urinal. Passed out for good.

Dick looks Eric over when he orders again. "Got anywhere to go?" he asks, pouring.

Eric's head shakes. "Probably never move."

"You fall off that stool, I'm gonna leave you on the floor."

"Deal." When Eric's eyes close, he can see the veins on his lids crisscrossing. Tawny. His heart is pumping pure scotch. "I gotta sit down," he says, aware that he's sitting.

Dick pours a beer and sets it down in front of someone else. "Want help to the john?"

"No. A walk around the parking lot, maybe. Back to finish the drink."

"Don't get run over by any parked cars."

Eric thinks that's funny. He hoists himself off the stool, using the bar because bars are for that, and staggers to the door like an ordinary drunk. It's still raining, and now it's dark. He walks a little way in the cool air, feeling the rain pop against his face. He leans against the wall; it's cool, too, and hard on his back. He stares at his feet as they slink out from under him. Until he's on his ass, holding the building up in the rain.

Eric slips in and out of silence, feeling his heart beat. He knows he's not asleep because he can smell the piss, freed by the rain and running down the wall. On occasion, cars pull up. Footsteps skip near him, sometimes over him, depending on where they park. He listens to the world again. There is more honking now, with a base note he can hear from a nearby bar but can't feel. People move faster at night, Eric thinks. They are revving.

He is all water now, down to his shorts, but feeling better. His heart's not so stuffed anymore. It's the rain, he decides, the cold of it mending him, shrinking his skin tight so he can't pour himself out. Now, when a car pulls up, he can open his eyes and watch. That will keep them away from him, he thinks. They'll see the danger that he is.

At least in prison, the guys are aware of one another, Eric thinks. They know where he is, that he's out. They know where to find him if they look.

Headlights catch him, then slim legs. A woman in a miniskirt gets out of her car. She dashes to the bar door with her coat flopping like a crippled bird to keep her head out of the rain. It's getting busy, he thinks, the Black Rose; it's a shame. Respectable people are going there.

Then there's another car; this time, a couple gets out. It makes him wonder if the car is green, if it's the grandparents he conned this morning. It seems long enough ago to be possible. He thinks of calling out, asking if they remember him, but they get to the door too quickly. He watches them go.

In the doorway, they trade places with the woman in the miniskirt, in that "after-you" dance people do. She is walking toward him, and he thinks he could talk to her, too. The alcohol has dried his mouth though—funny how wet can make dry. He tilts his head and opens it to the rain.

As he imagines the rain—silver, falling into the dark, onto his tongue—he thinks of hidden treasure. It sparkles above him in new headlights with the click of the woman's shoes. The shoes are wet, of course, the rain runs in tracks through tiny filaments from her ankle in a dip down her spiked heel. He wonders how he can see that in the dark until the headlights flash away again, and he realizes the woman is standing there. Has been stopped in front of him for a while.

They are slim legs, without stockings. He follows their flare from her shoes up to her knees. They aren't the pieces of her body he knows best, but he does know them. He wishes, suddenly, he was anywhere but here.

It is Talia.

Talia sinks down beside him on the ground. Close, but not touching. He keeps his eyes on her shoes because he can. They are new. He thinks, of course. Wet, green, and new.

"I did what you said," he hears. "I didn't come."

Eric always said she had a dirty voice. It is low, and textured like a fingertip. It's thrilling to hear her now between the raindrops.

"I almost went anyway," she says. "I was in the car, but never turned it on. I just can't keep playing your games."

"What games?"

"Oh God, I knew I shouldn't have come."

Talia shoves her legs straight out, knocking Eric's eyes to her hips. If she doesn't get too angry and leave, he thinks, he might see her face.

"Eric," she says, "it's raining."

Funny, he thinks, she's funny. He thinks of himself in her dark again. With all the pieces of her life, all the times, the loves—the answers. Of all the things, besides her diary, that he could have taken, he wonders if he would have stolen her shoes.

"Look at me," she says, and he does. Her mascara is smearing under her eyes. The rain sits in beads on her perfectly colored lips. "Am I really so scary that you have to push me so far away?"

"Scary?"

If he protests, he knows, he will lose her. He's about to answer when it hits him that she is actually, finally, here. "Umm," he begins, trying for moisture. He wants to stick his tongue out, but he knows it won't help. He flips quickly through his mind for something to say.

"Forget it."

She hasn't said a single thing about his hair—in fact, he can't tell if she even noticed. And the water, something about the way it crawls up her skirt, makes him worry. Over her thighs, into her lap. "Umm," he says returning to what he knows, "you didn't come."

"No. I took you at your word, for once," she says. "And if you dare say it was my choice, I swear I'll leave."

She will, he knows, and she's right. She stole his line: he was going to accuse her of not caring.

"I don't believe this," she says. "You're too drunk to speak."

Eric nods, realizes she's crying a little. Like she did when she moved into his house. Sad Talia, sad like he was when he was sitting with the grandparents and thinking of his blown-up buddy in 'Nam. He could speak—he should speak—but the conversation is going too slow to get lost in. It's full of sighs and quiet. Full of important things, taking him by surprise before they can come out of his mouth.

"I," he says, "can speak."

Talia's eyes are intent, the lightest things around—they are metallic, slightly, and misty. "Then say something," she says. "Tell me what I want to hear. What do you think is going to happen if you let yourself love me? How am I going to hurt you?"

How could she *not* hurt him? he wants to ask. He knows enough to say "I love you," but the words aren't coming out. Eric tries to picture the last time he used them, but he can't recall her face. Her hair, her clothes, he can't even remember the time of year. "Let me," he says, shaking his head, trying to clear the drink and feeling almost sober. "Wait."

The time before, then, what did he do? He searches his mind for any time when they were happy together, when he wasn't dirty, or muddy, or smelling like puke. Like now, dragging Talia with him. Watching her face wash away in the rain.

Eric has no tricks. Nothing to give her but the truth. "I," he says, "I was going to come home. To get my things. And yours. I was going to steal your stuff."

"You were going to steal my stuff." She forms the words like she's trying out a new language. "Well. That's not what I expected to hear, but at least it's honest." She looks surprised as she hears her last word. The rain has puddled in her lap. It rushes down her thighs as she rises.

Eric can't remember the last time he was honest. It feels both strange and good until he realizes she is leaving. It isn't until she rises that he begins to understand. He wants to be in her darkness, with all her dirt, all her cherished feelings. He wants to hold her from the inside where she can't escape him. Then he can wipe her tears away.

It's her tears that he feels now, all the way back to their high school prom. Talia's face at his car window as white as the moon. As he lay on top of Laurie then, watching Laurie's date pull Talia into the gym by her arm, he couldn't shake the feeling that he was more hurt than she was. He kept hurting in the next two years when she refused to speak to him.

All he could keep was the sight of her long, heavy hair.

He has never had anything to give her, Eric knows now. It's better for her if she leaves. She is moving slowly, so she won't slip, but it's okay, because it gives him time. He can say good-bye to each foot as it flexes, to each step. The puddles beneath her wobble, then rush back to fill the holes.

How many steps has she taken, Eric wonders. Two? Three? Her calves twitch, bunching and releasing, but so slowly as she moves. He could reach them, he thinks. He could stretch his hands. If only he had gone to her house, he would know how to keep her. Being unprotected with her couldn't be any lonelier than this.

Eric rolls over—he's wet anyway—and crawls. The gravel digs into his knees, but her shoes are in front of him now. The puddles catch him in the chest with a satisfying smack. The shoes' sweeping backs are in front of him, like wineglasses cupping her heels. They are stopped.

Eric isn't on his knees anymore, more like on his belly in the rain, but there's a new shoe in his hands. And Talia, just one foot of her—she can't leave unless he lets her go. He presses her skin the way she deserves and nestles his cheek on the ground.

As Talia looks down at him, streams of rain spill off her hair and into his face. He wants to turn his head to taste it, but settles for letting it fall in his eyes. One into the other, over the bridge of his nose. He needs her; she knows him so completely.

He's full of things he can't possibly ever say.

17

MARIKO

HORSE RACING, 1990

"Mari, I said I was sorry," Roger repeated. "I shouldn't have said anything to your mother, but I was concerned. You've been so depressed for the last two weeks, ever since that damn lunch with her. How was I supposed to know that you never actually went?"

"For once, Roger, I wish you'd let me live my own life." If only she had answered the telephone herself, Mari thought, already revising the last few minutes. She could still hear him saying, "You know, Emi, it's none of my business but . . ." It *wasn't* any of his business, but in a single unalterable sentence, Roger had chastised Emi for shutting her daughter out, only to find out that Mari had lied to them both. Mari's mother hung up, of course, with a tactful excuse about something that needed her immediate attention. Now Mari had no idea what to do.

"But you told me you had lunch with her. You said you asked her for the truth and she wouldn't give it to you." He sighed. "Christ, Mar. You *are* my wife."

"You don't own me."

"That's not what I'm saying, and you know it. You've been so unhappy—since Tyler left, but especially since you got those damn internment papers—and I wanted to help."

"I'm not a child, you know," she said, though she could hear how much she sounded like one.

"Look, I said I was sorry. I should have handed you the phone. But I don't get it, Mar. Why did you lie to me?"

Mari pressed her fingers against her eyes, cutting off Roger's words as neatly as if they were printed in front of her. Why had she lied? Because he would have accused her of running from her mother like she always did, and she would have had to defend herself once again. It had seemed like such a ridiculous thing to fight about when there was already so much between them that was wrong. Even so, she hadn't planned to lie, but he surprised her by returning home early. And with so much sympathy, at a moment when she needed it so.

She couldn't admit that she had lied because it was easy. Instead, Mari stared out the window at the leaves blinking in and out of the midday sun. She envied the trees; they were so constant and had so much room in which to move. Mari wanted to go to them, to let the sun search for her under the nodding branches, but she settled for admiring. She couldn't leave. Not anymore. She knew no one would invite her in again if she did.

Suddenly, Mari understood what she needed to ask. "Why didn't you take a day off to spend with Tyler when she was home?"

"Are we back to that? The day trip was your idea, Mar, not Tyler's. She had a million friends she wanted to see and a tan she just had to have . . ."

"Why haven't you ever played softball with her?"

"Softball?"

"Yeah."

"I haven't played softball in years."

Mari knew, even before she pressed him, that she was trying to gauge how far they had traveled. She needed to hear how much her husband loved them—her and Tyler—but he had no idea what she was talking about.

"I've been inundated at the office, Mar," Roger said. "All I get are questions, every time I turn around. What you have to understand is, it has nothing to do with Tyler. It's just that, when I've been busy in the past, you've been busy, too."

He was telling her that he was necessary and she was not. "So this whole thing is my fault because I have nothing to do during the day?" she asked flatly. "You know, I *did* try to have more children."

It was the silence around him that stopped her, the way her words slapped the surface of it and disappeared. Roger's face was ravaged; he looked the way he did the first time she miscarried after her abortion. She had been sure she was dying, but it wasn't until his tears fell on her chest that she realized he was afraid, too. Mari had insisted on calling her Uncle Carroll when she started bleeding. There were things she wouldn't need to say to him that a doctor would have to be told. They never went back to the hospital after that first time; they cried at home, trying to be philosophical until Mari couldn't bear to watch Roger hide his disappointment. After three years of trying, they finally had Tyler.

But Roger never knew how many times Mari tried to give him his son.

Where were they now? Mari wondered. Their conversation had moved far beyond her luncheon with her mother. They had come to a more dangerous place, though, a place Mari never would have brought them to on purpose.

Roger looked so tired.

"You look tired. I'm sorry."

Mari touched her face, surprised that the words came from her husband.

He held out his hand, inviting Mari to sit with him on the couch, and she took it, closing her eyes so that she could picture his and the crooked smiling lines around them. The vision helped her relax and remember how many years she and Roger had spent together. How much life they had weathered.

"I know it's hard," he murmured, taking hold of the conversation again. "The story is certainly much bigger now. Much harder to bury."

"But," Mari protested as the words dropped individually, like stones into dust, "I didn't bury it before. I didn't know."

"I think you did." He tightened his fingers around hers, as if he wanted them to listen. "Not consciously, maybe, but you've always known that you weren't legitimate. I'm sure you guessed there was something more."

The word *legitimate*, which her husband chose and delivered so mildly, was shocking. "How could I have known?"

"Well, you lived with Eric in the camps."

"Wait a minute. I was barely born!"

"The war lasted three years. I'm not saying you should remember, but I'm sure you knew him."

"Mom said he was my cousin."

"I'm not saying—"

"Jesus, Roger, you're blaming me for this, aren't you?" As Mari rose, her feet began to tingle. She was standing firmly on the ground next to the couch, sure she was about to fall. "I can't believe it. What could I have done? I didn't have anything to do with it. Nothing at all."

"But don't you see, Mar? You have the chance to do something now and you refuse to do a thing."

"I don't have a chance, Roger. I never did. My mother won't talk to me—not now, not ever. If I thought she would, I would have tried."

He let her words stand, though she could tell he didn't believe them. "Well, why don't you ask someone else, then? Your Uncle Jack, maybe. You said he raised the boy."

"Oh, sure. I'll just call and say, 'Hey, is Eric my brother?' And he'll say, 'Who the hell are you?'"

"He's not going to be rude, Mar. He has no reason to be."

"Maybe, maybe not," Mari said, but she felt herself slipping. He was right, of course. Roger's solutions were always so well reasoned. It was as if he was trying to make sense *for* her, so that she wouldn't have to think.

"Why are you pushing me, Roger?" Mari asked. She was hoping to provoke him, to find the energy to fight.

Roger smiled at her from the couch, inviting her to hear the sadness in her words. "Look at it this way, Mar," he said, holding out his hand once more, "what if it was you who had been abandoned? Would you want your brother to turn his back against you?"

The first sight would be important—when Mari had imagined it, her Uncle Jack stepped out of the crowd, his arms wide, and she recognized every strand of hair and fold in his face. It was a romantic image, true, but that was Santa Anita's fault. At home, staring at her telephone, the racetrack had given Mari the perfect excuse to call her uncle. She co-opted her old life as a reporter, telling him that her newspaper wanted a story on the internment as the fiftieth anniversary approached. The track would be a perfect place to reconstruct a faded memory.

Uncle Jack hadn't wanted to meet her. She could hear it in his voice, unfamiliar though it was and thinned out by the distance between them. Mari's new-found strength ebbed when he started making excuses, until she realized he couldn't refuse her directly; he was an old Nisei man after all. He would wait for her to retreat, or to suggest she was imposing, and all she had to do to resist the niceties she grew up with was to remember how important this meeting was to Roger. She owed it to him for all of her lies, and it was such a clear choice, between Roger and Jack, that she found it easy to let her uncle breathe into the line.

Besides, she was not going to harm him. She just wanted a few details to confirm that everything was fine so she could go home. This was her chance to be the peacemaker that Roger had always accused her of being. If her mother had left anything unresolved with Eric, Mari could settle it for her without Emi ever needing to know.

"Mariko?"

Mari's uncle came up from behind her, a good-size man in a short-sleeved shirt. His face was like her mother's with its smooth, flat planes, but his nose didn't have the broken bump that Emi's did, and his chin had been squared off by age. Each eye was marked on its corner by a stubborn thatch of wrinkles from years in the sun. Cozy-looking, Mari thought, appraising him, but nothing really to recognize.

"Uncle Jack?" She stepped forward to hug him; she was within inches before she realized he was making no move in return. She stuck her hands out to stop herself too late, pressing them to his chest as her body bumped his. Her stomach slid against her ribs as she stepped back, patting his shoulder, as if in thanks. As if she had tripped and he caught her. Then she stuck out her hand.

"You're so much like your mother," Jack said.

Mari couldn't imagine how. Emi's beauty was exact, while Mari's eyebrows may as well have been smudged there and her eyes themselves were too round. At first she thought he was just being polite, but the grains in Jack's voice rubbed the words raw as he spoke them.

It didn't sound like a compliment.

"Thanks for coming, Uncle Jack. Especially on such short notice. You know how newspapers are. Impossible deadlines."

"You want to interview me, eh?"

"I'd love to: a Santa Anita survivor. It's a good angle." Now that he was here with her, it was no easier to tell him the reason for her call. "Is there somewhere we could sit down?"

Jack laughed or maybe it was a cough. It was a short sound, devoid of mirth. They could sit anywhere, Mari realized. The area was lined with benches, most of them empty, and couched in a garden of flowers so perfectly placed that she was sure they would spell out words if she saw them from the air. Even approaching from the parking lot, the track had felt unreal to her; it shivered through the heat like a dehydrated dream. The buildings, Spanish in spirit, had been painted sea green with pastel bric-a-brac and yellow spires. They were as clean as the San Gabriels behind them and the sky.

Mari's uncle put his hand near her back to escort her toward the main building, not close enough to feel the heat of his skin or his touch. She looked around, as if she might need a few pictures later, and stepped onto the escalator in front of him. Fast-food storefronts fell away on either side. The world above her was beginning to roar.

"You've been here before?" she asked, raising her voice as she stepped onto the steady floor. It didn't seem like Santa Anita. It wasn't suitably fantastic. "I mean, recently."

"You place your bets there," Jack told her, leaving her to assume what she could as he swept his hand toward the crowd on her left. There must have been twenty rows of people in front of as many lined-up teller windows. Against the other wall, and around the freestanding columns, they made notes and checked their programs. She was surprised at how bored they seemed.

Jack rushed her up a short concrete ramp. "This is the grandstand."

Beyond the shell of sheltered seats that Mari stood in was the light. In it, the track coiled neatly around a field bright with flowers and dotted with roofs, then headed off in several directions. There were two concentric oval fences along the inside of the gravel, enclosing a trampled interior grass track, but no races were running on either one. "A playground," Mari murmured, taking stock of the wide, unprotected park contained inside the fences. She couldn't see any gates or crosswalks. There were people in it, but she could find no apparent way to enter or leave.

"This way," Jack said, leaving her to follow him down the row. The chairs were hinged, old and dirty. The grandstand itself felt used. Jack kicked a metallic hamburger wrapper down the stepped concrete and unfolded two seats. She was barely settled when he asked, "So why are you here?"

"I want to know if Eric is my brother." The midday sun must have made her rush things; it was bouncing off the mountain walls, onto the track, then into her eyes. The jockeys flickered as they steered their horses across the lanes toward the starting gate.

"I knew that was why you came."

Mari watched Jack dip his square hand into his chest pocket for a cigarette and a match, wondering if he was always this gruff. It could simply be his way, she told herself; after all, he was a man of a certain age and a former soldier. She waited while he held the smoke in his mouth; when he finally let go, his voice was rougher than before. "Of course he's your brother," he said, his eyes on the starting gate. And then, "Why do you ask?"

Mari held the news in her ears to see what effect it had on her. Maybe it was Jack's demeanor, but the relief she had expected wasn't there. "I got my internment records. He was listed with the family."

"And? So? What do you want to know?"

Mari paused. Now that she could ask anything, what did she want to know? "Is he okay?" she began. "What's he like?"

"Of course, he's okay. Now anyway. He's got a wife, three good-looking boys—got his own landscaping business. But something like that, well, you never get over it. It hurt him badly."

"What do you mean, 'like that'?"

"Like being tossed aside. Put in an orphanage by your own mother."

"An orphanage?"

"That's what she did, and before the war, too. You know what those places are like? It was just luck that Mama found out in time and saved him. If not, they would have sent him to Japan for sure."

It took Mari a second to figure out who Mama was. "*Who* would have sent him to Japan? The people at the orphanage?"

"No, the government. During the evacuation. They sent the people in the sanitoriums away. Tuberculosis. They got rid of everyone they could."

Mari felt like she had walked into a movie in the middle and Jack was trying to fill her in before the next character could speak.

He had summoned her brother in a few strokes, adding people and events she had never considered. She couldn't imagine her mother was actually so callous. "Do you think he would want to see me?"

Jack coughed again; it was definitely a cough this time. He wheezed shreds of it back into his lungs. Mari wanted to pat him on the back, but she was afraid he'd pull back, or worse, that it would encourage him and too much past would spill out. "Are you okay?"

"Yeah." Jack went through his pants pockets. "Just asthma. I have an inhaler somewhere." He put one end of a small *J*-shaped tube into his open mouth and pressed it. "What did you say?" he gasped, holding his breath in.

"Do you think he would want to see me?"

"Oh, I don't know."

Mari waited.

"Do you want to know the truth?"

It was a surprisingly good question. She wanted a story that made sense. Mari had always assumed that, whatever had happened, the trauma had been her mother's. She even imagined that, by finding Eric, she could set Emi's mind at ease. But in her mind, Eric had always been okay.

He had been happy.

"Yes," she said. "I want to know the truth."

"Leave him alone, then. Let him live his life. Eric has had to make do for so long now, I'm all the family he needs."

Mari kept her eyes on the park, with its hidden entrances and tightly wrapped rims. "Does he know about me?"

"Of course he does."

Of course, of course, Mari thought. It was all her uncle seemed to say. She had been sure that, if Eric did know about her, he would be pleased she was here at last. Now she wondered why, remembering her own reluctance to search him out. But she hadn't wanted to disturb him, and Jack was saying something different. It hit her then that her uncle was blaming *her*, as well as her mother, for Emi's actions. It wasn't a burden she was willing to carry.

"Did she send you?" Jack asked.

"What?"

"Is this Emi's way of trying to get past me?"

It was a strange question, but she answered it. "No. Why would she need me to get past you?"

"I'm his only protection. She could have taken him with her so many times, but she never did. Do you know what that's like, being rejected over and over?" Jack's voice gained speed. "I don't know how she lived with it. I really don't know. But that's Emi for you—thoughtless. You know, the first time she came back, she took you away with her. You, and not Eric. Can you imagine that?"

The question had become a recurring theme in the few short days since her fight with Roger, but neither her husband nor her uncle realized how easily Mari could put herself in Eric's place. At any moment, she could feel her mother leaving as thoroughly as if it was she who had been left behind. When she was young, Mari's deepest fear was of abandonment, so much so that she was almost always the first person to get into the family car. On picnics, even as a teenager, Mari was always there to pack their belongings, and often became sick enough, at the end of a meal, to have to lay down on the soft backseat in the dark. Until now, though, she had never understood why.

Jack hadn't expected an answer, Mari noticed. After trying so hard to make her feel guilty, he looked almost peaceful for the first time that afternoon. He even turned from the race that was lining up at the gate to give her a brief apologetic smile.

"You want to bet?"

"No."

"I could teach you."

Mari shook her head. She didn't want to be taught; she wanted him to take back all the things he had said, to cleanse her of his anger. But it was too late. In addition to rejecting Eric, her mother had clearly damaged Jack, too. They weren't the extent of the casualties caused by her mother either, Mari realized; she herself had grown up with the inexplicable feeling that something was missing, and with the very real fear that she, too, would be easy to lose. It was all so plain now. How many times had her mother refused to answer her questions? For how many years had she held Mari away?

Jack had been there when Emi left Eric; he said she had had plenty of chances to reclaim him, and she had never even tried. She could have done it for all of their sakes, but she'd been too selfish. Now that Mari knew what actually happened, she realized she was going to have to repair things after all.

But not by acting as a peacemaker.

No, Mari was determined, instead, to make her mother pay.

18

JACK

BASTARD, 1942

It's Mama in the doorway, her Sunday hat on. Her Sunday dress. Jack reached the living room first because his ears are good and his legs are young—now he stands on the opposite side, in front of the kitchen door, the first witness to her return. It won't be more than a few seconds until Papa comes roaring out of the kitchen to accuse her, and maybe slap her off her feet. Before Emi follows to find out why and how Mama left the house. For the first time in months. Without a word.

Jack has been waiting for this moment since he walked into the house after school and found it smelled like nothing—there was no noise. Will was gone, but what made Jack want to flee was the fact that there was no sign of Mama. He searched through the gutted house for her, faster and faster, thinking he was the last survivor, afraid someone lurked there for his return. Until he got to Emi's room—a place he would never ordinarily have entered—and plowed in unannounced. He found himself grateful, so grateful, that she was there, in her room, and alive. That she hadn't heard the FBI take their mother away, so maybe Mama was okay after all, mysteriously gone it was true, but just for a moment. Emi was calm.

"Then I better start supper," was all she said, and he could have kissed her. Emi rose from the chair by the window and began to brush her hair. Staring, Jack felt almost as if she were stroking his own hair, and he was soothed. He was soothed, too, when she made sukiyaki—Papa's favorite meal. Of course she'd planned it; she knew Papa would care more about his supper than where Mama disappeared to, so she put two hours into it while Jack hovered in the kitchen with her where the life was. As she hummed, and they talked, Jack believed he'd repaired the situation somehow, that things would continue on course. That his sister had started time forward again. However painfully and slow.

It is 7 P.M. now. Papa's been eating supper for a half hour.

And Mama stands in their front doorway, finally, only steps inside the house. She is wearing her blue Sunday suit and her hat with the fringe. She has on stockings and the good shoes she stores in a felt bag in her closet.

She holds a fat wrapped baby in her arms.

Terrible things come through his front door, Jack thinks. First it was Emi—a scandal gathering in the dark. Now it's Mama, like she was before Pearl Harbor when she used to dress up. Jack can hear yet another creature scratching outside, lurking and waiting for its chance to get in. He wonders what new disaster Mama has brought with her. If he could move, he thinks without hope, he'd slam the door.

Mama stares at Jack, impassive. She doesn't notice the noise, or the dead silence of both doors. She is ignoring the string of questions that lies between them.

Who is this child? That's the real question—and the only one Jack knows the answer to. It is "the other one" Mama referred to the night Emi returned. So she searched for Emi's other child and found it. But, he thinks, why?

Another sound springs up between them. Scraping. Jack cringes against a blow, but it's coming from the front of the house. Something dropped in the dusk. Jack hears a low male curse, and he leans forward, to test his feet, to see if he can uproot them, throw himself off balance and toward the door. If he can, he thinks, he could lock it. But it's still light enough for Jack to see that he would never make it in time. The thing has almost taken shape behind Mama. Her back, turned against it, is the family's last defense. She stands like a statue in the door.

Oh God, Jack thinks, expecting without reason to see his mother struck down. And then, oh God, oh God, but this time with relief, a painful flood of it that makes him dizzy, because he recognizes those potent eyes. It is his brother, Will, home again, his face disfigured as he drops two suitcases inside the door. Jack finds it eerie that when Emi arrived she had two also, and that she set them in the same spot. Emi's were battered, though, and these two match. Jack moves to help Will but stops when he realizes he hasn't been seen.

His brother's eyes, when they finally look at Jack, are flat. His mouth is set, as if he's cold, and his cheeks are flushed. Once he's dropped his burdens, he loosens the knot of his tie and releases the top button of his suit jacket in two movements so sudden that Jack is surprised his clothes are still intact. Will's eyes keep moving until they reach the kitchen door. No one has said a word yet.

There is nothing to say.

Will enters the kitchen first. Jack holds the door for Mama and the baby, close enough to see that neither Papa nor Emi have glanced up. He understands now that Papa is eating, will continue to eat, because supper is meant to be on the table at six-thirty, and the head of the family is served first. The silence, from Papa, is what tells him—it doesn't matter that Mama and Will are there or what they've done. When enough time has passed, Papa sets down his chopsticks.

"Who do you think you are, leaving me without supper?"

"I'm so sorry," Mama says. She is standing, jogging the baby, who has chosen this moment to begin fussing. It is huge in her arms. "I am worthless. A no-good wife."

Jack barely hears Mama's words; they are regulars in his small reserve of Japanese. Normally, she delivers them with her hands clasped and her eyes on the floor, but the baby has forced her into a less contrite pose. One of its little arms moves, up and down, as if charging its motor. Mama is following it with her eyes.

Will stands behind Mama's usual seat next to Emi, ready to take it but waiting for Emi to rise before he will sit—and to serve him. The tension, the fear that Jack tried all afternoon to shake, is stronger now, more like a river, and Emi has become a rock in hopes that it will flow around her. Jack marvels at how smooth her features are. She must hear the baby, but she hasn't looked at it. Papa has, but Jack knows he would rather die than ask questions in front of his sons.

Emi's hands have been resting on the bulge of her stomach. Now she puts them on either side of her empty plate and pushes herself up—she is much heavier than she seemed while she was cooking. As she picks up Will's plate, he leans toward her and says, conversationally, "Whore."

No one in the room acknowledges the word. Or the uncommon ugliness Will's voice gives it, which even Mama and Papa should be able to understand. Jack can see that it has struck by the way Emi slings her arms under her to help her lift her belly. Jack is the only one who watches her steps—rolling, almost off balance—as she walks to the stove.

The word continues to fill the room, but Jack doesn't dare erase it. He doesn't want Emi to serve him, to come near him, for fear that Will will see him at last. Since the FBI released Will, he has been looking for a target. Jack doesn't want to be there when Will unloads.

Mama says, "Fix a little rice for Eric."

While Emi does, the family begins to eat. Jack stares at the table, noticing flecks—not dirt but discoloration—on his bowl; the frayed ends of his chopsticks; and a stain, fading now, on their everyday tablecloth where he dropped a mouthful of spaghetti months ago. It is a mystery that he sees it now, a rebuke that even the tiny things in the room seem immense. He marvels that no one has noticed the limp carrot flowers Emi cut for the sukiyaki. He remembers the way her knife lingered, lengthwise, as she notched each one five times—how her fingers guided the blade as she released each papery slice. They fell neatly in a leaning stack, then she slid the knife underneath it and lifted it whole onto the waiting plate. When the carrots were finished, she cut the celery into boats.

Mama holds the baby in her lap and tries to eat. Jack can see it more clearly now. It has a broad face, pink and lumpy in its discomfort, but it is older than he thought it was. It has real hair. The fist waving has become a ritual, little pistons moving fast or slow depending on its position.

Mama keeps shifting.

"It's too hot," she says to Emi once she tastes the baby's rice. "Cool it down. Bring a spoon."

She has stirred the mood of the room, and Will is quick to take advantage. "Stupid girl," he says. "Not a very good mother, is she? Let's see, what is she good at? I can think of one thing."

Emi gets a second helping for Papa before she sits down with her own meal. She's taken only a small scoop of rice and a few vegetables for herself.

"What do you think, Jack? About our fine, upstanding sister? What's she good at, eh?"

Carrots, Jack wants to say. Fear shudders through his ears and—unaccountably—his groin as he waits to be rescued. By his parents? By Emi? But it doesn't matter what he says anymore. His sister is beyond his help. "Yeah." Jack forces himself to please Will. "We know what she's good at."

Will's nostrils flare. His eyes are wide. "So? What's she good at, Jack?"

He's being stalked, Jack thinks—Will's looking at him like he's a gift about to be opened. "Well," he mutters, "we know." He is humiliated. "We don't have to say."

"Whoring, Jack," Will says, the fun leaving his voice. "She's a whore. She's good at whoring."

Oh, Jesus, Jack thinks, if he could just leave. He's trapped until Papa finishes and excuses them. No one else is done, but Papa should be. The old man's been eating for hours, and so slowly, as if he's trying to keep them here.

Will leans toward Jack. "Say it, Jack. Be a man."

He feels the danger, coming not from Will, but from Mama and Papa and the fact that they are allowing this. Both of them continue what they are doing—Papa staring into space with his goofy grin, Mama clucking the baby to sleep. Jack hates them, prays they don't understand the words. "She's a whore," he says for his brother.

The baby throws its blanket back and begins to thrash. It unreels a thin wail that pierces Jack's head in dashes when his mother stops bouncing it. Mama looks confused, then annoyed, that it won't do what she wants. At last she says, "Emi, take Eric so I can eat."

"I can't hold a baby and serve, Mama."

"No one needs serving anymore," Will says.

Emi turns to Will, finally meeting his eyes. She is present suddenly, alive in the room for the first time, and Jack can feel that they are too close, that someone should have stepped between them, put Will in his regular seat. That someone should be between them now, because they are bumping into each other.

His brother and sister are falling out of control.

"Where am I going to put it?" she asks, keeping all but a touch of anger out of her voice.

Will stares deliberately at the bloated belly where Emi's lap used to be. The glee is back in his face. "Maybe you should have thought of that."

The baby spits out its rice. Its cries are louder.

"Shut that thing up," Papa says. Jack sees that he's put his chopsticks down, but not in the right place. He's only pausing, not finished. "Get me some tea."

Mama collects the blanket around the baby. "You're right of course. We should feed him later. Emi, take Eric upstairs while I get your father some tea."

Go, Jack urges her in his head. He's never wanted anything more.

"I'll get the tea," Emi says.

"I'll get it. You take Eric."

"Where do you want me to take him?"

"To your room. He'll sleep with you."

Emi seemed about to rise, but now she stops. She delivers her next words in apparent pain. "No, Mama."

Jack can't believe she is resisting. That she won't take the baby and escape. He finds himself hating her for that, too.

For refusing to save either one of them.

Will pushes himself away from the table and turns on Emi. His cheeks are flushed again; Emi's defiance has pleased him. With a stiff pointed finger, he strikes out at her. "Don't. You. Dare. Talk. Back. To. Your. Mother," he says, knocking on her shoulder with each word.

Emi shrinks from him until she is leaning. Her face sags, but she won't yield. "I told her I wouldn't take him," she says. "I told her, but she wouldn't listen to me."

"Take him upstairs!"

It is a roar—unfettered—and to punctuate it, Will sweeps his hand over the table and toward the door. A glass splinters at their feet. The muscles under Will's eyes are twitching, Eric is screaming, and Mama, thank God, has finally risen.

"Take him," Will says. "Take him."

When Emi doesn't move, Will stands. He grabs her arm so tightly it bulges around his fingers as he tries to yank her from her chair.

"Don't touch me," Emi says, but she's up, grabbing the back of her chair for balance, turning her face away from Will. She seems afraid to move her body.

"Don't touch me? Maybe you should have said that to the men, eh? All those men you've been rutting around with. Maybe you should have said that to them."

If only, Jack thinks, Will didn't have to do this. If only he would stop.

"Bastard," Emi says.

Will's right arm swings straight out like a baseball bat and hits Emi in the face. She looks surprised as his fist smashes into her nose, sending her backward against the table, her heavy back side smearing into her food, shoving the bowls into one another. Papa jumps out of the way as she slides into Jack's sukiyaki, launching it into his lap. More glasses topple. She scrambles upright and faces Will with a torn blouse. Her nose is bleeding into her mouth.

Jack is the only one seated. He can't rise without dumping the sukiyaki on the floor. He's trying to breathe, to talk, but he can't get enough air in deep. Papa is wringing one hand where he was hit with food. He is standing next to Emi.

Do something, Jack thinks. Anyone. Please.

"Shut that baby up!" Papa orders, as if he's just noticed the child is screaming. As if he hasn't said it once before.

"Bastard is right," Will says. He is pushing Emi backward with his steps, with his leer leaning into her face and with his spittle. "The little whore should know."

"Will," Mama pleads finally. Jack wants to cheer. She understands. If not the words, she sees the violence. He feels released now, enough to turn and see her, still standing beside her chair, the struggling baby on her hip.

"Will, please," Mama repeats. "The stove."

The wave of relief that Mama started with her first plea is crashing in Jack's head, through his ears, momentarily drowning the noises around him. The stove, he thinks stupidly, seeing that Emi is indeed within inches of the cooling burners. Oh, Mama. Is that all?

Jack watches, each movement shredded into pieces so he must see it, as Will reaches forward, both fists bursting open as he grabs

Emi by the shoulders. Jack sees her sway as he yanks her from the stove and shoves her against the wall. He sees Emi's shoulders hit first under Will's hands, then her head snap, forward and back. Her body follows. The wall creaks as she hits it, she seems to sink into it, then bounce off in a spasm. Then she falls back, her stomach spreading like a muted ripple.

"Now, take the little bastard upstairs."

Emi struggles to stand on her own, to get away, but Will's hands still pin her shoulders. Her face is smeared with blood. Neither one of them has seen what Jack has, that Mama has taken the baby and slipped quietly out the door. He could speak up, Jack thinks. With the baby gone, there's no need to argue. But his parents' silence is choking him.

Emi twists her neck and sinks her teeth into Will's hand.

With a scream, Will drops his hand and sends his knee smashing into Emi's stomach. It wobbles, kicking back weakly. Jack expects to see his sister burst. She falls forward, one hand wrapped around her stomach and one grasping blind to break her fall. The hand finds Will's tie, and like a dog on a leash, he jerks with her, falling on top of her on the floor.

The screams—Will's, Emi's, even the baby's—are everywhere. If he opens his mouth now, Jack thinks, he will scream, too. It will be a wail, a dirge, because no one is doing anything and he cannot, because his parents have accepted this and that means he must, too. The wallpaper is fading around him; the wood floor and even the ceiling are slowly turning black. He can't do anything to stop Will. He can't stand it, but he has to.

"Goddamn it. Goddamn bitch," Will is moaning and rolling on the floor. "Look what you did!" He's fallen off of Emi, but his red hand enrages him and he grabs her hair, tearing it out of the roll she wears it in, and slams her head on the ground, banging his own with the force. She arches backward, her belly rising like a mountain, trying to shove him away, but he has her pinned. Her glancing push does nothing but encourage him. Still lying on the ground, Will smashes her in the face again and she grunts, twisting her head in a smear of her own blood on the floor. She hits back in a flurry, her hands half open and flapping.

It's beyond stopping, Jack realizes. His father is sitting there, no longer watching anymore. His mother is gone. They didn't care enough; not even Emi cared until it was too late. Perhaps she didn't know, couldn't see herself trying to scramble away from Will, her legs kicking out but not connecting. He hates her for it, hates them all for doing this to him. Making him watch her lose her shoe, watch Will lunge for her, throw his body on her sideways, hear her grunt as he hits. Emi's shirt, stretched over her huge stomach, is dappled with the blood running off Will's right hand, where he has drummed her with his fists. He is pummeling her like something inside him is broken.

Emi has her arms safely around her stomach now, curled in a ball. Will staggers to his feet, his arms waving for balance. He wobbles, only steps from Jack, but doesn't see him. He lifts his foot, aims it straight for Emi's stomach.

Please, God, Jack thinks, someone has to stop this. Even if it means he is no longer part of this family. Especially if it does. He grabs Will's arm, afraid to speak—he moves between his brother and his sister, hoping that Will's foot strikes him, too. He wants to feel as bruised as Emi does.

He's so embarrassed by the fact that he's untouched.

"I don't think—" Jack says. Then, "She's not moving anymore."

Will looks at Jack like he's slowly recovering consciousness, then they both look down at Emi. Strands of blood-soaked hair cut across her face. Her lips are smashed. They part, peeling away from each other as she struggles to breathe. Her nose is twisted, as if Will has snapped it in the middle sharply enough that Jack can only thank God the bone isn't poking through her skin.

"Good," Will says. He throws an arm over Jack's shoulders, leans into him. Jack tries to move him to a chair, but he waves his hand in the direction of the living room. "Let's go in there," he says. "Get out of here. C'mon."

* * *

Jack helps Will because he is asked to. He doesn't turn around again until his brother does, until they've reached the door and are about to leave the room.

Until Will looks down at their broken sister and says, "I hope she's dead."

19

KAORI

FIRST HARVEST

It wasn't Will's fault, Mariko. Your mother understood that; she knew what life was like in those early years. Jack was too young to remember, but she was there on the farm in the shadow of our house each morning when the sun lit the top of our hill and began to crawl down. She was there in 1926 for our first harvest, when I had two black woks in front of me over a split drum your grandfather set up to make the cooking go faster, and twenty pickers waiting for their breakfast. They weren't Japanese, mostly Mexicans, so I made mush from rice and oats, like we were fed when we were migrants. I know now that the peace I felt that morning was an omen.

On that day, though, I thought it meant something good.

The scene around me looks like this. Your mother stands on my left side where the line begins. She is helping, holding bowls straight up over her head so the workers can take them without stooping. The women in the line often give Emi a smile; their own kids are milling around, quiet with big staring eyes. Some of them gather near me, looking respectfully at Jack, who's asleep on my back. He's not a year old, so it's a useful place to keep him. Away from the fire and out of my arms.

Will passes through the line with the others, then crouches with his back against the pear tree, bowl to his mouth. He sets his hat down; he's already brushed off the thighs of his overalls. Thinking back to that scene, it's Will's eyes I remember most, blazing over his thin, hairless cheeks each time daylight finds and lights another row of carrots. It was ours, this time. We had twice as much land in celery alone as my father ever owned, and Will helped as much as anyone. He was out there before breakfast dusting for insects with the backpack and the thin metal hose like a walking stick. Chasing the bugs around the roots. In the evenings, he was old enough to fire the edges of the fields to keep the weeds from drifting in. Will had spent an hour that morning picking in the half-dark to bring in his share of the crops, and I could see him savoring it, trying to memorize each tray of vegetables. I imagined that he was moving the sun as he replayed it in his memory, turning up the heat, as if the day was over instead of just beginning and he'd been allowed to stay home for it all.

The serving was done. Mitsuo called for the men to get the bamboo baskets and packing trays ready. The pickers left their bowls on the table and put their hats and bonnets back on as the children swarmed into a group to be cared for. I took the basin to the well for dishwater, walking out of the shade and into that lush late-season sun. Will had risen, too, more slowly than the rest. He was still gazing at the fields.

"School bus comes in twenty minutes," I told him. The smile I gave him said I was sorry.

"Do you need help, Mama?"

"No, you go on."

Will nodded and headed into the house. That's when I should have said to him, "*Shikata ga nai.*" If I had spoken, our lives—even yours, Mariko—would have been different, but there was cool water on my hands, splashing unexpectedly as I set the full bucket down, and it carried my thoughts away. My hands plunged into the water and awakened there, rubbing clean and new just for a moment. I patted my face, and all the cooking and the noise fell away until it was just me and the soft greens in the fields. I heard the baby's steady breathing on my back. I was swept with an absurd desire to set him down and run through the furrows. I wanted to haul up a fistful of carrots, and twirl, and hold it above me and up to the sky.

The night before, Will had walked into the front room and asked your grandfather if he could stay home just to get the harvest started. He'd done it on days past when the work was heavy, so I looked up in surprise when I heard Mitsuo refuse. Will was ten at the time—he was strong, though his arms looked like splinters. I knew better than to argue, but I also knew we needed every man we could get.

Maybe Will was thinking the same way I was, because he didn't hesitate or look down at the floor. "I won't fall behind, Papa," he said eagerly. "I'm smarter than all of them anyway." He didn't seem to notice Mitsuo's face, puffed and puzzled as it often was after dinner; if he had, he might have stopped boasting, and talked about the harvest, about wanting to see the growing cycle through. Instead he said, "Please could I miss Japanese school? All we do is snap to attention when the teacher raps his ruler. Besides, I know all the words already."

It was inexcusable, even to me. It wasn't just Will's pride, his disdain for us and our language. It was face too. Will's Japanese teacher was also from Kumamoto—he was Mitsuo's friend and an important source of sake in those Prohibition days. Perhaps Will was usually asleep when the man came to visit, so he didn't hear the sodden laughter and the crossing stories. I had listened to them one evening until I was banished from the room.

"On the boat!" the teacher roared. "Remember when we sighted shore?"

"I remember."

"You were so jolly. You were going to own the world. And now you have a good house."

"Not so good. Rubbish really." Mitsuo was proud.

"Good house, good farm," the teacher said, knowing that this was a point of agreement. We had two small rooms for sleeping, an outhouse and a bathhouse; even a half-kitchen with pipes running in through the walls. "Remember the steak?"

"No—"

"Yes! The steak. The dinner. You remember the steak!"

They were drunk enough they should not have noticed me mending a tear in Mitsuo's overalls, but the man needed an audience and a reason to talk. He got out of his chair and lurched toward me. On his way across the floor, he stumbled, pulling a cloth off a small side table. I caught my breath, then, but the table only teetered. The cloth floated harmlessly to the floor.

"Let me tell you."

"She should be working. Go in the back, woman. Sew somewhere else."

"Let me tell her. She can go after." The teacher had a grip on my arm. His words were blowing into my face as he tried to get the story out. "We had a steak, the night we saw shore. Okada over there, he was so jolly. He never had a steak. I never had a steak. But I told him it was the best thing in the world, so he picked up his big fork and knife. All ready. You should have seen his face!"

The teacher was giggling, then he was laughing so hard he let go of my arm and fell down. He thought this was even funnier. I could feel Mitsuo's anger building, and knew this, too, would be my fault. Still, I couldn't move. Even if he was on the floor, I couldn't leave the guest.

"You should have seen! Big hunks of fat. They were clear, wiggling, there was blood everywhere. We could smell it all along the table. Those Caucasians were so excited, and old Okada here, he just looked at that dead brown bone sticking up, then he jumped out of his seat and barfed right over the side of the ship!"

It was that night I was thinking of when Will announced that Japanese school was stupid. I saw the same savage eyes, the maddened fists that strung so many of our early days together. Mitsuo raised a hand and shook it above his head. He stared at it; for a moment he looked genuinely bleak. Then he remembered Will, and his voice lashed out with the rest of him. "Get out of my sight!" It was so raw; he wanted so badly to erase us all. Will barely escaped that time, but he clearly didn't learn. It was only me who recalled the teacher's laughter then, and saw Mitsuo's shame.

In my mind, I am picking radishes. It's fast picking, bending from the waist to twist the root with one hard pull, not squatting, like with peas or berries where you have to pluck each fruit. The tops start off soft in my hands, but they get rougher as the dirt flies and I can smell the earth drop off and lay down fresh and new in the rows. My gloves wrap around my middle finger to keep the backs of my hands from burning, but my palms are free to pick and tie the radishes into small bunches that I stuff into the bamboo basket and the pockets of my apron. I made my picking apron myself from old rice sacks. I made the bonnet with a ruffle to shield my neck, so it's only my back that beats with the sun.

Our farm is twenty acres, so we are spread out. We don't talk, except sometimes when a runner comes with a new basket, or if we carry them out of the fields ourselves. Even then, we don't say much because English is the only language we share. I'm on Mitsuo's hill, I call it that because it's why he chose the farm, and why we could afford it. A hill means handpicking, no machines. Between the brown and the green, at the exact point where one grows and the other shrinks, I can see light straw hats, denim shoulders, and jeans. We are trying to outrun one another. It won't all come in today, of course, but we are excited, and for a moment we've forgotten what we can't do. I know my row count, it beats in my head. Three. Then seven. Then ten. The hill rows are short and easy to pick. Then fourteen, and it's time to make another meal.

* * *

I tell you this, Mariko, to prove that I never saw Will that day until we had two good hours of light left and I was headed back to the house to cook supper. I found him in the carrot rows, wearing the clothes that he'd been in that morning, so eager to be working that he didn't look up when I passed by. Most of a full basket stood beside him, and I remember leaving him alone. School had not been over for long, and I was sure he had a goal to reach. Knowing my son, he would do anything to reach it, too.

So when the jalopy pulled up to the house that night and the teacher stepped out with a jug of sake in his hand, I wasn't worried. I was washing laundry in an iron pot on the woodstove. Will sat behind me, doing homework at the table so he could share my light. I put it near him. Gas light is weak and full of streaks; he needed it more than I did. I had my back to him and boiling steam in my face so I didn't see him recognize the voice outside.

Mitsuo had stepped out onto the porch to greet his guest. I could hear their voices, but I wasn't thinking about the words. The sake was a gift that day. They would drink it straight, I knew, so I didn't bother to take them cups. They sat on the bench.

I was fishing the clothes out, and the men were several rounds into their drinking, when the teacher first mentioned the harvest.

"It must have been a good day. Must have been a lot of acres."

"The trucks go in for the Monday market," Mitsuo said. "We have the weekend."

"Education is important, too."

I heard a grunt as the words settled down on me, then a swig at the jug which could not have been Mitsuo. I didn't think, at that moment, that Mitsuo could be moving. My hands were plunged into the steaming laundry, but my neck felt like ice. Will had skipped school, disobeyed us. I had no idea what Mitsuo would do.

"He's smart, your Will, but he has much to learn. It would be a shame if all he knew was farming."

Each word made it worse, until at last it was so bad that I could move. I turned to face Will and wasn't surprised to find he'd slipped away. His book was gone. Only the light and the shadows remained.

Outside, Mitsuo struggled to reply. "It was first harvest. Surely an exceptional day."

My hands were burning in the clothes. They came up red and puffy when I heard Mitsuo's words. It would have been worse for him to admit that he couldn't control his son, but then the punishment would have been determined by the teacher. This way, Mitsuo was required to do it himself.

As quickly as I could, I wrung the laundry and took it out the back door to hang. My hands shook as I put it on the line. The clothes were wrinkled. I could see them clearly, edged in moonlight, but I didn't have the time to shake them out. The children's room was dark beneath the curtain in the window. I kept my eye on it in case Will's head appeared. The men on the porch were quiet, following their thoughts, I guessed, and I knew how dark Mitsuo's were and how much he must have wanted the teacher to leave. I prayed the man didn't know and would stay. I prayed Mitsuo would drink until he couldn't move, pass out on the porch and do no harm. When the laundry was hung and cooling, I paused and looked out into the fields. I imagined I saw Will standing there, but I knew none of us could leave.

When I slipped back into the house and set the basket down, the men were still talking on the porch. I waited in the dark, until the children's breathing emerged beneath their words, then I felt my way into the bedroom. The children shared a single bed along one wall, with Jack in the middle so he wouldn't roll off. Will was in it, lying on the inside, since he got in last.

"What did you do?" I hissed.

He'd pulled the blanket over his mouth. I could see his eyes flinch so I yanked his arm. He opened them. They were shadows in the darkness.

"Answer me. Don't you know what your father will do?"

"I just—" It seemed all he was able to say.

* * *

We don't even hear the warning sound of the jalopy driving away. We hear the staggering footsteps and see the light swing from out of the hall. I am blinded by the yellow ball, and by the heat flying into my face as Mitsuo does. He is roaring a noise that cannot be a word. Emi and Jack scream: distinct, entwined sounds that pierce my head. They must see what I do—which is light, and angry gray motion—as Mitsuo reaches over me and yanks Will up by his hair.

Emi curls into a ball, throwing one arm over Jack. "Mama, Mama," she screams, in a voice so high and torn it isn't human. Her face is down, as if this will protect her. She doesn't know I'm there.

"Shush," I say as Will and the light disappear out the door. Her eyes open—they are wide and night-blind—but the pull of my son is too strong. I can hear his heels as they scramble and kick in the hallway, and I feel myself leaving. She doesn't want me to go.

I take the small hands she's raised to me and put them on Jack, whose tears have clogged any screams he might make. "Stay here. Don't move."

"Mama!" Emi's arms are up again and she is crying, but I'm backing to the door. I know she'll grab Jack once I'm gone and find whatever comfort there she can. In the hall, there is more light, and when I fling open the front door, the moon is so bright I can breathe it. I can hear Mitsuo cursing in the barn. And then, I hear the strap come down.

I followed them into the barn, Mariko, though I don't know what I planned to do. I ran there, letting my legs stretch under me, letting them stir the cool air until I believed, somehow, that I could stop the strap. The barn doors grew in front of me, but I didn't stop until they were three times taller than I was and I could see the warp in each one. If I had simply thought, I would have known I wasn't strong enough to change things, but I had to learn the hard way that fate had a way of snapping back.

The barn door was half open. Except for the silver block trailing off the edge of it and onto the dirt, there was no light inside, so I moved blind toward the sound of the strap until I could see it carve the air and flicker over Mitsuo's eyes. Will was coming into focus, too: he was thrown across the saddle rack, his naked buttocks high and gashed. His arms reached backward and held him on. It wasn't until he heard my voice that he started to cry.

"Stop it, I beg you. It's finished. Please."

"He's a disgrace," Mitsuo muttered.

"He's bleeding. We can punish him another way."

"Go away, woman. He needs to feel what he's done."

"Please," I said as another dark line sprung out of Will's skin, "he was only trying to help."

"Shut your mouth!"

I was giving him another target, so I didn't move when he dropped the strap and lunged toward me, but I didn't know how close his arm was until his elbow smashed my cheek. Red shot through my eyes and the straw rose around me. I dropped without breaking my fall.

"Go back to the kitchen!"

"Papa!"

Mitsuo was turning back to Will, so I sat up and tried to cover for my son. "You have to stop," I said. There was straw in my hands. I clenched and unclenched it to help myself think.

Will was hanging in the same place on the saddle rack. He hadn't risen or tried to dress. I wanted him to go and didn't understand why he wouldn't. My whole purpose had been to give him the chance to get out.

"Mama, please go back."

"You have to stop," I said again, but the words tumbled out without meaning. I knew we were maddening Mitsuo, trapping him between us. Will was fighting me and my attempts to save him. He was making me angry, too, so sure he could survive it alone.

As Mitsuo started toward me, I began crawling, thinking he would only try to strike me, and maybe I could get him out of the barn. But suddenly his hand snapped out and pulled me standing. I was being dragged toward Will and the saddle rack; I was relieved because I'd forgotten what he liked to do. Everything was so slow. I saw him shove Will off with his knee; I saw my son drop on his side. Will dragged himself forward, but he was caught in the straw and too weak to move. He'd crawled right below me, making the same kind of ball Emi had curled herself into. He might have felt my breath on his face as my husband flung me over the saddle rack, snagged at the waist, my head plunging almost against the floor.

My hair dropped over Will's eyes. My hands dangled. He was so close I could smell his breath, I could hear his whimpers as if they were mine. I was furious at Will for being there, for starting this and not going to school; furious that his eyes were open, they were right there, staring into mine. He could see my face sag and the blood rush to my head, but he wouldn't close them. He could see Mitsuo's legs as they lined up behind mine.

When I felt my skirt hit my head, I brought my right hand down over Will's eyes. It slid on his tears, tangled in his hair. I pulled back, snagging his ear in my fingers; my palm hit his nose. Will jerked his face toward the ground, burying his left eye in the straw, and suddenly the palm of my hand found the soft bowl of his eye socket and pressed into his right eye. His face was so slick, I thought I might have pinned his eyelid open, but I knew I couldn't risk the time to shift it when Mitsuo ripped my panties from the top down to my knees.

I rocked forward when Mitsuo probed me with his fingers, pointing himself into me but off to the side, where there was no way to enter except through the bone. One hand clutched my waist, then the other, as he tried to fit me on him like a shoe. I kept thinking he'd stop, that he'd give up or realize that his son was right there, but then he found what he was looking for and shoved himself in.

He tore me so hard I jerked against the saddle rack. Even as I tried to relax, the skin on my hip bones ripped on the rough wood. My hand skidded off Will's eye again, this time my thumb slipped into his mouth, but I recovered on Mitsuo's second thrust and managed to grab Will's hip with my other hand. He was limp; he rolled easily in my hands, as if he was stuck to them. My face was ringing. My hair swayed against Will and through the straw.

Mitsuo shoved himself in again, rocking me, scraping over and over until the pain was total and so unsurprising it may as well have been gone. I could feel everything else: the bones in Will's face beneath my hand, the toes of my shoes scraping the ground. I could taste blood on my tongue where I bit it when my head snapped back. I could hear the names Mitsuo called me. He wanted me to fight and feel the hurt, but I was too worried about what Will could hear. I could see Mitsuo's upside-down legs—shoed and bunched and jiggling—and I ground Will's cheek deeper into the filthy straw.

When it was over, I just hung there. I gave Mitsuo time to close his pants before I tried to lift my hand off Will. My fingers felt stiff. My hair against my face was filled with tears. Will stayed in place, in the same tight curl he'd been in since I swung down. Still naked from the waist. He didn't move until his father pulled him up with me and herded us both outside to the scrub trough. I tripped with him, the remnants of my panties dragging on one foot. I reached down to grab them and lost my balance; I remember seeing Will ahead of me and wanting to shove him, just for a second, as I fell. If he hadn't been out there, it could have been any other night, run together, forgotten. After all, it was on nights not unlike this one when Jack and Emi were conceived.

My fingers are numb, and fat as sausages in the icy water. There is plenty of light, for a change, from the moon. Will stands beside me, our shoulders touch to keep him up. I can feel Mitsuo's eyes on us, though I know the porch is empty. Will's hands clutch the brush, sawing at the vegetables until they are raw and their skin is broken. He jerks and fumbles like he's forgotten where he is.

The curtain parts in the children's window. Emi looks out at us from under the drape. Once again, she is watching me, observing my shame. I can't make out her face, only the crooked outline of her head up to her nose, as if she is balancing off the bed so she can see. In case Mitsuo is there with her, checking on our progress, I plunge more carrots in the trough, but I feel nothing from the house, no protest anywhere in the night. I wonder what she's doing there.

I wonder what she wants and what she sees.

Through Emi's eyes, I see my nose, dripping like water in the trough. My hair is ratted and hanging down; it covers my cheeks. But she doesn't see my ruined panties, or the mindless itching between my thighs. By now, she can no longer see me. I make sure of it: my tears are dry.

"Mama."

I turn toward my name, glad to pull away from Emi, and Will's face looks into mine for the first time since I closed his eyes. Deep red welts cut across his left cheek where it scraped into the straw. There are long, sweeping single lines in the hollow, and others that are bruised and braided on the rise of the bone. The eye that was on the bottom is swollen; the other is filled with questions, spilling with them just as Emi's are. I can't explain.

"Don't ever speak of this." It is my voice, ripped and frayed.

"Mama?"

"Don't disobey your father and it won't happen again."

It is just coincidence that Will chooses that point to sink to the ground. He does it slowly, a joint at a time, like he's being chopped at the root. He doesn't raise his hands to stop, and so he falls.

I caught him almost at my feet and lay him down in the slick grass where I could kneel beside him. "Shush," I whispered, but I was talking to me. I was the one who was crying, finding it hard to catch my breath. Will was still. He seemed to be sleeping. The bruises on his face were turned toward me, darkening as I watched them, accusing me. Without standing, I reached my hands into the trough and held them in the icy water past my wrists until they stung. Then I pulled them out slowly, like they were gifts, and brushed Will's bruises, his broken skin. I did it again and again, though I couldn't be sure if it was helping.

There was no other way to say I'm sorry.

20

MARIKO

SHIKATA GA NAI, 1990

"For God's sake, Mom! Can't you do one thing for me? Just put on a pair of shoes you can walk in?"

Emi was caught standing. Her ridiculous sling sandals glowed in a slice of light through the living room window. "One thing?" she asked.

Mari waited for the barrage. I've spent my life taking care of you, bailing you out of trouble—all the claims a mother who had been there for her daughter could make. Claims that would justify the anger Mari had carried inside her since her trip to Santa Anita, and release the power Jack had given her to yell. Instead, Emi remained silent, her face eclipsed, not bothering to point out that, at Mari's request, she had already changed into the only pair of pants she owned.

"It's important, Mom. Believe me," she said, softening. "There's pig shit out there."

Carefully, Emi picked up her right foot and flicked her sandal toward Mari. She repeated the motion with her left, her head dropping almost to her daughter's height. Mari watched the edge of light slide down her mother's legs as she moved them, then flash on her bare, twisted feet and fall into an empty parallelogram on the living room floor.

"I don't know what makes you think I can't handle a little pig shit," Emi said as she scooped up the shoes and headed toward her bedroom.

Mari wondered if the tone in her mother's voice was meant to be a warning. After all, they *were* only going for a walk in the backyard. On her way back from California, Mari had decided to ignore Roger's earlier advice about confronting her mother in public; she knew how easy it was for Emi to outwait her. She needed to find a place where she couldn't retreat, where she wouldn't betray herself by protecting her mother. That was when she remembered the waterfall in the ravine that ran behind her childhood home.

It wasn't a fall as much as a trickle, but the tumble of rocks had always been Mari's own. It was tucked away so that, unless you were looking closely enough to realize that you were seeing the tops of trees, and not bushes, you could walk right by. When Mari was a teenager, she used to sit on the warm, flat stones that were so abundant there and cry as she watched the frogs and tadpoles twitch in the thick pool below. It was where she had brought her fear, her anger and heartbreak—and all the other emotions she didn't dare exhibit at home.

Emi reappeared wearing flat canvas loafers and followed Mari outside easily enough. It was a perfect day to be outdoors. Bright clouds bulged high above them; the grass got deeper as they walked down the hill, nests of it crackling around their feet. The air was thick with forest smells and, from so far away that it must have been Mari's imagination, ocean spray. With each step, Mari felt lighter, as if she were less in her body and more a part of the place. When they turned the corner, she stopped to feel the differences. She had been afraid everything would be smaller, dingier, even littered, but it felt the same. Her feet still knew the path.

"Sit," Mari said when they reached the pool. She tried not to notice how fragile her mother looked as she perched herself, legs braced, on the largest, flattest stone.

"Is it Roger?" Emi asked after waiting patiently through Mari's thoughts.

Mari shook her head. "It's Eric. I flew to California to see him."

She had started with a topic sentence, Mari noticed, surprised at how easy it was to meet her mother's eyes.

"Oh." Emi seemed to nod. "Is that all?"

"What do you mean, is that *all*?"

"You scared me." Emi paused; she wasn't looking at Mari. "I was afraid you had cancer. So many people do."

"Don't avoid me. I know he's my brother. Why didn't you tell me?"

"You never asked."

Mari opened her mouth, then closed it, surprised to realize that what Emi said was true. She had dreamt the question; had translated each word so many times that it meant nothing with the others; she had lived inside it, smothered it, thrown it into the air.

But she had been unable to ask it.

"Tell me what happened."

Emi rubbed the lichen on the surface of the stone into a gray powder. A series of openings and excuses passed over her eyes. She seemed to be waiting for Mari to withdraw her request. When she didn't, Emi said, "It's been a long time."

"But you remember."

At last, Mari got a reaction. Emi seemed annoyed that Mari wasn't going along. "Sometimes, Mari, once you've made a choice—and made it public—you simply don't have the room to change your mind."

It was a cryptic statement, but Mari thought she understood what her mother was referring to. "The orphanage," she said, more to herself than to Emi. The law must have made it impossible for her mother to reclaim Eric once she had given him away. But that didn't explain why she wouldn't have taken Eric gladly once Mama adopted him and returned him to the family. Of course, Emi didn't know Jack told Mari about Mama's rescue. She searched for an appropriate tone. "You could ask for help, though."

"Yes. You could ask." Emi kept her words hypothetical, as if it was too painful for her to return herself to that time. Still, Mari heard just the slightest, misplaced emphasis—on the word *ask*, instead of *could*.

"Where was everyone else?" She pressed. "Your parents, brothers?"

Emi considered her for so long. Was she thinking about all the suffering her stubborn refusal to ask her family for help had caused? Mari wondered. Or was she simply trying to decide, yet again, what Mari did or didn't need to know?

"Things were different in those days," Emi said finally. "Your reputation was everything, especially if you were Japanese. You wouldn't understand."

Then she said, "It killed my brother."

It was too big a leap for Mari. "What did?"

"The war. Will was the oldest. My parents never recovered from it."

"You never talk about him. Were you close?"

"I don't?" Emi looked surprised. "There's so much to say." She paused, as if thinking about Mari's question. "Were we close? No. But he must have been a good man—just barely a man—until the FBI got him. They started arresting people after Pearl Harbor, because they owned a boat, say, or taught Japanese. We had already burned everything—letters, birth certificates, even Mama's family photos—but they came anyway and took Will away. Of course, there was no evidence, nothing to hold him on, but that wasn't the point. Will snapped. He couldn't bear the shame, I guess. He could never quite believe that it didn't belong to him, even after they let him go."

Mari wondered at the phrase "must have been." Emi said it

almost as if she hadn't known her brother before the war. She waited for her mother to tie the stories together. When she didn't, Mari prodded her. "What about my father? Was he arrested, too?"

Emi frowned. "Your father? George is your father."

"Not by blood."

"Blood. Lord. I hope he never hears you say that. It would kill him if he thought—"

"Mom, stop it. You know I love him more than anything. That's not why I'm asking."

"Well, why are you asking?"

Mari stared at her mother's face. Did it matter who her father was? She wasn't going to look for him, too; she had no desire to replace George with someone else. Of all her mother's secrets, her father's identity was the least important. But she needed to ask a question that couldn't be avoided. She wanted to hold on to a single tangible fact.

In reply, Mari shoved a stack of pictures she had taken of Jack into Emi's hands. The ones in the grandstand were shaded and hard to see; the better ones were near the fence on the stretch of tarmac that butted almost up against the track. Mari had pleaded to get Jack to take off his sunglasses, but those snapshots were the worst. She must have been distracted when she took them. She'd caught just a slice of his face in the crowd.

"You're going too fast." Mari took the pictures from Emi's hands and parceled them out, forcing her mother to hold each one until she was satisfied.

"That's Jack," Emi said, lifting one closer to her face. "I haven't seen him in years. He looks just like Papa. So old. God, I must, too." When she finished, she asked, "How is he?"

"You ruined his life."

Mari said it because it was true, but it didn't generate the remorse she was hoping for.

"*I* ruined his life?" Emi asked with some heat. For a moment Mari thought she'd found the key, that her mother couldn't resist the truth anymore. Then Emi asked, "What do you want, Mari?

Do you want me to cry? To claim I was the victim? Would that make me a better person in your eyes?"

Mari flinched. A better person was exactly what she wanted. "I want to know the story."

"You know the story. Why are you pretending this is all so new to you?"

Mari didn't answer, refusing to let her chance encounter with her birth certificate make her feel guilty.

"I didn't hide Eric from you. It's not as if you never met him."

"You and Roger, both," Mari said, taking the offensive. "I can't believe you. I was a baby in the camps. I must have been, what, two? Three? How could I have known he was my brother?"

Emi waved impatiently. "I mean when you were kids."

"Kids?"

"The summer we went to Los Angeles. You must have been, God, seven maybe? Or eight. My father died, and I took you to the funeral. I dropped you and Eric off at the cinema together after the ceremony. How could you forget that? It was your first picture show."

Mari stared past her mother. The image of the red dress returned to her. The memory had been real.

"No," she said, but the word was a reflex. Something to keep her mother from speaking. Eric must have been about ten, she remembered. His hair had been slicked back, and his eyes had just begun to float over his newly adolescent cheeks. She saw him clearly: awkward, admiring her. He had treated her to a soda before the show and had refused to take the money Emi had given her, though she must have had more than he. She could see it all now; she could hear him speaking.

It was the memory of his hand in hers that had almost sent Mari off the road that day. It was he who had made her feel so very loved.

"Yes," Emi corrected. "And then you came home and tore the house apart looking for your birth certificate. Don't you remember?"

"Oh, God." Mari was reeling. She must have known Eric was

her brother then, or at least suspected. And he must have known she knew, because he would have been the one to tell her. The truth Mari had been searching for was that she had sided with her mother and left him. What was worse, she had aborted her own baby years later, despite the fact that she had lived her life in the echo of a missing child.

"Mari."

Mari heard a whimper, something small, needing help. She had wandered along the stream without realizing it, but her mother was still with her; if she stretched out ten arms, they might be able to touch. Emi's feet were splayed and braced, as if they couldn't stand in flat shoes. She was an old woman, with flat breasts to her ribs and a dumpy back side. She was a chameleon, just as Mari was; it was impossible to see the selfishness that ate up so many lives.

Mari waited for her mother's triumphant conclusion. But Emi didn't seem to feel the need to assign her the blame.

"Mom?" Mari asked, "please tell me what happened."

"Come here," Emi said, making a motion back toward the waterfall. "Sit."

Mari couldn't move. Instead she dropped where she was, too ashamed to look at her mother. She could feel the grass beside her give when Emi sat down. The Emi that Jack described would already have left her, Mari realized. She tipped her head, trying unsuccessfully to find shapes in the clouds as she waited for her mother's words.

"Did I ever tell you about the piano?" Emi asked once she was settled.

"The one at home?"

"No, this one was my father's. He studied music in Japan."

Mari's mother plucked a blade of grass from the thick *kikuyu* blanket and put the soft, barely green stem in her mouth. "It's a long story, from before you were born."

"I was born—"

"At the racetrack. At Santa Anita, where we were interned."

That, at least, was a fact; the door between them was open at last. Mari waited for more details about her birth, but Emi had something else on her mind.

"It was 1942," she began, "shortly after they announced the evacuation. We were living in Los Angeles, and we were finally well enough off to own a few things. Papa had just bought the piano and was starting to teach himself music again. I think it was probably the best time in my parents' lives."

Emi sank back, letting her gray hair float on the surface of the grass. "Anyway, we couldn't take the piano to camp. We couldn't take much of anything, so we held a clearance sale like you wouldn't believe. We got offers on the piano immediately, which is amazing when I think about it now, but Mama wouldn't bargain. She figured that pianos weren't run-of-the-mill items, and this one was only a couple of months old."

"You couldn't store it?"

"No. We had to get rid of everything. And people knew we had to sell."

Her mother squinted under a protecting hand, then sat up. "As I was saying, on the second day a man with red hair came by and he really wanted that piano. Papa let him play it for a while. A Mozart piece, I don't know which one, but every once in a while I hear it and I'm back there, listening and packing, until all that's left is the man and the piano.

"Anyway, he offered the full amount—I think it was one hundred dollars. He said he needed to find a truck to move it. He didn't pay of course because he was afraid we'd sell it out from under him, and he'd never get his money back, since we'd be 'safely' away in camp."

"So your father promised to hold it?"

"Your grandmother did. She was the one in charge."

"Please tell me he came back."

Her mother smiled sadly and into the distance. "Not the next day, or the next. Then, the day before we were supposed to leave, a couple showed up, and *they* wanted the piano. Mama said it wasn't for sale. I was in my room—I spent a lot of my time there in those days—and when I heard that I came to the top of the stairs, ready to go down and sell it myself. Mama was standing in the middle of our empty living room. This tiny woman. The man wasn't bargaining, he was waving cash right in her face, but she still shook her head. She was always so proud. So true to her word. I tell you, I couldn't speak."

"And the guy with the red hair never came back, did he?"

"No, he came back. About an hour before we had to report to the church. He and two friends, and the truck he said he needed. He gave Mama five dollars, said the money was a favor. He could easily wait and take the piano for free once we'd gone."

"Oh, God." Mari could see it all. Her mother, her grandmother, the five dollars, and the man with red hair and straw-colored eyes. They were suspended, standing in a driveway, and Mari was unable to make them move. Her grandfather, uncles, even Eric were missing from the story, but Mari had a feeling that their absence was part of her mother's message. "I would have taken an ax to it."

"I thought of that. But we needed the money."

The story was still close enough to hurt her mother, but it seemed important to Emi that Mari understand. The way she held herself, and the way she spoke, were so unguarded. Mari was ashamed to realize that Emi's candor wasn't as unfamiliar as she would have thought.

"You know," she said, "my mother had a saying. '*Shikata ga nai.*' She used it a lot, especially during the war. It means, 'It can't be helped.'"

Emi paused, and Mari used the time to sound out the unfamiliar words in her head. Then her mother looked up, surprised and pained. "*Shikata ga nai*," Emi repeated. "You know, I never believed her."

After trying all afternoon to read the clouds, the piano was suddenly above Mari's head. Right over the tallest tree. It was a baby grand, just like theirs, with the top propped open concert-style and a low, uneven bench in front of it. It was a sign, Mari realized, and now she had to decipher it. She looked for her grandmother, a tiny woman in her early fifties, standing in the sky as resolutely as she stood against the back of Mari's eyelids. She looked for Emi, too, a young girl frozen in the doorway of the room that was her sanctuary, watching her own mother do what she thought was right, even at the expense of the family. The two women didn't say a word to each other, but together, they were trying to tell Mari something. About the war, perhaps, about the family.

The only truth she was going to hear was in the story, Mari realized. It was all either one of them could afford to bear.

21

JACK

TUMBLE AND FALL, 1990

Jack can't breathe. Tequila aloft, he drops into his La-Z-Boy, thinking he's got to stop moving, and thinking about his wife, Kay. His glass is high, so he can examine it without lowering his head. None of that straw-colored shit for him, that peppery Cuervo. He discovered this stuff years ago, the time he and some buddies decided they needed to cross a border—any border. A sure sign they were drunk. They hauled ass, made it in three and a half hours on the freeway, and that's where he found it. *Anejo*. Honey-heavy. A scalding mouth of gold.

Like Kay, he thinks. Just like her. He should never have fallen in love with her—she was Japanese on the outside, but different as a *hakujin* under her skin. A New Yorker, a true American. He'd known she was young, but thought she was like him and just rebelling.

He never should've followed her lead.

It was at Taro's house, not too long after the end of the war, that Jack met Kay. She was so out of place. She was wearing yellow, bright stop-sign yellow—he saw it the minute he walked in. She was in conversation, leaning forward to hear over some terrible music with a dragging "do-do-do" harmony that no one could actually dance to, and Jack was staring at her because yellow on a Japanese woman was so rude. Then she raised her head and caught him as she glanced at the closing door. Her skin was like cream, completely pure, which was the reason for the dress and which made it even ruder. Her hair was twisted up, loose and trembling and not at all stylish. It was almost bedroomy, but very sleek. Like oil. Her eyes, too, like oil. She was watching him, all black and white, all eyes, all yellow—she looked like the *tennyo* in his mother's stories. The angel wives. The thought made him blush. He looked away, and there were his friends, drinking and fiddling with cards—he moved into the shelter of their game. It wasn't until he'd won his first hand of five-card draw that he'd had the courage. Then he'd asked his host, casually, "That girl over there, who the hell is she?"

Jack rubs his face and the air in his apartment thins. He puts his asthma inhaler down and pushes back against the hollow of the chair. His feet kick up, bouncing a little, in socks, on the beaten velour footrest. And he hears Kay say, "Well, you can waste your own evening if you want to, but I won't let you waste mine." They were her first words to him, slid together like a poem, delivered from behind him on that night at Taro's house. Something about her voice was slippery. It had no home, no place somehow—it was hollow. And her words, what words she chose. Jack didn't know what in hell she was talking about.

He was sitting with two buddies, three if he counted Taro. There were five chairs—he'd dragged the extra one from the kitchen so he could rest his worse leg on its plastic seat. He wanted to drop it, so maybe she wouldn't notice, but that would've meant grabbing it with his hands to keep his knee straight, and even more attention. He checked the other guys' faces to see who she was talking to. They were all looking at him. They'd been talking about something, but Jack couldn't hear a single word in his mind except hers. There was nothing to keep him from turning around.

Kay tucked her head, like she wanted to see him from under her eyelashes. This close, her lips were full and uncolored—they arched like a bird's wings, one side higher than the other. Her mouth was completely lopsided. A beauty mark hovered over the highest point of her highest lip, the first thing to lift when she smiled.

"Excuse me?" he asked.

Kay wrapped her arms in front of her, her top hand circling a glass. "You know what I mean."

She'd seen him tracing her lips. But he had her, she'd chased him down in front of her cousin, and he suddenly thought he could do anything. "Miss," he said, playing to his friends, "I don't even know what you said."

The guys began to smile then, but they didn't crack up until she tilted her tiny chin and said, "Fine. I've only got three more days here, so if you want to ask me on a date, you'd better do it now." Then they exploded, even Taro, who was acting like she had nothing to do with him. Kay flushed. Then, as Jack smiled and tried not to pick a side, she slipped back across the room. In response to their laughter, or maybe because a good tune came on, someone turned up the phonograph. Kay was swept into a dance.

"Hey Jack, she likes you, too."

"You better watch it, Jack, she's a dancer."

"Taro better watch it. If I was you, Taro, I wouldn't let that one out of the house."

Jack let his friends' voices drift in the splashing piano keys around him as he watched Kay dance. Nothing forward, but she was graceful. Her heels were high. He could see the curling muscles on her calves flicker in and out of shadow as she moved.

He wanted to get up, cut in, but the guys were right. He couldn't dance. He'd sent her away, and now he had no excuse to approach her. Not that she'd welcome him. He didn't know the dance. He didn't know the music either. The last music he could remember, he'd heard in camp.

"Jack, you in?" Taro asked, dealing.

"Yeah." He counted the cards snapping behind him as he took a last look. The guy with Kay swung her around. Not too flashy, but the other couples were giving them room. Girls were frowning—Jack saw one touch the clean curl on the back of her neck as she watched Kay's hair bounce and strain against the magic that held it into place. Again, he willed, do it again. He wanted to see Kay's hair tumble, but it was stronger than that—deceptive. The count on the table was five, and he heard it clearly, calling him away from Kay, so he turned and joined the game.

"Ante up," Taro said.

"All right, all right," Jack said. He had nothing. Not even a pair. "Give me three."

"Hang on, Jack. Jeez. I'm not even in yet."

He could fill her drink, Jack thought. The glass in her hand had been empty. Or he could just apologize. For the guys laughing, he didn't mean to make fun of her. She was alone, leaning on the wall with one shoe flat against it like she was about to push off, her hands crossed behind her. He couldn't believe she was comfortable there. And—he felt a touch of Mama when he thought this—he couldn't believe she was marking up someone else's wall.

"I have nothing," he said.

"What a way to bluff, Jack."

"No, I really got nothing. I'm out." Jack eased his leg off the chair and stood. The music was over. He could hear someone requesting the Clovers.

"Good luck, lover boy."

"Get your own life," Jack said. "I gotta take a piss."

The heavy prosthetic heel on Jack's left shoe rapped the floor as he walked toward Kay. Any guy in the room would love a dance, he thought, just as long as their mothers and girlfriends didn't find out. She was that kind of girl—not loose, but the kind that didn't fit, the kind that made good girls secure their own hair when it was hers that was threatening to fall. She knew things, too, like how to get a guy to come to her without looking at him, but she didn't scare Jack. He wouldn't get too close, or ask for things. Besides, she was a visitor. She'd leave.

When he reached her, Jack saw the full bird in flight as Kay gave him a real smile. "I'm sorry," he said. "Kay, isn't it? The guys have no manners."

She cocked her perfectly oval face, completely unembarrassed. "See? I was right. You know my name. You *were* staring at me when you walked in."

"Oh, I wouldn't—I was just surprised. You were someone I didn't know."

"You know everyone here?"

"I—no. I stared at them all, though."

She chuckled and handed him her glass. "It was only soda water," she said. "That *is* why you came over?"

There are secrets, Jack knows, so many of them. Weak ones that come from weakness. Like with Eric, sitting over dinner—all subjects are closed, there's nowhere to get in. Especially when it comes to Mariko, what she said when she appeared. When Jack brought it up the first time, he didn't tell Eric his sister had wanted to see him. He was afraid, maybe stupid. But he couldn't bear to lose Eric, too.

Eric didn't want to talk about Mariko. Instead he put the brussels sprouts in Jack's hands and said, "You know who I was thinking of, speaking of ghosts from the past? Kay. Whatever happened to her?"

Talia looked up when she heard the question—she was far too interested in heartstrings. "She's in New York I think," Jack said. He passed the dish with his fingers crossed. Talia had a rule, everyone ate everything. Even the folded little eyeballs, the green Jell-O with cream cheese. Both of them were somebody's favorite. He couldn't imagine whose.

"Remember the time she made roast beef for Mama?"

"Who did, Kay?" Talia asked. "I've never heard this story."

"It was just after Jack proposed. She wanted to make Mama dinner because Mama had made her a dinner, and I don't know how it happened exactly. Jack, couldn't she cook Japanese?"

"Christ, I don't know." But he did. He remembered watching her lift the roast out of the oven. Her face was pink from the heat, her apron pink from her hands. He'd asked what she was doing, and she thought he was offering his help. She was so pleased at that moment—roast beef was her specialty.

For his mother, she told him, nothing but her best.

He let it go, and she stayed happy. By then, it was far too late to warn her. Too big a problem to know where to begin.

"I thought Mama was going to die right there," Eric said. "Big hunk of red meat. Bleeding and everything."

"She ate it though."

And Mama's face, completely still when she saw it coming. He sliced it thin, for her, so thin she could pretend it wasn't real. She covered it in mashed potatoes, and Kay was too content to understand.

"At least she waited until Kay left before she started yelling, 'She's not Japanese, she's not Japanese!'"

"You didn't help much, either."

"Well, I liked Kay's food. I liked Kay, too, for that matter."

It was all so clear. Mama telling Jack he needed a real Japanese girl, Eric injecting himself into the fight. He was such a brat in those days, not even ten and still telling Mama he was going to marry a white girl. That Japanese girls were dull. Jack could see the thick red and blue stripes on Eric's shirt, the white collar around his skinny neck. The tension shifted, and it was between them—Eric and Mama—like it always was. Jack could've walked away. He wanted to ask Eric now why he used to jump in like that to take the heat, but he was afraid of the look he would get. The sizing up.

"So what is she doing now?" Talia asked.

"What?"

"Kay. What's she doing in New York?" She looked innocent, like she thought Jack and Kay sent each other birthday cards.

"I don't know. I don't hear from her."

"But she was your wife."

"Only for a year," Eric pointed out. "In the scheme of things, she wasn't much."

"Oh," Talia said. Then, "I didn't mean to pry."

But it was strange Kay came up. Jack had been thinking about her himself. Wondering how she was doing. He wanted to tell her about Mariko's return, for some reason he thought she'd know what he should do. He thought of calling the old number he had, but there was no point in it now. He hadn't written when Eric got married, when any of the boys were born. He hadn't even written when Mama died—he had just waited, watched the church door.

Again with the inhaler. Jack lies on his recliner, trying to use no oxygen, let the attack pass. There's no sound around him—everything's in his body and his head. His nose is getting smaller. His chest so huge. He could suck forever on that thin thread of air.

He still remembers the night he said they could move. It was an odd moment even then, after dinner but before bedtime, and for some reason he was teaching Kay to drink tequila. Like the Mexicans. They were in their room, sitting on the floor. Kay was leaning on the bed, her legs parted and sprawled in front of her, her dress slid halfway down her thighs. He'd sent her downstairs for everything—glasses, lime, salt—and now she claimed she was too tired to climb onto the bed. So they were sitting there, tequila bottle between them. Between her legs. Her feet were bare.

Kay lapped the base of her thumb. "We have to move, Jack. We have to live on our own."

"We can't. Not with Papa. It's too complicated."

"It's not complicated. It's necessary."

"Name one good reason, then."

"We could, you know, have some privacy."

"We're private now."

"Jack. There's a million reasons."

"Then name a million." He was smiling. He wasn't even annoyed.

"I'd have to write them down," Kay said. Her hand had dropped so her mouth was clearly exposed. "We have paper?"

He reached for a stray piece on the desk behind him, knocking a pencil onto the floor. It rolled toward Kay, and she stretched her leg straight and grabbed it between two of her toes.

"We could get Papa a nurse," she said, bending her knee to bring the pencil to her hand.

"You grabbed that with your foot!"

"I'm lazy."

"I've never seen that. How'd you do it?"

"With my toes. You've never seen anyone use their toes?"

"I thought only monkeys could do that."

Kay looked at him, unsure whether to be offended. "My mother does it. I thought it was a Japanese thing."

Jack laughed. "You're real Japanesey," he said. "A real *ryosai kenbo*."

"And what's that supposed to mean?"

"I don't know. Good wife, I think. Wise mother."

"There's a reason right there. I want to be a mother."

"Now?"

"We can get him a nurse. We can come for dinner Sundays. We can put him in a home."

"We can't put him in a home."

"We can't keep him here like he's a baby. He's getting worse every day. He sucks his thumb, Jack. He puts it in his mouth every time he sees me and follows me around the house. It's creepy."

"You're creepy."

"I'm serious. It's like I'm his mother or something. And he wants to feed."

"You're making that up."

"I'm not, Jack. I swear." But she was smiling as she moved

toward him, her skirt falling to the floor. "He needs a nurse," she repeated, modest now. Her face hovered.

Kay won him over then. In their new bed. She slipped around and under him like she needed to touch every part. She rubbed her feet along his legs, stroked his arms. And when they were done making love, she lay in bed and wiggled her toes. Like she was trying to type. The first time he'd asked her, "What the hell are you doing now?"

"Hmm?" She lifted her head for a hint and her toes stopped.

Jack laughed, uncomfortable with spelling it out. "What were you doing with your toes?"

"Silly. I'm not doing anything."

"You were."

"Silly Jack," Kay said, sweeping her hair over his chest. "Turn off the light." She curled against him in the dark, one leg draped over his.

He could feel her toes nudging his calf. "There. You're doing it again. You're trying to pinch me, aren't you?"

"What are you talking about?"

They'd both scrambled up. Jack could see a trace of Kay's face, propped on her elbows.

"You were pinching me with your toes. You were doing this." Jack reached out and scissored his toes uselessly against her leg.

"Oh, that." She started to giggle.

"What do you mean, 'oh that'?" She was laughing, so he had to smile along with her. "You're crazy, you know."

"No, I'm not. I was just singing."

"You were singing? You were trying to pinch me. You were singing with your toes?" She was still laughing. "What were you singing?"

"A jingle."

"Like on television? You were lying in bed singing a commercial with your toes? Why? What does that mean?"

"It means I had a, you know. You know."

"Jesus, Kay."

"It means I'm happy, Jack."

He forgot himself, that's what it was. How he grew up. With a mother who planted, picked, pruned, hoed, cleaned, and cooked—with parents who, well, maybe love wasn't important. They did their best, followed Papa's lead. That's all anyone could do.

And in the end, Jack wanted to believe Papa was lucid, though he never knew what went through his father's mind. Sure it was crazy, to have broken the mirror. But Jack could see him standing there, looking into it. There must've been something in the image that he didn't want to see.

Eric had Papa locked in his room that day. Safe, as he always was. They'd never hired the nurse. Eric did such a good job, they didn't even try. He took care of the hygiene like a nurse, but he played with Papa, too. Took him outside. And the old man responded sometimes, because Eric was family. Familiar. He'd say things, sometimes, that almost made sense.

Jack and Kay were almost comfortable in their new apartment. Kay was sewing curtains, she'd drape the colors all over the living room when he came home. That night they were going to Mama's for supper, but Kay was out during the day, shopping for bedspreads, when Papa escaped from his room and carried his lamp into the bathroom. He must have picked the lock, and for some reason, Eric wasn't there to stop him. The kid must have run out to get something—Jack was sure there was a reason. An errand probably, it wasn't like Eric to leave him.

It was just bad timing, bad luck.

Papa left his locked room, walked down the hall to the bathroom, and shattered the mirror. Why he would do that, Jack still doesn't know. Jack was at work when Papa chose a long shard and climbed into the bathtub, tucking himself in on all sides. They said he held the glass just right. It didn't even cut his hands. It was maybe ten inches, the shard—the end sticking out of his chest was longer than Jack's fingers. There was no blood anywhere on the floor.

By some miracle, Eric was still gone—it was Mama who found the old man dead. It was her voice, too, that found Jack at his desk, on his way home, and asked him to pull the glass spike out.

It was an honorable way to die, Mama said. It wiped his life clean. But after the coroner left, Jack recognized her unfinished gestures. She shrank, hid on the couch. She didn't cry. Jack knew the signs, the oblivion, from the war. He knew Kay's, too, each one of them the next day when he finally returned. Blind to her own tears as she searched his face, looking for something just out of her vision. Her head darted, as if she needed to cross the highway, but cars kept getting in the way. She needed to find one straight shot, so she could take it. But there was nothing left in him to see.

Kay had called Mama's house the night before, so there was nothing to explain. They both knew he was moving back home. He wanted to speak anyway, wanted to sink into her, have her hold him—though he knew he'd be caught then, torn between her and his mother, neither of them asking for him but both wanting so much. It was tough to pull himself around like he did—he almost gave in more than once. Kay was wonderful, though. She followed him from room to room, close enough to touch, never trying to change his mind. Watched as he fell in and out of sleep. There was food—she gave it to him. She sat with him, helped him pack.

It doesn't even bounce on the floor, the inhaler. It thuds, because it's useless, no longer worth his energy. Jack's hand, on the armrest, is too heavy and too far from the rest of him. Jack's lungs are useless, too—nothing in, nothing out. He has to call someone. He will. For help. But the attack will break. Soon—it's at its peak. And there's something he likes now, something he's felt before. Not asthma. He wants to keep it.

It's that first night with Kay.

Jack is at Taro's again, handing Kay a drink. She is standing alone.

The glass goes up. And she wraps her hand right over his. In front of everyone. She doesn't care. She holds him there, she holds his breath—and he's sure she does it because she knows she'll disappear. She holds him dizzy, trapped between the icy glass and her fine warm hand. Her face turned, her eyes so fragile he can believe for a moment he is supporting her.

He doesn't want her to go.

Jack stares at the curve of her neck, the swell of her collarbone, and her hair trembling—about to tumble. He doesn't want her to go. Her hand burns, her fingers worse than the glass. He is falling, into a clear space, and he can hear someone say, "This is it." Someone somewhere. That's when he slips the glass out of their hands and sets it down. He keeps her hand in his, where it will always be. Her hair is like oil.

"Will you dance with me?" he asks, ready now after so many long years. She will nod—he knows it—so he keeps his eyes on her hair. Waiting. He is waiting.

Expecting, any minute, to see it tumble and fall.

22

ERIC

CLUES, 1990

"Hey, hey." Nudging Talia for more popcorn, Eric whispered, "This is it. The showdown."

"Yeah, I figured." She hooked her legs over the arm of the sofa, popping the bowl toward him with her belly. The half-human head growled, "*You should get out of here now*" as the mechanical fingers loaded the gun. The face, helmetless, floated in shades of gray, warning them. "Is he going to die?"

"You gotta watch. I'm not going to tell you."

"God, you really did love this movie."

"It's going to be a classic. I tell you—"

The phone in the kitchen cut in between them.

"*Hey, we're partners*," the woman on the screen said.

"We should probably answer that."

"No. Turn it up."

"Come on, Eric. What if it's important?"

"They'll leave a message." Eric grabbed the zapper. "*Get the car*," the deep television voice told them. Sharp blue eyes stared over the balcony at the bad guys. Gun cocked over the heart.

"Just put it on pause. Come on, Eric, it's after midnight. What if it's one of the boys?"

"All right, all right. We should go out from now on." Eric extended his arm, and the screen froze beneath the voice floating out of their answering machine. White static lapped at the top of the frame, pulling the eerie head out of shape.

"—McNeil. Hawthorne Police Department," the voice in the kitchen was saying. "I'm trying to reach Mr. Eric Yoshiko."

Shit, Eric thought. Cops. His hand dropped. The zapper clattered. His name in the cop's mouth was so familiar, all dislocated vowels and a "Mister" with no person behind the sound. The television shrank as the sick relief of being caught swept through Eric like a ghost. He used to raise his arms when he heard his name, not drop them. Put them up against walls, throw them over the hoods of cars. He thought, This is what being a parent is, dropping everything and hearing it echo in slow time. Talia had said it was the kids. She was past him and gone now—she'd picked up the phone. She'd left him alone, scanning the room for what had been safe: a clean sofa, turquoise chairs, a cactus. Big windows that Talia liked to open for air. On the screen, the white head and blue eyes crackled. It was just him and the eyes, watching him, waiting to move. Eric itched to press the forward button, or turn things back, but he was moving, himself, toward the phone.

When Eric finally got Jack's front door open, the air inside rushed them. Three whole days, that's what the air said as it clogged their mouths and noses, then went by. The room was almost cold. Eric stepped into dark; even when Talia flipped the light switch on, the dark lingered on Jack's walls, coloring the cracks, refusing to recede completely. There was a bruise on the frosted overhead shade where one of the bulbs had blown, and it was talking to him, too, asking how Eric could have let the man die and then lie there for three goddamned miserable days.

Eric didn't want to think about the smell. Old people, closed rooms—they both had an odor that could pass for this one. He was welcome to view the body, the McNeil cop had said, perhaps in the morning. They wanted him to claim it. It had already been identified.

"Fuckers don't even break the news face-to-face," Eric muttered. There was a buzzing sound somewhere. He had been so desperate to come here that he was surprised there was nothing to do.

"Well, what do you expect? You were screaming about your citizen's right to know what the hell was going on," Talia said. The words were angry, but her hand was not, and it reached up to Eric's shoulder and brushed his arm down over his elbow to his wrist. Her fingers joined his; they shifted to fit. Neither Eric nor Talia was ready to move from the spot they'd claimed in the center of Jack's living room. "He asked us to come to the station."

"Why should we have to haul our asses to their station? They should have sent a car."

"And what if we weren't home, Eric?"

"Then they could have waited."

He could hear how petulant he sounded, but he wasn't prepared. Not at one in the morning. He hadn't been able to find the car keys in his pocket, didn't think to leave a note for when the boys came home. Talia drove, and Eric let the trip to Jack's apartment slur into light outside his curving window. Red and green down some of the side streets, neon signs. It was soothing, watching them fall like stars. It was Talia's face driving, her muffled sighs, he couldn't bear.

Even Jack's door gave Eric trouble. It wouldn't take his key at first. Then the smell and the cold. It was the super's fault, Eric thought, the asshole. It took the guy two weeks to fix Jack's fucking stove when he was calling every day, but only minutes to turn off the heat when he was dead.

Talia slipped her hand out of Eric's and shoved it into the pocket of her cardigan sweater. The sofa was on her side of the room. If she lifted her foot, she could kick the coffee table. Eric went with the idea. If he stretched his arms, he could scrape his knuckles on the walls. The wall on one side, bookshelf on the other. He'd closed his eyes; open, the walls danced farther away. Still, the place was too small to have a dining room. Just a pass-through to the kitchen. A counter with stools.

Talia pushed herself toward the coffee table, away from Eric and the center. He felt her leave more clearly than he saw it. She stood, her purse still hanging on her shoulder, staring at Jack's magazines. He'd kept them in drifts, in an order he understood, in case someone needed an article, and Talia stacked them every time she visited. He always thanked her and joked about needing a wife. She bent now, and her purse swung—missing the table, hitting the air. She picked up a copy of *Time*.

"What are you doing?"

"I don't know. Cleaning, I guess." The magazine slipped from her fingers as Talia turned. She ran her hand through her hair, then stopped halfway and hung on. Exposed, the side of her face was all glassy slopes and curves. "I don't know."

"Why the hell does it need to be clean? The super's seen it dirty. So has Bill whatever-the-hell-his-name-is who got him to open the door. And the police, they've all seen it. They've all been here."

Talia kept on holding. She looked like she could leave. "You're a real bastard sometimes. You know that?"

"Yeah." He moved his eyes to the television, too wounded to keep himself under control. The top and the knobs were covered in dust. Jack had left a glass on one of those bona fide TV dinner trays, something from the 1960s set up next to his favorite chair. The tray was dull green and chipping, the glass marked on the bottom with a brown glaze. Eric wondered if it was stuck there, dried and forgotten, or if he could lift it in his hand. "So what else is new?" he asked.

Eric focused on the chair while Talia unzipped her purse and began sifting through it. For aspirin, he thought; he knew he gave her headaches. This time, though, she wasn't the only one. He couldn't even breathe.

Maybe it was the shock, Eric thought, sitting in Jack's chair. He put his feet on the little kick that jumped out, found himself pointed at the television, and closed his eyes. He tried to feel what Jack felt, but it wasn't what Eric liked, sinking so deep in a chair that he might disappear at any moment. The hush of velour on his neck soothed him until he thought of Jack's neck and couldn't remember exactly how long his uncle's hair was. An image came, of walking into the morgue and hearing a guy say, "Here he is, identify him from the back." He tried to think of Jack's shoulders, whether they were hunched or still tall. He pushed his own against the fraying chair, looking for a match from side to side and reminding himself that they hadn't been close. Especially not when Eric was a kid. In fact, Jack was kind of an asshole most of the time, so why did it matter if Eric didn't know him from the back?

Talia walked by without offering aspirin. He listened to her step but got hung up waiting when she reached the deep carpet in the hall. It was like she disappeared until he heard her fading sigh. Eric felt it quiver out of his gut.

He didn't know Jack, not until after the divorce, and then he hadn't wanted to know him. Jack had been the kind of guy you had to catch in passing, always yanking on his bad leg so he could get going and be gone. Once Kay left, though, he was back—everywhere and open—if you reached out and touched him, you could grab his insides. Eric hadn't been able to bear it; he'd thought of Jack as an octopus, all those tentacles waiting to take hold. It wasn't just the company he was trying to avoid, it was the responsibility—knowing he was the one who had inadvertently forced Jack home, and that Jack didn't know what he'd done. Eric knew, even then, that he was heartless, that Papa's death should have haunted him, but it was Jack who did—the slow way he fell apart before Eric's eyes. Jack only came to Eric's room once, and that was several years later, to tell Eric about the birds and the bees. Time had stopped for his uncle by then, too. He didn't know Eric either; he was too far behind.

Jack was so far behind that time that he believed girls still saved themselves for marriage. Maybe some did, but Eric knew a few who were pretty friendly in the right setting. Bathrooms were where it happened for him. During lunch break, Eric and Lonnie used to take these two girls to one house or another. Even they would only neck with protection—other people in the room—but if it got really hot, you could get them into the bathroom for a few minutes. It was a delicate thing. In the bathroom, you could close the door and go at your own pace, but you were usually crammed next to the bathtub or had the edge of the sink against your ass. The other couple had it made, they had the sofa and the danger of getting caught.

In those days, Eric's girl was a Latina, with big, soft lips. He couldn't remember her name, but then, they never acknowledged each other in public and in private they weren't talking. She and her girlfriend liked to pretend they didn't go below the waist, but if he could get his fingers on this girl's nipples, she'd be dragging *him* behind closed doors. She didn't make it easy, but he could tell she liked it because they had a whole ritual worked out. She'd wear a skirt always. She'd put the lid of the toilet down and slip off her panties so she could rub herself against the cold while they necked. She didn't look naked, that was important, but she wanted to be. Then they'd trade favors. He'd kiss her nipples if she'd kiss his cock. He'd suck her nipples if she'd suck him, usually only the head, but sometimes she'd let him in about halfway. Especially if he talked to her, if he said, "Baby you're so hot," or "You drive me wild." The last time they were together, she was rubbing herself all over the toilet. He watched her lips pull up his cock, slick, then slide back down. It felt amazing. Then it was her turn, and he was about to pull out when she let him all the way in, and he hit the back of her throat. She felt the change and started struggling, but he was burning up and there was nothing he could do but hold her tight. He always regretted it. It was years before he found another girl like her.

It was during that time Jack came up to Eric's room for his little talk. He'd asked, through the closed door, if he was interrupting anything.

"Just homework," Eric said, though he was stretched out on his bed.

Somehow, that was permission to enter. Jack pulled Eric's only chair up next to him.

"I'm memorizing something for speech class."

"This will only take a minute." Jack searched Eric's bare walls for a conversation opener. As if they'd be filled with trophies, Eric thought, watching. Or pictures. He had friends who did that, but not him. He'd never put up anything that could give him away. "I wanted to talk to you about, uh, girls," Jack said.

"What about them?"

"Well, you're getting to that age, you'll be dating soon, and I thought you might have some questions. Things you might not want to ask Mama."

Eric remembered then that his softball was under the bed. He swung his legs over the side and sat up, then hung his head between them, bouncing a little so Jack couldn't ignore him. He reached for the ball, but it was against the back wall. "I don't ask Mama anything," he said upside down.

"Eric, straighten up." Jack whacked his head, but only to startle him. "This is your chance to talk man to man. I'd think you'd appreciate it."

Eric sat up, but drew the line at smoothing his hair. "I know about the birds and the bees."

"About reproduction?"

"Intercourse. I've seen the pictures. Just the inside stuff, though. Drawings of sperm."

"Oh. Well. That's good." Eric thought he'd gotten rid of Jack by saying the word *sperm*, but there was more. "Did they talk to you about dating?" Jack asked.

"What about dating?"

He watched Jack search for his words, surprised at his uncle's resolve. "Well, there are, I guess you'd call them, rules of courtship. Ways to treat a girl. Ways to respect her."

"Rules of courtship."

"Yeah. Like when to hold her hand, when to kiss her good night. And what to do about, you know, stronger feelings you can't act on."

Stronger feelings? Eric thought. What he should do was ask if Jack was recommending masturbation. "Don't worry," he said instead. "I haven't been holding anyone's hand lately."

Jack rubbed his chin. He was angry, and trying to hide it. "Your smart mouth is going to get you in trouble."

Eric spread his arms wide. "I'm telling the truth, Jack. I'm not in danger of ruining anyone's reputation."

"It's not only a girl's reputation, Eric. People get hurt from doing things too soon. There are things better saved for marriage."

"Like sex?"

"Yes. Like sex," Jack said sternly. "Especially sex."

Eric had finally stepped over the line, but just to make sure he was there, he said, "Oh. Well, then, I'm sorry for you, Jack."

"What? Why?"

"Because I guess that means you're never going to have sex again."

The refrigerator hummed through Eric's remembrances, drowning the clock he hadn't realized he'd been hearing. The sounds, so constant, shamed him. He wondered if he had realized, when his uncle confronted him so long ago, that Jack was talking about his mother. Those things that were better saved for marriage, those people who could be hurt. Growing up, Eric assumed he was the one who could inflict hurt, and it was Mama and Jack—what passed for his family—who could be injured.

Pulling himself from his uncle's chair, Eric walked over to the bookshelf. It was black lacquer, with open ends to stick stuff on. Jack's paperbacks were swollen and yellow the way they got when you left them outside for the day. A hardcover, *A Taste for Death*, was lying flat on the end of a shelf, marked where Jack had stopped reading, almost at the end. Kinda grisly, Eric thought. And then he thought, at least Jack knew who the killer was that far in. As Eric opened the book to remind himself of the story, the marker released and slid down the page into his hand. It was a 7-Eleven receipt. He held it close so he could read the faded total. Eight dollars and three cents. The other side was blank.

A small *koa* bowl sat at eye height in an honorary arc cleaned of dust. A gift. Tchotchkes, Kay'd called them; she was full of strange words. The lid snuggled in the curve of Eric's palm as he lifted it to see what Jack kept inside. It was empty. He spun it, and the blond wispy wood blazed.

It was from Mariko, Eric knew. His sister. Jack told him about her visit several weeks after she had gone. Like he was waiting for any leftover pieces of her to drop out of the air, so they could no longer touch Eric. It had seemed silly, since he hadn't felt her betrayal in years, hadn't thought about his mother either, but then he realized, from the way Jack said her name, that Jack was jealous. It was yet another revelation, that he was afraid to lose Eric to his sister after all this time.

It couldn't have been more than a month ago when Jack finally raised the subject on the porch. It was after a dinner he'd been hinting for—over apple pie—and he said it so abruptly that Eric couldn't speak.

"So I sent her away," Jack said, "after all this time, I don't know what she thought she'd gain. That whole selective amnesia story. I just don't know." He waited for a response, but Eric couldn't give one. The night continued to fall around them as they struggled to find their words. Finally, Jack said, "Just in case, you know, anything happens to me," and gave Eric her address.

Eric could have said, "I know how to find her." It was a shock to realize that it was true, and it pissed him off; he liked it better when he didn't have to be responsible. When Jack wasn't hovering there, wanting him to say, I like you better. I choose you.

Would it have killed him to relieve Jack? To say, just that once, that he did the right thing? But the old pain had rung in his ears, muffled his trust. He hadn't been able to think, so he hadn't, and he was left now with books and tchotchkes. The fishing reel pencil sharpener his kids gave Jack years ago. What did it mean there on the top shelf?

"Umm, very nice," he'd said to the kids as they wrapped it. And then, yelling to Talia in the kitchen, he asked, "What the hell does he need a pencil sharpener for?"

"It's a fishing reel, Eric," she replied, annoyed that he hadn't helped. "He fishes."

Well, he did fish, Eric thought, picking up other things. A stapler. Something ceramic. A picture frame, big enough for one face, but empty. Some things he just cocked, didn't even lift them. They were all horribly still.

The magazines on the coffee table behind Eric were now half neat. Behind them was the sofa, home to a half-dozen needlepoint throw pillows Mama had made over the years. Over it were the only two photographs in Jack's house, neither of which he chose for decoration. The bigger one showed Eric and Talia on their wedding day. Talia'd had it enlarged and framed in the days when it was okay for the groom's tuxedo to match the bride's blue eye shadow, and Jack had kept it to embarrass them. He'd kept the other because Talia framed it to match, and he couldn't break the pair. The picture was of Jack's family. Prewar, the only thing left from those days. Five people, Mama and Papa and the three kids—Jack still in short pants. All of them in white. All five wearing white hats in different shapes. It was a picture Eric had studied often since he'd found it in a book with Mama's things. He'd fought Talia when she decided to frame it. "He'll love it, Eric," she'd insisted. "He's not exactly easy to shop for." She thought Eric was touchy because Emi was in it, but the truth was, he didn't see her there. It was just that they looked so dead. All of them, even before.

They weren't posed right, Eric thought now, tracing the figures with a finger. Where were the allegiances? Who was in control? Nothing of Papa was in that picture, nothing of Will, who Eric never knew. In a picture, you should be able to see who loved whom. Who remembered. But their faces were silent, unable to tell him how much they knew about what they would do.

Mama, so shy—she should have been at the center. It was she who held the family together, even as it dwindled. The mugging, of all things, was their inevitable release. Two guys jumped her only blocks from home one afternoon. She'd gone to the store, and if she'd given up her purse instead of swinging her grocery bag crotch high at one of the thugs, she'd have come out fine. Eric still remembered her in the hospital, so angry that she couldn't lift her cast without help. She started right in on how there was no milk at home for Jack because the *bakatare* took it.

"They took the milk," she yelled, as if he was the one who was going deaf.

"It probably fell, Mama," Eric said from the visitor's chair they'd set up in the opposite corner of the room. "We can buy more."

"They stole it."

"These guys can hurt you bad, Mama, worse than a broken leg. You can't fight about milk."

"Why? Why should they have my money? It's my money."

"It's okay, Mama, it's okay. You can't fight with thugs, though."

"I didn't fight," she said, but her eyes avoided his. "For no reason, they snapped my whole bone."

That was when the family truly fell apart. Maybe they should have kept Mama at home until she died, but she wasn't easy to follow. The doctors leaned on them. It was for her own protection. The first time she'd fallen, she broke both wrists and didn't even call Jack at work. They kept insisting. Old bones didn't heal.

The three of them picked a good home. Eric had it worked out so he and Jack could take turns visiting, with Talia there to spell them, but Jack was there every day, always waiting to see whether Eric showed up, and always first, too. On the day Eric was thinking of, the residents were in the god-awful yellow cafeteria for snack time. Mama and Jack were easy to spot. She was the smallest of the white-gowned ladies, and he, in a sports shirt, pressed pants and belt, was the only visitor. Jack was completely gray by then, but bigger than the older ones. He held a blue and yellow pot holder, the kind made from loops, in his hands.

"Hi, Mama," Eric called. It could have been a kindergarten, except for the watercolor landscapes and lush calligraphy posted between the proud stick-figure pictures. Eric ducked the construction paper hats, then poked his head into one, an origami Noah's ark, to see if he could make her laugh.

"Eric!" When he got close enough, she tipped her cheek for a kiss the way she'd learned from the other residents' visitors. "For you," she said, taking the pot holder from Jack.

"Oh. Thanks." He glanced at his uncle, saw him drop his empty hands into his lap. "Hi."

"You don't like it."

"No, I do. I do. Isn't it for Jack though?"

Mama stuck out her lower lip. "You don't like it." Turning away, she frowned at the room until she recognized someone. "Mildred. Mildred!" she yelled, waving frantically. "Come. Come here."

Hearing her name, the old woman looked around. She stood, the graham cracker she was licking still pressed against her mouth, happy to be called.

Mama pointed at Mildred's pot holder, punching her finger in the air. "Bring it. Bring it."

"Mama," Eric warned, but she ignored him, yelling, "Bring it, bring it," even after Mildred had picked up her pot holder and started toward them. As Mildred smiled, dropping the cracker to show her remaining teeth, Eric tried to guess her race. Without luck. That was the thing about old people, he thought, once they shrivel up, they all look the same.

Mama snatched Mildred's pot holder and gave it to Eric.

"You like this one better."

Mildred smiled and patted Eric's ear.

"You like it." Mama shoved the blue and yellow one into Mildred's impassive hand. "See?"

As Mama tried to close Mildred's fingers around the substitute,

Eric looked over at Jack, expecting to see a worried frown, but he seemed as amused as Eric was embarrassed.

"Jesus," Eric said, "she's got all of them as beaten as we are."

He might have said it on purpose, after all, they were old men, and if it pissed Jack off, there was no longer anything he could do.

This time though, for the first time, Jack didn't take offense. He laughed, and there was something so free in his face. "Yeah, she's a little dictator all right," he said.

"She is?" Eric asked, surprised at his relief.

"Sure," Jack said. "She's a mother, isn't she?"

In Jack's bedroom, the sheets had been stripped, the comforter folded and placed at the foot of the bed. The washing machine in the bathroom was vibrating gently against the wall. Talia's work. She'd thrown open both windows, too, and the smell had faded. The stains on the mattress could have been anything. Could have been coffee.

Talia was dusting the dresser, making a neat line of Jack's brush, hair gel, hand cream, razor, and four bottles of pills. Behind the line was a piece of wood. Polished dark. "I'm not destroying evidence, am I?" she asked.

Eric noticed she'd been crying.

"No. The cop said it was natural. The coroner's already done."

"So fast? They just called."

"They found him this morning. It was us they couldn't find. You know. Next of kin."

Looking around, Eric realized he'd never walked down the short hallway that led to this room. It had seemed so private, but it was the same carpet, same basic furniture as the rest of the place. Through the open closet door, he could see shirts flailing their long arms to get out of the crush of clothes. Would other people wear them? he wondered. Did you wear dead clothes?

"Do you think there's a will?" he asked.

"I'm sure. Jack is—he was—very practical."

"You think so?" Eric walked over to Talia and picked up the

piece of wood. It was cool in his hand and heavy. He'd thought it would be carved, but it was natural. "What's this?"

"Wood."

"Very funny." Eric rubbed it, feeling the knots and twists in the surface. There was no varnish on it. It had been rubbed to a shine.

"Your grandfather made it," Talia offered. She hadn't looked at him once in the face since he'd walked into the room, and she wasn't looking at him now. "It was a good luck charm."

"How do you know?"

"Jack told me."

"Oh." Turned right, it looked almost like a hand reaching, a forearm half the size of his own. Eric closed his fist around it, expecting to feel something living there. His grandfather, maybe; he couldn't remember him either. "What is it?"

"Just wood. He found it at camp. He liked the shape, I guess."

Camp, Eric thought. So long ago. Like the war, like the clues to who they were, why Jack would keep a piece of wood. It was something not even Talia could answer, it was allegiances again. Trying to figure out what was important. Or better yet, who was really who.

"Walking around here," Eric said, "I feel like I never knew him. Like he was a stranger."

"Oh, please." Talia turned toward the bed. She gave the blanket a last touch.

"What?" He put the wood down and turned to her, wanting to hear.

She looked up at last. "Why are you doing this Eric?"

"What?"

"Pulling away. Pretending like you don't care."

"I'm not."

"You can't simply let go, can you?"

"Because I said I didn't know him? That means I'm uptight?"

"Come on. You knew him, Eric. You know him." She wasn't angry, though; she was opening herself to her tears. "You two are exactly alike," she said, moving at last to touch him. "Exactly."

* * *

Men in white coats were passing Eric, but no one asked him what he was doing there. He was okay. It was routine. He was there for his mother. She was having tests, but there was nothing to worry about. Everything was quiet, no bustle to indicate anything was wrong.

He was walking down a hallway, and then he was sitting in a cafeteria. Like the one in Mama's old folks home, with the crafts and the drawings, but he understood this was a hospital. The light that filled the room made people's skin yellow. There was coffee in front of him and people around.

Talia was with him, too. She had the sharp blue eyes from the video but he knew it was her. She had the video voice, too—"Hey, we're partners, get the car." At first, he could only make out what Talia was saying, but now he could hear the others speak. They were saying his mother had died. Someone was patting his ear, Talia maybe, but he had lost her face. They were saying they were sorry.

"All for the best," someone said. He heard the words but wasn't understanding—he thought they'd made a mistake. He tried to conjure up his mother's face to see if it was true. Jack's face came to him instead, then his Mama's, but Emi's face was black and white and like a child's. "I'm so sorry," the person said again, but he didn't feel it. The hands kept stroking him, patting his ear. He couldn't see them, but he knew they were dark, like polished wood. "You're wrong," he said to the voice, but no one heard him. He was the only person in the cafeteria.

Then time spliced again and Eric was running. Up and down long hallways, stumbling a little, and he was asking, "Why didn't you call me?" "Why didn't you tell me?" He could hear himself, and he knew others could, too, but there was no one else in the hallway. His chest was being swallowed, he was panicked, yes, but there was betrayal, too. He was thinking, This can't happen. I didn't say good-bye, as he looked for her door. He needed to find it and open it, because if he did, she'd be alive. He could turn time back to when her tests were only routine. Three whole days, he thought. A lifetime. He was moving fast down the hallway, but it was long now, and fish-eyed, and there were no doors at all.

Then, suddenly, he was back in the cafeteria, only it was his dining room, and they were eating Thanksgiving dinner. His youngest son was there—Jason—he had three pieces of pie on his plate and he was scooping ice cream between them so they wouldn't touch. He waited, expecting to hear Jack tell Jason that it would all get mixed up in his stomach, but there was a party going on and Jack wasn't there. People were drinking wine in evening clothes. "We knew," they were saying. They all, always, knew. He was standing in the middle of the room in a tuxedo. Crying. He looked for Jack, thinking his uncle might be able to explain, but somehow he had slipped away. Someone put a wineglass in Eric's hand but he threw the glass away, listening for a crash, wanting them to hear it. "I didn't know," he said. The glass disappeared, and the people kept talking and drinking. "I didn't know," he said again, "I thought it was just another day." The party crowded around him, but no one would listen, and he couldn't seem to touch them. Their voices were like static, muffling him, freezing him in one place. He couldn't find Jack but he could see him clearly; he couldn't find Mama either, but he knew she was there. He was standing uselessly in the middle of the room, still crying, burning in the static. Together, they were his real mother, he realized. And they were with him now—somewhere—but he was also alone.

"I didn't know," he screamed again, feeling only the loneliness. His words bounced past him and came back, echoing, dislocated. They broke into pieces, into letters, they scraped his mind until finally they faded into the static and left him wondering if they were true.

"Eric? Honey?"

Eric jumped awake in his own room. His chest was throbbing. He could hear his heart, and the hot bruise inside.

"Um, okay?" Talia was facing away. She pushed against him,

groggy, for comfort. "Just dreaming," she assured him, falling back to sleep.

Dreaming, Eric thought. He sat up, sorting through familiar shapes to push the dream away. His legs were shaking, so skinny and mortal he could see the shadows on them where his flesh fell away from the bone. The round mirror over the bureau glowed with the outside light, and he focused on its blankness. He raked his hands over his ears, but it was all still there, he could feel it.

Every second of it. His tears were real.

23

MARIKO

REUNION, 1990

It was a small group gathering, hunched against the stained edges of the sky. From where she sat, safely inside her rented car, Mari could feel the wind bunch against them as they arranged themselves around the open grave. On one side, a handful of white-haired mourners swayed, their movements resigned, whispering. Their lives must be a series of funerals, Mari thought; they must seem reliable by now, trustworthy. It explained their calm.

On the other end of the grave, a younger nuclear family stood, without touching and in order of size, though whether out of habit or by accident, Mari couldn't tell. Parents and three boys. She felt an energy from them, and from the way each sought his own margin of grief, she knew it had to be Eric and his family.

Mari hadn't met them yet, but she was prepared to recognize them just as she had recognized Eric when he called to tell her Jack was dead. Her brother's voice had been dark, not a note was familiar, but her name in his mouth held everything, and she wasn't as shocked to hear from him as she might have expected. One of the first things he said to her was, "So what's new?" Then, "My wife says not to say anything else stupid. She's always telling me what to do."

"Yeah," Mari had said. "Women are like that." She laughed then because it seemed right that Eric would pick up, not from where they left off, but from where he was. She imagined him leaning against his kitchen wall, using a telephone mounted in the center of his family to show that calling Mari was a natural thing to do. That's why she made the joke—though she wasn't sure that she herself was "like that"—because everything was all right at last. She had to drag her laugh back in, every shard of it, when Eric spoke his next words.

"So, Jack told me about your visit here. Sorry it's taken a while to call. I've been busy, but the thing is, well, Jack is dead. I called because he would have wanted you at the funeral. That is, if you want to come."

Mari waited for the proper sorrow, but she felt only a crush in her chest that more of the past had disappeared. She knew Jack had lied to her when she saw him. For example, he claimed to know nothing about the horse stalls at Santa Anita, even though one of the few things her mother told her was that her family had been housed in them. He didn't want to go with her to see them either; he was tired and preferred to sit in the shade. When he said good-bye, though, he had told her, in a friendly way, not to get stuck in the past.

Mari had promised to keep in touch.

"He wanted me to come?" she asked.

"Sure! He liked you. Said you lied through your teeth but were feisty as hell! Oh, shit." Mari heard him put his hand over the receiver, then he was back. "Talia called me an asshole. Sorry, I didn't mean it like that."

It was Eric who brought Mari back to California. She needed to apologize. She hadn't given much thought to Jack, or prepared herself for the gravestones piled against one another, tipped by the wide underground embrace of the elms. As Mari stepped out of the car and picked her way toward her brother and his family, the older mourners began skirting the open grave to shake his hand. That acknowledgment of her brother, as the head of the family now, felt right to Mari. She watched the two groups mingle, each bowing, briefly and repeatedly, to console.

Once Mari was close enough to hear Eric's voice, though, her brother turned away. He walked head down, his arms twisted so tightly in front of him that his hands disappeared. She could see the energy she had felt earlier in action now; even his slightest movements were errant, out of control. He must have seen her, she thought, and was escaping. Maybe his memories were resurfacing too.

Don't do this, Mari told herself, it doesn't have to be about you. But even reminding herself that she was at a funeral didn't allay her fear that her brother had changed his mind.

Then she heard a woman's voice, woven in grief. "You must be Mariko," it said. "I'm Talia."

Mari stuck her hand out of her daydreaming; she had almost walked into Eric's wife. "Yes, Mariko," she said. The woman holding her hand was so poised. Mari's eyes moved from Talia's simple dress and pantyhose to her own twill gauchos. They were the only black pants she owned.

She should have bought a dress, high heels, Mari told herself; if she had them, it would be possible to speak. But any outfit she chose would have carried a message. Well-off, stodgy; she couldn't take the chance.

"Eric, ah," Mari started, "said you're hosting a wake this afternoon." What he had said was "she's adamant." He'd seemed to delight in the word. "I'm looking forward to it."

Talia nodded her beauty shop–twisted hair. "We're going to lead a caravan out of here afterward. You're welcome to come in our car."

Mari smiled politely, wanting to go after Eric. He was circling in on two nearby graves. When he finally stopped, near the foot of one, Mari counted the rows between her and the headstones so she could visit them later. Whatever he'd found there, she imagined he was gathering courage. Since she was doing it also, she took comfort in that.

"Jack planned the whole ceremony," Eric's wife continued. "Didn't want to burden us, I guess." When Talia sighed, Mari noticed for the first time that she didn't dye the gray out of her hair. They had that in common. "Of course, we had to make some changes, given, you know, the timing. How long it took for him to be found."

Mari didn't know, but before she could ask, an older gentleman in a black robe and baggy pants joined them, sparking more abbreviated bows on both sides. He was about Mari's height and weight, not hunched over but well-proportioned in a small way.

"Reverend Joya, this is Jack's niece. Mariko, ah—"

"Stone," Mari filled in. The man in front of her looked like an idle porcupine, not a priest; his bobbing gray hair had been styled with Dippity-Do and his fingers. He bowed from his hands, folded neatly under his rib cage and over the long embroidered sash that hung in a double line of dancing kanji from his neck. Each time he went down, Mari could see a double twist in the sash behind his head.

"My, uh, sister-in-law."

"Ah, Jack's niece," the reverend murmured. The crow's feet that crowned his high cheekbones, and his squeezed eyes, made him appear to be laughing, but when Mari met those eyes, she could feel his tears running down her own cheeks, and she knew that, though he could have been anyone, he was Jack's friend. She had no words to offer him, not someone who truly loved her uncle and was loved. Finally, she reached out, past the surprise on his face, and grasped the back of his sash in her fingers. Facing him, with her arm resting on his shoulder, she twisted it gently so it could lay flat.

It was the kind of wordless gesture her mother would have made, Mari realized. Sitting beside her waterfall with Emi, listening for what her mother couldn't bring herself to say, Mari understood for the first time how thoroughly Emi's silence had isolated her; Emi knew it, and accepted it, but Mari wasn't willing to let herself do the same. She wanted to go home, and to do that, she needed to confess her own lies to Roger. She needed to be brutally honest, so he could respond as he wished.

Mari pulled into the parking lot behind Roger's office as the sun dropped into her windshield. Objects began trailing shadows behind them as she moved. She was nervous, unsure of his reception; she hadn't spoken to him since she left for California, even to say when she would return.

She had imagined she would catch him in repose, but when Mari opened his office door, Roger was leaning over his desk, still working as the day shut down. She took a deep breath, ready to tell him everything at once.

"Mar! You're home."

Roger stood to greet her, but she stopped him, terrified that she was about to take something that wasn't hers. "I have to talk to you," she began. Then, "I don't want you to speak." In the order of his office, suddenly nothing was coming. "Could we go to the park?" That would give her time to gather her thoughts and make them real. She would also have the banyan tree she loved, with those cords in its trunk like the base of her neck. When she snuggled into it, as she had often done during lunch times years ago when she and Roger were dating, she could feel her pulse as clearly as if she were sitting in the hollow of her own collarbone.

"Please, Roger." He was coming toward her, and she knew, if he touched her, she would lose all her strength. Then, because there were no words to rely on, Mari fled through his open door.

A brass bell began ringing. Not a cowbell, or a meal call, but in bright, separate peals. Reverend Joya keened over it, his tones swooping into one another, sliding on their dissonances, adjusting their volumes. It was a blessing in a solemn, long-abandoned language. It was harrowing and beautiful, but Mari was left with nothing to hold.

The bell had pulled the group in toward the grave and up against Mari. Eric had returned and was standing nearby. As the prayer rose steadily higher, Mari checked around her. She felt like she was missing. There wasn't a single face she knew.

Their mother should have been here, Mari thought. She had spent days dreaming of ways to trick Emi into coming; she played great reconciliation scenes in her head. But Eric never asked once about Emi, not when he called with the news, not when he called back to suggest hotels where Mari could stay. It was Mari who raised the subject. And what she got was a sigh.

"If she wants to come for Jack," Eric said, "then she's welcome. But the past is past."

Mari had considered his words in silence, struck by how similar they were to something her mother would say. Regardless of who they came from, she couldn't quite grasp their meaning. Was Eric saying the past was full of trauma and should lie undisturbed? Or that the past was forgiven, and in the present they could start again?

Whatever her brother intended, Mari couldn't get her own past out of her mind. She kept seeing her red dress and the two of them walking out of the theater and into the sun. She was afraid that Eric wouldn't believe her memory had failed her; it seemed ridiculous, even to her. Listening to the resolution in his voice, though, she realized she had to know what, if anything, he had said to her.

"Do you remember seeing me?" she asked. "When I was about eight and our grandfather died?"

He hesitated for a long time. Then he said, "How could I forget?"

"Right," she said, fully committed now and at a disadvantage. "Well, I did. I mean, I'm having a hard time with the pieces, and I thought . . . What do you remember?"

"Your walk, for one." He chuckled. "Your knees knocked

together. I made fun of you and you were very serious. You said it helped you get through the tall grass and then you ran around swinging your calves like scythes so I could understand what you meant."

"You made fun of me?"

"Sure. You were funny. I took you to see something scary, didn't I? What was it? You know, I walked through every aisle in a video store once to try and jog my memory but damned if I could come up with it. I do remember I lied about our ages, though, and you screamed and hung on to me. Afterward, I took you out for ice cream."

"My God. I had no idea. When I got my papers and saw your name, all I remembered was my red dress."

"Blocked me out, eh?"

He said it easily, but it was an excuse she could no longer bring herself to accept. "Can I ask you a question? Did you—why didn't you say anything? About being my brother?"

He didn't answer, leaving her to listen to herself instead. She sounded so distant. She was asking him about his lost family, about a day when he had surely already been mourning his grandfather, and it was clear that, even then, she hadn't considered his feelings.

"Do you know what I remember about that day?" he asked her finally. "That it felt so good to have you there. We were together, I was a part of things after so long and I never thought—"

I never thought you would leave me again, she heard. His unused words were deafening.

"Listen, Mari, we can talk if you want, but Talia will kill me if I scare you away from the funeral. Why don't you just come?"

When Eric finished saying that, on the telephone, in the past, the real man began to speak. Whole words boomed in Mari's ears. His voice was slower than it had been over the wire, and the Nisei quality, not exactly singsong but slowing and surging in and out at the punctuation, was more pronounced. Mari could hear his commas and periods especially.

"A lot of you here knew Jack better than I did," Eric was saying, with none of the wisecracks she'd heard on the phone. "He spent the better part of his life trying to teach me about honor. I guess I've always been a slow learner. And when I did finally get it, it wasn't because of anything he said. I learned by his example. I don't have to tell anyone here that Jack was a hell of an honorable guy."

Mari could feel the sorrow swelling through her brother. She could see it in the way he picked his fingernails and shuffled his feet. Jack had talked about Eric like a son, and, for the first time, Mari realized her brother was mourning him as a father.

"I should stop there, right?" Eric asked, interrupting Mari's thoughts again. "I know Mama would think I'd already given Jack the best tribute. But the thing is, a lot of guys are honorable, and Jack wasn't like a lot of guys.

"Jack, as a lot of you know, was funny, too. He was brave. Foolish even. He got drunk sometimes—once he and I danced down the middle of the street. He loved a lot of people, and he worried about us.

"I'm getting off the track, but what I wanted to say is, Jack was real. If you ask me, the best way to remember him is to listen for him. Jack had the kind of life you could hear in his voice. I think that's important, too."

Roger caught Mari before she reached the stairs and walked beside her, without speaking, to the park. They passed an older couple feeding the mynah birds, but no one else; it was the time of day when Hilo emptied into the breezy wooden houses that ran away from the center of town—from the stink of gingko trees to the sweeter plumerias of home. Mari headed directly for her banyan tree and curled herself between its roots. Roger settled as close as he could without blocking her, on an angle so she could see him more in profile than head-on.

Even then, Mari could feel time stretch before her. The air around her was easing as it cooled, lifting the coos of the birds with it into the trees.

"Whatever it is, you don't have to tell me, Mari," Roger said, his words feeling sudden to her. "I shouldn't have tried to force you to talk to anyone if you didn't want to. . . ."

"No, I do have to tell you," she said, resisting the urge to accept his offer. She wanted to explain that this wasn't about Eric, but she was too afraid to stop. "When we met, I was pregnant. Do you remember that?"

"Yes."

"Well." She took a breath. "I had an abortion."

Roger's careful calm didn't flicker. "I'm not surprised."

"You knew?"

"No. It's not a shock, that's all. It fits." She had placed herself too far away for him to touch her, so he smiled instead. "Why don't you talk for a while, Mari? Tell me what you want to say."

She had thought that was it, that she'd had an abortion, but suddenly she was telling him everything that had happened. As her story unwound, Mari was sure she could hear the words Roger would use to soothe her; he would remind her of her trouble conceiving before the abortion, and how doctors had never found a medical thing wrong. She could feel herself being liberated, as if Roger received each piece of her confession and tossed it into the air. But when she was finished, finally, when she told him how her prayers to be punished were answered, over and over, he was absorbed in his own thoughts. He was intent on his hands, balanced straight out on his loosely bent knees. For a terrible moment, she thought he might never speak.

"So that's why this revelation about Eric upset you so," he said at last. "You think you did something worse than your mother did."

"That's not even a question."

He gave her a small, weary smile. "Sure it is, Mari. What if you had had that baby? Maybe we wouldn't be together; we wouldn't have had Tyler. I'm sure you've thought of that."

She shook off his question. "I wanted to be a mother. That's all. And you wanted to be a father and I"—her words trembled—"ruined it for both of us."

"How's that? We're parents. We have a great kid."

"Yeah. But not the one you wanted." Mari couldn't look at him. "I know how much you wanted a boy."

"Me? You were the one—"

Mari heard him, but dimly. Instead, she was caught, suddenly, in the clenching pain of her miscarriages; each one ran through her as she remembered cradling her stomach to keep her babies in. After all this time, the loss was so real. She felt the rush as her insides began to empty; the blood warm and plentiful between her legs. She wanted to melt where she was—onto the kitchen floor, into her bed—but instead she ran to the bathroom in her mind so there would be no telltale stains when Roger came home. She had to protect him, Mari thought, feeling her memories slow down to real time. She threw herself on the toilet, barely getting her panties down to her knees before she heard the blood splash softly into the bowl. This time, she prayed, let it only be blood. In seconds, though, she felt something more solid move inside and managed to slip one hand beneath her in a smooth motion. Just in time. Mari felt the soft touch, no more than a kiss, as her baby fell into her palm. The warmth of her body ran out and through her fingers, cooling in the indoor air. She closed her fist, pillowing the baby; even as she drew her hand up and out of the toilet, she felt the crazy urge to press it back in. It was a tiny, grape-size thing—peeled white and already beginning to pucker. She could see the head and back inside it, and a dark mark where the baby's heart had been.

"It wasn't me who wanted another child, Mar. Really." Roger's voice was scared.

"They're gone—all of them." Mari wanted, more than anything, to keep the wail out of her own voice, but the world was shaking beneath her words and there was no way to control them. She hadn't known what to do with the baby. She should have buried it outside; they had so much room. But she didn't want Roger to know, to grieve or blame her. A burial would have taken too much time.

It wasn't me, he had told her. He wasn't the one waiting for a son. Looking at him, at the growing horror on his face, Mari wanted to cry. She had tried so hard to hide her broken self from him, but now it seemed even her face was breaking down. It was as if he could see her thoughts clearly, see her wandering from room to room with her hands cupped before her, trying to keep the blood and water from dripping off her arms. She had kicked her pants off because she couldn't get them back on and her heavy sweatshirt looked so out of place. Mari couldn't remember how many useless door frames she had passed through, or what she had been looking for.

Mari raised her hands, forming an empty shield in front of her face so that if Roger tried to speak his words could never climb over. Her palms were far enough away that she could trace the lines that should mean something, after all this time. How many babies had she held in them? she wondered, watching blood flow again along her lifeline, along her heart line, under her nails. She should have put them in the ground, scratched the dirt out with her hands, but the exposure, her sheer nakedness even in the dark, had terrified her. It was morbid, she had told herself. Too permanent.

But she wouldn't have had to live in hiding. And her babies would be where they belonged.

"Oh, God—"

She didn't know what she was asking, and she never saw Roger move. Suddenly he was there, crouched over her. He had one arm around her back, yanking her off the tree and into him; he used the other to crush her head to his chest where she could feel his pulse pound her cheek. His lips were tangled in her hair, so it took a while for her to hear him speaking. Whispering, actually.

"Hush, Mari. I'm here."

Eric's speech prompted an odd wave of clapping that moved around the group and picked up speed. It seemed to mark the end of the funeral, though they had the coffin still to lower. Mari expected the mourners to cry, but they hugged and talked softly around her instead as Jack was slipped into the ground. The California sun had dried a gray-brown crust over the nearby mound, but its reach into the grave was limited, and the walls ran darker as they dropped. It was a violent sight, and a violated one, the way the earth was peeled back to take her uncle in. So different from the casket itself, polished as simply as a dining room table. She was thinking it wouldn't take long to split down the grain, she was thinking of Kim and her belief that artists "like to rub the dirt in." Kim didn't know her Uncle Jack. They'd never even met.

In the circulating crowd, Mari made her way toward Eric, and in the brief, weary look he gave her, she imagined that he was either growing older or becoming young.

"Mari."

It wasn't a question. Her brother's arms were around her before she could respond. There was nothing urgent in his embrace; it was comfortable, and Mari liked the way he leaned on her, as if he had expected her to be there.

"You're coming to the house, right?" he asked her after they broke apart.

"I'm going to meet Roger at the hotel and we'll come together."

"He's not here?"

"No. He didn't know Jack and—I guess I wanted to be alone. I think I'm going to stay here for a little while. Think about things. Roger's probably landing now, so I have some time."

"Well. Looking forward to meeting him." Eric chopped his sentences short for the mourners shifting patiently behind her. "Plenty of time later to talk, right?"

She could agree and withdraw; it would be the polite thing to do, but Mari had waited so long to speak. She had no explanations or excuses to offer. "I'm sorry, Eric. I'm so terribly sorry."

Her brother nodded. "We all have to go sometime."

"I wasn't talking about Jack."

"I wasn't talking about Jack either," he said. Mari was amazed at how easily he could joke about being left behind. She was apologizing for her role in it, and she thought it was possible that he didn't understand until he asked, "Mari, what could you possibly have done?"

She didn't respond right away. Eric's small smile stayed on his lips as the other mourners handed him away from her, from one person to the next until he had taken the lead. They fell in behind him, in twos and threes, trailing between the same graves, as if they could lose one another forever with one missed step. From where she stood, they became a snake, bulges running down it as the graveyard shifted, then disappearing with a snap in the tail.

When the last car left, Mari sank to her knees, relieved to be grounded. She sensed someone with her and wondered if it was Jack, beginning his forty-nine or however many Buddhist days of waiting before his soul was set free. She smoothed the dirt with her hands, but felt nothing. Then she rose and found her way to the two graves Eric had visited earlier.

As Mari suspected, they belonged to her grandparents. Mitsuo and Kaori. The stones were sharp and equal, as if they'd been placed together yesterday, not five years ago, not forty. Each grave cradled a spray of orchids, by-products of Jack's passing no doubt. Mari wondered who would tend them now that he was gone.

Nowhere nearby could Mari find a marker for her other uncle, Will, the one who died in the war, but there were stories everywhere, coming from the ground. She could hear them, overlapping, in a chorus around her head. So many little babies, as the years rolled backward, so many people dying young. Mari listened for her grandmother's story. Mama, as Emi called her, would know the truth, especially about her own daughter. But Mari's grandmother could have been standing beside her, Mari realized, and she wouldn't even recognize her. The past had become memory; it was no longer real.

What could you possibly have done? Eric had asked her. His question reminded Mari of walking through the parking lot at Santa Anita once she had tried to peer past the horses in the stables and had found nothing at all to see. She had been searching for the barracks, listening for old echoes behind rows of modern cars. She had no idea where to look, but she was certain that if she tried hard enough, she would find the right place. It couldn't all have been erased: where she'd been born, where she had lived.

Mari had been given a sign that day, but she didn't recognize it until now. What she had seen was two children, no more than ten, wandering among the cars. They were a boy and a girl, clearly lost, but unable to admit it. The girl was tired; the boy anxious. He was older, pulling her by the hand.

Mari didn't understand, at first, what they were doing. The boy and girl had made several zigzags before she realized they were looking for a blue sedan. They moved from one to the next at random, without any thought for how big the lot was or how many times they might return to the same car. The little girl teetered on her feet, most noticeably each time they turned away without success. The boy was in charge of peering into the windows at the backseats. Sometimes she forced him to prop her on his knee so she could see inside, too.

Normally, Mari would have helped them. She would have waved first so they knew she was coming, then pointed out the overhead numbers and organized some kind of a plan. But she was too weary that day, too disappointed. She could do nothing more than stare from where she was, leaning against a lamppost, and watch them try to decide how to select the next car. Mari knew the little girl was failing by the way she tripped more frequently and gave up looking into the windows. Maybe it was the distance or the sheer number of choices, but Mari had felt as powerless as the children.

It hadn't struck her until this moment that she, too, had once been so impossibly small.

24

KAORI

BIRTH DAY

It happens only two days after I chased Emi from the latrine. Two weeks after we arrived at Santa Anita.

I am standing in our horse stall with your grandfather as the last of the day falls out of the sky, folding clothes and weighting them to push out the wrinkles. He is quiet. It's as if he's gone. A tin radio sound floats up to the ceiling, where it can cross the partitions and drop into our stall. It keeps me company until we hear Eric scream.

I know his voice, I know his step, too. He's running faster than his legs have gone before. He's bouncing off the walls, into doors, trying to find our stall, and I hear the sound—his body banging into wood. I drop the shirt that I'm holding and run to the door.

Eric whirls toward my voice when I call his name. He grabs my legs, sobbing. He won't let go. It's sunset, but we're inside and I have to see through the hay and dust hanging in the shadows of our lightbulb. Eric is howling, no words. I run my hands down his back to see if it makes a difference to his cries. I turn his arms, looking for a broken bone.

He's too young to be here alone, I think, and he isn't. Your mother has returned. She's standing near the stable doorway, tottering a little, but holding on the best she can. Her shoulders are pulled forward. She has one hand slung under her belly like she's trying to keep it from falling to the floor.

I think maybe they've been attacked, but I can't see a trace of it from the front and I curse the dim light. It doesn't matter. I know she's hurt.

Then she buckles. I see her knees go. She folds, a piece at a time like a pocketknife, smashing her stomach on her thighs. She grunts and clutches for something to hold her, but nothing is around.

Eric lets go of me and runs halfway to Emi, wanting to help her, unwilling to leave. He's crying and screaming again. He stops between us, dancing and stamping his feet. He looks from one to the other, not knowing where to go.

Your mother's almost on the floor, but she's struggling against collapse. We draw the neighbors' attention again, and this time it's too much to ignore. They come out of their stalls and someone reaches Emi, a man. He's pulling her. There's a crowd.

"We better get her to the clinic," someone says. "She's having her baby."

I know by then, but the words move the others. One of the neighbors tries to lead Eric away. He screams "Mama," but I can tell he means Emi, and I know that, if he's scared now, things are about to get worse. He kicks out at the woman who drags him away at my gesture, still trying to save his mother, but Emi doesn't see him. Her eyes are squeezed into tight white circles. She's too deep inside herself even to know that it's me who reaches out next to grab her arm. That in itself is a blessing because, almost immediately, I pull away.

Her arm is just—so strong. Like a man's, even under the cloth. It could be skinless, the way the muscles shake and move. It isn't anything like I thought my daughter was, and I realize I haven't touched Emi since she came back to us. The last time I touched her, she was a child.

That's when I feel it—regret. And a fear that I misjudged her, the sharp realization that maybe I didn't know all there was to know. I do know that if I tried to play back our past then so I could understand it, I would weep. Instead, I reach out again, giving my fingers a courage to match her own.

The man holding her pulls against me as I begin to lead her to our stall. "Ma'am," he says, "this woman is having a baby. We have to get her to the clinic."

"No," I say. I have yet to see a doctor. "Our place is clean. She can have the baby there."

As we help Emi into our horse stall, I can see the threads of blood and water on her dress and down her thighs. It will soak the straw in our mattresses, I know, but she can't give birth on the floor. I don't want her lying in her blood all night either. When she sags toward her bed, I pull her toward mine. I free one of my hands and yank the sheets and towels aside. I know I can sleep anywhere. There will be plenty of time to fix things in the morning.

"No!" Emi twists, trying to protect my bed. "Over there."

The poor man doesn't know what to do, but tensed up like that, Emi is heavy, and it's a simple thing for me to push her down.

"It's okay. It's just for now," I tell her. Then I turn to him. "Could you get a doctor?"

"But I thought you said—"

Emi cuts him off. "Mama, this is your bed!"

"Please," I say, ignoring her, trying to get the man to focus his attention on me. "I need help." It must be clear that I do, especially with Emi complaining. "Hush!" I scold when he finally leaves. "It's too late, Emi. You've already ruined the straw."

I am abrupt because I'm worried. There are too many warning signs. Like the pain she's suffering. It bothers me, since I don't know her labor began on her way to the mess hall, but she decided to keep going, and then stayed so Eric could eat. She's also more than a month early from what she told me, and there is no reason for her to lie, since it doesn't make any difference to me when she conceived. I am afraid there is damage, that's the word that comes to me—damage—and I don't want to think about why. Then I remember all the hauling she's been doing since she returned to us, and how it could have brought the labor on. It doesn't have to be the beating Will gave her. That explanation helps me breathe.

When the next contraction washes over her, we both reach out at the same time and grab each other's hands. It's less shocking this time, the touch. Her fingers are stubby in mine, but alike. We have the same knobby knuckles and nails.

"Squeeze," I say, and her nails leave impressions in my skin. We are facing each other, so I shift my hands to fit hers. "Just your hands," I tell her as her legs flex and arch her back off the floor. "Relax your body and it won't hurt so much. Squeeze your hands."

It's the only advice I have, and I can't remember far enough to know if I followed it myself.

We stay that way a while, hands joined, keeping quiet for the neighbors. Emi holds on, squeezing and puffing, groans and sometimes yells escaping. Her face is red and white, the lines of her grimaces fading more slowly after each contraction. I tell her everything will be fine, that the doctor is coming, and she nods and cries a little when I speak. Her legs are splayed open, knees bent, like she's getting ready to give birth. The contractions seize her body and roll down.

Finally, the door opens. Our neighbor has returned. He couldn't find a doctor, so he brought George Hamada, a medical student with three years of school completed. George is the only choice, and he's barely older than Emi. It's my guess that he's never delivered a baby before.

George strips off the sport coat and tie he is wearing, not even asking permission, and right away he begins talking, soothing Emi and giving me directions in the same silky tone, so I have to listen carefully to hear what he says. Even in that most intimate moment,

Emi doesn't seem the slightest bit embarrassed. So despite his fresh grin and his age, I decide to let him stay.

George introduces himself, we all introduce ourselves, and he starts telling little stories. He tells us he was on his way to an interview for a place on the clinic staff, which explains the fancy clothes. The pay is lousy, especially for the internees. At first, I think he's just full of himself, but then I realize he's trying to put us at ease. I don't hear much of interest, but Emi seems to be listening. Time picks up speed.

"Oh, Christ," Emi yells the next time a contraction hits her, "Oh God, Jesus—" She isn't praying, of course; she has chosen the worst possible time to take the Lord's name in vain. George doesn't flinch, and I admit that, with him moving around and talking and me released from Emi's fingers, her curses don't seem so bad. At least we are building for something, no longer waiting. George pulls the sheet out from where it's tucked at the foot of the mattress so he can get underneath it and still keep Emi covered. He compliments me for putting a bucket of water on the potbellied stove.

"Mama knows these things," Emi says in a weak voice.

"Do you have a clean towel?" George asks me. "Something to wrap the baby in?"

I show him the towels I gathered before he arrived. "This is all we have."

"See?" Emi asks. "I told you. She's a pro."

She's talking to him but her eyes are on me. It seems so important to her that I answer, but I don't understand what she's referring to. There's nothing to say about my births, I want to tell her. Just that I had three children and survived.

"I remember," Emi continues, "what you taught me when Jack was born. Don't you?"

I remember. Myself on my knees in the mud, begging my daughter to take me inside. I can't believe that she has mentioned it with a stranger there to hear.

Not even Emi is so cruel.

"Hush," I say to shut her down. "Don't bother with that now."

"She talked me through the whole thing like it was nothing special," Emi says, talking to George. "We were out in the middle of nowhere. It was just the two of us when my brother was born. And then, when I ruined one of her dresses, she didn't even get angry. She was fearless. So in control."

George murmurs something soothing, but I can tell he's not listening to her words. It's only me, trying to reconcile her memories with my own. I rejected them for so long that the ones coming back to me seem unreal. I was on the farm . . . Jack was born . . . and I may have crawled into the house, but it was so long ago.

Using the sheet as a cover, George slides his hands over the top of Emi's stomach and down the sides. Then he puts them between her legs.

"You're doing great, Emi," he says. "Everything looks great. We're almost ready to go."

She tries to smile, pulling her eyes toward his while I clutch at the towels from the corner. Does she truly remember my labor like that? I know, even if I can no longer envision it, that I brayed, whined, and rutted. But without that memory, there is nothing between us. If she is being honest, there is nothing for either of us to forgive.

I can't ask her about it then. It's too new; we have no privacy; I can't even help her, since I already called for George. All I can do is to give George the knowledge I have that he doesn't. A warning. I can tell him the baby is early and I promise myself that, if I have to, I will explain why.

"Everything's just great. Emi's doing this like a pro," George says in the cheerful monotone I am beginning to appreciate. "How early?"

"A month or so."

"That's okay, that's just perfect." He puts his hand down between her legs again and keeps it there. "The head will be a little soft, but we're going to be okay on this one. We've got perfect position here. Make sure we're ready to wrap him up tight and keep him warm."

He looks so encouraged. Not like your grandfather—always so scared by what he couldn't do that he would have tried to push the baby out. That's when I know George is special and put Emi into his hands. He's prepared, more than I am, for what is to come.

Emi starts screaming. It's a relentless sound, impossible to soothe, impossible almost to bear. She is all voice, trying to lift herself out of her body.

George pushes the sheet gently up your mother's legs, baring them so I can see.

"Okay, here we go," he says. "When I tell you, I want you to push down, like you're going to the bathroom, okay? Mrs. Okada, why don't you come sit with us. You can hold Emi's hands again. That will be nice for her. Emi, listen to my voice, okay? It's almost over. You've got your mother's hands? Good, that's good. This will only take a second."

Emi cuts him off with another scream.

"Okay, push!" he says at the same time, and she does.

It goes on like that. Over and over, Emi pushing and screaming and tearing at my hands. Her hair is wet, slinging sweat in all directions. I rock back and forth with her, twisting as she tries to push sometimes and to wrench away from George and me and the whole process at other times. I try to stay with her, I put all my energy into that. It isn't a second, it's minutes—probably thirty minutes. George tells us what he can see, which parts he can see. Emi says "Mama" a couple of times, but she can't get out the words that she wants to follow. Toward the end she is shrieking, "Help me, damn it!" and several other well-chosen phrases. I'll spare you the details. Your mother's mouth can be foul.

Then she relaxes, and I hear you scream.

You shatter the room for such a tiny thing. The whole stable hears you. George holds you in his hands and turns you like a prize. He puts his finger in your mouth, and wipes you down with warm water, checking and washing you at the same time. There's a whole ritual after birth that I have never seen before. It's the doctor's ritual, not the woman's. It's about cleaning, and waiting for the placenta and cutting the chord. The woman lies with no energy, like your mother lay in my lap. In that moment, there's nothing left for us to do.

Emi's eyes are closed, no surprise after what she's been through, but I remember thinking that she looks so young, like she did in the early days on the farm when I used to sneak in and watch my children sleep. I smoothe her wet hair back, knowing she'd want it to be straightened; I want to express my pride, even though it's not the first time she's had a child. Forever more, that moment is special; it's not like my other memories, which unwind like movies on their own. This one is filled with texture: her skin soft as a custard just out of the oven; the rich smell of her blood wrapping us so tightly I can taste it in my throat.

Emi has almost passed out when George gives you to her to hold, but she struggles to sit up. When he puts you on her chest gently, your face looks so fragile and light against her skin. Your mother is so exhausted, George has to wrap her arms around the blanket to keep you from falling. He stays with her, too, on his knees just behind her. She leans against him and he helps her hold you so I can see.

Mariko, I see you exactly as you looked that day. You are pink and baggy as an old man, with thick, flat hair. You have cloudy eyes, set like jewels under blue lids. And your mouth is a puddle changing shape. You use it to let us know you have arrived.

Emi shifts the blanket. "Oh," she says. It sounds like her last puff of breath. "It's a girl."

"A beautiful baby girl," George says. He is so proud, anyone would think you are his own. The three of you together are beautiful. "Ten fingers," he tells Emi, "and ten toes."

I know now that I broke a promise to your mother and our lives spilled out of it. I promised to help her if she stayed with me during Jack's birth, but when she needed me years later, I turned her away. When Emi came home that night after Pearl Harbor, it was because she trusted me. And I punished her for intruding, hated her for seeing me as I never wanted to be.

But I can see all of us more clearly now, and remember who we were. Who we still are, because without our pasts we aren't complete. When I think back over everything I did—what I thought I knew and what I hid—the person I understand best is your mother. She is here, in front of me. Always. And I cannot change a thing.

My daughter doesn't count your fingers. I can no longer see her with you and George. When she returns to me, she is with Jack, cowering over him across the dirt floor of our two-room shack on the day he is born. Her mouth is near Jack's ear—she is puffing in it rhyming words and nonsense noises. She turns to me then and tells me proudly that she saved me. She has fulfilled her half of my bargain. And I can't say what I should have said.

"Mama," Emi says idly. She is too absorbed in the baby to see that I have finally rallied myself enough to turn. I can still watch her rub Jack's smooth chest with the back of her own hand. I am with her as she touches his fingers with her other hand, over and over, the same five.

What I am doing, each time I return to her, is waiting for my daughter to speak. And she is taking her time, but we both know there's no hurry now. She always waits until I begin to drop off. I have been fighting unconsciousness for so long.

But before I can go, there is something she must say to me. So I remain, behind the dark of my eyelids, and listen to her count. It is devoted, and soothing, and I feel like it will go on forever. In her young voice, I feel myself relax.

I do not open my eyes when she finally speaks, but I hear her words. They grow as they leave her and come to me, until they are bigger than the room. She asserts her claim to something I never gave her. A love I spent my lifetime trying to ignore.

"I'll be your baby," she says softly, sure that I hear her. "And he can be mine."

Her words give me a passage to her heart. I can find it, the way I never could before. There is a small smile on her lips, and though she has curled herself around the baby, it is my weary face she sees. Then Emi slips one of her hands in my cold one.

At last, she is where she wants to be.